BENEATH THE SKY

BY

DAN THOMPSON

QUANTUM FORGE PRESS

BENEATH THE SKY

Copyright © 2012 by Dan Thompson
Cover art by Martynas Latušinskas

ISBN: 978-0-9854146-0-3

Blog: www.DanThompsonWrites.com

www.QuantumForgePress.com

For my daughter, Catherine

BENEATH THE SKY

Chapter 1

"They call us heretics for fulfilling God's promise to manifest heaven here on the earthly plane. Have pity for them, my friends, for they are not among the Chosen of God and will not be welcome in His paradise." - St. Mason's epistle to Ganymede

Margaret Pritchard's life was saved at 7:43 on a Tuesday morning, but she never knew it. Her savior was a navigation computer almost a light-year away, and its action was noted only in the automated logs. For Margaret and her world, it was everything.

At that moment, she was glancing up into the sky at Lake Harmony. It was four kilometers away, but she could see the core lights glinting off a boat's wake as it made its way towards the docks on the spinward side of the lake. At this time of the morning, the lights were still patchy and dim, but they were starting to burn off a wispy layer of clouds that had formed towards the aft of her little world.

She turned her attention back to the path as she cut across the corner of the park towards the aft entrance to the school. A young boy was running towards it but stopped and fell into line behind her respectfully. She suppressed a smile over that. It was only her first year, but the teacher's uniform had an impact.

After a quick climb to the third floor, she whisked into her classroom to find her class seated and waiting, all but one. Time would tell if little Ashton was out sick or merely late again. Turning to the board at the front, she wrote out the date in high script: March 28, 1049. Her students fidgeted behind her, but she had been taught to take care with such things.

After embellishing the final mark, she turned her gaze on them. "Now, can anyone tell me what's special about this date?"

A few hands went up, and she selected Belli. "It's my brother's birthday."

The class burst into a sporadic fit of giggles before settling down.

"I'm sure it is, Belli," Margaret replied, "but I didn't mean special for you and your brother. I meant March 28 in general. Anyone?"

Three hands remained up. "All right, Sarah, what do you think is special about it?"

With a bragging smile, little Sarah pronounced, "It's Turning Day!"

"Turn Over Day," she corrected, "but yes, some people call it Turning Day, too. That was the day *God's Chariot* reached the halfway point on our journey to New Providence." She surveyed the class. At a range of seven to ten, they were a mixed lot, but it would be many years before she could have her pick of the students. "Does anyone remember what year Turn Over Day was?"

Only one hand remained. "Yes, Mary?"

"Eight hundred fifty-five, Miss Pritchard." Mary came from a very proper family, and it showed. Teaching Mary would serve Margaret well within the local tier, but she also knew any help would be limited. The Pritchards and Ellises had maintained a quiet animosity since her grandfather's time.

"That's very good, Mary. Eight hundred fifty-five, almost two hundred years ago. Now, if you all did your reading last night, you should be able to tell me who the High Reverend was. Anyone?"

The review eventually led into a quiz, catching out four who had ignored the assignment, and then the day moved on into math and grammar. In the afternoon she focused on her specialty, teaching three different classes on environmental systems. Today it was recycling protocols for common metals. She finished off the day with her morning class again, and assigned that night's history reading, the Captains of the ninth century. When they were older, of course, they would get to read of the two Great Mutinies and the three minor ones, but these little ones were still too young for that.

After that, it was a quick trip back downstairs, and she was almost out the spinward doors when Tier-son Joseph Mackenzie called after her. "Maggie! Wait up a moment."

She stopped and waited patiently as her supervisor huffed through hall, trying to navigate his girth around children. She knew her place well enough to wait for him, but she wasn't going to retrace her steps to meet this man, even if he was a tier-son. "What can I do for you, sir?"

Mackenzie slowed up as he approached, his rounded cheeks red with the exertion. "I wanted to remind your father about tonight's tier meeting. He hasn't said anything about the budget yet, has he?"

"Not to me, he hasn't." It was only a half-truth. It had been discussed openly with Aunt Jen at dinner the night before, so she knew very well that Father planned to argue strongly against Mackenzie and his plans for Charity Lake, but technically, the conversation had not been with Margaret. "But you had best try his link. I was going to be having a picnic with my Cal, so I wasn't going to see Father until after the meeting anyway."

"I did try it, but he's locked out. I couldn't even get through with an emergency page."

Margaret took a step back. That was not like her father. "Is it actually an emergency?"

Mackenzie grimaced and shuffled his feet. "Well, not really an emergency, but it is important. I was just hoping you might be able to get through with your code."

"Well, Father doesn't like it when I interrupt him on duty, but if I can reach him, I will be sure to pass on your message."

"Thank you, Maggie. You're a good girl."

She turned to head out the door, already deciding that she would only use her low priority page. In addition to being a

Tier-son himself, Father was Third Navigator, a position of significant respect and responsibility within the crew, and if he was busy on duty, no little toady like Joseph Mackenzie was going to interrupt him.

Captain Akahele Kalas had been skimming a novel in her command chair when the little bridge of the *Jinley* turned from peaceful monotony to the chaos of multiple alarms.

"What the fuck was that?" She leaned forward over Semi's navigation console. The chart was still updating, trying to make some sense of the data pouring in from the close encounter.

"Not sure," he replied, "looked like some kind of rock, a big one."

"At that speed?" She moved over to the other console and called up the data herself.

"All I'm saying is what it looks like on scan. Mix of metals, judging from the surface spectrum, and its magnetic field pegged the instruments. Not sure of the actual size... not enough mass for anything that wide. Might be hollow or something."

"But nothing on the charts?" In sixteen years, she had never had a surprise like this.

"No, ma'am, nothing. This part of the channel is rated green-three, nothing above twenty microns."

Akahele thought it over for a moment. She thought about calling down to Victor, but the tach-drive status was nominal, all greens barring that intermittent alignment glitch on the port sail generator. Whatever it had been, they had come away unscathed. "I just don't see how something like that could be moving so fast."

Torin Graylock stepped through the rear hatch and crowded into the bridge. "It might be a transient, something from outside the galaxy."

Semi turned back. "You've got to be kidding me. The odds of something getting that far, let alone crossing our path —"

Torin held up his hands. "I'm merely stating the possibility." He turned to Akahele. "It would be quite a find, Captain."

Semi looked back at the plot. "Well, look, it's already half a light-day behind us. If we're going to break tach, we should do it soon while we still have a good chance of finding it again."

Akahele shook her head. "No, we've got a time-bonus on this run, and I'm not going to fool around trying to match courses with this thing. I don't even know if we're rated for that kind of reentry."

Torin started to object, but she waved him off.

"No. Just log it, Semi. We'll report it when we get to Answay and let those survey guys check it out. That's what they're paid for."

Semi dumped it all to the backup holo-core and returned his gaze to the boards. "Everything looks clear from here on, Captain."

"Keep a sharp eye out anyway. We've had enough excitement for one day."

The bridge of the *Chariot* was much more subdued. There were no alarms. The overhead lights were dim, and most of the ambient light came from the various displays arrayed around the crew. Nevertheless, Captain Ackerman was far more worried. He leaned over his officer's shoulder and stared intently at the display. "Let me see it again."

Lieutenant Commander William Pritchard dutifully played the recording again. The burst of color could not really be called an explosion as much as a streak, blue in one direction and red in the other, fading out into the near X-Ray and the radio at the extremes. "It's the same as the others, but this is by far the best look we've ever had." It was a remarkably good recording. He had been working with the sensor techs for the last two years to boost this kind of sensitivity in the extended spectrum.

"And it was right across our bow?"

"Close enough... seventy-three degrees, and probably not more than a million kilometers away."

He looked back at Pritchard's display, frozen at the brightest moment of the burst. "And when we passed by that point?"

Pritchard shook his head. "Nothing, sir."

"Who else has seen this?"

"Conners in scan, Commander Soze, and myself."

Ackerman nodded. "Well, what do you think?"

"If you're asking for my analysis, I really don't know, but I don't like it. It worries me."

Ackerman chuckled. "But we've been seeing these off and on for almost five hundred years. We're still running at over forty percent the speed of light these days. Perhaps this is merely another unexpected relativistic effect."

Pritchard pressed his lips, holding back his answer. "Perhaps."

Ackerman scanned around the bridge. A few of his crew were making furtive glances in his direction, but Commander Soze was officer of the watch, and his pacing through the control aisles was a calming influence. Even so, he continued in a quieter voice. "Speak your mind, Bill."

Pritchard also glanced about before continuing in a hushed tone. "I mean, yes, we've seen a few things that have led us to refine old Einstein, even trusty Jacobs, but there's nothing in the theories for something like that."

The captain shrugged. "There's always room for new theories."

Pritchard shook his head. "It's not that. If it's a relativistic effect, then I would expect them to be dropping off now that we're slowing down. It's not simply that our sensors are getting better. I think we're seeing more because there are more, and they're getting closer."

Ackerman took a deep breath but kept his tone calm and quiet. "Are you suggesting this is some kind of a sign?"

"A sign from God or a sign of something else?"

He shrugged. "Your choice."

Pritchard stiffened. "Well, that's not really for me to say, Captain, but either way, I don't particularly relish the idea of taking this to the reverends."

"Neither do I," the captain replied with a frown. "But I don't really have a choice in the matter."

Cal Johnson wrapped his left arm around Margaret as they lay in the mesh hammock. It was strung between two branches of an old oak tree. It was only a mild climb to the spot, but it was enough to tuck them out of easy sight, both from below and from any curious eyes on the ground curving above them. This was one of their favorite spots, a secluded niche in Ballard Park, fully three kilometers from their mutual parents' neighborhood. It was good for talking as well as more amorous activities. Such unions were politely frowned upon, but there was little actual risk of shunning.

"So how did your mother take the news?" Margaret asked. "I know she's been praying for this promotion." Beyond mere praying, Margaret knew she had also been pushing on two of Cal's uncles.

Cal smiled contently and pulled the blanket a little higher. "I haven't told her yet. I wanted to tell you first, Mags."

She kissed him on the cheek. "That's very sweet, but why?"

"Because the promotion comes with a raise, and more to our future, a better housing allotment."

"You mean...?"

He gave her shoulders a little squeeze. "Yes. I can get my own place now."

"You have someplace in mind?"

He looked up and pointed through open patches in the leaves. "Right over there, in Wilson tier, just a block from the tram line. It's not grand or anything, but it's quaint."

"Oh, I love that area," she replied. "Grandma Noreen lived there when I was just a little girl." She shifted to lie across him a little more. "Of course, I do like this little spot of ours."

Cal shrugged. "Cousin Patrick told me about this place when I was only fifteen. It's time for me to pass it on to someone else."

"I don't know, Cal, it's one thing for us to meet in the park. There's a tradition there, but for me to just come to your place... well, that's not done."

"That brings me back to the raise, Mags." He took a deep breath to steady his nerves. "It's enough, with what you make at the school, we could get married."

She gave him a playful kiss. "But we are getting married, silly. Or did you want to propose all over again?"

He replied with a short tickle. "No, once was enough. What I meant was that we could get married now, this year."

She shifted, backing away. "You know I can't do that, not until I'm twenty. Father says."

"You wouldn't be the first, you know. Just last month a girl in my tier got married at eighteen, and it's not like we're rushing into it."

She sighed, remembering the last time she had had this particular argument with her father. He was a loving father, to be sure, but when angered he was a force to be reckoned with. She had learned long ago not to provoke him. Aunt Jen said he had once been far gentler, but it seemed that had died with her mother. "You know I can't, Cal. Besides, it's only eight months. We can wait."

He set his jaw. "Maybe I should talk to him."

Margaret giggled. "If you want, but let's not forget what happened at last year's Launch Festival."

Cal could not help but smiling, and that spread into a broader relaxation. "I still say that wasn't my fault, but all right. We can wait, at least a little while."

Above them, the core lights were dimming into an evening sky of houses and parks. Margaret peeked out through the branches, looking towards Tier Wilson. Perhaps it was time to give up the park after all.

Captain Ackerman relaxed in the High Reverend's office. It was comfortably suited, with fine woods and soft leathers – real leathers from some of the *Chariot's* few herds, not the more common synthetics. He had sat here many times, and he scanned about looking for any changes but found only one since his visit the previous Friday. The small portrait of his daughter had been updated, her visage as a young woman finally replacing the lanky teen that had graced the wall for years.

The wait itself was not unexpected. This was not their regularly scheduled meeting, and Ackerman knew Hathaway's schedule had been reasonably full today. Earlier captains might have seen the wait as part of a larger game, a subtle jab in the interplay between the crew and the reverends left over from the last Great Mutiny three centuries before. Captains officially deferred to the High Reverend in all matters, of course, though the High Reverends had usually been wise enough to avoid any decrees on the operations of the ship itself. It was an arrangement that had worked very well for Ackerman and Hathaway, but he knew that friction had been common between both of their predecessors.

Before long, however, Hathaway swept into his office, his swift movements in contrast to the age in his face. "So sorry to keep you, Jim. You know how Reverend Haggerty can be."

Ackerman rose and clasped him by the forearm. "Indeed, but with far less patience than you show. Thank you for seeing me on such short notice."

Hathaway sat in the chair next to Ackerman, eschewing the formality of his desk. "For you, anytime," he replied, "except, of course for —"

"Except for Thursday nights," he finished for him. "Yes, I remember."

Hathaway responded with an embarrassed grin before gathering up his thoughts with a long sigh. "So, you said it was important but not urgent."

Ackerman nodded. "We had another sighting today."

"That's what... three this month?"

"Three confirmed. There were perhaps another dozen possibilities, but we don't always get such a good look. This one was close, though, very close."

"How close?"

Ackerman shrugged, knowing that Hathaway was weak in this area. "Close in astronomical terms, but if you'd been looking at it, you could have seen it with your naked eyes."

"And you still think it's something real, not just some trick of the light."

"Yes, and I'm not the only one."

"Who? Not that fool... Rickman, was it?"

"No, no. Rickman is gone, promoted into retirement I would say. No, this was my Nav-3, Bill Pritchard."

Hathaway nodded. "Yes, I believe I met him once... seemed like a reasonable fellow." He rose and strode to his bar. "Would you care for anything?"

Ackerman was a Roxa drinker, preferably the double-malt variation they made in Olsen tier. He knew the Reverend despised the taste, but he usually kept a small decanter on hand. "My usual, but just a thumb. I'm officially on duty until seven." He accepted the glass while Hathaway poured himself a bourbon. "And yes, Pritchard is a good man, very level-headed."

"Is he a family man?"

"He has a daughter, a teacher I think, though he's a widower, some ten or fifteen years now."

Hathaway returned to his seat and took a sip. "Something you two have in common."

Ackerman nodded and sighed. "Of a sort. I recall that it was Glonic syndrome for her. You don't see much of it anymore, but at least they had time to say goodbye."

"True." Hathaway did not press on that matter, and Ackerman was quietly thankful for it. "So tell me, what does Pritchard think of all this?"

He suspected very much what Pritchard had thought, but he owed it to the man not to put such words into his mouth. "He did not offer an explanation, but he cannot attribute it to the relativistic effects of our speed."

Hathaway nodded. "But you do have an explanation, I take it?"

Ackerman took a sip. "Yes, High Reverend, one that borders on heresy."

He raised an eyebrow. "Now this should be interesting. Go on, Jim. Taint my soul with your heresy. Between the two of us, I can use a little from time to time."

"Thank you, High Reverend. These sightings, these flashes, they have grown more and more common the further out we have gone, the closer we get to New Providence."

"Perhaps a sign of blessing," suggested Hathaway.

"Perhaps. Or perhaps a sign of danger." Ackerman took a deep breath before plunging ahead. "I know it is the official position of the church that Earth alone was blessed with life by

God and that only Man was blessed with the mind to go forth unto the other worlds, but what if we're wrong? What if there truly is some other life in the Universe, alien to us, but still capable of traveling the stars? Perhaps these flashes are signs of their ships passing, or maybe a flare to warn us off."

Hathaway considered it for a long moment of silence. "As heresies go, it's big, but there have been bigger. These flashes, you believe them to be artificial? Man-made, or rather alien-made?"

"Certainly artificial. While it is difficult to prove they are not natural, it is what I believe. I can only speculate at their source."

"Are they something that we could produce ourselves?"

"Perhaps a small one, though even then not quite. There's just too much energy in these things."

Hathaway nodded. "I'll have to take your word for it, friend, but I trust you in these matters."

"Thank you, High Reverend."

He sipped at his bourbon. "So tell me, have you shared this particular heresy with anyone?"

Ackerman chuckled and finished off his glass. "I rarely find the time in my schedule for spreading heresy, so no, I have not."

"And do you feel the need to do so?"

He shook his head.

Hathaway drained the rest of his bourbon. "Then what would you have me do?"

"I hesitate to advise you on guiding our mutual flock."

Hathaway smiled. "But you came here to do just that, so don't stop."

Ackerman nodded. "I may have been the first to reach this particular heresy, but if these sightings continue, particularly if they increase, I will not be the last."

Hathaway replied with a quiet grunt. "From anyone else, Jim, that would sound unpleasantly like a threat."

"I understand, High Reverend, but you know I don't mean it that way. It is a warning, one I feel I must give, just as surely as you would warn me of a gap in the core fittings."

Hathaway rose and stepped over to his desk. Certain times demanded a formality between the two of them. "Well said, Captain, and I thank you for bringing this to my attention."

Ackerman rose and stood before him. "My pleasure as always, High Reverend."

"I would ask, though, that you do what you can to limit the discussion of such things amongst your crew." He began fidgeting with some papers on his desk. "You know how it goes. Rumors are the only things that seem to outrun our ship."

"I will do my best."

"And this Pritchard fellow, I think I'd like to meet him again. Nothing formal, you understand, just something where I can take him aside for a moment. Please arrange it with my staff."

"Certainly, High Reverend."

"Thank you, Captain. You may go."

Ackerman nodded once, and turned crisply on his heel to leave. He was lucky to have Hathaway, and he knew it. He could think of at least two High Reverends out of history who would have had him under arrest before he could reach the door.

Captain Akahele Kalas fidgeted in her seat as the Survey administrator scanned over her report on the screen projected over his desk. At first, he seemed to be giving it only a cursory read, but he stopped partway through and rewound to the start, taking it in more slowly the second time. Eventually, he closed it and met her gaze.

"It's a rock. I'll grant you, it's an interesting rock but still just a rock."

Akahele had expected as much from the Survey branch, especially from a has-been like this Belikovsky. Nothing in the inner systems ever interested them much. It lacked the glory of charting new systems on the frontier. "Aren't you going to investigate?"

He shrugged. "We might. I must confess that your first officer's theory is intriguing, but right now we're down to one survey ship in this sector. It's tied up charting the asteroid belts around Lasko-Gamma for the next three months, and even when the *Buscador* finishes refit, she's been committed to the colonization board for the first two months. By then your rock will have passed the Jasper shipping lane and will no longer be a pressing concern. Still, I'll bring it up at the next scheduling session. We should be caught up on our backlog by next summer."

Akahele sat back. "And in the meantime?"

"We'll post an advisory. From the data here, a ten light-day deviation to coreward for the next three months should be more than enough to keep even the sloppiest navigators safe from harm." He rose to see her to the door. "We thank you for bringing this to our attention."

She walked outside into the cool air. They say that the Answay sky is always overcast, and today was no exception. The canopy of clouds extended down even further on winter mornings like this one, almost completely masking the towers that rose from the city's center. Torin was waiting for her next to their rented pod, poking at the pebbles in a rock garden with his foot.

"Anything?" he asked.

She shook her head. "They're posting an advisory."

He pushed a stray stone back into place. "That's it?"

She opened the pod's hatch and climbed in. "They might send a survey ship next year."

Torin joined her and punched up the destination code for their dock. The pod slid smoothly out into traffic and hooked onto the main transit line. "So, it's just going to be sitting out there for a year."

She nodded. "Not quite just sitting there, but I hear you."

"You're thinking about it, aren't you?"

She chuckled and gave him a hard stare. "Yes, I am thinking about it. That doesn't mean I'm going to do it."

"I understand."

She looked out the window as they followed the long curve through the spaceport. "After all, I'd need solid assurances from Semi that we can find it again, not to mention some kind of down-tach program from James to get us in at that speed."

Torin nodded, trying hard to suppress his grin. "Absolutely."

Akahele looked at him again. "Now why do I think you've already worked it out with both of them?"

Torin's smile broke through. "Because you're very perceptive, Captain."

Chapter 2

"We have broken down contact into nine categories, created full taxonomies of hypothetical life forms, and crafted an encounter decision tree that fills volumes, and yet we are fundamentally unprepared for a true first contact situation. Why? Because quite simply, no one has ever had one." - Vincent Caruthers, *opening address to the Joint Conference on First Contact, 3375*

Bill Pritchard waited in the foyer as calmly as he could manage, but he found himself pacing in fits across the marble tiles. This was the first time he had ever been to the High Reverend's estate. In fact, he had only met him once before, back when he was promoted into one of the eight prime navigator slots. Now he had been invited to a private party, and he was late. Two officers of the Divine Mark stood silently just inside the front door in full dress uniform, their ceremonial sabers brightly polished.

Captain Ackerman stepped in from a side room. "Pritchard, good, there you are."

"I'm sorry I'm late, sir, but—"

"Oh you're not that late. These things always start late. We're still circling over the hors d'oeuvres."

"But sir—"

"What?"

"We just had another sighting," Pritchard paused to eye the Mark officers before lowering his voice. "Another close one."

Ackerman motioned him back towards the door. "As close as that one last month?"

He nodded. "Just shy of a million kilos off our stern, but what really concerns me is that it's different from the others. It was just blue. The red half wasn't there."

"What do you mean? Was it the angle?"

"No, sir, the angle was fine. It just wasn't there."

Ackerman chewed on it for a moment. "Look, don't say anything about this over dinner. Later, perhaps, you and I can discuss this with the High Reverend."

Dinner itself was a lavish affair with real steaks and a huge central dish of vat-shrimp with a rich cream sauce. Four of the Reverends were there with their wives, along with six tier-fathers. Pritchard was the only tier-son, and he knew it was a not so subtle breach of governmental etiquette for him to be here without his own tier-father. The High Reverend headed the table, of course, and he was joined by his wife and eldest son, Arthur. Pritchard and Ackerman were the only crew present, clearly set apart by their uniforms.

Despite the power assembled at the table, the evening grew more casual as the night wore on. By the dessert course, the jokes were raucous, and the liquor was flowing. Pritchard noted that the Captain was only sipping at the various toasts, his glass never dropping to the point of needing a refill. That alone was an ominous sign of the conversation to come.

Eventually, they moved out into the great hall and into several smaller groups. While the hall was ostensibly for dances or private performances, it was ideal for these informal talks. Typical of other ninth century architecture, small alcoves surrounded the perimeter, while three sets of French doors led to balconies overlooking the gardens.

Pritchard found himself pinned in one such alcove by Reverend Morris who was expressing his disapproval for the park policies in Pritchard's tier. He disagreed with them as well, but he was still forced by loyalty to defend Tier-father Boland's decisions, especially given his conspicuous absence. It was a delicate act, because he still hoped to someday reverse those same decisions. Pritchard was on the verge of saying just that when High Reverend Hathaway sauntered in, a half-empty wine glass in his hand.

"Oh, there you are, Tony. I believe your wife is looking for you."

Morris nodded. "Thank you, High Reverend. It is probably getting on time for us to head home anyway. As always, I am humbled by your hospitality."

Morris left, and Pritchard glanced around at the portraits in the alcove in a futile attempt to find a way out from under the High Reverend's gaze.

"It's Bill, isn't it?"

"Yes, High Reverend. Lt. Commander Bill Pritchard, third navigator."

"And tier-son, not to forget."

"Yes, sir. I do what I can."

"The other tier-fathers speak well of you." He stepped back, beckoning him with his wine glass. "Come, we should talk, you and I."

Pritchard followed him back out into the main hall and off towards one of the balconies. He glanced around the room and spotted Captain Ackerman standing near Reverend Lansbury and Tier-father Baker. The Captain nodded towards Bill and stepped away from the others.

Outside on the balcony, Hathaway settled himself into a seat by the railing while Pritchard stood stiffly by a bench opposite him. Before either could speak, Ackerman stepped through the doorway, closing it behind him. "I thought I might find you two out here," he said.

Hathaway raised an eyebrow at Ackerman's presence but made no obvious protest. "Yes, I was just getting to know this officer of yours, and since he is also a tier-son, I suppose he is also an officer of mine, so to speak. Are you here to chaperone, my dear Captain?"

Ackerman returned the smile. "I mean no interference, High Reverend, but the reason for my presence will soon become clear enough."

Hathaway looked back and forth between them, Ackerman standing firmly by the door, Pritchard eschewing the bench beside him. Their stance made it clear. They considered themselves to be on duty. "Well, then, let's get to it. Bill, I understand you were watching the sensors last month when we had that big flash, the close one."

"Yes, High Reverend."

"And what do you think of it?"

Pritchard looked over at his captain for support but found none. "It is difficult to say. Clearly, they are unexpected anomalies."

Hathaway shook his head. "Even I know that, but I think you know more. Or at least, I think you suspect more. So, for the moment, try to forget that your captain is eavesdropping on our conversation, and try to forget that I am the High Reverend. What do you think they are?"

"Well, I... I think they are ships, High Reverend."

Hathaway nodded. "It's an interesting theory, though you are not the first to suggest it."

Pritchard glanced at Ackerman who merely nodded.

Hathaway took another sip from his wine glass. "So, if they are ships, where are they from? We're too far out from Earth for it to be them, not in such numbers."

Pritchard's eyes widened at the heresy the High Reverend was suggesting. "I confess that the notion of aliens did occur to me, but I also had another thought. If the ships were fast enough, they could be from Earth."

Hathaway scoffed at it. "How much faster could they be? After all, your captain always told me that the really high speeds were impractical over anything less than intergalactic distances because of the relativistic mass and whatnot."

Pritchard nodded. "Yes, but they could have found something new after we left. If they could find a new energy

19

source, or a new reaction to push with, they might be able to get enough acceleration to approach light-speed even over distances as short as a few dozen light-years."

"Other colony ships?"

"Not like our *Chariot*, I wouldn't think. I would suspect smaller ships, just enough for a modest crew. At those speeds, they could do it in a single generation. Or for that matter, they might not even be manned. After all, our own automations have improved significantly since we launched. Earth could have achieved much more with its resources. It might be as benign as an automated terraforming wave."

Hathaway considered it slowly. "I see you've put a fair amount of thought into it. How certain are you of it, that these flashes are ships?"

"It's more of a gut feeling than anything, but we might be about to find out in light of..." he trailed off and looked to his captain.

Hathaway followed his gaze over to Ackerman. "What? Has something happened?"

"We've had another sighting, even closer, and different from all the others."

"When?"

"Just before dinner," Ackerman replied. "Our Mr. Pritchard here was on duty when it happened."

"And what makes this one so special? You say we're about to find out... what?"

Ackerman nodded to Pritchard who answered for him. "Well, High Reverend, this flash was lopsided, and given how close it was, we know it wasn't just a sensor glitch."

Hathaway looked back to Ackerman. "And what does that mean?"

Ackerman allowed himself a little smile. "If these things are ships, then this one didn't fly by. It stopped."

Hathaway lurched to his feet, spilling the rest of his wine in the process. "You mean there's a ship here now?"

"Nearby perhaps, a million kilos or so. I put in a call to Commander Soze, and he has all the scopes sweeping the area. Nothing so far, but I should really be getting back to the bridge myself."

Hathaway was flushed. "Yes, Captain, I think you should."

Ackerman turned to Pritchard. "I know you just came off your shift, but I'd like to see you back on the bridge as soon as you're able." He then gave a curt bow to the High Reverend and departed, leaving Pritchard under Hathaway's quiet gaze.

"This ship," Hathaway said, "did you know about it through this entire dinner?"

"No, High Reverend. I think I only put it together during dessert."

Hathaway chuckled. "Blueberries stimulate your thinking?"

"I think it was the color," he offered. "In truth, I'm still having a hard time believing it."

Hathaway shrugged. "Well, it might turn out to be nothing after all."

"Perhaps, High Reverend."

"But you don't think so, do you?"

"No, with respect, I do not."

Hathaway stared at Pritchard a moment as if taking measure of the man. "I don't want to demean your fellow officers, Bill, not at all, but you are not like the rest of the Captain's men."

Pritchard bowed his head slightly. "I'm not sure what you mean, High Reverend."

"You must already sense it. You are a tier-son, after all, and from the sounds of it, you'll be a tier-father soon enough. You see the larger picture beyond merely following Ackerman's orders, and you have the good judgment to act on it."

"That is kind of you to say."

Hathaway shook his head. "Humility doesn't suit you, Bill. Your captain needs men like you, but you can't limit yourself to merely following one man's orders, loyal though you are. Your real loyalty must be to the colony and its mission. You do understand that, don't you?"

Pritchard nodded gravely. "Yes, High Reverend, I do understand."

Hathaway stood and walked over to embrace Pritchard by the shoulders. "Then don't deny me or your captain your good judgment. If you're going to be a tier-father, or perhaps even a Reverend, it's time you start thinking like one."

"I will do my best."

Hathaway released his grip. "Well then, my good Tier-son Pritchard, I send you back to my friend. I am sure you will serve him well."

Pritchard nodded one last time and took his leave. He was growing more certain there was indeed a ship out there, and no matter who was on board, the implications for his world were staggering.

Margaret relaxed in her bench swing on the back porch of the Pritchard home. Father had built it for her mother long ago, before she died, but over the years it had become her place to sit and enjoy the view. They lived in tier Bennet, only three kilometers from the rear engineering sections, so she could see almost the entire length of the Chariot from there, the furthest bits fading into a haze around the core lights.

Her father sat on the steps leading down into the side garden. He had been going through the motions of polishing his shoes. It was an old habit of his, and one he usually did with vigor, though he had spent five minutes reworking the same shoe over and over. He paused and caught her staring at him. "What is it, Maggie?"

"I said Cal got his promotion. He's no longer apprenticed to Mr. Welles."

Bill Pritchard set down the left shoe and picked up the right. "That's nice."

Margaret let the silence stretch until her father's brush had reached the toe. "He's moving too. He found a sweet little apartment down in the Wilson tier."

Her father's brush continued on. "Well, I'm sure he'll make the effort to come back and visit."

She pressed her lips together and summoned her courage. "I think he wants me to visit him... well, more than just visit."

The brush stopped, and he looked up and met his daughter's eyes. His intensity startled her, but she did not look away. "Maggie, we're not having this conversation now."

"But Father, I am going to marry someday. I want it to be with your blessing."

He sighed and set down the shoe and brush. "No, my little Magpie, it's not that. Cal's a fine boy —"

"A good man," she corrected.

"Yes, a good man I suppose, but..." he looked out over their little garden and the sweep of the ground up into the sky. With a shrug, he turned back to her. "It's just that I have another shift now, and it's not a good time for such talk."

She leaned forward in her seat, balancing precariously. "But you just had an extra half-shift last night."

He looked back down at his shoes and wiped away the remaining polish with a cloth. "It's just a busy time, you see. We're upgrading some equipment, and you know I've got a new apprentice to oversee."

Margaret leaned back. "That's all right, then. It can wait, though I've got parent meetings tonight. Tomorrow?"

He looked up at her as she swayed gently on the bench and shook his head slowly. He set the shoes down and crossed over to her, taking her hands and smudging her pale skin with the black polish from his own. "Maggie, I want you to listen carefully." She nodded. "If anything happens in the next few days, anything sudden, I want you to head for the closest shelter immediately. Don't wait for the alarm. Don't wait for instructions. Just go."

She looked at him closely, seeing the fear she could only remember vaguely from her childhood. "What's wrong, Father?"

He shook his head. "No, no questions this time. I just need you to promise me you'll go to the shelter."

She nodded. "I promise."

The five of them had gathered in *Jinley's* crew lounge. Akahele sat at the head of the table opposite Torin at the far end. Semi, James, and even old Victor were gathered around. According to association regulations, one of them should have been on the bridge, but this was not the first time they had ignored that rule. Floating above the table was a magnified view of a rough cylindrical asteroid, perhaps twenty-five kilometers in length. Its rotation was slow, but even in the real-time feed it was visible.

"So, Semi," Akahele began, "tell us about our rock."

At the far end, Torin could not completely suppress a smirk. "Our rock, yes, tell us about it."

"For starters," Semi said, "it's not a rock, but I think we all know that now." He was met by nods of assent around the table. "The fact that it's decelerating was the first sure sign that something was up, but in this augmented view…" he paused to toggle a mode on the projector. It zoomed out and highlighted a broad cone extending for hundreds of kilometers out in front of the asteroid. "Here we can clearly see the magnetic field they are projecting. At this distance, we can't make out their thrust jets, but this is clearly a Bussard ramjet, and the biggest I've ever heard about."

"So, definitely a subluminal design?"

Semi nodded, and James chimed in. "I don't think you could make a tach sail big enough to support that thing, at least not a stable one."

"Can you tell where it's from?"

Semi shrugged. "Well, there are no obvious markings on the surface. As for its course, you have to understand there's a fair amount of stellar drift over the kind of time frames we're talking about, and we don't really know when it began its deceleration or how long it might have cruised just on its momentum."

Victor gave a little harrumph. "You're telling us all what you don't know. How about what you do know, or at least, what you might know."

Semi smiled. "Given its current vector and rate of deceleration, it would have passed through the vicinity of Sol within the last twelve hundred years."

Akahele wanted to pin him down. "Passed through or launched from there?"

"Yeah, it could have been launched from there. Tannis Proxima is another possibility, about four thousand years ago."

Clearly, no one thought much of that possibility. Both Tannis Proxima and Tannis Beta had been settled colonies for over a century with no signs of any previous civilization anywhere in the system.

Torin finally broke his silence. "Well, we should at least be able to tell where it's going, right?"

Semi nodded. "Callista Prime. If they maintain their current deceleration, they'll arrive in another six hundred and eighty years or so."

Akahele thought it over. Callista was a loose binary system, with the Prime as a main-stage star holding twelve planets, including one very hospitable, and another too harsh for anything but environment suits but rich in heavy metals. Between its native resources and its central location in the Gemini basin, it was one of the wealthiest and most populous systems in the Confederacy. Even without the current economic realities, it would have made for an attractive colony.

No matter how she came at it, it was a messy situation. "Well, gentlemen, it looks like we have a ship of errant colonists here, and in another six hundred years or so, their grandkids or whoever are going to be pretty disappointed." She glared across at Torin who remained silent. "Or, we could pop on over and say hello."

Victor shook his head. "This is too much like a first contact situation. That's what those survey guys are for."

"Not that they've ever actually done it," James pointed out.

"But they're trained for it at least," Victor responded. "We're just guessing."

"It's not first contact if they're human," Semi argued.

"But we don't know that," from Victor.

Quiet settled over the room, and Akahele looked over to Torin. "You've been pretty quiet. What do you think?"

"I think if we don't make a decision soon, we won't be the ones making it. We've been closing with them for almost a day now. They probably know we're here."

Torin did not have to defend his argument. The computer made his point for him. "Warning," its voice chimed, "sensors detect an object moving towards us." The display interrupted to show a dim, boxy vessel thrusting towards them. "Estimate intercept in six hours."

Akahele looked to the rest of the crew. "Torin, you take watch. James, I want you on the bridge. Semi and Victor, you're off-shift for four hours. Sleep if you can." They nodded their assent and left their captain and first officer alone.

Torin shrugged. "Sorry. I like to be right, but not that right."

The next four hours passed slowly. Akahele stayed off the bridge, knowing that she would just be crowding in on Torin who had the watch. Instead, she stayed in her cabin, officially taking a rest period. She draped her uniform jacket over the back of her desk chair and stretched out on her bunk. As captain, she had one of the two full-size beds on the ship, though she took advantage of it far less often than she would have liked.

Sleep did not come. She had suspected as much, so she tried to meditate instead. She focused on her breathing, willing herself not to count down the time herself. In and out, slowly, just like the waves of the incoming tide. Even then, sleep did not come, but at least it kept her from pacing the floor, six steps to the door, six steps back. She had not done that since her days as a journeyman navigator on the *Cappella*.

Finally she gave in and brought up a computer display of the closing gap and recorded a long log entry. She laid out their history with this particular object, referencing the relevant log entries from the Ringway-Answay leg, but also fleshing it out with anything else she could remember. Some it was trivial details that only now seemed particularly relevant, but after a while she realized she was rambling. With thirty minutes before shift change, she closed it with, "So I don't know if this is my last log entry, the first chapter of something huge, or merely something I'm going to look back on later and laugh. We'll see in a few hours. Captain Akahele Kalas, commanding."

With that done, she took a quick shower and dressed in a fresh uniform. Standing in front her mirror, she checked the part in her hair and hooked her collar again, straighter this time. She never liked the way Takasumi's dull green went with her olive-brown skin, and she still thought the diagonal arrangement of buttons added five kilos to her appearance. Yet it was still her captain's uniform, and she would not trade it for the world. At one minute to shift-change, she strolled down the hall to the bridge and stepped through the hatch as calmly as she could.

James sat idly at the navigation station, while Torin was half-buried in the sensor bay. Without looking back he greeted her. "I could set my watch by you, Captain."

"Especially today. Status?"

He emerged from the electronics and sealed the panel behind him. "I presume you've been monitoring from your quarters."

She nodded reluctantly.

"It still looks like two hours to rendezvous. Whatever is over there, it's already decelerating to match course with us."

She glanced at the panel behind him. "Any problems?"

"No, not at all."

She turned to James, who immediately wilted under her glare. "We thought we would have heard something by now, you know, some kind of communications. Not a tach-burst, of course, but a comm laser or at least some kind of EM chatter."

"And?"

James shrugged. "Nothing. After a while we started wondering if we were having an equipment problem."

She understood. Torin had been running a diagnostic suite on the signal processors. "I appreciate your diligence. Now, both of you take a break."

James sauntered out without any objection, but Torin lingered. "I presume you're not going to tell me to get some sleep."

She shook her head, knowing that would be an impossible order. "Get a meal though. I want us all sharp when that thing gets here."

She had the bridge to herself for a moment, and while she flirted with a nervous stomach, she also had confidence in herself and her crew. Semi wandered in five minutes later with a half-eaten Brunshwick wrap in his hand. "Sorry, I overslept."

She eyed him incredulously as he sat at the navigation console. "You actually slept?"

"Sure, didn't you?"

She suppressed a laugh. "No, you know... paperwork."

He nodded and made a few adjustments to the display. "Who do you want to do the final maneuvering on this, us or them?"

She thought it over. This kind of ship-to-ship rendezvous was rare, at least amongst legitimate merchants, but when it did happen the standard procedure was for the smaller ship to yield control of its maneuvering thrusters to the larger ship's computer. There were exceptions, of course, for emergency situations or when surrendering to boarders, but it was always predicated on the assumption that one ship would hold its vector while allowing the other to close in, preferably under mutual computer control. That was not going to happen this time.

"Let's let them do the final closing. We're still matching the deceleration of the main ship with a short thrust every few minutes. When this little one closes to twenty klicks, I want you to stop that and just let us drift. We can position the dorsal airlock towards them and see how close they want to get."

Semi swiveled around in his chair. "And how close do you want to let them?"

She shrugged. "Say a hundred meters, but if you think for even a second that they're going to collide, you back us off. Do not wait for an order. Is that clear?"

"Yes, ma'am, very clear."

"And once they close to within five klicks, I'll have Victor warm up the tach drive, and you be ready to throw that too."

"But Captain, at that range a ship that size might not survive the backwash."

She nodded. "Better them than us."

The next two hours passed even slower than the previous four, though there was a brief moment of excitement when she belatedly ordered everyone into their vacc suits and sealed all the compartments against the possibility of a hull breach. Torin was back on the bridge by then, and she was wishing she had eaten something before. She told her suit to add a slight nutrient mix to her water and sucked nervously on that.

At twenty kilometers they made their last corrective burn and reoriented with the dorsal lock towards the interloper and waited. The incoming ship seemed to hesitate for a moment, slowing down much more sharply, but then it continued on in, already assuming that they would no longer be matching the mother ship's deceleration. It was dragging out even longer. Whatever was over there, they clearly did not want to spook

Akahele or her crew, but if anything, the long process was having the opposite effect.

At twelve kilometers, Torin turned to Semi. "Say... if this thing didn't come from Sol or Tannis, where was the next likely origin point?"

Semi shook his head, the shoulders of the vacc suit relaying most of the gesture. "There wasn't one."

"What do you mean, there wasn't one?" Torin pressed.

"Well, not in this galaxy anyway."

That got Akahele's attention. She toggled the ship comm. "James, Victor, let's get the tach drive on standby. I want it ready to engage if Semi asks for it."

Torin looked back at her. "Sorry. I guess I should have asked that earlier."

She just shrugged and waited.

At three kilometers, the other ship switched off its main thrusters and continued in on what appeared to be little more than attitude controls. At two hundred fifty meters, it finally came to a relative stop.

The silence on the bridge stretched to almost a minute before Torin broke it. "Well now what?"

"Still no kind of signal?"

Torin checked his displays again. "Nothing that we're recognizing."

She thought about it, staring at the dim image of the ship resting above her. It was edge on, but angled off to the side, its main thrusters paralleling her own. She punched up the high-resolution radar overlay, and then she saw it. "There it is," she highlighted it on the main display with a hand motion.

Torin looked closely. "I see it." The lines of the ship and the indentations made it clear. They had come to rest with their airlocks pointed at each other.

Akahele rose and headed for the hatch.

"Captain... where are you...?" Semi let the question trail off.

"They clearly intend a face to face meeting, so I'm heading up to the airlock to invite them over."

Torin stood. "But, shouldn't I? I mean, don't you think you should stay on the bridge?"

She just chuckled for a moment. "Really, Torin, if you were Captain, would you stay here and send your first officer? Would you pass this up?"

He gave her both a grin and a sigh. "Not a chance, ma'am."

What would have normally been a quick trip to the airlock was slowed by the need to key open several hatches and seal them behind her. By the time she had started the lock cycle, Torin was on the comm, "There's some extra light over there. It looks like... yeah, their lock is opening."

"Understood."

She hooked her boots under the toe holds on the deck and keyed the lock from her wristpad. The doors above her slid open and the center floor of the airlock rose up to lift her out of gravity and onto the level of the ship's skin. Above her, she could see the other ship, and the window of light that must be the open dock. As soon as the lift locked into place, she hooked on her safety line and gently kicked herself free. There was a moment of disorientation before she could stabilize herself with the suit thrusters, but then she was essentially on her back, facing upwards to her visitors.

The light flickered and she thought she saw a hint of moment. She punched up the magnification on her visor and held her eyes steady. The form was at first gangly and misshapen until she realized that it was merely upside down. A gentle roll on her part fixed that, and she could see the form was clearly humanoid: two arms, two legs, and a reflective bubble for its head. "Are you guys seeing what I'm seeing?"

"Yeah," came Torin's reply.

"So much for a different galaxy," Semi added.

In her visor's view, she could see the figure pull something metallic up from its belt and place it against its own visor. She guessed it to be some kind of external magnifier, so she waved. The figure waved back. She was not terribly eager to invite a potential boarder onto her ship, but she was even less eager to have this face to face meeting in the unseen interior of their ship. Seconds ticked away, but she decided on the known.

Opening her arms almost in an embrace, she waved the figure towards her. The figure tapped its head twice and released the viewer, letting it retract back to the belt. She was not sure what to make of the gesture, but soon enough she saw the jets fire and thrust the figure towards her across the gulf. She passed a quick word to Semi not to hit any panic buttons and then pulled herself back down to the lock's deck.

By the time the figure came to a rest near her, it was almost obviously human. Even under the bulk of the suit and its oversized thruster pack, the proportions and joints were too close for some quirk of evolution. She hooked her boots into the rings and watched the figure rotate into another set with a practiced grace. She keyed the lift back down, and they sunk into gravity, her companion rebalancing with a sense of surprise.

She held up a hand to wait as the airlock began to cycle, and she took a moment to really look him over. It was most certainly a him, she guessed, judging by his height and the proportions of the suit. Various symbols cluttered around suit displays and hookup points, many of them even using a fairly standard character set, but what really caught her eye was the viewer dangling from his belt. This close, she recognized it immediately. Her first captain, old Carston Schmidt of the *Cappella*, had once shown her an antique replica. It was a sextant, the ancient tool of the navigators.

The status light went green, and she swung her face plate back, letting the air in. She could not gauge his reaction through the reflective coating on his helmet, but he reached up and unsealed it, lifting it over his head. His head, the hair slick with sweat, bore the unmistakable bearded face of a man.

She held out a suited hand. "Captain Akahele Kalas. Welcome aboard the *Jinley*."

He held out his own and grasped her by the forearm. "Third Navigator Bill Pritchard. I must say it is both an honor and a surprise to meet you Captain Kalas."

Chapter 3

"I fooled around a lot in my college years. I never really stuck with one program long enough to call it a specialty, studying only the subjects I liked: music, journalism, electronics, sociology, and so forth. Eventually, though, my advisor reminded me of an eternal truth. There is no escaping History."
— John Kealing, accepting the Clio Medal for his volume, "The Caspian Road: Warnings for the Next War"

Akahele handed their visitor off to Torin while she got back into her Takasumi uniform, and when she caught up with them in the galley, Bill Pritchard sat on a bench, the bulky upper portion of his suit set out on the table. Torin had provided a bottle of water, which the visitor had almost finished.

Torin was leaning against the galley counter, still in his vacc suit with the helmet hanging over his back. "A thousand years..." he was saying. "It blows my mind that you could keep a ship going that long, let alone one that big. I've never seen anything like it."

Pritchard nodded. "It is our home. We take pride in it." He glanced around the room just as Akahele took a seat across the table from him. "And this is a fine ship as well. How fast does it go?"

Torin hesitated, looking to his captain.

She shrugged. "He may as well know everything." She looked him in the eye. "We broke through light speed about seven hundred fifty years ago. The *Jinley* can go roughly six hundred times the speed of light.

Pritchard's eyes went wide.

Torin grinned. "That's nothing. Some of the military couriers can do over four times that, but they don't give out exact figures for that kind of thing."

"But... but, Einstein..."

Akahele put a comforting hand on his wrist. "He did pretty well for an Earthbound observer. I mean, surely you've noticed a few anomalies out here, especially pushing that big of a magnetic field around."

He nodded slowly, his gaze dropping to the table and Akahele's hand.

Torin stood. "If you'll excuse me captain, I'm going to change." On his way out, he pointed to the intercom on the wall, and Akahele nodded.

Pritchard just sat for a moment, and she let him, but eventually his eyes returned to hers. "You're everywhere then, aren't you? Ships... colonies... even nations?"

"Yes. There was a strong push to get out. Twenty-eight billion was a lot even for three planets."

"And New Providence?"

"Your destination?"

He nodded.

"Callista Prime, settled about three hundred years ago from what was then the Hudson district of the old Republic. Current population is about eight or nine hundred million." She could see it in his eyes. A lifetime of dreams, gone in an instant. "I'm sorry."

He sighed. "It's not your fault."

"Can I get you something to eat? That might make it a little easier."

He shook his head and sat upright. "No, I need to be getting back to the shuttle."

She moved back towards the kitchen. "Surely you can take a little time."

"No," he stood. "I left some systems running on automatic."
He went over to the rest of his suit and hoisted the torso up
over his head. "I have to get back."

She stared at him as he suited up in haste. "Nothing critical
I hope."

He forced the waist clamps down one by one. "Very
critical."

And then it hit her. "You took precautions, didn't you? In
case you didn't come back in time."

He picked up his helmet. "I'm sorry, Captain. I was under
orders. We didn't know."

She thought about her own precautions, the tach drive
holding on standby, ready to shred the little shuttle with the
backwash. "It's all right, Bill. We can take care of it together.
How much time to we have?"

He looked at the readout on his wrist display. "Oh, actually
about six hours," he admitted. "I suppose I could have had that
meal after all."

Akahele smiled nervously and shook her head. "I think
we'll all eat better once your critical systems are a little less
critical." She called out to Torin, knowing he would have been
monitoring, "I imagine you're getting the airlock prepped by
now."

"Yes, ma'am," he responded, "and I'm standing by at the
lock with your suit."

At the lock, Torin was suited up. She suspected he had
never actually unsuited in the first place. She eschewed the
more intimate hookups and just pulled the suit on over her
uniform. "Let's not keep this waiting," she urged as they
stepped into the lock.

Torin made one fleeting attempt at stopping her. "I really
think that this time, I should —"

She shook her head. "Captain's prerogative." She patted
her thigh through the suit to feel her Jansky-7 in her pocket. "I
can take care of myself, Torin. You just take care of things
here."

The ride across went smoothly. She let Bill take the lead with her using her own jets to follow behind and off to his left. The airlock on the shuttle was smaller, but the two of them could still fit, mostly because her suit was so much more compact. She noted that the final safe status light was blue instead of green, but she took her cue to break the seal on her helmet from him anyway.

Bill gave a nervous smile. "I'm no Captain, but I do welcome you aboard."

There was no gravity inside, so they drifted in on various hand rails. Bill seemed at ease in the environment, but she moved cautiously, afraid of bumping anything "critical". When she caught up with him, he was braced against the walls in a small storage compartment. Bolted to the floor was a roughly cylindrical device about a meter in length. He had just pulled a large electronic plug from a socket, and the various lights on the display reconfigured and one by one went out. From the size of the device, even the most powerful chemical charge would have done little but shower the *Jinley* with debris.

"Nuclear?"

Bill nodded grimly. "Again, I apologize."

"No need," she assured him. "I... I had taken steps of my own."

"Nothing critical, I hope."

She thought about it and punched in the suit-comm on her wrist. "Torin, tell James to take the tach offline for now. And Semi, you can ignore my earlier orders."

Bill drifted out into the short passage and sealed the storage hatch behind him. "Perhaps I should offer you the meal."

She shrugged. "Sure, but what I'd really like is a tour of your ship." She saw Pritchard's eyes glance about the close walls and low lighting. "No, not this ship. Your main ship."

He smiled. "*God's Chariot*, though it's not really mine. I'm merely an officer."

"Then I look forward to meeting your captain."

37

She strapped herself into the copilot's seat and folded her arms to keep them off the controls. Bill opened a communications channel beside her. It was audio only, and he motioned her to silence. After a few cursory queries and acknowledgements, a stern voice came. She knew instinctively it must be Pritchard's captain.

"Pritchard, what's your status?"

"All is well. Sorry for the communications dropout. I had a bad motor on the antenna array. It's fixed now."

"Good. Did you find anything?"

"Yes, Captain, as a matter of fact I did. I have an interesting dust sample here I think you'll enjoy examining."

There was a pause. "Dust? You're sure?"

Bill looked over at Akahele's quizzical stare. "As sure as I can be without a lab."

Another long pause. "Well, yes, that should be interesting. Come on back as soon as you're ready. Oh, and your daughter's been asking after you, pretty insistently."

"I'm sorry, sir."

"No," there was a chuckle. "Not at all. I believe she is merely eager for your return, as are we all."

"Of course, sir. Please tell her I'm on my way and not to worry."

"Will do, and thank you, Pritchard. In fact, God bless you."

Bill took a deep breath, letting it out in a ragged sigh. "God bless us all, Captain. Pritchard out."

She gave him a moment to recover before asking, "Dust sample?"

"The signal is not encrypted in any way, and you're something of a secret. The captain and I worked it out ahead of time."

"I gather our arrival will cause some political problems."

He shrugged. "It could have been worse."

"How?"

"You could have been a gas sample."

Docking bay twenty-three had been cleared of most of the normal personnel, but two techs stood by as the lift slowly brought the shuttle down to the hanger deck. Margaret stood as patiently as she could, but the low gravity of the hanger levels made it hard. She was so anxious to see her father that she literally floated off her feet at times, the long lines of her dress swaying around her legs.

Beside her, Captain Ackerman was outwardly more at ease, but she suspected he was a little nervous as well. He was in his full dress uniform, and Margaret had only seen him wear that at the high festivals and her father's last promotion. He even wore the real Peace cluster, the formal badge of Captain since the Great Mutiny of 774. It was so enticing that it was all she could do not to reach out and touch it.

"Thank you for letting me come," she told him.

He smiled at her, still with a formal air about him. "Your father has done me a great service. For all of us, really. And I just thought he should have a proper welcoming party."

"Though a small one."

"The best ones are."

The lift finally locked down into the deck, and the shuttle hatch cracked open with a short puff. Margaret could no longer restrain herself, and she started towards the shuttle as fast as she could push while still keeping some contact with the floor. She was halfway there when her father came into view.

"Watch your step," he was saying, "we still don't have full—"

"Father!" she cried out, flinging herself through the air the last two meters.

Bill Pritchard turned just in time to brace himself for the impact of her embrace. He caught her and squeezed tight. It was the best thing she had felt in two days.

"I was so worried, Father," she whispered into his shoulder. "After what you said, and then you didn't come back after your shift, and no one would tell me where you were, and Captain..." she trailed off as she saw an exotic woman behind him in the shuttle's airlock. "I'm sorry, I just..."

"It's all right, Maggie." He held her by the shoulders and maneuvered them out onto the deck. The woman stepped forward gingerly, hesitating at the threshold. Ackerman had also come forward, somewhat more stately, but held off a few steps. Pritchard came to attention. "Captain Ackerman, I present to you Captain Akahele Kalas of the *Jinley*."

Akahele met Ackerman's gaze and saw a brief double-take. "May I come aboard?" she asked.

Ackerman began a slow nod before thrusting out a hand. "Oh, yes, of course. I apologize. It's just a little unexpected."

Akahele took the outstretched hand by the forearm and was repaid with a firm grasp. "It's an honor to be here," she said.

Margaret stood by, looking closely at the green uniform of her father's guest, so different from any on the ship, both in its fabric and insignia. "Father," she whispered, "why do you call her Captain? And what's a *Jinley*?"

Akahele heard her and turned with a warm grin. "The *Jinley* is my ship, and I am her captain."

"Your ship?" She looked back to her father. "But..."

"Come," Ackerman beckoned. "I have a private tram car waiting." Akahele and her father followed behind leaving Margaret standing alone by the shuttle.

"But Father..."

Ackerman turned to see her. "Oh, Miss Pritchard, you come along too. There's no harm in it. Today is a celebration."

She rushed forward, forgetting the gravity for a moment and flying to them before regaining her feet. She pressed down the skirt of her dress and took her father's hand. "Why thank you, Captain Ackerman, Captain Kalas. I would love to join you."

By the fourth time around, Akahele realized that they were taking a very indirect route, mostly making latitudinal circles while only occasionally sidestepping towards the front of the ship. She might have noticed it earlier if not for two things: the incredible vistas it provided and the constant barrage of questions from Captain Ackerman. Most of it was ground she had covered before with Pritchard on the flight back, and he was helping to translate some of the technologies into better metaphors.

"Like a sail," he was saying, "on the old ocean vessels of Earth and Mars. Apparently the wind is everywhere, though it's apparently stronger in some directions than others."

Ackerman nodded. "The wind, eh? Storms, too?"

Akahele pulled her gaze from the tinted window. "Yes, actually, shifting disturbances in the tachyon field are a common navigation hazard." She glanced briefly at the little communications strip on her jacket's arm, the status showing green. The *Jinley* should still be picking her up. "I'm curious, Captain, is this just the scenic route, or are we hiding?"

Ackerman sighed. "Well, it had been agreed that if Pritchard found anything, or anyone, that I would bring you to see High Reverend Hathaway immediately. I was just trying to buy a little time first, to get a handle on the situation."

"I see." She had gotten the civics lesson from Pritchard on the flight over. The colony was divided into eighty-four districts called tiers, and the people in those districts elected a number of tier-sons to represent them in a local council, usually prominent community members or local clergy. Each of these local councils would eventually promote one of their own as their tier-father in a lower legislative body. Barring recall, retirement, or further promotion, tier-fathers served for life.

The twenty-two reverends were drawn from the tier-fathers, but they were selected by the existing reverends. In addition to forming some kind of upper legislative body, the reverends sat as judges and also had leading positions in the church. The High Reverend himself was a lifetime position and was selected from and by the lower reverends. She had likened it to the cardinals and Pope, but Pritchard had suggested it would be wise not to repeat that analogy.

Pritchard had also hinted that there were long-standing political issues between the Captain and the High Reverend. It was nothing personal, he had assured her, just something lingering from a mutiny hundreds of years before. Looking into the eyes of this captain, she wondered if this feud was truly history. "Is there anything else you need to know before we meet with him?"

"No. Well, I'm sure a thousand things, but mostly I want to caution you. Your news of New Providence, your ship, even your very existence represents a threat to our way of life, something we have protected for over a thousand years at great cost. The High Reverend is a good man. I assure you of that, but he is also very much a man of faith. He believes in God's promise of a new world, of a heaven on this earthly plane, and you..."

She nodded. "And I have come to break the promise?"

"I'm afraid that is what he will see."

Akahele looked to Pritchard who accepted the words with no visible reaction. The girl was somewhat aghast. "Tell me, Captain Ackerman, what do you believe?"

She could see Pritchard's eyes go wide with that, but she waited for Ackerman's answer.

"It's complicated," he hedged.

She shook her head. "That's not a good answer."

He set his jaw. "Sufficed to say I am required to answer that I also believe in God's promise of a new world, but I am open to practical matters. Know that not everyone will be as open."

She looked out the window again on a colony of over three hundred twenty-five thousand, all keeping the hope of a New Providence alive for future generations, a hope she knew to be dead. She could sense the size of the stakes now.

The High Reverend's home would have been considered a wealthy estate back home on Naria, but in the limited space of the *Chariot*, it was clearly the seat of power. The gardens were colorful and well manicured, and the architecture itself was as ornate as the old Governor's Palace on Lannex. Servants escorted them quickly through various foyers, past a grand hall, and finally to a more modest and comfortable anteroom.

"I must speak to the High Reverend for a moment first," Ackerman explained and excused himself with a curt bow.

Akahele observed her two remaining escorts. Bill Pritchard seemed nervous. She suspected he had had brushes with power before and did not enjoy them. His daughter, on the other hand, seemed alert and curious, watching her intently. Akahele flashed her a courteous smiled.

"Excuse me, Captain Kalas, but when did you last eat?"

"We ate on the shuttle."

"Shuttle paste?" she accused her father. "Surely you could do better than that." He attempted a response, but Margaret waved him off annoyed finger. "Captain, when did you last have a real meal?"

She had to think about it. It had certainly been an unusually long day. "I had lunch about... fourteen hours ago."

Margaret shook her head disapprovingly. "You must be exhausted."

She sighed, realizing how right the younger woman was. "Well, it has been a full day."

Margaret turned a stern face to her father. "We know how to be better hosts than that, Father, so when you two are done here, you bring her right home where we can put an honest meal into her and a real bed under her." Then turning back to Akahele, "That is, if you would be so kind as to grace us with the honor."

Akahele had arrived to turn their insular world inside-out, and this young woman was the first to go past it enough to show her the genuine warmth of compassion. Certainly Bill Pritchard and his captain had responsibilities and duties to preoccupy them, but it was a welcome change to feel it coming from someone. "Of course, Miss Pritchard, I gladly accept your offer."

"Then I must be off to prepare," she said, turning to go.

"Maggie," he father warned, "not a word of this to anyone."

She shook her head. "You know I can keep secrets," she replied with a sly wink. "Even from you."

Alone again, Akahele whispered to Pritchard. "A daughter that can keep secrets from you?"

He chuckled. "And Job thought he was tortured."

The far door opened and Captain Ackerman led them into the High Reverend's private study. Hathaway rose from behind his desk to greet her, opening his arms to embrace her. "Oh sweet angel of the stars, how you have blessed us with your visit," he intoned as he released her. "While I weep for the loss of our New Providence, surely you are another providence personified."

She was overwhelmed by both his warmth and inherent charisma, thinking more than anything of her father back on Naria. In her mind, she knew it to be at least partly a show, that he was a politician, but that did not for a moment diminish the emotional rush she felt in his presence. "It's... it's been wonderful to find you."

They sat in a small cluster of plush leather chairs, though it was clear from the arrangement that Hathaway's was in the dominant position. "My good Captain Ackerman has given me a sketch of your news, but please, indulge me by sharing it again. Tell me of your ship, of your world, for that matter of all the worlds."

She plunged into it again for the third time, though the previous sessions with Pritchard and Ackerman gave her some clue of which areas to dwell on and which to avoid. Hathaway seemed far less interested in the technical ratings of her ship or others. He was more interested in the scale of it all, so she did her best, scraping up what she remembered from her school days as well as her day to day adult life.

The Thousand Worlds benchmark had been passed with great fanfare some two hundred years before, just before the splintering of the great Republic of Man. Of course, even then it was more accurately a thousand star systems, and over thirteen hundred worlds. The three largest political unions were the Hudson Confederacy, the League of the Catai, and of course, the Solarian Union. The Solarian Union was really just the remnants of the once great Republic after splintering again and again over fifty years of civil war. The League had survived the wars largely intact, transitioning from rebellious province to nation state with ease. The Confederacy had suffered far worse and was still struggling with the political aftermath, having had two smaller civil wars of its own since then. The *Chariot* itself was passing through space that had nearly been ripped from the Confederacy during the Caspian Rebellion a quarter century before.

These three giants still dominated much of the core systems, while a few dozen smaller coalitions filled in the gaps. Another few hundred small independent systems spotted the frontier. Her home world of Naria was one of them, situated on the far side of Sol, perhaps five hundred light years from the *Chariot*. Primarily an ocean world, its key industries were sea-based agriculture and tourism for the wealthier League citizens.

"You're such a long way from home," Hathaway commented.

She shrugged. "There was no real future for me there. Dad is seventy-two standard and still piloting a harvester in the northern seas, but I had my fill of it during breaks from school. Apart from that, I couldn't see myself living off the leavings of the rich visitors coming in from Windsland or Barrons. Maybe it was simply youthful wanderlust, but I got out."

"And you've done very well for yourself, a captain of a starship. Have you ever been back?"

"There's usually a big family gathering for Tidal Blessings. That's about every two standard years. I've been back for two of those, but that was all. It's far enough that I have to take a leave of absence, and that means taking myself out of rotation. That's going to be much harder now that I'm a captain."

Hathaway beamed at her with those ever-loving eyes. "Yet I sense you will make it again."

"At some point, yes." In truth, she could have visited home more often if she had taken a job in the League, but most of the shipping in the Catai region was dominated by half a dozen large shipping lines running bulk freighters over established routes. Here in the spinward fringes of the Confederacy, there was a lot more flexibility. Captains of the Takasumi Line operated with a great deal of autonomy, and she liked that level of freedom. It was that, more than anything, that had led to their meeting. "Mostly, though, I've been staying here in Confederacy."

"Have you been to this Callista Prime?" Hathaway asked.

"A few times. I rarely get past the port, but I did once go on a camping tour of the northern mountains."

"And you're quite sure about it being our New Providence?"

Pritchard had resigned himself to the technical matters only lightly discussed, but now spoke up. "I am certain, High Reverend. I showed her our charts and course plot in the shuttle. This Callista Prime is, in fact, our New Providence."

"And I suppose we have no legal claim on it?" he asked.

She shrugged. "I'm not a legal expert, but I doubt it. Any government that would recognize your claim is long since gone. But Callista is not full by any means. The primary has a land mass almost as large as Earth's and by your standards, it is lightly populated."

"No, while such an offer would be generous, the promise of New Providence was to have a world of our own, a separate place to practice a righteous life without interference." He paused with a heavy sigh. "To live amongst the others... no, that would never do."

Silence settled over the room as the news finally hit home for the High Reverend. Pritchard shifted in his seat, the leather squeaking awkwardly. Ackerman had relaxed back into his seat, one leg draped casually over the other knee. "Perhaps..." he trailed off, though from the intensity of his eyes, Akahele had no doubt that he knew precisely what he wanted to say.

"Yes?" Hathaway roused himself.

"Perhaps we could find a new world," Ackerman suggested. "From what dear Captain Kalas has told us, there is more than sufficient passenger and shipping capacity to transport us somewhere new."

Hathaway furrowed his brow. "But without the *Chariot* where would we live? It was to be our home for four hundred years of terraforming."

"Surely," Ackerman countered, "with over a thousand worlds in just six hundred years, terraforming must be much faster."

Akahele nodded. "Definitely, if a planet is close enough, well, I've heard of frontier worlds becoming livable in just thirty or forty years with enough of the right algae strains and atmospheric plants."

"And do such worlds exist?" Hathaway asked. "One we could claim?"

"Well, sure, they exist. That's the main purpose of the various survey forces, though it's less of an issue to claim one. It's more about who's willing to fund the effort."

Hathaway slumped in his seat. "But we have nothing, or rather, all we have is what we need for our new home."

"But, sir," Ackerman continued to press, "the church, the rest of it. I would think they could afford it, if they were willing to help."

He started nodding with growing vigor. "Yes, it might be time for reconciliation. That wound has festered long enough."

"What reconciliation?" Akahele asked.

Hathaway sighed. "Oh, there had been something of a schism just before we left. As I understand it, it was over our departure. Our forefather's felt it was our purpose to live God's way as His ordained servants, and the best way to do that was to leave. The rest of the church felt more of a calling to minister to the rest of humanity, to convert them really. A number of them were quite vocal about it, and..." he trailed off. "Well, I wasn't there, of course, but it was apparently quite a difficult time, pitting brother against brother, splitting families, even marriages." He gave a short chuckle. "Who knows, perhaps they've already pursued our choice after all, making their own New Providence. Might they have done so?" he asked.

"Forgive me, Reverend, but just what church is this? I don't quite recognize the, uh, well the trappings."

Hathaway's smile returned, beaming with its full charisma. "Why, my dear Captain Kalas, we're disciples of the blessed St. Mason, the true children of God."

Akahele's eyes went wide. "Masonites?"

"Yes," Ackerman answered. "You're familiar with us then?"

Her heart started racing. Yes, she was quite familiar. Like every other child, she had read the history books: Great Father Calloway of the Masonite Army, Calloway the would-be savior of mankind, Calloway the Butcher of Titan, the Ganymede Massacre, and more than anything else, the madman behind Martian Holocaust. She glanced around the room, thinking about exits. Torin would have heard, but it was a long winding path back to the docking bays. She felt her small Jansky-7 resting in her thigh pocket, but it was only good for a dozen shots, less if she had to go against armor. Adrenalin was already fighting at the fatigue, but she did not think she could make it, not against any kind of organized security. Her eyes darted back and forth between her three inquisitors as ancient horrors flashed through her mind.

"Tell me," she demanded quietly, "just when did you leave Sol?"

"Well, it's year 1049," Hathaway answered, "though I'm not sure if we kept the same monthly schedule since Launch Day falls conveniently on January first."

"No," she shook her head gravely. "On the Earth calendar. What was the date?"

Ackerman leaned forward with a questioning look. "Our official launch date was November 13, 2287."

"And you've had no contact since then?"

"I understand we did for the first couple of years," Hathaway replied, "but well, relations with the rest of the church were so bad that we just gave up. I remember reading once that they even disassembled the Sol-facing antenna array."

Ackerman nodded. "It's true. I was rereading the old logs last night. The last contact was in early in year 3, or about 2290." He turned towards Akahele sharply. "Tell me, Captain Kalas, what happened after we left Sol?"

She took a deep breath. There was no going back. "There are no more Masonites," she told them. "Not since 2302."

Ackerman reached out and grabbed her by the wrist. "What happened?"

"We killed them," she spat it out. "Every last murderous son of a bitch."

Chapter 4

"We can forgive our brothers and sisters for leaving us. Perhaps God truly did call them away to a New Providence. But for the heathen filth that we are left with, there should be no such compassion." - Nathan Calloway, 2289

"We didn't start it," she told them. "It was that butcher, Calloway. Sometime in that last decade, he started pushing people out of the Saturn colonies. First Titan, and then the others. It wasn't anything overt, at least not enough to pull in the colonial board, but by 2297, it was clear. Saturn's moons weren't safe unless you were a Masonite."

Hathaway was still grasping. "But... Calloway. I never heard of any Calloway. Jim?"

Ackerman shook his head. "I saw nothing about him in the logs."

"You'd have no reason to know him. He was just some preacher on the Titan frontier when you left, but by the time the colonial board finally took action in 2298, your church, your brethren, had named him Great Father of the Reclamation, and he declared that the inner system was to be cleansed."

"Cleansed of what?" Pritchard asked.

She looked at him in disbelief. Could these clueless innocents truly be of the same church? "Of us," she replied, "the heathen, those not chosen by God, according to that butcher."

Hathaway shook his head. "Surely, this is some kind of misunderstanding. I know our forefathers wanted a world of our own. Perhaps this Calloway fellow merely-"

"No!" She pounded her fist down on the table. "It was no misunderstanding when he was burning domes on Titan." She pounded her fist again. "It was no misunderstanding when he nuked the settlements on Ganyemede or when he dropped that asteroid on Paris." She held her fist up in fury. "And let me assure you that the billion lives lost in the Martian Holocaust were not simple misunderstandings!"

"I sympathize with anger over the losses in war," Ackerman eased in, "but was this Calloway truly pursuing such a campaign, or was this merely a war that got out of control?"

Akahele turned her rage towards him. "No, it was not out of control. It was most definitely under his control." She shuddered. "The records, the survivors' testimonies... Calloway took a personal interest in the plight of many of their prisoners, and he wasn't called the Butcher for his actions in battle. If you would even think to defend that madman... he had other nicknames, you know. The Widow Killer. Father Executioner. The Zoo-Keeper!"

"Enough!" Hathaway cried, recoiling in horror. He sank into his chair, burying his face in his hands. "Enough," he whispered. "Dear Lord, please, enough."

Akahele was still leaning forward in her chair, her fist poised above the table to strike again. She looked around at her audience, three men who had never known the histories that forged the once great Republic of Man. She shook out her hand and leaned back from the table. "I'm sorry, Reverend, Captain. They drive this one pretty hard in school, and most of us can trace our lineage to the family members who died in the war."

Hathaway looked up from his hands. "And with the annihilation of the old Masonite Church, I suppose we can as well."

She took a deep breath and sank in her seat. The fatigue was hitting hard. "You're right, and I know you're no more the perpetrators than I am the victim. Still, you have to understand that Calloway... He is the ultimate sociopath in our histories, and the rest of the Masonites don't fare much better in public opinion."

"Then perhaps," Ackerman offered, "we just have to work harder to change some opinions."

"Yes, yes, you're right," Hathaway replied. "Captain Kalas, I have been a poor host, needling you with questions and ultimately scaring you with history's worst monster. I can see now that you must be exhausted. Let me have food and a room prepared for you. We can talk more tomorrow when you've had a chance to rest."

She chewed on it for just a moment before deciding to reward the purer of the options. "I thank you for the offer, Reverend, but I already accepted an invitation from the Pritchard family."

Both Hathaway and Ackerman turned to the silent fourth simultaneously.

"It was... actually, my daughter..." he stammered before gathering himself. "I did not mean to presume such a position of honor, High Reverend, but my daughter and I wanted to assure Captain Kalas that a warm meal and a soft bed were waiting for her at the end of your meeting. We will, of course, defer."

Hathaway opened his mouth to speak but stopped, his jaw hanging awkwardly. "Your daughter, eh?"

Pritchard nodded quickly.

"Then no, good Tier-son, it is I who should not presume. Truly such an offer should have been my first words to our guest, and your daughter has taught me a lesson in charity and hospitality. I only ask that you spare no effort for our guest and that you return with her tomorrow so that I may show that I have learned your daughter's lesson."

"Certainly, High Reverend."

They rose, and Hathaway clasped Akahele's arms in his own. "Tonight you sleep in the womb of God's Chariot. I pray it to be a night of peace and rest."

"Thank you," she replied and followed Pritchard out.

In the anteroom, he paused to lean against the doorframe.

"Are you all right?" she asked.

He nodded and stood straight again. "I suppose it has been a long day for me as well."

"I hope I didn't cause you any problems by asking to stay with you."

He shook his head and led her down the hall. "Not at all, though I confess Maggie surprised me."

"Does she do that often?"

He laughed. "With increasing regularity, I'm afraid. Come, let's see what surprise she is preparing for us now."

Hathaway stared at the closed door for a moment before going to his small bar. He got out two glasses and poured them both drinks, giving Ackerman his usual Roxa, but not merely a finger's worth. "Tell me, friend, what do you think?"

Ackerman accepted the glass and took a healthy sip. "It is a situation ripe with opportunity."

"Yes, and with dangers. It seems we have inherited, what... a trillion enemies?"

Ackerman shook his head. "It's been a long time, over eleven hundred years for them. How long could they hate us?"

"How long did they hate the Jews?" Hathaway settled into his chair and sipped at his bourbon. "Well, we have time to worry about that, but for today, I'm more worried about the internal problems. Clearly, her arrival and what she represents..." He sighed. "How many people know about this?"

"A few of the bridge crew, perhaps three or four on the hanger deck, another one or two scattered about. I'd say a dozen in all, plus Pritchard's daughter."

"Yes, I was going to ask about that. Why was she... well, given the security, what were you thinking?"

Ackerman drained the rest of his Roxa. "Perhaps I wasn't, but then again, after what we asked our good Pritchard to do, don't you think he deserved a proper homecoming?"

Hathaway nodded. "I'll grant you that, but how long do you think we can keep this secret?"

"I have confidence in my bridge crew, but the rest, well, let me just answer that the secret won't keep as long as we think it will. Sooner or later you're going to have to make some kind of announcement. If I may be so bold, I would not wait even an hour."

"An hour? Perhaps you're right, but I would like to consult a few of my Reverends." He glanced at the ornate clock on the far wall. "Would you be able to join me for dinner? I would appreciate your thoughts."

"Of course, though I would recommend-" He stopped at the sight of a light flashing on the desk.

Hathaway moved to his desk and hit the intercom. "Yes?"

It was his private secretary. "Sir, Reverend Terrence is calling. He said it was an emergency."

"Put him through." Hathaway stood and circled around his desk. It was always an emergency with Reverend Terrence, remarkable for a job as mundane as colony communications.

"High Reverend, thank you for taking my call. I've got something for you here, rather unbelievable actually, verging on heresy."

"Go on."

"There's a rumor running through the peer network that there's a ship outside, a human ship."

Ackerman stood and moved quietly to stand near the desk.

Hathaway put on his best laugh. "We have shuttles, Jim, and those maintenance whatnots. Those are human ships."

"But, sir," Reverend Terrence insisted, "there's video, almost an hour of it. I'm no expert, but it sure doesn't look like anything of ours."

"Video?" Ackerman demanded.

"Yes… is that you, Captain?"

"Yes, Walter, the Captain is here. Now tell us about the video."

"It's very good quality, high dynamics. My technical lead tells me it's the same format as used by our shuttles."

Ackerman lowered his head in anguish. "We used an inspection shuttle. The video is on by default."

"Sir, I have three of my best men working on different denials, but I'd like some kind of guidance on —"

"No," Hathaway replied. "No denials."

"But, High Reverend, there's no truth to this, is there?"

Hathaway took a deep breath, letting it out with a whispered, "Lord, give me strength."

"High Reverend?" came Terrence's plea.

"Post a notice that I'll be delivering an important sermon soon."

"When?"

"Just soon!" Hathaway threw the switch on his desk and locked eyes with Ackerman. "An hour, you said?"

The Captain shrugged. "I also said it wouldn't last as long as we thought."

Tier-father Alexander Boland sat silently in his den, trying to take in the news the High Reverend was delivering on the screen before him. It was something out of a nightmare, surely. He would wake at any moment.

"It is this last bit of history that is the most troubling, but at the same time, my children, it should not come as too much of a surprise. Our forefathers left home not only to separate ourselves from the unbelievers but also to separate ourselves from the rest of the Masonite church, from those who had lost their way and strayed from the call of God's true path. It would seem now that our fathers' decision was truly divine wisdom. Those who stayed behind have paid for their sin, for their blasphemy, while we remain as the unblemished flock.

"Still, we may now find ourselves blamed for their crimes, to be the pariahs of humanity, yet this is no great burden. Remember that we were charged with forging a new path, apart from the others. It is no great shame to be shunned by those we desire to leave. That the rest of Eve's children fought with those we left behind... yes, even that they were forced to kill them, this is no reason to view our visitors with mistrust. Their ancestors had the strength and will to do what had been, perhaps, our own responsibility. That our own forefathers were too few to have accomplished this peacefully is the real tragedy.

"As for our children, the ones who will look back upon us for the decisions we make now, they will still do so standing beneath the sky of our New Providence. Yes, the star we are currently sailing towards is inhabited and now seems unsuitable for our purpose, but that planet was always just a planet. New Providence is still our destination. It may just take us a little longer to find it. This is not something to weep for. Rather, it is joyous news, an affirmation of God's promise.

"Tomorrow shall be a day of celebration, a new holiday for our calendar: Reunion Day. All non-essential personnel, with the exception of crew E3 and above, should take the day off for celebrations within your tiers. I have authorized the release of the necessary resources. Enjoy yourselves.

"But the day after tomorrow, we must return to our lives. Oxygen levels must still be monitored, crops must be tended, and the trams must still run. Yes, today's news portends great changes, but these changes will not come tomorrow or the day after. They will not come this year. In fact, they may not even come in our lifetimes. We were all born here into an obligation to carry our colony forward so that our children's children may reap what we sow. That has not changed. I pray it will never change."

The image faded and was replaced by the concert he had been watching before, but now the tier-father was on the floor, the pain in his left arm beyond imagination. By the time the symphony reached its climax, Alexander Boland had slipped into unconsciousness. He did not wake.

Akahele woke rested and hungry. The bed had been luxuriously soft, though she dreaded what it would do to her back if she slept on it every night. The hunger was a result both of how long she had slept and of the aroma drifting into her bedroom from the kitchen. She sat up and saw that her uniform, which had been tossed aside carelessly the night before, was now hanging in a small alcove by the door. Her comm was still on the nightstand.

"Comm check," she said into the pickup.

"Good to hear from you, Captain." It was Torin. "We were starting to wonder if there had been something in the food."

"No, just a lot of it, and a draining day, too. Have you managed to listen to all of it yet?"

"Most of it, ma'am. We lost some of it in the docking areas and the tram. I'd be happier if we could close in."

"I'll talk to their captain about it. Did you get the research I asked for last night?"

"Some of it. They don't really release the full survey database, of course, and even then, there's probably another three of four thousand systems that have only had private surveys done. No idea on those."

"I'm not asking for a map of the known universe, Torin. Just tell me what you've got."

"You didn't take a pad did you?"

"No."

"I could download it into your suit computer."

"I think that's still back in the docking bays. Just give me the rundown."

Seven available worlds fell into the parameters she had provided. Two were claimed by the Adren Union, but with no inhabitants on them it was not considered to be a strong claim. Another lay within in Confederate space but was so marginal on the habitable parameters that the terraforming cost would be prohibitive. The other four were out among the independents, and little was known about them beyond basic planetary statistics and atmospheric mixtures. The closest to their current course would still require a seven degree correction and likely take another two thousand years to reach.

"Two thousand?"

"And that's relativistic ship time. For the rest of us, even longer."

"Hell, in that amount of time, the Republic could rise again and move the capital there."

"And fall and rise again, ma'am. For that matter, I read last year that it may only take another three or four millennia before we've settled the majority of the galaxy."

She scowled. "And the other option?"

"Well, the shipping capacity is no problem if they can afford it. I think it's beyond Takasumi to handle the volume on its own, but I'm sure Helliker or perhaps Schneider and Williams would be happy to take on the subcontracts. The real problem is at the other end. Even if you wait until after the terraforming, you're still talking about a lot of structures."

"And the terraforming itself?"

"That one is tough to say. It's not a one-size-fits-all task, but I did find a quote from a news dump about Verig being done by a consortium in the Gemini Basin. The total cost of the project is being estimated at sixty trillion over forty-five years."

"Is that Confederate currency?"

"Yes, and it's being backed by Callistan bonds, so there's no real premium there."

"Damn, I knew this kind of thing was expensive, but not that expensive. Maybe they could at least hope for some more flexible terms."

"For Masonites?" Torin scoffed. "I wouldn't count on it."

"Yeah, it is a pretty visceral reaction." She heard movement in the hall outside. "Ship status?"

"All systems nominal. The hull is taking a radiation pounding from moving this fast in normal space, but nothing the shielding can't handle for a while. If it would be all right with you, I would like to move us in a line behind the *Chariot*. There's a lot less interstellar gas in their wake."

"Do it in a couple of hours. I'll want to give their captain a warning about it. Anything else?"

"Not really, but we're wondering just how long you're planning on staying over there."

"Two, maybe three days. There's going to be some kind of party at the Reverend's today, and then I suspect they'll want another day of more organized talks. I figure it's the least I can do, but I'd like to cut it as short as possible. There are a lot of folks that these people need to be talking to, and in reality, we're pretty far down the list. Best that we get going and try to hand off the larger problems to someone who knows what they're doing."

"Need me to come over and help?"

She chuckled. "Sorry to be stealing all the glory, Torin, but the situation here isn't exactly stable. With just me, I know we can pull out on short notice."

"But—"

"Don't worry, Torin, I'm sure we'll come by again soon. I'll try to come up with a valid business case for Takasumi to underwrite adding them to some kind of trade route."

"Aye, ma'am."

She got dressed but left the comm unit in the bedroom and went out to sample the local breakfast. Margaret was alone in the kitchen, pulling a mountain of rolls out of an oven. "I don't think I can eat all that."

Margaret laughed. "Of course not. Most of these are for the tier's celebration later in the day. I haven't been very active in the Youth Auxiliary for a couple of years, but Gregory Solomon still calls me when it's time to bake."

Akahele sat and began eating, amazed at how hungry she was. "Where's your dad?"

"He had to go early to see Tier-father Boland about the festivities. Normally this kind of task would fall to Father, but today he'll be escorting you to the celebration at the High Reverend's."

"And your mom?"

"She died when I was five."

"I'm sorry."

Margaret sat across from her and shrugged. "It was a long time ago. I wonder what she would have made of this... you sitting here at her table eating the rolls from her recipe. A captain, and a woman at that."

"Has there never been a female captain here?"

"Not since the last Great Mutiny. She was a woman, you know, Captain McMurry."

"Your father mentioned something about a mutiny, but he didn't say much. What's it all about?"

Margaret smiled and sat up straight. She almost wished she had her projector from class. The original colony government, she informed her guest, was a largely bureaucratic structure dominated by a council of Reverends with no true executive. The crew of the time were strictly functionaries, and the captain had no real authority other than that of a high-level manager. The First Great Mutiny came in 463 when Captain Watson seized control during a food shortage. He formed the tier structure and established the tier-fathers as his council of advisors, but the Captain himself retained full authority. This lasted another three hundred years through two minor mutinies where the Captain was killed by his, or in the latter case, her successor. The Second Great Mutiny came in 742 when the Circle of Reverends took over from Captain McMurry.

"Why?" Akahele asked. "I mean, why her and not the captain before?"

Margaret frowned. "Apparently, she was a very bad captain, very harsh." She gave conspiratorial glance around the room. "But her history was written by the Reverends, you see. Personally, I just think they got fed up with having to bow to the will of a woman."

"I see, and how did it happen?"

"Oh, they murdered her along with most of her senior officers. In the history books they're officially called executions for crimes against the colony, but I've looked it up. There are no trial records. But, you see, it was a mutiny."

"And how did it end?"

"Ah, now there's an interesting story. Even after most of the senior officers were killed, it was still quite a fight. The Reverends had everyone whipped up in a frenzy, but a lot of people were crew or had family that were crew, so it was starting to look like there would be open fighting in the streets themselves." Margaret paused to make a violent chop with her fist. She was clearly enjoying the telling of the tale. "But McMurry's senior environment lead, James Watson, a descendant of the first true Captain Watson, had survived."

"What happened? Did he threaten to cut off the Reverend's supporters?"

"Oh, no, just the opposite. He threatened to cut off the crew areas. He made a big speech about the need for peace in the colony, for compromises and such. 'We need only look at our sky to see that we are one colony, one world, and if we fly apart, surely our world will follow.'" She said it with a flourish and then blushed. "Sorry, we make all the students memorize the speech in their sixth year."

"And did he? Cut them off, that is?"

"It never came to that. Personally, I always thought he was bluffing, but the crew surrendered. Watson became the new

Captain and was awarded the Peace Cluster by the first High Reverend. It's that gold brooch Captain Ackerman wore yesterday. I mean that was really it. I'd never actually seen the real one up close before."

"So, that's how you got the High Reverend?"

"Yes, and it's very important to always address him as High Reverend, not merely Reverend."

Akahele nodded, sure she had already given offense. "You have such a unique culture. It's hard to take it in all at once."

"To us it is merely who we are, but you're something none of us ever known, a foreigner, and it really shows."

"Do I stick out that much?"

Margaret lowered her eyes to the table. "I'm sorry, Captain Kalas, I meant no disrespect."

"No, none taken. I'm just curious. What is it, the uniform?"

"No, it's…" she fidgeted in her chair. "It's your ears," she said at last.

"My ears?"

"Yes, your ears. The way your hair hangs, your ears are covered." She looked up at Akahele and grinned. "In fact, around the Reverends, it's almost scandalous."

Akahele noticed that Margaret wore her hair in a traditional French braid, pulled tight across her scalp and then cascading down her back. Thinking back, she had seen similar styles at the High Reverend's home amongst the various staff. "What's taboo about covering your ears?"

Margaret shook her head with a sigh. "Because we must always keep our ears open to hear the word of the Lord."

Akahele reached around and felt at her loose hair. "It's not quite long enough for much of a braid."

"Oh, I have just the thing," she answered fleeing the room. She returned a moment later with a set of long pins and clips and took up position behind Akahele. "Trust me. I can make this work."

She relaxed into it, enjoying the sensation of Margaret's hands moving through her hair, tugging here, twisting there. "You seem to know what you're doing."

"I sometimes do this for the girls at school. Now, Captain Kalas, tell me of the worlds you've visited. Which was the most beautiful?"

"Roney," she answered without even thinking about it. "It's the sixth moon of Herradon in the Alston system. The orbit is unstable, so it won't last more than another million years, but the view of the rings..." She took a deep breath, remembering. "I'm not enough of a poet to describe them, Margaret. You'll just have to go see them yourself."

The High Reverend's grand hall was large enough for Akahele to recognize it as such, but it was still undersized for the task. Mostly, it was exquisitely ornate with decorative columns leading up to carved figureheads, each different but stately. She gathered that they were High Reverend's from previous generations. They made for an impressive gallery staring down at the assembled guests.

Akahele was certainly not a statesman, or even much of a public figure, so apart from her sister's wedding she had never had to endure being in a reception line, certainly never one this long. She had been greeting the upper crust of Masonite society for over an hour when the wife of one tier-father pulled her close for an embrace.

"I'm so glad you're getting us out of this rock," she whispered. She pulled back and smiled. "And your hair is lovely, very stylish."

Akahele did her best to suppress her dismay. "Uh, thank you. Young Miss Pritchard was kind enough to make it presentable." She glanced further down the line where Margaret stood near her father. Margaret herself was beaming with the excitement of attending the High Reverend's own celebration while her father was doing his best to look comfortable.

"I'll have to compliment her on it," she replied as the next tier-father moved into place, an elderly man who looked afraid to take her hand.

"It is an honor and a privilege to meet you," he intoned. "It is truly an auspicious day for our fine colony."

She smiled, trying not to laugh at the awkwardness of it all. "And I am honored by the warmth of its welcome," she replied. As his wife moved into place, she glanced down the line. It still stretched into the foyer.

Akahele spent that night in the High Reverend's guest house, a three bedroom home near the back of his gardens. There was a full kitchen, a chef, and two maids to attend to her. The bed seemed just as soft as the Pritchards' while offering a more comfortable support. It was in all ways the more luxurious of her two nights thus far, but she found that she was missing Margaret and her unguarded honesty. The staff at the High Reverend's was all "Yes, ma'am," and "Certainly, ma'am." They were as honest and courteous as a sullen crew.

The next morning she began a long serious of meetings with the High Reverend, Captain Ackerman, and various members of their staffs. Torin had spent the day of celebration researching the shipboard databases for appropriate contacts. His list included four major terraforming companies, seven law firms specializing in colonial law, and dozens of regional authorities ranging from survey to legislative affairs. This time, she made no effort to hide Torin's virtual presence. In fact, she laid the flat strip of her comm unit out on the table before her and introduced Torin as a full participant of the meeting. It was much more convenient that way, since Torin was clearly recording it all and using one of the *Jinley's* computers to organize the results into a structured action plan.

Most of the Reverends from the day before cycled through, presenting their particular areas of governance and putting forth their prioritized lists of queries. The only person that the High Reverend had throughout was his personal secretary. Hathaway frequently made cryptic comments to him, and he would nod and scribble a few notes on paper.

Captain Ackerman, on the other hand, had only a few of his officers attend, and mostly they seemed to be lower level technical experts on various aspects of the *Chariot's* systems as well as her terraforming equipment and technologies. The only senior officer present through the day's sessions was Pritchard, and the Captain rarely relied on him or restrained him. Ackerman took no notes, yet his memory seemed up to the task. He was able to answer almost all of the ship's systems questions himself, and he even corrected Torin on a few points when he misspoke.

They had been discussing various colonial security arrangements, the kind of patrols that kept pirates and mercenaries from harassing new outposts, and Torin had commented, "You would have to take that up with Admiral Doyle of Survey, Captain."

Ackerman had taken on a quizzical look. "Survey? But in this morning's session you explained that all frontier military patrols were coordinated through the sector admirals, which in this case would be an Admiral Nelson, I believe. Could you clear that up?"

Torin had paused for a moment, clearly checking his own notes. "My apologies, Captain. You are correct. The military units are not under Doyle's direct command. However, Doyle is more likely to be sympathetic to new colonization efforts and can act as your advocate with the sector admirals."

Ackerman thanked him for the clarification and then proceeded into queries on various pirate activities, dispositions, and resources. Akahele had rarely seen that kind of grasp, and almost always it had been in either politicians or military commanders. She was not sure which of the two best applied to Ackerman.

"Are they really humans?" little Mary Ellis asked.

Margaret leaned against her desk at the front of the classroom, the board behind her filled with new words like tachyon and names like Akahele and Callista Prime.

"Now why would you say that?" she asked. "You've seen her picture. Did you think, perhaps, she was a goat instead?"

The class giggled, but Mary was resolute. "No, I thought she might be an angel sent to take us to New Providence."

Margaret slid off her teaching stool and knelt down before Mary, taking her hand. "That's a very sweet thought, Mary, and Captain Kalas is much like an angel. She is kind, honest, and I think she truly does have a love for all of us, but she is not an angel of God. I have seen her eat, and sleep, and do all the things we have to do. She is an extraordinary woman, but she is just a woman."

Mary nodded. "Ok, I believe you, Miss Pritchard."

Margaret rose and patted Mary on the head. "Anyone else have a question?"

Charlie Hunter perked up and asked, "Did she even have to... you know, use the toilet?"

Laughter spread through the room, and hands on hips, Margaret glared at him. "Of course she did, Charlie. Just for that, we're going to do some math problems." She strolled to the board to the sound of groans. "Now," she said, pen in hand, "if a ship can travel at six hundred times the speed of light, how long would it take to travel from here to Callista Prime and back?"

The groans softened as her students worked it out at their own desks and began to realize what the answer really meant.

Akahele pushed back from the table and slid the comm unit back onto her sleeve. She shook hands with the last few Reverends and officers departing. In the end, it was just Captain Ackerman and the High Reverend left in the conference room.

"It looks like we covered everything," she said.

"Yes," Ackerman replied. "I imagine we'll have quite a few visitors in the coming months. It's sixteen days to the sector capital on Latera?"

"Give or take. There's a mild storm on the charts that we might have to divert around."

Hathaway patted her on the shoulder. "I pray you a safe and uneventful voyage, but before you go, I had hoped to have a small, private dinner."

She cocked an eyebrow. "Private?"

Hathaway smiled. "A small family affair." He turned to Ackerman. "You should come, of course, and bring your son."

She wondered what she might be getting into but then flashed on her salvation. "I was wondering, High Reverend, if I might invite the Pritchards. They were so kind to me, especially Margaret. I would like the chance to see her again before I leave."

"Yes," he replied with a slow, thoughtful nod. "Yes, that would actually be quite appropriate. We'll dine in about two hours."

The various parties left to attend to their duties, and Akahele retired to the guest house. The maids waited on her, fixing her hair again, pulling the short strands tight and far away from her ears. They even gave her what was apparently the traditional welcoming foot washing, which was as luxurious as it was awkward.

They had also prepared a beautiful strapless dress, adorned with intricate lace trim, but she opted to stay with her uniform. It had been a long time since she had worn anything that revealing, and she had never been comfortable with it before. Ultimately though, she did accept a flowing green cape that at least made her look a little more feminine. She was worried about the time, but the maids insisted that she wait, informing her that the guest of honor is expected to arrive last at this sort of gathering.

When the time finally came, it was Margaret Pritchard who arrived at the guest house to escort her in. "I'm actually your guest," she explained, "so it's appropriate for us to arrive together." She wore a daring blue halter dress with a wide train that flirted with the floor. She had the kind of beauty and vitality that came with youth.

Akahele gathered the cape behind her and followed. "And your father?"

"Oh, it's a different rule for men," she replied as they took their time walking past the gardens. "He's already at the main house." She stopped for a moment. "I just wanted to thank you for inviting us. A private dinner with the High Reverend... it's the kind of thing you only read about." She resumed their stroll. "Cal's never going to believe it."

"Cal?"

"My fiancé – I showed you his picture."

She nodded. "The blonde, I remember. You should have brought him."

Margaret gasped. "To dinner? Under the High Reverend's roof? Now that would truly be a scandal."

Akahele chuckled. "There's so much I don't know about your people."

Margaret extended her arm and walked beside her, linked arm in arm. "Well, then, I shall just have to keep an eye out for you."

The other guests milled around in the great hall, and Ackerman pulled Pritchard aside into one of the many alcoves. This one in particular was lined with portraits of some of the early captains. Notably, it did not include any captains after the first Great Mutiny. "It looks like Captain Kalas will be on her way in the morning," Ackerman said. "Tell me, Bill, what do you make of her?"

"I trust her intentions, certainly. As for her capabilities, her judgment, she is only human, and humans are not perfect. Our case will be a difficult one to represent, for anyone really. I worry, perhaps, that she might not be up to the task."

Ackerman nodded. "I have had similar concerns, but she does seem quite competent as does her first officer, both very rational, professional. They seem the kind of crew I would want to rely on."

"They certainly are, sir."

"And I have come to rely on you, Bill."

"You are too kind, sir."

Ackerman waved him silent. "No, far from it. Your honesty on these sightings, your ability to maintain security, your analysis, your willingness to carry out difficult orders, all these things have shown me you are far more than merely my Nav-3." He reached into his pocket and pulled out a small glass-topped case. "Your new insignia, Bill," he said, handing it over. "I'm promoting you to full commander."

Pritchard accepted them into his hands. "But sir, there isn't an open spot on the commander rotation."

"I know, but with everything that's happening, I am designating an officer to focus on these external matters, to act as my liaison and such. You are that officer."

Pritchard stiffened, growing perhaps an inch in the process. "Thank you, sir. I won't let you down."

"Of course you won't, Bill. Now, the whole thing is unofficial until I run it past the Reverends, but that's always been a rubber stamp. Just don't wear them in public until then."

Pritchard's eyes went wide. "The Reverends! Captain, I—"

"Captain, sir," a servant interrupted them. "Begging your pardon, but Captain Kalas has arrived and everyone is gathering in the dining room. If you will follow me."

"Captain, there's a complication..."

Ackerman shook his head. "We can talk about it later. Tonight is a night for family. Ah, there's my son now."

Pritchard cursed quietly but followed, tucking the insignia into his pocket.

A servant held Akahele and Margaret in a side room as the guests assembled, and on signal showed her into the dining hall. The table was set for ten, and the seating arrangement was laid out carefully according to the proper rules of Masonite etiquette. High Reverend Hathaway, as host, took one end of the table, while Akahele, the honored guest, sat at the opposite end. Hathaway's wife sat at his right, while Margaret sat at Akahele's right. The rest of the long table was filled out by Pritchard, Captain Ackerman and his son, Hathaway's own two children, and his brother Victor. Akahele noted that of the four younger guests, all single and of marrying age, only Hathaway's son and daughter were seated together. She could see now that Margaret's warning of taboos was not overstated.

Hathaway opened the evening with a blessing. It was clearly a traditional ritualized blessing, complete with two response sections from the other guests, but there were a few miscues. Akahele thought back to what she had read of the Masonite's beliefs of their special chosen status, and she suspected that the High Reverend was censoring the traditional prayer in deference to her presence.

Then came the wine and a series of toasts to her, given in some order of seniority, first Hathaway, then Ackerman, and so on. Most were overstated and friendly and a little long-winded. The most interesting came from Hathaway's son, who stammered out, "To Captain Kalas, the loveliest captain I have ever seen."

Though by far, the one that struck Akahele as the most heartfelt came from Margaret, who apparently fell last in this particular hierarchy. She raised her glass saying, "To Captain Kalas, who came so far to be my — to be our friend."

She would have loved to respond in kind, but a nod from Margaret made it clear that her own toast must be back to the High Reverend as host. "To the High Reverend," she responded, "who has brought you all closer to home than any had ever hoped."

The meal began in earnest then, and it was something of a free-for-all on the toasts after that, though they were far less formal. "To young Richard Ackerman on his impending nuptials," and "To Madam Hathaway and her roses – I hear they will fare well at the competition this year." It was a general sharing of good news, with each calling out the fortunes of the others. Hathaway's son had placed second in an archery tournament. Margaret's fiancé Cal had been promoted recently. Akahele thought it a wonderful tradition.

Hathaway's brother lifted his glass and with a half-mouthful of mutton proclaimed, "To Tier-son Pritchard and his impending promotion."

Madam Hathaway cheered on. "Here, here, very true. You are certainly moving forward in the world."

They all took sips, and as Ackerman set his glass down, he asked, "Excuse me, Victor, but how did you know?"

"I told him," Hathaway replied.

Ackerman turned to the High Reverend. "But, High Reverend, how could you have known?"

"I've known since yesterday morning. Bill told me about it himself. Terrible news of course, but the *Chariot* must still spin."

Ackerman turned towards his newest commander. "Yes, terrible news, right Bill?"

"Oh, but you might not have heard," Madam Hathaway went on. "We didn't want to ruin the celebration and all. Tier-father Boland died two nights ago."

"And I have no doubt," Victor nodded to Pritchard, "that your fellow tier-sons are going to send you into the House of Fathers with blessing and haste."

"Most certainly," Hathaway agreed. "And well deserved." He took another sip of his wine and turned a serious eye towards Ackerman. "But I gather, dear Captain, that this was not the promotion you thought we were speaking of. Tell me, what other good fortune has fallen on our humble servant?"

Ackerman set his wineglass down and sat a little more straight. "I just promoted our humble servant to be my newest commander, with the Reverends' blessing, of course."

Hathaway sat back in his chair. "Commander, eh?"

"But Father," Hathaway's daughter chimed in, "there's never been a tier-father above the rank of lieutenant commander."

"Forgive me," Ackerman's son Richard replied, "but that's not quite correct. Captain Emerson was also a tier-father until the day he assumed command himself."

A silence settled over the table, broken only by Hathaway's sigh. "Well, things were different then."

"Yes," Ackerman replied, "I suppose in many ways they were."

72

Akahele began to ask how they had been different, but as she opened her mouth, she felt a sudden squeeze on her right wrist. Margaret's grasp was firm, and her eyes made the message clear. Captain Emerson must have been one of the captains from between the two Great Mutinies. She nodded, and Margaret released her arm.

That was when Akahele saw it. There, on the back of Margaret's left hand, lay the tell-tale blue mark. She snatched Margaret's hand and pulled it close. "This spot, tell me, Maggie, where did you get it."

"This? It's just an ink stain."

"Did you wash it?"

All eyes had turned to them. "Well, yes, of course I washed it."

"Did you scrub it?" Akahele insisted.

Margaret glanced around nervously. "Why yes, I even used a brush, but the ink we use at school, you see..."

Akahele grabbed at Margaret's arm, twisting and turning it to examine it. She found another mark on the outside of her bicep. "And this one?"

Margaret craned her neck to see it. "Oh my, I hadn't even seen that one."

Pritchard leaned forward. "What exactly is going on, dear?"

Akahele grabbed Margaret's shoulder and spun her around in her chair. She leaned in close, staring at the skin on her exposed back. She found three more with the clear daisy pattern, two of them along the spine – already along the spine. As quickly as she had seized her, she released her, backing away from the table and knocking her chair to the floor. "Sweet Ocean, no, don't let it..."

Margaret stared at her. "If I have given offense..."

"No, no..." she collapsed onto the floor, sobbing into her hands, her deadly hands. "Sweet Ocean, no, take this into the sea. Do not leave this on my shore."

She felt a hand on her shoulder and looked up to see Madam Hathaway leaning over her. "What's wrong, dear?"

"No!" she shouted, slapping the hand aside. "No, no women!" She forced herself to take deep breaths. She thought about every hand she had shaken, the maids washing her feet, and yes, sweet and generous Margaret fixing her hair and washing her uniform. Blinking away the tears, she fixed on Pritchard. "Bill, I need you to get my vacuum suit right now."

He stared at her, confused. "But..."

She clenched her jaw to suppress the shout. "Right... now!"

He nodded firmly and darted from the room.

Hathaway stood over her. "My dear Captain Kalas, what is wrong?"

She glanced up at him, at Captain Ackerman, and looked on to poor Margaret rubbing at the blue spot on her arm. "Teruvian Pox. None of you have had it. No vaccines, no immunity." She buried her face in her hands. "You haven't even fucking heard of it."

Chapter 5

"Father, why have you forsaken me?" - *final words of Tess Fletcher, Teruvian Pox index case*

The silence held for a moment while they all stared at her, but it was her communications band tucked into her sleeve that broke it. "Comm check. Captain, is something wrong?" It was Semi from the ship. She must have left it in transmit mode after the meetings were over.

"Umm," she looked at the faces around her, some beginning to realize their plight. "I'm going to need an immediate evacuation, and I think we're going to be taking on passengers. Pull in close to the rear docking bays. No slow and easy approach. I expect you in range for ship-to-ship transfers within the hour."

"Aye, ma'am."

Margaret was still rubbing at the spot on her arm, and Akahele wracked her brain trying to think of when she could have caught it. She had not seen her much since the day before, but she remembered the morning she woke at the Pritchard home. Margaret had washed her uniform, and she had braided her hair. Who knows, it could have been the simple handshake at their first meeting. That meant she was a day and a half along, two days at most. She was no doctor, but she knew that in a grown woman, untreated Teruvian Pox was usually fatal in five days.

Five days, and two of them were already gone.

"She needs to be quarantined," Akahele said at last. "Shit, but a lot of people need to be quarantined... anyone I have touched, even shaking hands, anyone who has handled my clothes or bedding, anyone they may have touched, anyone..." she trailed off. She had shaken hands with hundreds just the day before.

Hathaway held his own hands out before him. "Everyone?"

She shook her head. "Mostly just the girls and the women. They're the only ones susceptible to Teruvian, but even the men could carry for an hour or two on their skin or clothing."

"Exactly how serious is this?" Ackerman pressed.

She locked eyes with him. "You've read about the old Black Death on Earth?"

He nodded.

"This is worse."

And it was worse. The first documented case had been on a small mining colony three hundred years before. Almost a thousand women and girls were infected. The prepubescent girls fared well, surviving with only mild scarring along the spine. For the older ones, the teens and their mothers, the mortality rate was ninety-seven percent. In nine days, two generations of women were wiped out.

It killed the colony. The survivors gathered up the remains of their shattered lives and fled back to their homes, carrying the young girls to dozens of different worlds. That would have been the end of it, except that the Teruvian Pox is not so kind. It did not happen right away, but as they grew into young women, they became active carriers, spreading the Pox wherever they went.

Tragically, they were no longer on a tiny isolated mining colony. Many had returned to densely populated worlds throughout the old Republic, and once it started moving, the Pox was everywhere. By the time they got it under control, over two billion women had died and over a third of humanity were potential carriers.

"Captain," came Torin's voice, ragged but alert. "I'm on duty now. What's your status?"

"Are you inbound?"

"Yes, we'll be there in about twenty minutes. I repeat, what is your status?"

"I brought the Pox, Torin." Her voice threatened to break. "I brought the fucking Teruvian Pox."

"You're a carrier?" It was equal parts question and accusation.

"It seems so." She was not supposed to be. In modern times, Teruvian Pox was quite rare. Like most girls, she received her first vaccination for it when she was two. She got her second at age five, and she was only a year shy of her third and final shot when she caught the Pox from her great aunt Hani at age seven. With her body mostly prepared, it was a mild case. Even so, she sat it out with a full course of anti-viral drugs and all the ice cream she wanted. The local doctors assured her it was so mild, in fact, that she could never pass it on. Even the medical screening for the Academy had shown her to be clean. They were all wrong.

Torin's muffled voice came back with a few curses, but eventually he settled himself. "Captain, they need to set up quarantines immediately, and I mean right now."

She scanned around for Ackerman and Pritchard but saw neither. "I know. I think they're working on it already."

"Is there anything I can do before we get there?"

She looked around. Most of them were still in shock. Poor Margaret still sat at the table. She seemed to be crying, but no one would comfort her. They could take Margaret, but they could not take everyone. There could be hundreds of cases by now. The *Jinley's* life support would only handle another four passengers, six if they pushed it. They could save a handful if even that. Margaret was already two days along.

"Go through the med-room. Look for anything that might help – Taranex if we have any – and dump the entire medical database into as many spare pads as you can round up."

77

"Aye, ma'am. See you soon."

Hathaway kneeled next to her. "Are you sure about this? I mean, maybe it's just an ink stain after all."

She wanted to grab his shoulders and shake him, but that would be touching. "High Reverend, you need to come to grips with the fact that you may be about to lose half of your colony."

"Attention! Attention!" a voice blared in through an open window. "This is Captain Ackerman speaking. I have an emergency message for all members of the colony. Our new guest has accidentally exposed us to a deadly virus for which we have no immunity. It apparently infects only women and girls, and it is spread by touch. I am ordering an immediate quarantine until future notice for all female colonists. Stay home and do not travel. Do not touch anyone, even family members. To all male colonists, it seems that you are immune, but try to avoid all unnecessary contact. Wear gloves when possible. Be prepared to cover extra shifts.

"The infection can be identified by persistent blue marks on the skin. If you believe you or your daughter are infected, contact your tier's medical office but do not travel without authorization. Tier constables will be enforcing the quarantine, and they can expect their orders through proper channels shortly. Above all, remain calm and avoid contact."

Ackerman returned during the last part of it, and closed the window as it began to repeat. "That should do for the immediate quarantine."

Hathaway stared at him in dismay. "What were you thinking, James? Did you decide that all on your own?"

"I mean no disrespect, but I had to act."

Hathaway was still taking it in. "By unleashing a panic?"

"Forgive me, High Reverend, but look at the clock. It's 19:33. How many mothers are about to put their daughters to bed? How many more infections were we about to have?"

He opened his mouth to answer, and then stopped. He lowered his eyes to the floor. "No, I... I'm sorry, friend. You may have just saved a lot of lives."

"I was only doing my duty, High Reverend. Now, may I suggest if you do want the quarantine, the confirming orders should flow down through your office."

Hathaway nodded. "Yes, I'll do that right now," he replied and whisked out of the room.

Ackerman turned to Akahele, pinning her to the wall with his eyes. "And now, Captain Kalas, what are you going to do?"

She set her jaw. "I'm going to fix it."

"That's the right answer."

The two captains stood in the observation deck of one of the central docking bays, their boots hooked into the floor rails in the low gravity. Akahele was already suited up, and speaking through her helmet comm. Outside, the last of the cargo pods was sliding out from *Jinley's* main hold, drifting towards the rocky surface of the *Chariot*.

"We'll have it secured with netting within the hour," Ackerman said. "Forgive me for not storing it internally, but after... well, I don't want to take any chances."

She nodded. "Don't worry, it's all vacuum sealed and fairly well rad-hardened." She sighed. "Six percent isn't much of a boost, but it's more than enough to make up for the unloading time."

A figure approached, jetting across the gap from the *Jinley*, a modest crate trailing behind on a cord. "Your first officer?"

"Most likely."

He twisted around and braced himself against the crate before firing the suit jets again to decelerate. It was a tricky maneuver, but he was skilled enough to bring it into the grasp of a cargo arm that guided them both into the smaller personnel airlock. The two captains greeted him there after it cycled him through.

"Captain Ackerman, this is my first officer Torin Graylock."

Torin did not unseal his suit but had triggered his suit's external comm. "It's an honor to meet you, Captain. Forgive me for not giving you a proper greeting. I don't want to risk anything."

"I understand."

Akahele was already unbolting the crate. "Did you get everything?"

"Aye ma'am. Really, Victor just ripped out the pharmacy cabinet."

"Any Taranex?"

"One vial. It's technically expired, but Victor said it was still good. The date's more for liability than real safety."

Sixty milliliters of Taranex. The standard course of treatment was twenty.

"But the medical database is there. Victor highlighted a few sections on emergency Teruvian treatment. Not as good as Taranex, but something."

She closed the crate again and dragged it out of the lock. "Ok, Torin, you've earned your claim of the second boot prints, now get back to *Jinley* and prep for departure. I'll be over within ten minutes."

"Aye, ma'am." He nodded to Ackerman and stepped back into the lock.

Akahele saw the crate off to a couple of uniformed workers and then turned to Ackerman. "Captain, there's a small supply of Taranex in there. It's the standard treatment for Teruvian Pox, but it's not going to be enough, not enough by far. The medical text should give you the best strategies for spreading it out for survival. That will be the key, survival, not treatment and cure."

"I understand."

"No, listen, Captain... James. The kids are going to get it. Young girls, daughters. It's going to look bad, almost as bad as the adults. Everyone's instinct is going to be to give the Taranex to them, but don't. They'll survive without it. It won't be pretty, but they'll survive."

"That's not going to go well. Our children, they're very important to us."

"I understand, but don't waste it on them. You've got to make that stick. Margaret is depending on you."

"I will."

Pritchard came shuffling down the corridor already suited up. "Sir, I'm ready."

"Sure you're up for this?" he asked.

"Yes, Captain, I am. Let's just get going."

"Then I'll see you soon. God speed, Captain Kalas. God speed," he said, and backed away to speak with the dock master and his aide.

Akahele and Pritchard stood silent for a moment, waiting for the lock to cycle back to their side. "I'm sorry, Bill. I don't know what else to say."

"It's not your fault, really. None of us thought about it either."

"How is she?"

"Calmed down now, a little scared. She lost her mother when she was very young, so she's always hated the hospital."

"How? I mean, how did she die?"

Pritchard sighed. "Glonic syndrome. By the time she noticed the symptoms, it had already advanced to the brain."

"That's too bad." Too bad because a real hospital probably could have cured her anyway. She let the silence stretch for a moment. "I still say we should bring her with us."

"It's been decided."

"I know, but I still say we should."

He turned on her, almost grabbing her. "Don't you think I want to?"

"Then why not?"

The airlock door unsealed with a puff and began to slide open. Pritchard stepped back from her, calmly. "The calls are already coming in. Over four hundred suspected cases so far. You can't take everyone."

She stepped into the lock. "No, I can't."

He joined her as she recycled the controls. He paused before bringing his helmet down. "She is my bond, my oath. There can be no doubt that I will bring back help."

The lock cycled through and they were jetting across to the *Jinley* in minutes. With no cargo, the navy base at Arvin was just under four days away. A Confederate carrier group was supposed to be stationed there, and even a light cruiser would have a real sick bay with a full pharmaceutical lab. And a cruiser would be faster than the *Jinley*, even twice as fast.

But six days was a long time for someone with Teruvian to wait. To some, it was a lifetime.

The main hospital filled in the first day, and much of it was the cream of the political society: reverends' wives, tier-fathers' wives, and their daughters. The hospital was only designed for twelve hundred patients at a time, but by the end of the second day there were no private rooms. Colonists were asked to bring in mattresses that were then lined up on the hallway floors. In all, over thirty-seven hundred patients crammed in, almost half of them children.

They knew they were dealing with only one strain, so cross-infection between the patients was not a concern. As a result, the patients were allowed to move freely through the hospital. The staff was down to seventy percent capacity, even with everyone working to their limits, but the newer patients were still quite mobile and able to help. Some of them were actually medical staff themselves that had been exposed before the quarantine.

It was one of these that brought Margaret an injection on the morning of the third day. She was resting in what had once been the third floor surgical waiting room, drapes from the ceiling providing her a hint of privacy. She had helped set it up the day before, but now she was restricted to bed, her legs numb and weak. The blue spots had radiated outwards into a mesh of blue lines that covered everything but the soles of her feet. "Sarah, it's you again."

"I've got your next dose right here, Maggie."

"No," she replied. "No more Tara... Taranex."

"Doctor's orders, Maggie. It's just a small dose, and you're still the most advanced case."

"Don't waste it."

"Good morning, Miss Pritchard," came a cheerful call from the door. It was Mary Ellis from her class, with one arm already covered in blue, and a streak running up along the neck.

"Morning, Mary, what are you doing here?" Margaret asked.

"Just making my rounds," she replied, smiling. "I'm gonna be a doctor when I grow up."

Margaret sighed. "Going to be."

"Yes, I'm going to be a doctor."

Sarah waved her over. "Well, young Dr. Ellis, I have to give our patient her morning shot. Would you like to help?"

Her face lit up. "Oh, wow, do we get to stick her and everything?"

"No, silly, she already has an inline infuser, so we just put it into the port here." She held up the little plastic Y-valve in the tubing.

"Oh, ok. I'll help anyway."

Sarah brought the syringe to the line, and Margaret let out a weak, "No, don't."

Sarah pushed it in anyway. "Your teacher doesn't want to take her medicine."

"But Miss Pritchard," Mary scowled at her, "you have take your medicine if you want to get better. You taught us that."

"Here, Mary, you can push it in. Slow, but be sure to push it all the way."

Mary followed the instructions precisely. "See, Miss Pritchard, I'm already a doctor. You'll be all better soon."

She took a breath, trying not to take in so much as to induce another coughing fit. "Thank you, Mary. You should go see your next patient."

The little girl nodded and skipped down the hallway.

"Sarah," Margaret motioned her close. "I read the file, and I know it's too late."

"Maggie, don't—"

"No," she whispered. "Once the paralysis starts, death follows in two days. My father won't be back for another three, maybe four. Save what you have... for someone who can last."

"That'll be up to the doctors, Maggie, but I'll tell them. Is there anything else I can do?"

"Yes. When the pain starts, put me somewhere she won't find me."

"Maggie, I told you I can get you into a room. You're a tierson's daughter, for God's sake."

She shook her head. "Just don't let her see me. Promise you won't let her see me."

"That I'll do, Maggie, but don't give up on us. I know your father isn't."

The *Jinley* made the down tach very smoothly, despite how close to the planet they made the shift.

"Excellent work, Semi," Akahele commended him.

Semi just nodded and made a quick adjustment, bring him more in line with the surrounding approach orbits. "Yeah, but I'm sure you're going to get dinged by port authority for it."

"My license can stand it." She turned back towards Pritchard who was leaning against the hatch frame. "Come have a look, Bill. How's that for your first planet?"

He stepped up and peered out through the forward window. Arvin was laid out before them like a tapestry. The land beneath them was a lush green with stony mountains peeking up at intervals. In the distance, a ribbon of turquoise water marked the shoreline of the deep blue ocean beyond. An encroaching storm formed a line across the sea, the clouds rising higher than the mountains had been, flashing from the lightning inside.

"Bill?"

"I've seen pictures, but…"

"Not the same."

"No, but I don't have time to go sightseeing."

She nodded. "You're right. So, let's see who's in port. Torin, can we get a line of sight on the naval base from here?"

Torin sat at the sensor bay, peering down at the screens. "Yeah, the station's just a few thousand klicks up ahead. Looks like most of the squadron is in-system."

"There's no time to waste. Let's see who we can get hold of over at the station. Make it a priority distress call."

"Hold on a second, Captain," Torin was making some rapid adjustments on the screens. "We might be in luck. If I'm reading the beacons right, that's the *HCS Henley*. She's a hospital ship. We might have better luck simply starting with her captain."

She thought it over. "How fast is she?"

Torin shrugged. "Faster than us, but she's not going to be leading any strike forces if that's what you mean."

"Good idea, Torin, but speed is going to be the biggest factor. We'd better stick to asking for a cruiser or an escort frigate if they've got one."

"What about one of those couriers you were talking about, Torin?" Pritchard was standing in the back of the bridge, leaning against the hatch frame.

Torin nodded. "Yeah, I've got the beacon for one of them, the CFS *CP-1822*, no real name. Sure, it would be fast, but they don't have the kind of facilities we need, no more than we have them."

Akahele rolled the two around in her head, remembering the promise she had made to Ackerman. "Let's get both. Torin, you open a channel to the *Henley*. Talk up the medical emergency, talk about the potential number of casualties, but just don't tell them they're Masonites. It would just piss them off, and they probably wouldn't believe us anyway."

"And the courier?"

She punched up engineering. "James, keep the tach hot. I'm going to be sending a directed burst message." She pulled up her keypad and typed it in. "Captain of *Jinley*, Takasumi freighter, to Captain of CFS CP-1822, I have top priority information in need of immediate relay. Information is highly sensitive. I will not transmit. Request docking for face to face meeting."

Turning back to Pritchard, she said, "That ought to get their attention."

Ackerman sat with Hathaway in his private study, waiting. There were no casual drinks this time. Ackerman looked up at the clock again. "They should be there by now."

"I know. I just hope our Mr. Pritchard can make our case, and quickly."

"He's a good man. I trust him."

"I know... I can see that now. When he gets back, I'll see to it the Reverends approve his promotion, tier-father or no."

"I appreciate that, High Reverend."

Hathaway shook his head. "For now, it's just John."

"Then let me tell you, John, how sorry I am about your family."

"Thank you," he replied. "It's early yet, of course. Louise says it hasn't reached her spine yet, and my Jenny... well, it's still only on her arm."

"That's good news then. It's going to be a rough few days, but they should make it."

"If Pritchard succeeds."

Ackerman nodded. "He will."

Hathaway looked at the family portrait on the wall and frowned. "Have you seen his daughter?"

"Maggie? Not since yesterday."

Hathaway frowned. "I saw her this morning when I took Jenny in."

"And?"

"It's bad, Jim. They had to set her up in an operating room because the screams were so..." Hathaway shivered. "I don't think she's going to last out the day."

"She's strong-willed, John. I have hope. I need to, for her father's sake."

Hathaway looked briefly towards the decanter of bourbon but did not stand. "Jim, tell me, how did you... well, when you lost your wife..."

"It wasn't like this, John. It happened too fast for worry, and afterwards I..." Ackerman stared down at his hands, remembering. "Like I said, it wasn't like this at all."

"Still."

"Yes, still." He stared blankly at the wedding ring he still wore. "It is a grief no man should know."

Hathaway nodded slowly. "Jim, I know you're not much of a religious man."

Ackerman stiffened. "I assure you —"

Hathaway waved him down. "I've known you too long, friend."

"Yes, I suppose you have."

"Yet would you... would you pray with me, today, for my family, for all our families?"

Ackerman looked up to meet Hathaway's eyes. "Yes, John, today I will do anything."

Lieutenant Larkin's office was small and overcrowded with knick-knacks collected from his twenty-seven years in the service. He had diamond bookends from the detonation of Carlson-5, a thirty-centimeter shard of polysteel from the *R.S. Jupiter*, even a piece of crumbling concrete from old Ft. Baker on Triton. Most of it was war memorabilia spanning most of humanity's history in space, but there were also a few handmade gifts from his daughter.

His two uniformed visitors, Captain Akahele Kalas and a Commander Bill Pritchard, sat anxiously across from his desk. "So, let me get this straight. You just found them by chance, this old colony ship that we have no record of, and you happened to give them the Pox, even though you'd passed two medical screens clearing you of it."

Akahele nodded. "Yes, sir, that's about the size of it."

He leaned back and propped his feet up on an open desk drawer. "And uh, just how is it that such a massive colony ship was launched without it ever showing up in the histories?" He waved his hand around the room. "As you can see, I know a little history."

Akahele considered her answer carefully. "I'm sure you know that the Sol system wasn't under a single government then. Even Earth wasn't. It could have been a secret, or maybe the records were just lost. It was over eleven hundred years ago after all."

He shook his head grimly. "Not likely. The four major Earth powers came through both the Masonites and the aftershocks just fine. No one else had the resources, not even Mars what with all their infighting."

Pritchard leaned forward. "Sir, I'm begging you. My daughter is sick, perhaps dying even as we speak."

Larkin nodded. "Yeah, so you said. I just want to clear up this question of your supposed colony's origin."

"But we don't have time," Akahele pressed.

Larkin folded his hands across his wide belly. "I have plenty of time."

Pritchard sighed and looked to Akahele, and after a moment she nodded. "We're Masonites," he said.

Larkin sat forward, dropping his feet to the floor. "Masonites, you say?"

Pritchard nodded. "Yes, disciples of St. Mason, the True Children of God."

Larkin kept a straight face for a moment before bursting out in laughter. "Oh, that's rich. I've got to admit, you had me going until the Masonite bit. You have to tell me, who put you up to this? Was it Captain Ascot? Or maybe Lieutenant Galloway?"

"No, sir," Pritchard replied. "I am being completely honest."

Larkin shook his head, still chuckling. "Come on. Everyone in the squadron knows I'm an old war buff, especially about the damn Masonites. What? Were you going to try to impress me with your behind the scenes knowledge? Are you going to tell me you're a descendant of the great War Reverend Melville?"

Pritchard shook his head. "No, sir, we left in 2287, before the war. I know nothing more than what Captain Kalas has told me about it."

"That's a nice out, gives you plenty of cover, but I have to admit you did a good job. I mean, the whole uniform, your service ribbons... it's top notch. I bet that's even a St. Mason medallion around your neck."

Pritchard lifted the chain over his head and held it out for Larkin. "It was given to me by my grandfather at my Renunciation ceremony when I was nine."

Larkin accepted it and looked it over in his hands. "Nice work, aged enough to not look freshly minted, but uh…" he let the light play over the smooth edge of outer ring, "clearly not old enough to be period."

"Sir, please, for my colony, for the life of my daughter, I'm begging you."

Larkin opened a drawer and pulled out a small magnifying loop. "Yeah," he said, distracted, "so you said." He put the medallion down on the table and peered at it through the loop. The inner symbol was worn, the finish clearly having been updated once or twice, an earlier one appearing to be silver rather than gold. "Where'd you say you got this?"

"My grandfather. It has been in my family for eighteen generations."

"Eighteen, eh?" One of the spokes was thinner than the others, not from wear, but clearly a manufacturing defect, perhaps even handmade.

"Please, sir. Do you have a daughter?"

"Daughter… uh, sure." He looked closely at the hatching on the second ring. It had the double crisscross pattern that most imitations lacked. "She's getting married in the spring."

"So is mine, if she survives."

And there it was, the symbolic break in the pattern, the one flaw that reminded "the chosen" of the original sin, and this was the part of the medallion most worn, as it would be from the ritualistic kiss supposedly required whenever it was put on. Larkin looked up at Pritchard and for the first time saw the pleading eyes of a father. "Oh my God," he said. "This is real, isn't it?"

Pritchard merely nodded.

Larkin banged his fist down on the intercom. "Chavez, get me a priority channel to the captain of the *Henley*. I'm on my way to the bridge."

Margaret sat on a cool stone bench. The dark granite contrasted against her smooth, pale hands, and the rich texture felt good against her palms. The garden around her was brightly lit, though she herself sat in the shade of a broad oak. The sky above was a real sky, deep and blue. She had seen a simulation on a childhood visit to the planetarium, but it had been nothing like this.

Laid out before her was beautiful garden filled with all manner of flowers and ornamental trees, many of which she had only seen in the records. A series of cobblestone paths wound though the garden, making little islands of lush green and brilliant blossoms. The fragrances wafting towards her from across the nearest path were the richest she had ever experienced.

"Maggie?"

She turned her head to see the other woman approach, and she recognized her immediately. Her hair was still dark, and she was dressed in her favorite yellow sheath dress. Margaret knew that Father kept that dress boxed up in his closet, but it still seemed perfectly reasonable to her. "Mother, it's good to see you again."

She sat on the bench beside her and took her hand. "It's good to see you too, Maggie. You've grown so much since I left."

Margaret looked around. "What is this place, Mother? I don't recognize it."

"It's New Providence."

"So we made it? I didn't think we would."

"Of course we did. Did you think your father would lead us astray?"

"No, but I never thought we'd get here so soon." Something about that troubled her.

"Remember, Maggie, we can go so much faster now. It didn't take that long at all."

"That's right! Captain Kalas and the *Jinley*. Did she bring us here?"

"In a way. She's brought you a gift."

"Then this is Callista Prime?"

"No, my little Magpie," she answered with a squeeze to her hand. "This is the real New Providence, a promise from the heart of angels."

She looked again at the flowers. A moment before they had been so tempting. "Then it isn't real."

"Not yet."

Margaret looked down at her hand again, her fingers twisted between her mothers'. The skin was clear. There were no marks, no scars. "I remember being sick, Mother."

"Yes, very sick."

She had no memories of her recovery, only of a fiery pain that would not stop. "I didn't get better, did I?"

Her mother smiled, but shook her head.

"You've come to take me then, haven't you?"

"No. This is only a visit."

"I don't understand."

"You don't have to, but do look at our garden and try to enjoy the moment. Accept it as a gift."

A spring breeze flowed between the trees carrying the smell of cherry blossoms, just like the orchard in Burton Tier when she was little. The rose bush shifted as a squirrel moved through, and a bright yellow butterfly spread its wings to ride on the wind. The squirrel popped out a moment later, flicked its tail and darted across the stone path. "It's lovely."

She felt the hand squeeze again. "Someday you'll sit here with your daughter."

"I would like that very much, but how can we have a world so lovely?"

"Have faith, Maggie."

"I'll try," she replied, but then the sun grew brighter, washing out the colors. Even in the shade, it was becoming too bright.

"I'm sorry, Maggie. Our time is up." The light grew even brighter, her mother silhouetted against it.

"Please, Mother, let me stay." The lines returned to her skin, and the fire began to burn again.

"No, you have to go back." All that remained was her mother's face against the light. "You have to tell them."

"No, Mother, please, it hurts. Make it stop."

"Goodbye, Maggie. Tell your father I love him." And then she was gone.

Margaret woke up screaming. "Mother, make it stop!"

An overhead light glared down on her. A doctor she did not recognize stepped into view briefly holding a large syringe. "Don't worry, Miss Pritchard, it'll all be…"

She never heard the rest. Her world went dark and silent.

Chapter 6

"Yes, I trusted my Captain. That's part of shipboard life. But trust has limits." – Lieutenant Horatio Nelson, court-martial proceedings for the Victoria mutiny

Margaret woke to see Akahele sitting in the chair beside her bed. Instead of her uniform, she was clad head to toe in surgical wraps including a mask across her face, but Margaret recognized the eyes. She was sitting quietly, going over something on one of those electronic pads of hers. The room itself had changed. From the look of the view out the window behind Akahele, they must have been up in the private rooms on the fourth floor. This was where her mother had died.

"You're back," she said at last. The coarseness of her voice surprised her.

"Good morning, Maggie." Akahele set the pad down. "I've been back for four days, don't you remember?"

She shook her head and became conscious of the fact that the pain was gone.

"That's all right. You've been out of it most of the time."

"Is that your new uniform?"

Akahele glanced down over the light green scrubs. "For now. At least they let me out of my environment suit."

Margaret raised her arm slightly and saw that the web of blue lines were still there but fading. The skin around them was dry and flaking. "What happened?"

Akahele stepped over to sit on the edge of the bed. "You made it, that's what."

"And this?" She looked to her arm.

"It's temporary. It was the same for me when I was a girl. It wasn't as bad, of course, but it healed." She gave a soft laugh. "The worst part from here on out is the itching, especially on your back, but it only lasts a few weeks. You'll feel it when they start weaning you off the meds."

She nodded once. It took so much effort. "And everyone else?"

Akahele looked out the window. "Seventeen," she said softly.

Ultimately, only seventeen of the infected women had died, including the wives of two tier-fathers and of Reverend Wallace. The low mortality came from a rather gruesome discovery about the nature of the drug Taranex. Its primary purpose was to deliver an agent that blocked key sequences of the Teruvian virus directly, but its secondary effect was to boost nerve efficiency. This second element kept the patient's heart and lungs from shutting down in paralysis while the virus was slowly destroyed. The colony doctors had no hope of replicating the anti-viral agent quickly enough, but they could boost nerve efficiency using other drugs at their disposal. Their thinking was that it would at least improve the patient's chances of surviving another day or two. The price it extracted was that the patient experienced the fiery Teruvian pain far longer than any of its previous victims had ever endured. Only the arrival of the courier ship had stopped it from becoming any worse.

Margaret reached out her hand and rested it on Akahele's arm. "It's not your fault. You know that, don't you?"

She sighed. "That's what everyone keeps telling me."

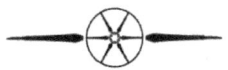

Lieutenant Winchester looked the young girl in the eye. "Now, your mommy took the shot, and she didn't cry. Didn't hurt a bit, did it, ma'am?"

The mother smiled at the lie. "That's right, my little Rinny-Poo, just a little pinch."

The three-year-old nodded while her mother held the girl's leg steady, and he gave her the same, quick and efficient jab that he'd done almost three thousand times since his arrival. In about four hundred of them, he got the same result as this one. The screams could be heard all the way out the door, down the hall, and out through the lobby.

"How many more?" he asked of no one in particular.

"None," came the answer. Pritchard stood in the doorway. "That little girl was the last resident of my tier. I have personally verified the list."

"Oh thank the..." he paused, cutting short what was likely a blasphemy in present company. "How many more of these am I signed up for?"

"Two more, but Tier Carriden is more industrial. It has far fewer actual residents."

"I assume you realize you're going to have to go through this again next year, and another five after that. I'm pretty sure we won't be around then."

Pritchard nodded. "Our doctors are quite capable of administering the booster shots as well as the other new vaccine schedules. I believe it was your chief of staff that insisted on this."

Winchester gave a snort. "Commander Ramie is an..." he paused and started packing up his gear instead. "He's very strict about controls."

"Personally, I'm more worried about the pace." Pritchard shrugged. "But I'm not a doctor."

Winchester glanced at him sidelong as he pressed his bag closed. "Pritchard... you're the one who came to get us, right?"

"Yes. I was one of them."

Bag in hand, he faced off. "Your daughter, how is she?"

"She's recovering. They say she's come to once or twice, but I haven't talked to her yet."

"That's good to hear, Commander Pritchard, but the next time you're worried about how fast we're doing our job, I suggest you remember that we blew off shore leave and hauled ass out here just to save that little Masonite cur of yours."

He walked out, not waiting for a reply.

They had not shown her a mirror yet, but Margaret saw all she needed to know in Cal's eyes when he came into the room.

"No, really, Mags, it's not that bad. Mostly it was just... you look so tired." He smiled as lovingly as he could, but it was mostly covered by the mask he had been forced to wear.

"Well, I am tired." She tugged at his surgical over-shirt. "What's with this? Was I asleep so long you became a nurse?" she chided him.

He laughed, the smile reaching his eyes. "No, Mags, you did not sleep that long. They're just being extra careful with you and some of others."

"But they said I was getting better."

"Oh, you are. You definitely are, but you'll still be contagious for a while, and those... those foreign doctors are being very strict, something about hybrids."

"Hybridization?"

"Yeah, that's it." He leaned in for a whisper. "Personally, I think they just like pushing us around. I hear their head doctor is a Hindu."

"No he's not," she scoffed. "You're making that up. They don't still exist, do they?"

Cal shrugged. "I don't know for sure, but that's what I heard."

"I'm sure you've heard lots of things," she prodded him with her finger. A fine trail of her skin was left behind.

He straightened up with a smug smile. "I am fairly well connected."

"What else have you heard? What of Father? I haven't seen him yet."

"I'm sure he'll be by again. They've kept him very busy."

"Who?"

"The Captain, the Reverends. He's quite the hero."

"Father? A hero? Now I know you're making things up."

"No, truly, on St. Mason I swear it. They're calling him the savior of the colony. They made him a tier-father. Even old McKenzie voted for him. Can you believe it?"

"I suppose," she yawned.

"I should go. You need to rest."

"No." She pulled at his arm. "I'm not that tired. You could stay with me for a while, maybe even scratch my back?"

He shook his head. "The doctors won't let me. Besides, I have to go cover another shift. The quarantine's still up."

"All right, but you have to come back tomorrow, and if you see my father, tell him... you know. Just tell him."

"I will."

He left the room reluctantly and was halfway to the decontamination station when he recognized the tall figure coming towards him in an identical set of hospital scrubs. "Tier-father Pritchard," he called. "It's me, Cal Johnson."

Pritchard stopped, grabbing him firmly by the shoulders. "Is she awake?"

"Yes," he nodded eagerly. "She was asking for you."

Pritchard released him and walked on.

"I'd like to talk to you sometime, sir," he said, following a step behind.

"I know, Cal," he replied, not breaking stride. "But not now." He paused only at the doorway to look at him. "Just not now."

Pritchard walked in to the welcoming cry of "Father! Father, it's you!"

Cal turned slowly and walked away.

Admiral Wozniak stood next to Captain Ackerman on the central platform of the bridge. Two dozen crewmen filled the lower level in its various nooks as they monitored the scattered system displays. Large screens blanketed each of the upper walls, cycling between different displays. Only one at the rear even gave the illusion of a window, providing a view of the colony interior from a camera mounted on the central core.

"Thank you very much for the tour, Captain. I confess I am envious of the amenities your ship provides."

"Well, thank you, Admiral, but it is of course as much colony as it is ship. I, on other hand, am envious of the speed your ship provides. You arrived very quickly."

The admiral shrugged. "It wasn't that far. Recalling everyone from shore leave, that was the real challenge. I let Larkin pull out with the *Henley's* surgeon without all that much information, but when he came back with tales of a Masonite vessel twenty-five kilometers long, well, I figured I should see it myself."

"Not quite what you expected, was it?'

He chuckled. "Well, I suppose I did flash on visions of some vast war machine, but I didn't take it too seriously. Still, it's a relief to come through here and not see any ship to ship weaponry."

Ackerman thought it best not to point out that the forward ionizing laser could be focused to deal with minor navigational hazards. "Well, we hardly thought we would need weapons out here. We left Earth secure in the knowledge that no one could outpace us and the faith that we were alone in the universe."

"And barring the occasional bit of fungus, your Reverends have been right about the latter."

"Nothing?"

"Well, we hear the occasional rumor out of the Catai, but nothing ever comes of it."

"Then tell me, Admiral, now that you've found the closest thing to an alien vessel that you're likely to see, what are you going to do?"

"I don't know," he sighed. "I think we'll stay for a week or two at least. Certainly, I'll want to have the *Henley* and its doctors at your disposal for a little while, perhaps even a couple of frigates to keep an eye out, but soon enough I imagine the rest of my carrier group will be moving on. In the meantime, I'll file a report back to Arvin and see what they have to say. Nothing personal, Captain, but I would rather you be someone else's problem."

Ackerman responded with a tight smile. "I understand, Admiral. We, of course, would rather not be anyone's problem."

Margaret sat in her hospital bed scratching at her back through her gown the best she could. Her father sat at the foot of the bed silently wincing at the sight of her contortions.

"There's this one spot I just can't reach," she complained. She tried once more and collapsed back onto the reclined bed in frustration.

"Why don't you use the back scratcher they gave you?" Pritchard asked. At least if he kept his distance, the doctors allowed him to keep his mask lowered.

"It has no bite to it, more of a rub than a scratch. That actually makes it worse if you can believe it."

Pritchard offered a gloved hand. "Can I help?"

She shook her head. "The gloves are even worse." She sighed. "Akahele told me this was going to be the worst part."

He gave a slight shudder. "I won't argue it, but it's hard to imagine anything worse than how we found you after we got back. You were so close to death. You'd lasted though the fire so long, longer than anyone, but even that Dr. Washington was doubtful."

She nodded. "I know."

"They told you?"

"No," she replied. "Mother told me."

Pritchard blinked twice as his jaw went slack. "What did you say?"

"I saw Mother. She talked to me." She looked past her father to the closed door. "I didn't want to say anything about it before, with others to hear it."

He lowered his voice. "I understand. Such a claim would be dubious at best."

"I know. Some might even say heresy."

He shook his head. "I wouldn't worry about that. Most would say it was just a fever dream. They can be tricky, you know, and you'd been through so much."

"Of course," she replied. "I did have quite a fever."

Pritchard stole a glance back at the door. "And what was the dream like? What did your mother say?"

"It was about New Providence but not Callista Prime. She said something about Akahele and gifts... and angels, I think. There was something about my daughter." She looked out the window. The core lights were dimming into night. "And there was something I was supposed to do."

"Your daughter?" he asked.

She looked back to her father. "It's still fuzzy, but I do remember this much. She wanted me to tell you that she loves you."

He allowed a smile. "For a fever dream, it sounds quite lovely."

"Yes, it was."

He looked at the clock on the wall. "I should let you rest, and I'll see if I can come up with a back scratcher with more bite."

Margaret laughed. "That would be wonderful. Thank you, Father."

Hathaway sat in the hospital's waiting room near the window. The day was already wearing on towards noon, and he had work to do. Parson Phillips in Wilson tier was being considered for a promotion, and he was reviewing several of his recent sermons. He was not terribly impressed, so it was a welcome interruption when Ackerman approached.

"High Reverend, I heard you were here," he said, walking over to the window.

"Ah, my dear captain, did you come all the way up here looking for me?"

Ackerman shook his head. "I'm here to check on one of my crew, Lt. Commander McKinnon from environmental. And you?"

"Louise and Jenny," he replied. "In fact, they're letting me take Jenny home today, but it's taking longer than expected."

"And your wife?"

"Maybe tomorrow." He glanced around the room and lowered his voice. "Between you and me, the way Louise has been complaining about the itching, I wouldn't mind if she stays a few more days."

Ackerman smiled wistfully but did not comment on it. "All in all, not as bad as I had feared."

Hathaway nodded. "Indeed. Tier-father Pritchard served the colony very well."

"As did Captain Kalas."

"Ah, yes, Captain Kalas," he replied with a frown.

Ackerman sat in the chair opposite him. "You don't approve?"

Hathaway shrugged. "It's not that I disapprove of her, or at least no more than any other of the heathen she brought back. Certainly she acted decisively to help us, but she also acted carelessly in bringing this pox upon us in the first place."

Ackerman nodded slowly. "I suppose. I asked the Confederate doctor about that, but he was as surprised as she had been that she could be a carrier. Even now she passes their Teruvian screening test as a non-carrier. He's going to write it up as a case study for some medical journal. In the meantime, he's putting her on a low-dose regimen of that anti-viral drug as a precaution. That seems enough precaution for me."

"Perhaps," he replied. "Even so, I appreciate that you found other lodgings for her. Twelve of my household staff caught this pox of hers, and nine of them are still in the hospital. Apart from being short-handed, it would be hard for us to make her welcome in my home right now."

"I guess I can understand," Ackerman replied. "Though again, your thanks should go to Commander Pritchard. Or I suppose I should say Tier-father Pritchard. He has been coordinating all the lodgings for our guests, mostly in his own tier."

"Commander... tier-father... indeed he's been quite the useful servant. I imagine we should make use of him again as we move forward."

"And how shall we do that, High Reverend? Move forward, that is."

"I suppose much the same as we had planned before," he replied, looking back at the papers in his lap. "But first, I'm going to have to teach Parson Phillips that the parable of the ice cave is not an appropriate homily for a wedding."

103

Pritchard and Akahele sat in the back corner of the diner, around the bend from the kitchen door. It offered them a nice bit of privacy, but the real reason was that the waiter had insisted on it. He had also taken away the tablecloth and was serving them with plates and utensils clearly intended to be dropped directly into the recycling feed. The quarantine had officially ended two days earlier, but those who had been infected were still expected to exercise care, especially Akahele.

The colony's textile industry had responded remarkably quickly, creating a new head to toe uniform for the survivors. It made Akahele feel even more of an outcast than before, but she did not see much of a social stigma being attached to the victims – her victims. She still thought of them that way.

"I stopped by to see Maggie this morning," she said, "but they were running some tests on her."

Pritchard nodded. "I just got a call from her doctor. With luck, they'll release her on Friday."

"You must be looking forward to bringing her home."

"It's going to be hard to get away to take care of her the first few days. I have so many more duties now."

"Let me help with that. It's the least I can do."

"No, I'm sure you have even more to do."

She shook her head. "Not right now. Plus it would be a real pleasure."

"Then I'm sure she'll enjoy the company, but if you really have time to spare, maybe I can get your help with this new communication gear. It's been a lot to learn, especially since it's not my background."

"I can offer what little I know, but isn't there another officer with that kind of expertise?"

"Not really, not above ensign, and even then it's not entirely applicable. After all, who were going to be talking to all these centuries?"

"I see your point. Are you going to be able to make it work at all?"

"All except for this tachyon burst mode. We don't have the polarizer, and frankly, it sounds like that's the kind of thing we wouldn't want anywhere near us."

She shook her head emphatically. "Absolutely not." She suspected the sail would tear through even the *Chariot's* hull. Theoretically, a receiver could be established without a drive, but she had never heard of it being done in anything short of spaceports. "Besides, there's no point, really. Tach bursts are only good for fairly short range – too much noise for interstellar distances. So, why the misgivings?"

He took another bite of the grata-steak. It was an artificial meat, muscle-tissue grown in a nutrient vat. "I'm worried more about maintaining it. I mean, I'm thankful for the equipment, but they're not giving us much in the way of spare parts, and it's going to be a while before our industrial base can make something this advanced."

"Well, it's military grade, so I'm sure it's even more advanced than normal."

"That's the other thing that worries me. Most of the compatibility adjustments have been on their equipment, not ours. It's like they don't want us to know how to use it. What happens when it breaks?"

"Maybe we'll just have to get you some civilian gear. Actually, there's a lot of stuff you folks are going to need."

"Well, yes and no. Remember that we got along fine for over a thousand years without outside assistance."

"I'm sorry. I didn't mean to imply you were a charity case."

"No offense taken, but you're right. If we're going to change, we'll need any number of things. Even then, it keeps coming back to money." He glanced down at the coins he had set out for their lunch, twelve parsons and a wheel. "Apart from adding to that Larkin's collection, I don't think Masonite coinage carries much value, here in the Confederacy or elsewhere."

"Well, money aside, the big question is whether or not you and your colony even want to change."

He shrugged and took another bite. "Some want to. Others oppose it. Mostly we just don't know enough."

She finally pushed her plate away, only half eaten. "What about that action plan we had before the pox? It's not exactly moot."

Pritchard nodded. "That's not been forgotten. In fact," he said with a smug expression, "as I'm a tier-father now, I've been going to the House of Fathers. Some of us are pushing for the Reverends to send an expedition."

"What's stopping you?"

He shook his head. "For starters, the relationship between the Fathers' House and the Reverends' Council is complex, but what's more troubling is that even if we convince the Council, we're not sure we'll be allowed to."

"Allowed? Your High Reverend seemed in favor before."

"Well, I suppose the High Reverend has a few more doubts now than before the Pox, but I didn't mean him. It's this Admiral Wozniak who may be stopping us."

"Why? What's he said?"

"Nothing definitive, but enough little things." He paused with a thoughtful frown. "The other tier-fathers think I'm reading too much into it, but I think he wants to keep us here, contained and under control."

"Maybe." She thought it over, remembering snippets from her own interactions with naval officers. "Though it's possible he simply doesn't want to do anything that can't be undone."

"Perhaps, but that keeps the decision in his hand. Understand that our ancestors left Sol to get away from that situation."

She locked eyes with him. "Just what are you suggesting?"

He glanced about to make sure the waiter was far away. "Can you leave?"

"I don't see why not? I mean, Torin's been having the time of his life as the local celebrity, so he's in no rush, but yes, we could leave. I have a request from the Admiral to see him before I depart, but even that makes it clear he expects me to."

Pritchard smiled. "You have room for some passengers?"

She nodded. "As a matter of fact, I do."

Torin took the glass from Commander Soze and sniffed at the liquor inside. "Roxa, you say?" He took a sip as the older man poured one for himself. "Damn but that's smooth."

"It's a favorite of the captain." Soze set the bottle back in the rack. They sat in the officer's lounge in the basement of the crew's academy.

"What is it exactly?"

"In historical terms, it's something of a double-malt made from..." he trailed off in a chuckle. "Trust me. You don't want to know where it comes from. There are some questions you just don't ask an environmental tech."

Torin took another sip. "Is that your specialty?"

Soze shook his head. "Power systems, though I imagine over the years I've pulled a shift every department there is."

"Is that common?"

"It happens. In the early years, I think they were grooming me for the Captaincy. You go around. You learn the ropes. It helps you not look like an idiot."

"But you never made it that far?"

Soze shrugged. "On a ship like this, most don't. For me, I knew it when I met Ackerman. I was pulling a stint in the docking bays, already a full lieutenant, and Ackerman was a freshly minted ensign. We had a twin failure with a jammed lift and the docking door, and the next thing we knew, we were venting air from the full section. He was only twenty-six years old, but he saw the solution and made the decision."

"And?"

Soze held out his left hand to show the missing two fingers. "Well, I got off with only this. Twenty-eight others weren't so lucky, but he saved over a hundred of us. If he'd waited any longer, we'd have lost the whole section. That's when I knew I was never going to make it past Commander."

Torin took another sip. "Wow. I mean, I want to be a captain someday myself, but I don't know if I could have made such a hard call as that."

"It was a harder call than you think, young man. His wife was one of the ones that didn't make it, trapped on the wrong side of the lock." Soze threw back the rest of his drink and reached for the bottle again.

"You're making that last part up, aren't you?"

Soze shook his head and poured another glass. "Pregnant, too. Hit him hard. Most of us expected him to buckle, but he pulled through. I'll tell you this, Mr. Graylock. When the shit hits the fan, that's the man I know who will keep it together."

Margaret checked her skin in the mirror one last time before leaving her hospital suite. The quarantine had been officially over for five days, but she still had to wear the extra layers of protective clothing. Even with that, the scarring along the back of her neck was still visible.

Akahele waited patiently in the doorway. "I'm afraid the scars may never go away entirely, but they will fade over time."

"I know," Margaret replied. "I'm not worried, but it's going to take me a little time to get used to." She gathered up the last of her things. "Shall we go?"

"You're sure you don't want to wait for your father?"

"No, I want to get home before he does and check the kitchen. I don't know what Aunt Jen has been feeding him, but he's getting fat."

"You're not planning on cooking dinner your first night home?"

"No, but if there's a bag of her sweet rolls in the pantry, I'm hiding them."

The trip home was made simpler by one of the few ambulances. Margaret was the last of the pox patients to be released, so they could spare it for her. She felt fine, but after almost a month in bed, the walk from the local tram station would have been too much.

Akahele carried Margaret's bag into the bedroom and then joined her in the kitchen. "Any sweet rolls?"

She shook her head. "A couple, but I suspect he's eaten most of the evidence."

"Let's get you settled in."

"No, I've had far too much of being inside. Let's sit out on the porch."

Margaret stretched out on the porch swing while Akahele took the seat traditionally reserved for Father. "Is it good to be home?"

Margaret closed her eyes and breathed it in, listening to the slow creaking of the swing. "I didn't realize how much I'd missed it. And you? Do you miss your home?"

Akahele shrugged. "I do miss Naria, but after a while your ship becomes your home. The worlds are merely places to visit."

"How many have you seen?"

Akahele pondered it a moment. "I don't know for sure. Two or three hundred. After a while you stop counting."

Margaret shook her head in amazement. "So many... are any of them like *Chariot*?"

Akahele glanced up at the sky and chuckled. "No, nothing quite like this, but there have been some remarkably beautiful worlds. Millisor, for example, lies within a stellar nursery nebula, so the night sky is incredible. Foralk has these cliff-face gardens that you can really only appreciate in flight, and then there's Oxidia with its three kilometer waterfall."

"Three kilometers? You've seen it?"

"Only in pictures. I never made it past the spaceport, and that place was a cesspool." She shook her head with a frown. "I was a cargo handler then, working my way across the frontier. I got caught up in some gambling scam and was almost left behind. Don't believe the postcards. It was not a pretty place."

Margaret shuddered. "You lead such an exotic life, but I don't know if I could manage it. Even these Confederate officers are so very coarse. I'm frightened by what else might be lurking out there."

She nodded. "I can see that, but after Oxidia, I learned to always carry a little protection with me."

"Protection?"

Akahele reached into a side pocket on her pants and pulled out a small black cylinder. She held it out to Margaret in the palm of her hand. "My Jansky-7."

Margaret poked at it tentatively with her finger. "Is it a weapon?"

Akahele nodded.

"But it's barely bigger than a roll of parsons."

Akahele shrugged. "It's just for self-defense. It's really not meant to be lethal."

Margaret took it and turned it over gingerly in her hands. "It looks harmless. How does it work?"

"Do you want me to show you?"

Margaret's eyes went almost as wide as her grin.

"I'll take that as a yes." She stood and led Margaret out into the tree-lined back yard. Standing behind her, she guided Margaret's hands over the Jansky. "You twist the safety off like this," she said, showing how part of the outer surface telescoped out into a stubby barrel. "Now aim at the branch over there and squeeze the two blue circles."

She did as she was told and was rewarded by seeing the oak branch jerk suddenly and sway back and forth as it settled again. "That's amazing," she gasped.

"Useful, though. That will definitely give someone a push. At the higher settings, you can even knock someone out."

Margaret turned it over in her hands, twisting the base up the power scale until it stuck. "It won't go past the greens."

Akahele put her hands over Margaret's again. "You have to pull and turn, see?" The base shifted further, but Akahele forced it back again. "But Maggie, you'd never want to use those red levels. They're really for use against someone in body armor. On anyone else, they'd be lethal."

Margaret let the Jansky slip back into Akahele's hands. "I didn't realize it could be so dangerous."

"Well, it's not really. If you're careful with how you use it, it's perfectly safe."

She perked up a bit. "If you say so."

Akahele chuckled. "Here," she said, pushing it back into Margaret's hand, "you keep this one."

"But what about the next time you're in, what did you call it, a cesspool?"

"Oh, I have two more back on the *Jinley*. No, you hang on to that one. You can use it if any of those Confederate officers get out of line."

Margaret did her best to suppress a smile. "I might, at that. You won't believe what one of them called me, and to Father, no less."

They heard a door close in the distance. "Speaking of your father."

Margaret pushed the Jansky into her pocket. "Quietly now. If Father heads for those sweet rolls, I want to catch him in the act."

Gregory Solomon sat quietly on the anti-spinward shore of Lake Piety watching the waves steadily roll in. A two-man sailboat tacked slowly against the wind in the distance, and a trio of joggers made their way along the aft shore. On a holiday, the lake would be teeming with people, both playing on the shore and swimming, but today was merely another Tuesday. Most of his fellow colonists were either at work or at school.

He was not. In fact, he was missing Dr. Hurst's lecture with only one more week before final exams. He was not worried about it. Normally this would be because he was confident in his growing engineering knowledge. Now he simply did not care.

The sailboat made a leisurely turn back towards the other shore. Gregory watched the wind push the sails open fully. He had never sailed. He did enjoy the water, and he could appreciate the technical challenge of managing the rigging, but it was not a real ship. It was slow and plodding, even by old Earth standards. It was little more than a curiosity.

A backpack dropped to the ground beside him. "You missed plasmas again." It was Tori Costello. She was technically a junior, but she was still in two of his classes. "Hurst asked after you."

Gregory shrugged.

"You weren't the only one. Michael and Quentin were gone too."

"Figures."

She sat down on the shore beside him. "Quentin said he had a cold. What's your excuse?"

He looked out at the sailboat heading back across the lake. It was making better time with the wind, but it would still take another ten minutes to reach the docks. "I've spent the last seven years working towards this, both at school and at university. I was third in my graduating class, and I'm on track to finish first here. I even have Dean Fields arguing with Commander Noland over whether I should go into teaching instead of crew, and Noland is offering me junior lieutenant on my first day. But now..." He shook his head. "I don't see the point."

She put her hand on his shoulder. "Propulsion engineering is a respectable career, Greg, and you heard what the High Reverend said."

He sighed. "I know. The wheel must keep turning and all that."

"Besides, you're not going to let Allison Parsons walk off with the valedictorian slot for algae studies, are you?"

He chuckled. "I suppose it's worth it just to spite her."

"That's more like it. So, do you want to borrow my notes?"

He took one more look out at the sailboat. It was not a real ship, but he imagined it could be pleasant for at little while. "Sure."

Pritchard jogged along a path paralleling the Lat-14 tram line. Margaret had been at least partly right. He might not actually be getting fat, but he could tell that his age was catching up with him. He had chosen to run in the anti-spinward direction this evening. He knew the physics well enough to know that the difference in effective gravity was minute at best, but his knees were thankful for it.

A young man approached him from the other direction, probably eager for any added effort that the spinward run would bring him. His shirt identified him as a student at the university, and he slowed as he approached Pritchard. "Tier-father Prichard," he called out. "Good evening to you, sir."

Pritchard nodded in return but kept running. He might have recognized the younger one as someone from his own tier, now far above on the other side of the core, but it was hard to be sure these days. He had never thought anonymity to be something of value until it was gone. Now he was recognized everywhere, especially by the younger colonists, eager for tales of his brief expedition to Arvin. He could understand their interest, for even he was not immune to their growing wanderlust. Still, as he jogged along the path, he was thankful he was old enough to value their colony for the home that it was.

He passed a few other people as they walked to the side. One of the tram stations was just ahead. It was still early in beta shift, so these were simply folks heading home after an evening out. One of them, however, stood out. Pritchard almost tripped trying to salute. "Captain," he said, gasping for breath.

Ackerman waved down the salute and fell in beside him. "Shall we see if I can keep up?"

Pritchard slowed to a walk. "I'm done. It's been months since I did this regularly. I used to be able to make it around twice, but not tonight. Maggie tells me I'm getting fat."

"How is she? I heard she was sent home last week."

He nodded. "She seems to be recovering well. She's even talking about going back to work on Monday."

"So soon?"

Pritchard shrugged. "I think she'd have gone straight from the hospital if they'd let her. Such is the passion of youth."

A young woman passed by, running ahead of them. They both paused to watch her, not so much with admiration, but with suspicion. There was something a little off about her. "Is she…" Ackerman asked.

"Yes," Pritchard replied. "I think she's from the *Regaldo*. The admiral has been cycling a number of officers through. He has not said so explicitly, I but I think they are treating it as repayment for their interrupted shore leave. I've been billeting most of them in my own tier, the *Jinley* folks as well. We were lucky to have been refurbishing that block of apartments at Carson and 37th. They were mostly unoccupied."

"Sounds reasonable, but you need to find someone to keep an eye on them."

"I've been taking care of it myself, coordinating between the rear dock officers and my local constables."

Ackerman grinned. "You're going to have to learn to delegate that, Bill." He glanced around, seeing no one near. "The mission is on, and you're going."

"Me? I'm just a tier-father, a junior one at that."

"No, you're a commander who happens to be a tier-father. I'm the one sending you. Reverend Cooper is officially leading the mission, and he's bringing along Reverend Morris to assist him. The three of you will head out on the *Jinley* next week."

"Morris is a good choice," Pritchard said absently. They had both grown up in tier Wilson. "But I don't think Cooper is going to be happy with having me along."

"I know, but don't let him hold his status over you. He reports to Hathaway. You're representing me and the crew. Don't forget that."

Pritchard made his own conspiratorial glance around. "But sir, you also report to the High Reverend."

Ackerman chuckled softly. "I know that, Bill, but remember that you and I bring things to the table that they don't. Crew life forces us to see things more clearly. We have to make them see it too."

"Make them, sir?"

"Make them, help them... you know what I mean, Bill. Give them the benefit of your reasoning without insulting their own."

Pritchard sighed with relief. "I see, yes. Forgive me, sir, but for a moment I thought you were hinting at something more."

"More?" he asked. "What... mutiny?"

Pritchard pressed his lips together and nodded silently.

Ackerman gave a hearty laugh this time. "Hardly, Bill. Certainly, the High Reverend and I don't always see eye to eye, but we're too close to ever let it come to that, especially now with the end so near at hand."

"That's good to know, sir."

They arrived at the next tram station, and Ackerman took his leave. "Let's keep this mission quiet for now, Bill. I don't want Wozniak and his lot to have a chance to object."

Pritchard nodded his assent and tried to resume his jogging, but even running against the spin, his footsteps felt far heavier than before.

Admiral Wozniak's office was much more spacious than Lt. Commander Larkin's had been, but it was also filled with his own personal collection of souvenirs. Wozniak's passion seemed to be models, and from the looks of it, he had a detailed replica of every ship he had ever served on. Akahele sat nervously in her chair looking at the miniature arrays of weaponry that surrounded her. It only made matters worse that two Confederate marines waited outside the door. The admiral himself sat behind his desk ignoring her as he read over a few files and stamped them with his approval.

"I understand you'll be leaving us soon," he said at last, still gazing over a few final details.

"Yes, Admiral. As exciting as this has been, I have cargo to deliver, quotas to meet, that sort of thing. You understand the nature of obligations."

"Yes, Captain Kalas, I do, and I take my obligations very seriously." He finally set down the last item and faced her directly. "I have many, of course, to my family, my fellow officers, but firstly, I have obligations to the Confederacy, and it is these obligations that I would like to discuss."

"I'm sure you know, Admiral, that I am not a Confederate citizen."

"No, but you have lived within our borders for over twenty years, and you sail under the flag of a Confederate shipping line. Unless you intend to declare your hostile intentions, I will consider you to be at least a friend of the Confederacy."

"Certainly, Admiral, and it was with that friendship in mind that I came to you on behalf of this colony."

"Yes, and that has put me in a rather delicate situation. You have placed into my care some three hundred twenty-seven thousand Masonites, the very scourge of humanity, and yet they are completely innocent of the atrocities we associate with that name."

"Of course, Admiral. Surely you see that."

"Just as I am innocent of the rebellion that first split us off from the Republic long before I was born, but that does not fill my heart with love for the Solarian navy. These Masonites are of the same cut as their forefathers, and their distaste for us is palpable.

I think many of my officers would like to see them dealt with now before history has a chance to repeat itself."

"But... Admiral, they left before the war. They weren't even with Calloway."

"So they say."

"You think they're lying?"

He shrugged. "There was credible evidence after the War that many of the Masonites had escaped somehow. No one knew how or precisely how many, but the numbers did not quite add up to the 2280 census. Still, how hard would it have been for them to just change the logs and never tell their children? Or perhaps the knowledge has been passed down after all. That Captain of theirs seems to be a crafty devil. Who knows what secrets he's hiding?"

"So, what, you're going charge them with war crimes from over a thousand years ago?"

"I doubt it, but that's not my job to decide. My job is to see to it that the Confederacy has the time to make that decision, and that brings me back to you, Captain. I don't want news of this getting out prematurely. Three hundred thousand Masonites hurtling towards Callista Prime – you can imagine the panic."

"Are you telling me I can't leave?"

He grinned ever so slightly. "You know, Captain, I could simply have you and your engineer detained and deported as foreign agitators. The rest of your crew are Confederate citizens who could be pressed into service. I would be completely within my rights."

"I appreciate your candor, Admiral, but I don't think you're really going to do that."

"No, I'm not," he admitted. "I would rather you had just filed your Survey report and been done with it, but I must recognize that your conduct in this matter has been honorable. I intend to rely on that honor for the time being."

"I'm glad to hear it."

"So, as a condition... no, strike that, as an understanding, I would ask that you not speak to anyone about your discovery here. No press, no local officials, no one."

"Not even a ghost writer?"

The Admiral chuckled. "Oh, I'm sure your footnote in history is assured, but for now, I want this contained. Will you give me your word as a captain on that?"

She considered it, knowing full well what she had already planned. "I appreciate your position, Admiral, and I promise that I will not speak publicly about the Masonites until I hear something official from the Confederate government."

"And your crew?"

She nodded. "They've worked with me for three years now. They can keep a secret, at least for a while. They won't be talking about it either."

"Very well then, Captain, I wish you a speedy and profitable journey. You are a credit to the Takasumi line. The navy values such accommodating captains."

"And Takasumi values its good relations with the navy, Admiral."

He gave one last smile, almost feral in nature. "Then I suggest you don't do anything to jeopardize them."

She was about to respond, but he had already signaled the door. The marine's presence behind her was both immediate and oppressive.

"Corporal, please see our guest to the shuttle."

Margaret had given herself time to walk to the school slowly, but even then, she was tired by the time she arrived. Instead of the stairs, she opted for the elevator to reach her third floor classroom. Tier-son McKenzie had offered her a first floor room, but she had been too proud to accept. She was beginning to regret it.

She arrived at her room to find many of her students there, but only the girls. Even though the quarantine was officially over, the Confederate doctors had urged them to keep the younger pox patients segregated from the rest of the population. To make up for her lost boys, she had eagerly accepted as many of the young pox girls as they would give her. A few more trickled in as she set up her desk the way she wanted it. The last one came in with a fresh roll call from the front office. She had twenty-three girls in total, all dressed in drab grey quarantine suits and tight fitting scarves. Of her original class, all but three of the girls were present.

As usual, she began the day by writing the date on the board in high script: May 14, 1049. "Can anyone tell me what happened on this date?"

Mary Ellis, sitting front and center shot up her hand. "It's the day Miss Pritchard came back to school!"

Even Margaret joined in the laughter. "That's true, Mary, but I was thinking of something much longer ago. Anyone? Ok, May 14 was the day they disconnected the Sol antennas. Does anyone know what year?"

Samantha Rollins raised her hand. She was one of her new students. "In year 6?"

"That's right." She opened her lesson plan for the day. "Does anyone know why they did it?"

They went over the various possible reasons from the practical to the theological, and at Nel's suggestion, they actually read through the captain's public log for that period. Her history assignment for the next night was whether or not they thought the early colonists had made the right decision, and a full page explaining why. With the Pox-induced segregation rules, the girls weren't rotating to other teachers in the afternoon, so in addition to her usual specialty of environmental systems, she also had to teach music and scripture. She was supposed to have included a small piece on etiquette as well, but she felt a better use of the time would be to read to them some selections from the history of the Confederacy. Akahele had loaned her one of her little computers with a large database.

By the end of the day, she was exhausted, and she could tell that the girls were too. It seemed as though they had not been pushed much by the other teachers. Still, they had all made it, and life must go on. Mary Ellis stopped on her way out. "I'm glad you're all better now, Miss Pritchard."

"Thank you, Mary. Besides, I had to come back and help you become a doctor."

She giggled. "Did you forget, Miss Pritchard? I'm already a doctor!"

The windows of Reverend Wallace's home were still draped in black, but Hathaway had come to visit anyway. It had been a month since the Lady Regina's funeral. It was time.

A servant led him to Wallace's private study where the mourning Reverend sat in an overstuffed chair, a bottle of bourbon and a copy of the *Chronicles of St. Mason* on the table beside him. Both where open. Upon seeing his master, he tried to rise, but Hathaway waved him down.

The two sat in silence for several minutes. Eventually, Wallace reached out for the bottle, and Hathaway spoke. "Brother Wallace, I know you are seeking the strength to carry on, but only one of those two carries true strength."

Wallace hesitated, but his hand did turn towards the open book. He pressed his fingers into the holy text for a moment and then withdrew them. "I was reading St. Mason's epistle to the Titans."

"Chapter four?"

Wallace nodded.

"Wise words," Hathaway replied. "Did you find comfort in them?"

He sighed. "No, High Reverend, I did not."

"I see. And if you cannot summon forgiveness, my brother, what would you have instead? Would you prefer vengeance on Captain Kalas? Or perhaps you would wish to make war on this entire Confederacy?"

Wallace met his eyes briefly before looking away. "In my weaker moments, yes, I confess I do, but I will not follow the likes of Calloway. I will not deepen the stain he made upon our names."

"Your beloved Regina would be proud to hear to you say that. Remember her love, Christopher, not her pain. Only then will you find your way back to God's path."

Wallace closed his eyes and nodded. "I know, John. I just get so angry sometimes. These heathen... I wish we could be rid of them."

Hathaway nodded gravely. "It may come to that, Brother, but for now I am keeping the door open."

"I know. Brother Cooper told me. He even sounded excited to be going."

"You don't approve?"

Wallace reached for the book again though he began to quote before he even reached it. "'The heathen's table is adorned with jeweled plates and sumptuous beasts, but for the Chosen, it masks a cup of poison.'"

"The parable of the rings... yes, I know it, Brother. However, our dear captain feels strongly that we should learn all that we can of this new world around us."

Wallace turned sharply back to Hathaway. "Our dear captain, indeed. And you agree?"

"It seems prudent for now. His arguments are sound, and I value his council. I know you have never cared for his company, but you know other crew – Regina's family if nothing else. Ackerman is well-liked and respected. I believe him to be a good fit."

He nodded. "Yes, that is true, but I know some of his officers disagree with him on this matter."

"As I would expect with such complexities, my Brother."

"Of course, High Reverend, but—"

"This is enough for now, my brother." Hathaway reached out, and took Wallace's hand. "Come with me now. Let us walk once again into the light and speak of joyful things."

Wallace nodded and rose. "That would be most welcome."

Petty Officer Jenkins was unloading the last of the crates she had brought over from the *Henley*. She was likely to stay on station for quite some time, but this was the last scheduled supply run for now. It was hard work made more awkward by the low gravity in the *Chariot's* docking bays. Ensign Branson was supposed to be helping, but he was too busy supervising. With the last crate onto the dolly, he sat down on it to rest.

Across the bay, she saw six suited figures hooking up to a small zero-g scooter unit. Five of the suits looked modern while one was clearly one of the crude Masonite models. The Masonite latched on at the controls, and the lift took them up towards the launch deck.

"What are you watching?" Branson asked.

"Not sure. Looked like some mad-hatter taking five of our guys out for a tour of the hull or something."

"Our guys?"

"Well, maybe. They were real suits, you know, but they looked more civilian."

Branson looked up to catch a glimpse just as the lift reached the next deck. "Probably that freighter crew. I heard they'd be leaving soon."

"Five? That must have been one big shore leave party."

"Not at all," he replied. "I bet a ship that size must have a crew of twenty, maybe thirty."

Jenkins thought about it. The freighter was not that much smaller than a patrol boat, and those were crewed by forty-five if you counted the marines. "Yeah, you're probably right."

With that observation, Akahele, Torin, Pritchard, and Reverends Morris and Cooper slipped away without anyone ever noticing.

Chapter 7

"As a boy, I read that politics is the process of deciding the important matters. As I grew, I learned that politics is more accurately the process of deciding what actually is important. By the time I reached office, I knew that the process of politics itself is the only thing of importance. Looking back, I don't know if I was ever right." - from the memoirs of the Honorable George Brighton, 32nd Prime Minister of the Hudson Confederacy.

Latera had not been the closest or the most populous world they could have chosen, but it was something of an unofficial outer capital. Of the Confederacy's two-hundred twenty members of parliament, nineteen lived on Latera much of the time, and another hundred and seven maintained offices there. It was a fairly wealthy world, with a highly technical industrial base, but it was really the convergence of trade routes and the associated banking activity that drew most of the attention.

It had made for a long journey, and by the midpoint of the sixteen-day journey, social conditions on board the *Jinley* were deteriorating. Reverend Jacob Cooper clearly considered himself to be the lead of the expedition and treated the crew with an imperial nature. It was no single incident, but nothing was up to his standards. His bunk was too hard, his cabin too small, the ship's rations too plain. Even their air offended his taste. "With so little room, it grows stale even from the eight of us."

Reverend Anthony Morris, on the other hand, was a much more accommodating passenger, even offering to take a hand at galley duty, but he made the mistake of discussing religion with Captain Kalas. It was after breakfast on the ninth day, and she was lingering over a cup of tea and a manifest report.

"I'm curious, Captain. The smell of your tea is rather unusual. Is that a Confederate herb of some kind?"

She set it down and pushed it his way. "No, it's from home. My cousin sends me a crate of it couple of years at Tidal Blessings."

He sniffed at it closer, but declined to take a sip. "Tidal Blessings, you say?"

She reclaimed her cup and wrapped her hands around it. "It's the first spring tide of the new year. It's a bit like Christmas on the Catholic calendar."

Morris nodded. "I confess I find your traditions fascinating. You frequently make reference to the ocean as though it were an entity unto itself. Is this a variant on the Genesis creation story, or perhaps something from Jonah's travails?"

"No," she explained, "but on a world where we all must live with the sea, it has earned a certain reverence."

"You mean respect?"

She shook her head sternly. "I meant reverence. She can hurl storms that drown the land, and the strength of her tides when Adrian laps Helen is like nothing you can imagine. She has no mercy for those too proud to acknowledge her power. But," she paused, letting a small smile settle on her face, "there is also such generosity. The fields of algae can stretch past the horizon, and the terra-cod can reach a hundred kilos. And in the southern summer, there is a stillness... a silence. On a calm day, the sweet Ocean takes all and forgets. She holds no grudges."

Morris had nodded thoughtfully before responding, "I see now. You're more properly pagans, sun-worshipers, that sort of thing. I have read of such primitive notions, but of course, I'd never encountered them personally. Did the original colonists come with those ideas, or were they invented afterwards?"

Akahele took it in silence, blinked a few times and stood. "Excuse me, Reverend, I have duties to perform."

To Morris' credit, he realized his gaffe just moments after it had passed his lips. He attempted to apologize before dinner, but it was clear the damage was done. He spent most of the rest of the journey in his cabin immersed in reading, though he did still perform his promised galley duties.

Pritchard was left as the uncomfortable go-between, both apologizing for and defending his Reverends and doing everything he could to lower their expectations. "Remember," he explained to them, "it's as though you're on crew territory. Don't push things you don't understand."

Morris had accepted it, but Cooper still resisted. "You forget, Tier-father, that even in crew territory, a Reverend's word is law. It is the Captain's oath."

"Perhaps for Ackerman, but Captain Kalas has no such bond."

By the end, it had even soured the camaraderie of Pritchard and Akahele. What had begun as a conspiratorial venture had slid into a testy partnership of compromises. She knew he was in a difficult position, but that did not make her dislike the Reverends any less. The fact that he continued to show deference to their authority only lessened him in her eyes.

The sixteenth day arrived at last, and they down-tached at a respectful distance and spent the next eight hours decelerating through three ever-shrinking orbits. The *Jinley* had no observation deck, so Akahele allowed her passengers to rotate through the bridge one at a time, pushing them all the way to the front, ahead of Semi's navigation console. Dawn from orbit was always a treat, and even though it had been a difficult journey, she did not want to deprive her guests of that experience. She let them go in their order of seniority, knowing that Pritchard would see the best of the three dawns as they were just about to drop into the atmosphere.

Landing was perfunctory and efficient, with the last hard brake and then the slow spiral down into the spaceport at Stonefall. As usual for the *Jinley*, they were berthed on the outskirts of the port, far away from the bulk carriers and passenger liners. Victor and James started immediately on the cargo unloading, though she did not expect to fetch a good price for her raw goods here. She had a few precious industrial metals, but mostly processed titanium that would have done fetched a much higher price at the shipyards of Arvin or Pino's Hammer. Akahele and Torin opened the starboard lock and led their passengers down to the polysteel landing pad.

"This is it, gentlemen, a real planet."

Reverend Cooper squinted up at the afternoon sky and the few white clouds spotting against the blue. "It's awfully bright. Do we need any kind of protective clothing?"

Torin assured them that they would not.

Pritchard stepped out and walked a slow circle, his arms spread wide. "I've had dreams of horizons, but never like this."

Reverend Morris had stepped off the ramp but was still lingering beneath the shade of the *Jinley's* sweeping wing. Torin waved him on. "It's perfectly safe," he said.

"I know," he replied. "It's just that part of me is, well..." he chuckled, trying to ward off the embarrassment. "I almost feel like I'll fall off," he said, nodding upwards to the sky that truly went up forever.

Torin's eyes went wide. "You're right!" he shouted, and jumped. He came down a moment later with a devilish grin. "Come on, let's get you guys started on your entry visas."

The plan was to list them as honestly as possible without creating a problem at customs. They were to be from the colony Chariot, and independent government between the Solarian Union and the Confederacy. Their purpose of entry was to discuss further colonization efforts with Confederate officials.

Torin led the two Reverends away, but Akahele caught Pritchard by the arm. "A word of advice: don't let them do the talking. There's a limit as to how much I can do for you now that we're here." She had, of course, told them of her promise to Admiral Wozniak, and she intended to keep it, at least to the letter of her promise.

"I can hardly tell them not to speak. I am a mere tier-father."

"But you said you were here as Ackerman's representative."

"Yes, and he is ultimately accountable to them, or at least to the High Reverend."

She shrugged it off. It was clear that her tolerance for Masonite politics was wearing thin. She gripped his arm one last time. "Find a way."

Captain Ackerman drifted amongst the color-coded fittings of aft-thruster four in silence. Once in a while the slow rotation caused him to misjudge a jump, but this close to the core he was essentially weightless. He paused at each joint and looked closely at the seal using his pocket light. About a third of them had gone brittle.

Ensign Weston looked on from the hatch. "Do you need a little more light, sir? I could ask Lieutenant Tomlin to turn on power in this section."

"No, I'm fine as it is. Tell me, Ensign, when were these seals last serviced?"

"I'm not sure, sir. I'd have to check the logs."

Ackerman twisted around a pipe and shone his light back at Weston's face. "Is this your section, Ensign?"

"Yes, sir, it is."

"Then you had damn well better know when these seals were last serviced."

"Sir, I have been in charge of this section for four years. In that time, the seals have never been serviced."

Ackerman turned back to his inspection. "That's what it looks like… probably longer. Why not?"

"Well, sir, I was never given the work crew, and besides, it's never been a priority. We haven't used these thrusters in almost two hundred years."

"No excuse for sloth, Ensign." Ackerman reached the final seal in the section and prodded at it with his fingernails. Tiny chips broke off under the pressure. He turned back to Weston. "Please tell Commander Noland to get down here on the double."

"Excuse me, sir, but I believe this is his off-shift."

Ackerman shone the light at him again, making him squint. "I don't care if it's his son's first communion, you tell him to get his ass down here."

"Aye, sir."

"And Ensign," he called after him.

"Yes, sir?"

"I hope you don't have any plans this month, because you're about to get that work party."

Pritchard made his way hastily out through the door to the street followed by Reverend Morris. Reverend Cooper was a moment behind, being pushed forward by a security guard. Undeterred, Cooper kept up his tirade. "And the volcanoes shall rain fire and ash upon the worlds of the unbelievers, for they have not been marked as the chosen, so says the Lord our God!"

The guard shoved him roughly out on the sidewalk and closed the door behind them. It was the third meeting that had ended similarly, but it was the first time they had been forcibly removed from the building. Perhaps the only reason they had escaped such a fate the first two times was that their hosts had been little more than interns.

Morris helped Cooper back up from the pavement. "That could have gone better, Jacob."

Cooper was still steaming. "Well, what would have had me do, Tony? They didn't even believe we were followers of the blessed St. Mason. Do you expect me to just sit there and be mocked by that... that heathen?"

"No, but I'm wondering if it might better for someone else to state our case."

Cooper looked at him incredulously. "Reverend Morris, if you think you can do a better job with..." He paused to take a calming breath. "You are welcome to try."

Morris shook his head. "Actually, I was thinking of our good Tier-father Pritchard. What do you say, Bill?"

Pritchard jumped at it. "Reverend, it would be an honor to perform such a duty."

Cooper stammered for a moment but accepted it. "Yes, that might work well, Tier-father. You do have a certain humility that might work better with these young power-seekers."

It did work better, and it did so promptly. Taking a cue from Lt. Commander Larkin's keen interest in Masonite history, he spent a few hours searching for historical societies. In particular, Sons of the Early Republic had a strong focus on the decades before and after the Masonite war. The club's treasurer, Neville Kramer, was also listed as an administrator in the local department of Colonial Logistics and Finance. With a few calls, he was able to get a lunch meeting for the next day.

Kramer had been much more willing to accept their story than the courier commander. In fact, he seemed quite pleased with the prospect. "I always thought something like that had happened. Charlie too, but he thought you'd gone to ground, maybe in the aftermath on Mars."

"Charlie?"

"Ah, Charles Kingsley. He's one of our better researchers. He writes the newsletter."

Lunch arrived. Pritchard had ordered the same spicy steak sandwich as Kramer, while Morris and Cooper opted for some of the local soup. Pritchard took a bite. "Ah, we have something much like this back home," he observed, "but I suspect this is actual cattle beef."

Kramer cocked an eyebrow. "Is that a dietary restriction? I always wondered, but I never found anything about that in the texts."

"Not at all," Pritchard assured him. "It's just that most of our meat is 'grata'. It's a special vat-grown muscle tissue. Very efficient, and very tasty."

Kramer's face went sour. "Vat-grown? Pardon me, but that sounds revolting."

Reverend Cooper stirred in his seat but kept sipping his soup quietly. That in itself showed surprising restraint. Back on board the *Chariot*, Cooper oversaw the Agriculture Board.

"You'd be surprised," Pritchard replied. "Sometimes we even grow the spices inside on these little vines. It's astounding what they've done."

Kramer kept chewing. "Really, spices grown in the meat?"

"Oh yes," he replied. "My personal favorite is the onion and garlic steak."

Reverend Morris nodded vigorously. "Especially if you get it from the fatty vats down in Grayson tier, with the garlic marbled right into the juiciest parts." He looked up wistfully. "I wish we'd brought some. I mean, it's certainly a treat getting real animal meat, but I miss the home cooking."

Kramer nodded thoughtfully. "Is it hard to do?"

Pritchard gave a nonchalant shrug. "We've been doing it for hundreds of years." He was careful not to say they had been doing it since the first Great Mutiny.

Kramer looked at them for a few moments, at the clear hunger in their eyes even as real meat sat steaming before them. "You know, Charlie's wife works over at Bioculture. She's the Undersecretary's aide, and I'm sure she would love to hear about this. Would you mind meeting with her?"

Pritchard smiled. "We'd love to, and the next time we're back, we'll be sure to bring you a selection of our finest grata."

The Bio-culture meeting led to a meeting with the assistant director of the local Colonial Ombudsman office. That got them invited to an after-concert party with Governor's brother-in-law. Also in attendance was Geniform's vice president. He was quick to point out that Geniform was the second largest pharmaceutical supplier in the Confederacy and was fascinated by Pritchard's telling of their mad dash to save his daughter's life. By the end of the week, they had an appointment with the office of the Honorable Charles Kirkpatrick, a senior member of Parliament and currently chair of the Colonial Allotment committee. The only problem was they had been told to bring Captain Kalas, their as-yet-unseen benefactor.

Serenity Park was filled with graduates milling around in their green robes. Gregory Solomon sat with his friends at one of the reception tables.

"What did Allison want to talk to you for?" Tori asked. She was the one junior at the table, her floral dress standing out from the sea of green.

"Probably to kick him in the shins," Quentin suggested.

Gregory repressed a smile. "No, not at all. She was very congratulatory. 'Nice speech' and all that. After all, I only beat her by two-tenths of a point."

Neville nodded. "It was a good speech at that. These are indeed auspicious times."

Quentin snorted a laugh. "Auspicious. That's a pretty big word for us plasma jockeys, Greg. This doesn't mean much to us in the here and now."

"But it does," Tori said. "I think it means a great deal, and Gregory knows it. You know Tier-father Pritchard has been gone for three weeks now."

Gregory nodded. "And Reverend's Morris and Cooper, too. I think this is really going to happen. I'm just going mad waiting for them to tell us."

"Me too," Neville agreed. "But instead of waiting I think we should be doing something about it."

Gregory leaned forward onto the table. "I was thinking the same thing myself."

Serj Mattima sat behind his desk with his hands steepled before him. His office was small but uncluttered. The only two departures from the spartan décor were the Takasumi Lines logo on the wall and the hologram of his daughter by the window. Across from him Akahele slouched in an uncomfortable metal chair with her feet propped up on a wastebasket.

"I'm curious, Captain Kalas, is there anything you want to tell me?"

She yawned, still adjusting to the longer days on Latera. "My numbers are a little off," she replied.

"I noticed, particularly this last run, this rather long last run."

"So I made a bad cargo call. It happens."

"I understand, but what I fail to see is how it could have taken you over two months to get from Answay to here when the normal travel time should have been no more than fourteen days. Were you having engineering problems?"

"No, the *Jinley* is running fine."

"Were you meeting someone?"

She did not answer.

Mattima put his hands down on his desk. "Captain Kalas, the Takasumi line takes pride in the fact that our ships run with independence, with captains capable of finding profitable opportunities. You have excelled at that in general, and we have freed you up from all but the lightest of schedules and consignment duties. However, a discrepancy such as this is difficult to overlook. We take a very dim view of smuggling."

She remained calm, merely shifting her feet on the wastebasket. "Mr. Mattima, I arrived here with the same cargo that I left Answay with."

"But two months is too long a gap to go without an explanation, Captain. If you cannot offer one, I will have to demand your logs. As the legal owners of the *Jinley*, that is within our rights."

She sighed and sat up. "I've been asked not to discuss it," she said. "You can have my logs and see where I've been, but as a favor to the Confederate navy, I agreed not to talk about where I've been."

"The navy?"

She nodded.

"It wouldn't be Admiral Wozniak who made this request, was it?"

"Um, yes, it was."

He shook his head and sighed, slowly turning his obvious disappointment into a chuckle. "You're the one, aren't you? You're the one that found the Masonites."

She cocked an eyebrow. "Masonites?"

"There's a rumor floating around town about some old sub-light ship out there filled with Masonites, like a colony or something, and that a freighter found them."

"Interesting story."

"Don't get coy with me, Kalas. The rumor also says that three of these Masonites are here on Latera trying to set up diplomatic relations. I'd even heard that they came in on a Takasumi ship, but I thought surely if any of my captains had done that, they would have told me by now."

"Unless..."

"Unless they had been asked not to talk about it. Does Wozniak know you brought them here?"

"No," she replied. "He asked me not to talk about it, but he issued no restrictions against carrying passengers."

Mattima shook his head. "That's a mighty thin line you're walking, Captain."

"I have good balance."

"You'd better, because the harsh reality is that Takasumi would rather lose you than our navy contracts."

She thought it over. Even if it cost her job, it had been worth it. After what she did to Margaret, after she had erased seventeen names she had barely met, she had no choice. Besides, there were always other opportunities back in Catai territory. For that matter, there were surely other opportunities even closer. In fact, one was staring her right in the face. "What if I could replace those contracts?"

"With what?" he scoffed. "Are you planning to open a concession on gawking at the Masonites?"

She leaned forward, her hands jumbling together as she began to weave her pitch, as much to herself as to Mattima. "These guys are serious about founding a colony. It's been the center of their culture for a thousand years. Think about that. Generations have lived and died on that ship, never seeing Earth and never seeing this New Providence of theirs, all so that some distant descendant of theirs will get to live on a rock they'd only known about by telescope."

"Then fine, go pick them up and drop them off somewhere with a tent and a tractor. There's plenty of new colonies that would accept a few more."

She shook her head slowly, the grin irrepressible as the numbers rolled through head. "You haven't heard, have you? There's over three hundred thousand of them on that ship."

"Three hundred thousand? Most colonies don't start with even a quarter of that." A smile started to spread across Mattima's face as the numbers hit him as well. "You're talking about a whole new colony. That's a huge effort."

"Yeah, it will be, but who do you think they're going to want as their primary shipper, some faceless conglomerate or the shipping line that cut six hundred years off their trip?"

Mattima nodded with growing eagerness. "I see your point. Of course, it's really too big for us, even if we freed up most of the fleet, but we could subcontract out a lot of it and still make a nice commission." Then he hit the disappointment. "But how are they going to pay for all this?"

Akahele shook her head. "I don't know, not yet. They don't know either, but at least with them here, they can try to get something started."

Mattima frowned. "It's a good angle, Kalas. I've got to give you that, but it's a long shot with no sign of an immediate payoff. It's up to you. If you think you can still make your quarterly numbers, then fine, but I think you're going to have to sink a lot of time into this, time that the *Jinley* will be sitting idle. Sooner or later, we'd have to put it back on the schedule."

"I know," she replied. She had reached the same conclusion on the trip from the *Chariot*, though she had not seen the answer until this meeting. "We should probably get it going now – no point it letting it sit idle any longer than necessary."

"Good to see you thinking of the bottom line. I think we have four captains waiting to get back into the rotation at the moment, though I don't think any of them are in-system right now. I could get you their dossiers to see which would make the best match for your crew."

"Actually, Mr. Mattima, I was thinking of my first officer, Torin Graylock. He's been with Takasumi for eight years with an impeccable record."

"Yes, I'm familiar with him. Do you think he's really ready for a command?"

Akahele smiled. "He was ready when I got him three years ago."

Mattima chewed on it for a moment before nodding his assent. "It's skirting company policy, but I'll approve it. Can you do what you need from here?"

"Hardly. I'll need to get back out to the *Chariot*, probably a few other places as well."

"Is it something you could arrange with another commercial transport?"

She laughed. "And let another company get involved? No, I was thinking more about one of the executive yachts."

Mattima shook his head. "Promoting your first officer is one thing, but borrowing one of our yachts for an indefinite period? You overestimate my indulgence."

"Not at all. I'm counting on your pragmatism. I need something small and fast that won't take cargo off the line, and the yachts are what we have."

Ultimately, he agreed, but she would be accruing lease charges to be credited against any captain's bonus she got on this venture. That was not her concern. If she could actually pull it off, she could afford to buy the yacht with that bonus. She had come into his office worried, but she walked out briskly, her eyes intense and alert.

Torin was waiting in the front lobby. "Captain," he nodded. "Victor called to say the last of the titanium blanks were delivered to Arsenault Mills, and Pritchard wants to see you. I told him you would be available this evening. I wasn't sure how long you would be in there."

"Good, walk with me," she told him. "I want to get back to the ship. There's a lot to do."

He followed her out. "What happened in there?"

"Plenty," she grinned. "For starters, you've been promoted."

He stopped in his tracks and grabbed her arm. "No, Captain, you can't. I appreciate it and all, but you're grounding me. I'll be on the list for at least six months. You can't do that to me, not right now."

She looked him in the eye. "Are you through, Mr. Graylock?"

He stiffened. "Yes, Captain Kalas."

"Then get back to the ship with me. You've only got three days to get the *Jinley* ready, and you don't even have cargo yet."

His eyes went wide. "You're giving me the *Jinley*?"

"Sort of," she replied. "Come on, Torin, I've got a job for you to do, and I need your help sorting out just what it is."

He followed her to their rented pod, listening in a daze. "You know, Captain Torin Graylock had a nice ring to it."

The view of the *Chariot* from the core was quite different. The ground lay in all directions, and the lack of gravity made for a strong sense of vertigo. There was no up or down, only in and away. In was safe. Away was best not contemplated. Commander Soze had dealt with it off and on for forty years without ever quite getting used to it. Even with the safety line, he always kept his good hand on something solid. Commander Noland floated nearby, attached only by his tether. A dozen other crew floated in the distance, slowly erecting an array of safety nets.

"I think these ones are going to be in much better shape," Noland said. "They also serve as emergency vent channels for the main power plasma conduits. We test them about once a month, all the way out to the thruster mix chamber and back."

Soze stared out at a collection of tall buildings next to Lake Virtue and tightened his grip on the handhold. "At what pressure?"

"I'll admit, not much, but it gets overhauled by section on a twelve-year schedule. If there are any problems, we shouldn't have much trouble fixing it. It's the actual thruster conduits I'm worried about. Some of those joints have been dry since before we were born."

"Do what tests you can for higher pressures, and then we can move this crew back onto the thrusters." He shifted his eyes back to Noland. "The thrusters will be the key. I think if we can get even modest pressure back there the captain will be happy."

Noland tugged his cable to draw him in closer to Soze. "If he's serious about this course change idea, I think we should go ahead with a complete overhaul now, all eight sections."

Soze shook his head and regretted it immediately. This was not a good place to move your head too much. "There's not enough time, Stephen. You saw the schedule."

"By why the rush? I haven't heard the High Reverend say anything about changing course."

"Me neither, but the Captain says he wants to give Hathaway options."

"That's what he told me, too, but that still doesn't explain the rush."

Soze shrugged, an odd motion in weightlessness.

Noland moved to the same handhold. "Aaron, do you know something I don't?"

Soze set his jaw. "Apparently. For starters, I know an order when I hear it, and after all these years, I know how to follow it."

"Okay," Noland replied, "but I don't like it."

Soze laughed and waved his free hand out at the distant ground. "Yeah, and this is my idea of a picnic!"

It turned out that meeting with the office of the Honorable Charles Kirkpatrick meant meeting with his chief of staff, Evelyn Hopkins. It also had the scent of an unofficial meeting as it had been scheduled in the evening when most of the office was empty, especially with the local members of Parliament on one of their two annual breaks. Akahele drove the three Masonites in her rented pod, and they were met in the parking garage by a tall, dour man. Pritchard pegged him as security immediately from the way he eyed them on their approach. He extended a hand in greeting, but the man merely keyed open a private elevator and rode with them up to Kirkpatrick's office suite in silence.

Hopkins was waiting for them in a windowless conference room near the back of the suite. Pritchard found her moderately attractive, but also somewhat manly with a short bob-cut that was the current fashion in the heat of Stonefall. She greeted them in turn, recognizing that Cooper was the senior member and should be first, yet once they sat she addressed Pritchard as their spokesman.

"Mr. Jansen relayed the story of your recent brush with the Teruvian Pox. Tell me, Commander Pritchard, is your daughter well now?"

"Yes, she has made a full recovery. She returned to work shortly before we left."

"That's good to hear. What is her profession?"

"She's a teacher. For the time being, her class is entirely young Pox survivors. We're still practicing elements of the quarantine until the second round of vaccines next year."

"That's very noble of her. I understand there were a few deaths as well."

He nodded. "Regrettably yes, but mercifully few."

"Seventeen," Akahele noted softly.

Hopkins sighed. "It's a pity, but it was probably inevitable – if not now, then in six hundred years when you are scheduled to reach Callista Prime."

"I suppose," Pritchard agreed, and then he realized what her comment implied. They had not yet told anyone about the location of their New Providence. That had been agreed en route to Latera. "You've been briefed, haven't you?"

She smiled, though it was unclear if she was masking her disappointment of being caught or pleased that Pritchard had taken the bait. "I read the Admiral's report yesterday. It's not yet being distributed to the full Parliament, but after speaking with Mr. Jansen I made a few inquiries." She turned to

Akahele. "As his report reads, Captain Kalas, he expected that this subject would remain secret for some time."

"I have not spoken of it publicly, nor has my crew," she replied, knowing that even now it was verging on a lie. "That was my promise to Admiral Wozniak."

Hopkins nodded. "Yet here we are."

Akahele shrugged. "Indeed."

"Well, Wozniak was foolish to think he could keep this bottled up for long. The rumors are all over, both here in Stonefall and down in the Strings, and I'd bet at least half of it is leaks from his report. We haven't received any word from the prime minister yet, but he's on a goodwill tour of the spinward systems. In due time there will be an official statement here on Latera, but it will probably be another week or two before the resident members can agree on it."

"And what will that statement say?" Pritchard asked.

"I suspect it will merely acknowledge the truth to the rumors, that we have found a sublight colony ship filled with Masonite refugees from before the War."

"That's all?" Morris pressed.

"Well, we're not exactly going to announce the evacuation of Callista Prime if that's what you mean."

Pritchard silenced the others with a glance. "And we would never expect you to do so. However, I have been reading your press since my arrival, and I notice that your government announcements never seem to be a mere confirmation of facts. They are always put in an emotional context. Back home we call this giving it the proper illumination, and with due respect to my fellow reverends, it often dictates the desired result before official debate begins. I sense the same practice is used here."

Hopkins smiled. "It seems we are not as different as one might think. We refer to it as shading."

"And can you tell me how this will be shaded? I presume you will be the one to draft this release."

"It will be a group effort."

141

"But led by you."

She stared at him for a moment before nodding. "Yes, I will likely be charged with the task. I already have two polls in the field, one gauging people's historical knowledge of the war and one testing their emotional reaction to various Masonite terms and images. Those will help me craft the message, but I have not decided just what that message should be. Tell me, Commander Pritchard, what would you have me say?"

"That we left in peace, and we return in peace. We're only looking for a world to call home."

"You paint a very simple picture for such a nuanced situation, Commander. For starters, not everyone is going to believe that your ancestors were all that peaceful. Wozniak, for example. He thinks either you're lying to us, or your ancestors lied to their children. To some extent, I think he sees you as hostile enemies."

Pritchard shook his head. "I don't know what would change his mind then. Are you asking us to surrender?"

She laughed. "As if that would make it any simpler. I don't know who would want to take charge of you. But as it is, you've come with your hands held out for charity while some of us would rather cut them off."

"And which would you want to do?"

She looked them over, each in turn, including Akahele at the end. "If it were up to me, I'd want to help you. My father was a first-generation Talun, so I understand your desire, not just for a home, but for a place to make your own. But it's not really up to me. Surely, I can advise and craft a message, but I won't put Kirkpatrick into a politically untenable position, especially when he has nothing to gain here."

"Another world in the Confederacy," Akahele suggested.

"Would it be?" Hopkins asked.

Pritchard sensed the flash of anger rising in Cooper, and he knew Hopkins had seen it too. "That would be for our children to decide, at least if I understand your colonial law correctly."

She nodded. "Remind me not to play Hun-luck against you. Still, beyond our initial statement of support, which I am not promising, there is very little we can actually do to help you. Colonies are primarily private ventures."

Akahele sat forward. "But doesn't the Confederacy underwrite some of the loans? I know they did for Clarkston, and that was just eight years ago."

Hopkins shook her head. "Clarkston is a special case. In addition to having a rich asteroid belt, Clarkston is strategically located near the Shiantic Ribbon. We need that system more than the colonists do, but we need them there to claim it. But that's beside the point. We only guaranteed the loans. We didn't arrange them. The industrialists back on Ringway did that. You don't even have that."

"Not yet," Pritchard replied.

"Yet?" she asked.

He did his best to put on a friendly smile. "Well, we've only been here ten days, and yet here we sit."

Hopkins returned the smile. "Well said, Commander. I confess it is a compelling story. It could play well with the masses, but I have long-term political realities to contend with." She stood and nodded to them. "I'll be in touch."

In the parking garage outside, their analysis was not optimistic. Akahele's was the worst. "She's not going to help us. She's right about the politics, particularly the party politics."

Morris was more confused than anything. "You'll have to educate us on your politics."

"They're not mine," she replied with distaste. "Never mind. Kirkpatrick has been working his way up through the party ranks for twenty years. If he keeps his nose clean, he could be Prime Minister in another decade, but one bad call could put him out of consideration. This is too risky for him, and Ms. Hopkins knows it. We'd have a better chance with some nobody in one of the opposition parties, the Soil Registry or maybe even the Caspian Sons."

Cooper shook his head. "Our way is better, simpler. These foreigners are a maze of closed hatches. And you, Captain Kalas, you have no solutions for us either." He opened the pod's door and lay back on the bench seat, his legs hanging out.

"Well," she sighed, "I do have one idea, but it's a long-shot, risky too." Their eyes prompted her to continue. "If we beat them to the press, get the story out ourselves, then we can put our own... illumination on it. If we can get a good public reaction, then Kirkpatrick will need to get out ahead of it."

Pritchard considered it. "How would we do this?"

She shrugged. "We'd have to start at the bottom again, and we're racing the clock. Still, if we could find some hungry vid reporter, it would be just the thing to make his mark."

Morris chuckled. "This free press thing sounds so much like the biblical pack of wolves, yet so many hold it in high regard." He turned to Pritchard. "That Kealing fellow from the party – remember him? He went on and on about it."

He nodded. "Yes, his love of the subject was only surpassed by his capacity for alcohol."

Akahele stared back and forth between them. "John Kealing?"

Pritchard nodded.

"Tall guy, gray hair, deep smooth voice?"

Morris looked to Pritchard. "Yes, he was even taller than Bill here, and yes, he did have a fairly deep voice. Reminded me a little of the High Reverend delivering the Sunday sermon. Why, who is he?"

"He's probably the best known news man on Latera, maybe even in the whole Confederacy." She shook her head in disbelief. "By all the tides, John Fucking Kealing... and you actually talked to him. Did he try to set up any kind of interview, anything like that?"

"No," Pritchard replied. "He seemed rather out of sorts. Frankly, I think he was too drunk to listen."

"Damn! Did you at least get his contact information? His direct link addresses, that sort of thing?"

Both Morris and Pritchard shook their heads.

"I did," Reverend Cooper called weakly from the pod. He sat up and flipped through several of the small contact cards he had collected in the last week. "Wretched man... here it is. Jonathan E. Kealing III, Transstar Media." He handed it over. It was the standard card containing the desired link with its priority rating, the encrypted signature buried inside.

"Then he did want to set up an interview, right?" Akahele asked.

Cooper shook his head. "No. He said he understood how hard it was to be so far from home, that he was sympathetic." He paused, trying to remember. "I'm not sure I want to know, but just what is meant by a 'marrow club'?"

"He wanted to take you to a marrow club?"

"Well, he implied I was in need of one, and that he was a member of a particularly good one."

She let out a low whistle. "I'm sorry, Reverend, but I don't think I can explain it without violating several of your taboos."

He lay back in the seat again. "I thought as much."

Pritchard fingered the card idly between his thumb and forefinger. "If the path to our salvation requires a sinner as our guide..."

Morris nodded. "Then we should walk briskly."

After classes were dismissed, Margaret reported to McKenzie's office as requested. It was a spacious room on the fourth floor of the school's central tower, and it appeared even more so given its minimal furnishings. She took a seat in the stiff chair next to his desk. "You asked to see me, Tier-son?" Normally, she would have merely addressed him as Mr. McKenzie, but his posture hinted that this was more serious.

"Yes, Miss Pritchard. I have received a few queries about your recent lesson plans."

"I'm more than willing to share them with the rest of the staff."

"No, Miss Pritchard, not that kind of query. I spoke with an irate mother this morning and two more parents earlier in the week. They are concerned about the reading assignments you have been giving lately. They are not from the standard texts."

"No, I took them from the *Jinley's* files before it left. I thought our students should learn about the advancements in terraforming technology since we left. These atmospheric bacteria are simply amazing."

McKenzie folded his hands on the desk. "It's more than the choice of the subject matter, Miss Pritchard. It is the manner in which you are presenting it. You seem to be preparing them for immediate departure. This is contrary to the High Reverend's statements. Some might say it hints of sedition."

"Sedition? I don't understand how you can call it that. I am merely trying to prepare them for the possibility that we may have a new home soon."

He picked up a page from the file on his desk. "Let me quote. 'Using Prallis and Riverland as guides, how long would it take Endaza-4 to support crops in the open air? How old will you be then? What kind of job would you have?'"

"That's hardly sedition, Tier-son."

He frowned. "Let me continue with the assignment you gave to your more senior girls. 'The Hudson Confederacy recommends three different constitutional forms for its new protectorate colonies. Compare them with the three forms used over the history of our colony.'" He glared at her. "As if teaching about the centuries of the Captains' Tyranny weren't bad enough, you go on, 'What are the differences in these other forms? Is there anything that would work better for our colony?'"

She sat stiffly. "Tier-son, I fail to see —"

"Obviously you do fail," he shot back. "You're asking these girls to suggest a... well, a mutiny. If this got out, far more than your job would be at stake."

She had had just about enough of this nonsense. "I would remind you, sir, that my father is your tier-father and a Commander as well, trusted by the High Reverend himself."

McKenzie chewed it over for a moment. "I am aware of who your father is, Miss Pritchard, but he is not the High Reverend, and he is not here."

She gave an angry harrumph, but let it go for the moment. Father was definitely going to hear about this upon his return. "Are you firing me?"

"No, Miss Pritchard. I am willing to let this go as poor judgment following your recent illness."

"Then what would you have me do, Tier-son?"

"Stick to the standard texts for starters. If you need help with lesson plans for the older girls, Mr. Hess has offered to share his with you."

She bit back her initial response, nodding a "Thank you" instead.

Pritchard felt uncomfortable under the lights, but the technician assured him it was necessary for the imagers to capture him from all the angles. Kealing sat serenely across from him, making a few last notes on a pad.

"You've had enough time to go over the questions?" Kealing asked.

"Yes. We appreciated the chance to prepare," Pritchard replied.

"It's all background material anyway. I just wanted you to have some nice stock answers ready. We'll have further details available for those who want to drill through, so try not to dive into the minutiae. Once we get rolling I'll mix it up with a few new questions."

He nodded. "What other questions?"

Kealing flashed his trademark smile. "But Commander, that's half the fun."

The director called out, "Okay, John, we're recording."

Kealing turned his head to some specific unseen point in space, and began his monologue. "The Masonite War is a distant subject for most of us, a collection of dates and places we had to memorize in school, and why not? The Masonites are long since dead and buried, or so we thought. Joining me tonight is Commander William Pritchard and his two Reverend friends, three Masonite travelers from our distant past."

Pritchard had heard most of it before. They had already done the interviews with both Cooper and Morris, and in each the lead-in gave top billing to the man seated across from Kealing. Most of the questions were repeats as well, drawn from the same prepared list. Pritchard did his best to keep it short, but he took the time to express his dismay at the discovery of what his ancient cousins had done. "It's been a shock," he stressed. "We're still coming to grips with it ourselves."

It was going smoothly, but Pritchard found that he was getting more extra questions than the Reverends had. While some were open-ended, many painted him badly. "As a military man," Kealing asked, "were you really that shocked to learn of the tactics employed by those you left behind?" It had come as a minor follow-up question, but it definitely caught him off guard.

"Oh, I'm not military," he replied. "I'm crew. Our colony has never really had a military."

Another that had been for him alone was, "How does it feel to live in a theocracy? Given the experience we've had with the Shiantic Ribbon on our border, most of our viewers would find it an ordeal. Does it bother you?"

He had almost laughed at the absurdity of it. "Not at all. The High Reverend is a good and able man, and our lives are hardly ruled minute by minute. After all, the scriptures say very little about oxygen reclamation or electromagnetic buffers."

"But nevertheless, you do not elect your High Reverend."

Pritchard smiled. He had already thought of this analogy while discussing politics with Akahele. "No more than you elect your Prime Minister. Your parliament does that, just as our Reverends do." He did not point out, however, that he wished he had more control over who the Reverends were.

Nothing in the prepared questions covered the Teruvian Pox. He knew the question would be coming, but he was not expecting it to come from the angle it did. "I understand there was an outbreak of Teruvian Pox in your colony shortly after the *Jinley* arrived. Your daughter almost died. How did that make you feel? Weren't you angry?"

"No, I was terrified."

Kealing leaned in earnestly. "I understand completely. My little granddaughter got it just last year. They caught it early enough for her to be spared the worst of it, but even that much was quite frightening. Personally, I was furious at the woman who had exposed her. She was a known carrier, and she'd taken no precautions at all. Come now, Commander, weren't you a little angry?"

The truth was that he had been furious, and it still ate at him. He had since learned that the Survey branch maintained a theoretical monopoly on first contact situations should anyone ever find an alien. They had protocols for just such biological problems, and Akahele had blundered forward anyway. Beneath the glare of the studio lights, he was aware of the silent seconds ticking by. "I..." he stammered.

"It's all right, Commander. I had a hard time talking about it, too."

Pritchard closed his eyes and sent up a quick prayer for strength. "I've forgiven her, you know."

"You have?"

"Yes, it wasn't easy, but we are taught to forgive."

"We all are, Commander."

Pritchard smiled at Kealing and in that moment saw his game for what it was. "Tell me, Mr. Kealing, have you forgiven her, the woman who infected your granddaughter?"

As Kealing's eyes went wide, Pritchard worried he had gone too far. "Well, Commander, I guess I'm still working on that."

After that it was just a few more of the prepared questions. In all, it had taken only thirty minutes. Kealing thanked Pritchard and the Reverends for coming and promised them that their story would get an extended slot on his weekend's show.

Back in the control room, his producer patted him on the back. "That was prime stuff, John, especially about his daughter."

"Yeah, it was, but he tripped me up at the end."

"You could have just said yes."

He laughed. "No, my son still has a suit pending against the bitch, and my deposition is in two weeks. I don't want to get asked if I was lying on air."

"We could always cut it. You got some great fire and brimstone stuff from that Cooper guy."

"No, no, it plays well. We'll stick with Pritchard as our central figure. He's got that whole uniform thing going – really evokes the old Masonite imagery. It's a pity we couldn't get that Kalas woman in for a response."

The producer gave a sly grin. "I'm way ahead of you there."

Chapter 8

"Your enemy will watch you move, so move for him. Entertain him. But also move where he is not watching." – from The Path of Fury, by Master Shiana, 3209 – 3258.

Akahele was waiting on the lower subway platform. The interviews had already gone thirty minutes over schedule, and another likely train had just arrived without them on it. Not much could have gone terribly wrong, but every minute passing was one in which she did not know. She began to pace the length of the platform, distracting herself. She was just about to make her turn at the end of the when the reporter first called to her.

"Captain Kalas, can you talk to us about your discovery of the Masonites?" she asked.

Akahele spun around to find a short, blonde woman facing her. The yellow imaging band across her forehead was clearly labeled Transstar Media. She glanced around trying to find a way out, but she was pinned at one end of the platform. She tried to step past the youngster, but she moved quickly to block. "I think our viewers would like to hear your side, Captain."

"I have no comment," she replied and tried to zigzag back the other way, but the reporter was quicker.

"Is that because you don't want to talk about it, or is it because you've been ordered to keep it a secret?"

She resigned herself to the futility of escape. "I'm a civilian. I don't take orders."

"But isn't it true that Admiral Wozniak compelled your silence with the threat of deportation?"

She glared at the reporter. "I really have nothing to say about this. Please leave me alone."

"Admiral Wozniak must have pressed you hard. Do you think it's because he's afraid of the Masonites and what they represent?"

"I don't even know the man. I can't guess his inner thoughts."

"But why else would he be keeping his entire carrier group surrounding the Masonite ship?"

Akahele almost answered, but instead, she grabbed the little woman by the shoulders and moved her aside. "Why don't you ask him?"

The reporter let her go, calling out afterwards. "Do you have a message for the Admiral?"

Akahele spun around for a moment and made a rude gesture. It was really more of a Catai thing, with sexual mores in the Confederacy being somewhat different, but she knew Wozniak would understand it. She ran all the way to the far end of the platform and ducked into a bathroom. She splashed water on her face to cool down, but when she looked up, she saw the reporter standing behind her in the mirror.

She glared at the reflection. "Can't you take a hint? Get away from me."

The reporter pointed to her bare forehead, the imaging scanner gone. "We're done, Captain. I just wanted to thank you. That's exactly what my boss was looking for. It plays well to the whole government cover-up sideline."

To Akahele, it still smelled like a trap, but she turned to face her anyway. "I told you I can't talk about it. I meant it."

"Oh, no, I completely understand. I've even read parts of Wozniak's report. Besides, the story will be out in a few days anyway, and you'll have your public moment of fleeing from the little reporter, clearly under the threat of some overstuffed navy type."

"What are you talking about?" For someone who had been so obnoxious a moment before, this young woman was being far too cheerful.

"I mean you're off the hook. It's so obvious you were keeping your promise. The shoving was especially good. We couldn't have staged it that well."

Akahele chuckled. "Government cover-up, eh?"

The reporter shrugged. "It's always a good story in an election year, but personally, I'm more intrigued by the human-interest angle. That girl, the Commander's daughter, I'd really like to interview her."

Akahele braced herself. She was not going to let this predator get to Margaret. "That's too bad. She doesn't seem to be here."

"But you're going back. I know you are. I'd like to tag along."

"Even if I am, why should I take you? What's your special interest in her?"

The reporter sighed, the permanent smile fading. She turned around slowly and pulled her blonde curls away from her neck. It was only visible for a moment, but it was clear enough to Akahele: Teruvian Pox scars from the base of her neck all the way up, disappearing into her hair. She dropped the hair and turned back around, her face down, ashamed. "I missed my last booster shot and caught it when I was fifteen. They gave me Taranex, of course, but it was still pretty bad." She looked up with a brief grin. "It's always hardest on those of us with freckles."

"Does your boss know? Was this his idea?"

"No, absolutely not. Ever since that thing with Kealing's granddaughter… well, they can't make you disclose. It's the law."

"My friends call me Akahele," she said holding out a hand. The reporter took it firmly. "I'm Marcy Clark."

The sanctuary was almost empty. The lights over the altar were off, and the pews were lit only by the illuminated paintings in the side alcoves. A junior parson was cleaning the holy font at the entrance, while a solitary officer sat at the end of the third pew. In due course, Reverend Wallace emerged from a side door and sat beside him. "I understand you wanted to see me, Lieutenant."

"Yes, Reverend. I wasn't sure who to come to, but I knew your wife."

Wallace nodded. "Family?"

"On her father's side."

"Then what can I do for you tonight, my son?"

"I'm worried about the captain."

"Is he ill?"

"No, Reverend, it's not that. I'm worried about what he's doing."

Wallace shifted in his seat to face the officer directly. "And what is he doing that concerns you so?"

"He's talking about changing our course, taking the *Chariot* somewhere else, but I have not heard the Reverends speak of this yet. Is this something being discussed privately?"

"While I'm not at liberty to share my private discussions with the High Reverend, I will certainly mention your concerns to him. Tell me, son, is our captain merely discussing this course change as a possibility for the years to come, or is he pressing it as an agenda?"

The officer looked Wallace in the eye. "It's more than talking, Reverend. He has Commander Noland and most of the engineering teams working around the clock on getting the engines ready for it."

"Are you certain?"

He nodded. "I haven't seen the actual schedule, but from the pace of things, he means to have this ready in weeks, not years."

"Weeks?"

"Do you want me to try to get the schedule?"

Wallace leaned back and pondered it. "No, not yet, though I want to thank you for bringing this to my attention. It is indeed a pious act on your part, but for now, I would like you to keep to your post and keep an open eye for anything else of this nature."

"Certainly, Reverend."

"And we can visit again if you find anything. You don't have a problem with that, my son, do you?"

The officer shook his head. "I know where my faith lies."

The waves broke against Morris's legs before rushing back out around his ankles. He had originally rolled up his pant legs to keep them dry, but that had long gone by the wayside as he ventured further into the surf. Even his shirt was half-soaked from the spray of the sea, and his bare feet sunk further into the sand as he wriggled his toes in the muck. The young boy who had guided them down past the sea wall rode one of the waves, waved to him, and headed back out into the surf.

Pritchard waited further back along the sea wall, peering out at Morris silhouetted against the setting sun. He had opted to stay dry. "We have lakes and waves aboard the *Chariot*," he had said. "I don't see how these could be much different." Akahele and Reverend Cooper were back by their rented pod arguing about schedules.

Pritchard called out to him, saying something about the time, but Morris cared little for that kind of thing. In that moment, the steady rhythm of the waves spoke to him of a different timetable. He knew this heathen world of Latera was a far cry from their promise of New Providence, but this taste was very welcoming.

Pritchard called again, his words finally getting through. "We need to go," he said. "Kealing's interview should be released any minute."

Morris nodded but did not start back immediately. He took one last look out to sea as the sun sank towards that thing they called a horizon and bade it farewell.

Saint Gregory's Cathedral was an ornate complex, harkening back to the styles of the twenty-sixth century on Mars. The upper spires almost seemed to float, though of course some aspects had only become practical under standard gravity with recent advances in materials. It was the largest cathedral on Latera, capable of seating over four thousand, though this was rare except for state affairs. It also housed the offices of Cardinal Mueller who oversaw the spinward reaches of the Confederacy as well as several independents beyond. In all, he was charged with the well being of over two billion Christian souls. By ancient standards, he was a Pope in his own right, but in modern times he was still a faithful servant of the order.

He sat at his desk in his private study, a small unadorned room. Its only luxury was a broad window overlooking the cathedral itself and the Talas river beyond. The news of recent days troubled him, this resurgence of an old war once thought long gone. This ill-named *God's Chariot* was within the bounds of his territory, but he was unsure of what to do. The longstanding position of the Church was that the unfortunate followers of the heretical priest Mason Sanders were forever excommunicated, not merely from the Catholic Church, but after the Third Reformation, from all of Christendom. Yet the last statement on the matter was a minor footnote from six hundred years ago. Was this excommunication truly forever, or had the position merely not been updated because there were no more Masonites for it to even be relevant? Could he, a mere Cardinal, change the Church's position on it, and more to the point, should he?

At times like this, he was glad he was not truly a Pope, that he had an earthly authority to pass this on to. He took out a traditional sheet of linen parchment and an antique ink pen and began to write. Passing on the physical communication would add a few days to his message's journey, but he felt that some things still required the formality of a handwritten letter.

> Most Holy Father,
>
> News of the Masonite discovery may have already reached you by the time you receive this. I have attached the recent news items as well as our own internal intelligence on the matter. What is most pressing for me at this time is what the official church position should be on this. I have prayed for wisdom, but I am torn. Should we remind our flock of why these so-called chosen of God have been cast out, or is it perhaps time for a rapprochement? I seek your guidance and your holy orders.
>
> In faith and humility, your servant,
> Gabriel Mueller

The church had its own courier ships, built at the finest shipyards in the Solarian Union, but even then, it would be at least four months before he could expect a reply.

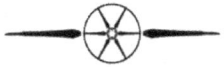

Akahele inspected the forward landing strut on the *Rachael's Luck*, rubbing at a brown discoloration running down the length of the locking brace.

"It's just a stain," Hannah Reynolds told her. Her tiny form wriggled into the space between the wheel and landing gear hatch. "We had a hydraulic pump blow out last year, and the fluid soaked into some of the parts. We replaced the pump immediately, but the rest of the unit's fine, just not as pretty."

"And it's passed inspection?"

"Yes, ma'am. Once after the refit, and our annual inspection was just last month."

Akahele nodded to her. "You and Mr. Burris run a tight little ship here."

"Thank you, Captain Kalas. It's a sweet gig, so Jake and I like to keep it running smoothly. I just wish it paid more."

"Have you ever thought of applying for one of the freighter slots?"

She shook her head. "I'd never rate past a first officer. I don't have a head for business. Profit, loss, overheads... no. I just want to fly." She looked off to the berth's gate. "It looks like the rest of your passengers are here."

Pritchard and the reverends walked up the incline slowly, encumbered by luggage filled with souvenirs, mostly little trinkets of consumer technology that were almost magic by comparison to what they had at home. Akahele waved, and Pritchard led them over, a pad in his hand.

"The second round of press just came out," he said, holding out a text story. "Kirkpatrick's Office Confirms Masonite Story," the headline read, "Following initial Teruvian relief effort, government in confusion over proper aid channels."

"Is it all like that?" she asked.

"Mostly. There's a few troubling bits, but the shading, as they call it, is mostly positive."

"That's very good." She motioned towards Reynolds who stepped up promptly. "Bill, I'd like you to meet Hannah Reynolds. She's the pilot of our new ship."

She thrust out her hand, still enclosed in a work glove, but Pritchard took it firmly. "A pleasure to meet you."

The introductions went around, though it was clear the Reverends were tired, especially Cooper. "I'm almost done out here," Hannah assured them, "but if you go on up, Jake can get you settled in your staterooms."

Pritchard led them up the ramp, and as soon as they had passed, Hannah turned to Akahele, "He's cute."

"Bill?"

"No, that Reverend Morris." She let out a satisfied sigh. "Is he the type to uh, you know?"

Akahele shook her head. "I very much doubt it," she replied and made her own way up the ramp. Inside, she heard agitated voices and found Pritchard facing off against Marcy Clark, his stance a notch or two down from hostile.

"Akahele, isn't this the reporter who ambushed you?"

She spread her hands in an act of appeasement. "Yes, but she's really okay. Remember how I said she wanted to interview Maggie?"

He nodded, his posture relaxing some. "Yes, though I didn't realize you meant she was coming back with us now."

Marcy Clark raised her hand meekly. "I didn't want to wait, so I told Transstar I wanted to get some extra imaging, you know, background stuff from their follow-up stories."

Pritchard set down his bag and sat opposite her. "So Kealing sent you?"

She shrugged. "Not really."

Jose laughed. "What she means, Commander, is that they said no. The word in the office is that they're putting together a big media trip with Kealing, Rodriguez, maybe even some Parliament types, but they're waiting until after the holiday season on Crestin – another three months give or take."

Akahele took her seat alongside Pritchard. "Then I'm confused. Just what are you two doing here?"

"Well, technically we're on sabbatical," Jose hedged, "but our contracts make it clear that as long as we pay our own way, anything we do now is freelance. It's the standard arrangement for us footstools."

"But Commander," Marcy asserted, "what it really means is that I'll be able to tell the true story, not just what some Transstar executive thinks will draw the biggest ratings or embarrass some politician. I want our viewers to see you for who you really are, not some overblown caricature from the old days of the Republic."

Hanna came up the ramp. "Good, I see you're all getting settled. We'll be leaving in just a few minutes, so if anyone wants a last look at Latera, I suggest you go to the observation deck."

Marcy sprang from her seat and headed forward. "I always love these!" Jose merely leaned back into the couch and waved her on.

Pritchard turned to Akahele. "It looks like this is going to be an interesting trip."

"At least it's only ten days this time, Bill. Play nice."

The movement of the tram was soothing, but Gregory Solomon did his best to stay awake. He had been more than happy to pitch in on the engine refit after graduation, but the long hours were starting to wear on him. He did not even notice the young man sit across from him until he spoke.

"I see they started you at junior lieutenant after all," he said. "Congratulations. Even dad started at ensign."

Gregory stared at him a moment, willing his eyes to focus. The man across from him was Richard Ackerman. "It's Richard, right? You're the captain's son."

"Guilty," he replied. "It looks like Noland is putting you through the grinder."

Gregory shrugged. "More like your father, and I'm not the only one. We're all pushing hard. This whole course change thing is surprising. What did your dad say about it?"

"Nothing," he replied. "You do know I'm not crew, right?"

Gregory rolled it around in his head. "I remember now, no favoritism. You went with recycling, right?"

He nodded. "Dr. Caruthers and I think we're on the trail of a new polymer. So, what's this about a course change?"

"It's your dad's idea, so we're getting the rear thrusters back online. If you ask me, it's a waste. I figure if we're going to do anything, we're going to use these new tachyon ships."

"I suppose," he replied, "but my father must have his reasons."

Gregory stifled a yawn. "I'm sure, but wouldn't you rather just get on another ship and go there now. I mean, it's probably going to be us anyway. Why wait?"

Richard chuckled. "And you have these ships already standing by?"

"No, but I'm starting to think we should get ready for when they are."

The tram slowed to his stop, but he did not get up. He looked across at Richard. There was an argument to be made here, and even through the haze of sleep deprivation, he could see a course of action.

Xavier Foshey was publicly known as a member of the Captains' Guild advisory board, a dabbler in the Lateran racing circuit, and a generous supporter of the arts. To the majority of the Yoshido piracy syndicate, he was known only as Father Chessman, the regional boss for the Caspian sector of the Confederacy. Only five people knew him as both, including a senior member of Parliament and a financial analyst well-placed within the Confederate intelligence community. All five worked for him, though they did not necessarily see it that way.

The man sitting beside him in front of his fireplace was Jiro Yu, one of his trusted inner circle and a useful intermediary. In addition to displaying a rare mixture of competence and ruthlessness, Jiro was also the great-nephew of Foshey's ultimate employer, the aging Mr. Yoshido himself. His particular talent was a knack for making problems go away. Today, Foshey had a problem.

"You've read about these Masonites I presume."

"Yes, Father Chessman. I have also gone over the latest intelligence reports in some detail."

"As have I. It is an amazing tale, and unfortunately, an opportunity lost for us."

"I had thought of that as well. It would have made for an excellent base of operations: large, mobile, and secret."

Foshey took a draw on his cigar, more to keep it going than anything else. "Without that last, it is gone to us, and it has become a problem for some."

"Who?"

"The names are unimportant, but sufficed to say that there are elements in the current government who would be happier if this problem went away, and soon."

Yu nodded. "That could be difficult. Wozniak's carrier group is still there."

"Not for much longer. He'll leave a minimal picket in place, but I've been assured its command will be friendly to our mutual goals."

Yu knew better than to ask for the details. "Should the problem go away completely?"

"That seems to be the idea, but a little plunder would add to the profit."

"You think they have valuable cargo?"

Foshey chuckled. "Of course, Jiro, the most valuable cargo of all, but try to get some of their engineers, too. We just might have to build a base like this ourselves."

"That, Father Chessman, is true wisdom."

The chamber holding aft thruster four was now filled with the echoing cacophony of two dozen uniformed engineers disassembling fitting after fitting. The once cavernous chamber had been transformed into a maze of webbing and safety lines. Captain Ackerman and Commander Stephen Noland stood near the entrance watching as a crew of four maneuvered a two-meter section of pipe through the last of the turns.

"This one is behind schedule," Ackerman told Noland, trying to be heard without resorting to shouting.

"I know, sir, "Noland replied. "One of the exhaust couplings was fused. We ended up using a radial torch to get it open."

"Two days for a torch?"

"Once we had it, it only took two hours, but the torch itself was in pretty bad shape. After all, no one has needed to use a radial torch of that size for a while." He shrugged. "Probably not even in my lifetime."

Ackerman shook his head. "You need to do better than this, Commander. I know there are going to be some glitches, but I want this refit back on schedule. If it's a matter of manpower, I can divert maintenance crews from other parts of the ship."

Noland watched as the crew moved the pipe past them and out the larger maintenance hatch. "I'll look at the allocations and see if I can use any more, but this would be a lot easier without the tight schedule."

"The schedule is what it is." Ackerman peered up through the webbing at some of the crew working. "I like it better this way. People are busy now."

Noland chewed on it for a moment. "Idle hands, idle thoughts?"

"That's part of it."

"And the rest of it? The course change?"

Ackerman looked back at his officer. "I'm still hashing that out with the High Reverend. In the meantime, you have your orders."

Noland nodded. "Yes, sir, I do."

Margaret and Cal swayed gently in their hammock in the shade of an oak tree that dated from before the last mutiny. She was still clad in one of her quarantine outfits, but it had already untucked itself in several places.

"I'm still angry at him," she said. "Teachers have always had control over their lessons. It's what allows us to attract the students we want. I think that McKenzie is trying to get control just for the sake of having it."

Cal rubbed at her shoulders through the cloth. "Oh, you shouldn't think that of him. Perhaps he's merely trying to smooth things over. He might have saved you a student or two."

"Well if they're not ready to deal with the future, then I do not want them in my class."

He kissed her head through the cap. "I'm sure that after the quarantine rules are over next year, you'll have your choice of students lining up to get into your class. In the meantime it's a hard situation. Only three other teachers got the Pox, so there's going to be some mismatches. You're going to need to compromise for now."

She sighed. "I know. I just wish Father were back."

"Me too. He owes me a talk."

"It might not be the best time, Cal."

"It never is, Mags, but that's not going to stop me this time."

She resisted a laugh. "It's your life."

"Yes, it is, and I'll risk it for you." He slipped a hand along her waistband. "But in the meantime..."

"Cal!" she protested. "You know what the doctor said: no unnecessary contact. You could still pick it up and carry it to someone else."

Cal pulled his hand out from beneath the blanket. It was covered in a tight glove. "No I won't."

She shook her head. "Sure, you've got a glove on your hand, but that's not enough, and you know it."

Cal kissed the cloth of her shoulder. "And just what other young lady do think is going to be touching me there?"

Her eyes went wide. "It had better be no one, you silly boy, and if not, then she deserves it for stealing my Cal." She reached down and started pulling on his belt. "Oh, I've missed this."

"You're not the only one."

The courier ship *CP-1261* performed its down-tach to a relatively stationary location in open space and dumped the encrypted data packets to the flagship via a tachyon burst as it swept past at half the speed of light. As soon as the courier had received the confirmation code via another burst, it set course for an up-tach to the base at Ringway, the next stop on its courier run.

On board the *CFS Regaldo*, Admiral Wozniak read the orders twice to make sure he was not misinterpreting them. Satisfied with his understanding and feeling some justification that it was the correct course of action, he called his fleet communications officer. "Radisson, I need a fleet readiness check, planned tach in one hour."

A few minutes later the answer came. "All ships report tach-ready except for the *Henley*. Her captain reports they have several crewmen and officers on board the *Chariot*. Should he recall them?"

"No, *Henley* can stay, but tell Captain Wallace he should shift to standby status. He may receive new orders within the week. Tell everyone else to be rigging for tach. I'll be issuing fleet orders soon, and get me that Captain Ackerman. I'll need to talk to him immediately."

Ackerman appeared on the viewscreen promptly. "What can I do for you, Admiral?"

"We've received new orders."

Ackerman nodded. "Yes, we saw the courier. You'll be leaving?"

"Very shortly. We've been ordered to the border of the Shiantic Ribbon. It's not much more than showing the flag, but it's been tense there the last few years."

"I understand, Admiral, though I believe there are several members of the *Henley's* crew on board. Do you wish me to expedite their departure?"

"No, I'm going to leave the *Henley* here for now, though I'll be urging her captain to start wrapping up his business. She's not really armed, so just to be on the safe side I'm going to leave the frigate *Goliad*. She should be able to sort out any troubles that come up."

"I appreciate that, Admiral. I wish you luck, and I look forward to seeing you again sometime."

"The same to you, Captain," he replied, suspecting that it was likely to be their final exchange.

He pulled up a fresh screen on a pad and wrote up the fleet orders. The simplest was to the bulk of the fleet: up-tach at 16:40 on a speed-run to the Shiantic Ribbon via Clarkston. The orders to the *Henley* were equally simple: hold station but maintain ready-level B. He tacked on a personal note for good measure. "Jim, don't expect to linger."

The final set of orders to the *Goliad* was much more difficult. His own orders had been intentionally vague, even though their underlying message had been clear. *Goliad's* captain, Patrick

Conway, was a weasely little snit who might or might not know how to read between the lines. He issued the standard convoy rules of engagement but also tacked on two more stipulations. "Do not engage against superior forces. Alert Fleet command at Arvin instead. Additionally, these Masonites are likely to draw all kinds of visitors, and not from the Confederacy. Exercise caution in this area. Do not risk an international incident unless it is a clear threat to the Confederacy."

He thought it was both clear and vague enough even for the densest of officers. Then again, he reflected, young Conway probably knew the score better than he. After all, his own orders had identified the *Goliad* as the ship to leave behind, and those orders came directly from Latera, bypassing sector command entirely.

Within the hour, the fleet did its up-tach in near unison. High Reverend Hathaway had joined Captain Ackerman in one of the aft observation bays to witness it, the sudden flash and the receding streaks of red. Hathaway turned to lean against the railing, his back to the polyglass bubble that looked out and down. "Personally, I'm glad to see them go. They were making me nervous."

"I've had similar feelings, but part of me wishes they were still here."

"Why? We're almost alone again. Don't you feel at least a little restored?"

Ackerman looked out into the void. "To be honest, High Reverend, more than anything I feel exposed. At least we still have the *Goliad* for protection. We should be all right."

"I would think that God will protect us, dear Captain."

Ackerman smiled and nodded. "If only I had your faith in that, High Reverend."

Hathaway patted Ackerman's hand on the railing. "Hopefully I'll have enough faith for the both us of."

Ackerman merely nodded but kept his gaze fixed into space.

Hathaway released his hand and glanced back out at the view of their empty wake. "Tell me, Captain. What's this I hear about a course change?"

Ackerman chuckled. "Oh, I'm simply putting options on the table. A course change is merely one of them."

Hathaway considered it. "You seem to be putting a lot of effort into it."

"I am, though I suppose more than anything I'm trying to keep my people busy. You know, idle hands and all that."

It was Hathaway's turn to chuckle. "Idle hands, indeed. I should have been doing some of that myself. Good thinking, my dear Captain."

Ackerman shrugged. "All that matters is that one of us thought of it."

Chapter 9

"I loved a girl once. This was before seminary, and I was little more than a boy, but I did truly love her. Ultimately, we went different ways, following our different callings, and I know that my life has been blessed by God in that calling. And yet, whenever I think back upon her, it is with regret for the path not taken." - His Holiness Julius IX, 3396 AD.

Rachael's Luck dropped out of tach a little on the fast side, but far enough behind the *Chariot* to make the adjustment. "Sorry, Captain Kalas," Reynolds said, her hands flying over the controls in a series of rapid commands. "It's just that I've never down-tached at this kind of velocity."

"No worries," Akahele replied. "I had my engineer going over the figures for days before we made our first attempt." She was sitting at the spare console in the tiny bridge, little more than a cockpit. The first scan sweep was just finishing, but it was not what she was expecting. She saw the *Chariot*, of course, and there was a transponder for the *Henley*, but that was all. "Where is everyone?"

A small blue light flashed on Reynolds' control. "We're getting a tach burst message, that might explain it. Can you handle it?" she asked, still adjusting their deceleration.

Akahele shunted the message to her console and read it.

"*CFS Goliad* to unidentified vessel: you have entered a restricted space. Hold your current position relative to the asteroid and prepare to be boarded. Repeat, match course and prepare to be boarded."

"We may get company, Hannah," she said aloud, pointing out the last phrase to Reynolds. She prepared to reply, but she was not sure to whom to reply. There was no *Goliad* on the scan, and the directed tach burst had seemed to come from the *Henley*. They must have been bouncing the signal to help hide the *Goliad*. In the end, she just set up for a unidirectional burst and began typing. "*Rachael's Luck*, Takasumi Lines, to CFS *Goliad*. We are matching course at present. We are unarmed and are not hostile. Repeat, we are not hostile. We have Masonite officials on board and request docking with *Chariot*."

The return burst again came through the *Henley*. "*Rachael's Luck*, hold course and prepare to be boarded."

She captured the message log and forwarded it directly to the *Chariot's* new traffic channel. She appended a final plea. "This is Captain Akahele Kalas with your representatives on board. We are being held for boarding by a CFS *Goliad*, but we are unsure where this ship is or if it is legitimate. Please advise."

Six long minutes later, Captain Ackerman's voice came on the speakers. "Kalas? Is that you?"

"Yes," she replied, "I dispatched the *Jinley* on some errands. Commander Pritchard and Reverends Cooper and Morris are on board."

They had to wait for the lightspeed delay for Ackerman's response. "Yes, the *Goliad* is legitimate, and they've relayed their query about you. I'm sending back your clearance, but I recommend you wait for them to give it to you before proceeding."

"Understood, Captain." She clicked it shut and waited.

Reynolds relaxed from the controls. "We're at a relative stop now," she said with relief. "This isn't exactly the response I was expecting."

"Me neither."

The clearance came a few moments later, again by a directional tach burst relayed through the *Henley*. "*Rachael's Luck*, you are cleared for docking. Do not deviate from direct course. Do not exceed two kps on approach. Shut down tach now and relay further communication through *CFS Henley*."

Reynolds complied, ordering Burris to spin down the sail generator. To be safe, she kept her approach well below one kilometer per second, dropping to almost a drift towards the end. Within ten kilometers, they started receiving guidance instructions directly from the Chariot and were led to docking bay six. Unlike the *Jinley*, *Rachael's Luck* was actually small enough to fit even in that modest sized bay, and within a few minutes of docking, they were being lowered on a lift down into a pressurized hanger deck.

Captain Ackerman was waiting for them when Akahele opened the hatch. "Permission to come aboard?" she asked.

Ackerman stepped up to join her. "Glad to see you again, Captain."

She greeted him with the traditional Masonite forearm grasp, though they both wore gloves. "Where's the rest of the carrier group, and just what is going on with the *Goliad*?"

He shook his head ever so slightly. "We'll talk."

Marcy Clark had chosen the Pritchard's back porch for her interview with Margaret. It combined an intimate homey feel with the breathtaking backdrop of the *Chariot's* interior, the horizons sweeping upwards around the brilliant lights of the core. Jose had set up the imagers along the railing and the window sill, so she could go without the mobile imaging headband. The lighting was imperfect, but she never liked the studio look in the first place. It was too artificial. This was real.

Margaret glanced about at the tiny imagers. "Which one do I speak into?"

"No, you don't have to. You really just speak to me. We balance it all out into a holographic projection later."

"Oh," she replied, pressing out a stubborn fold in the way her skirt fell across her legs. "I've never been interviewed before. I mean, I was interviewed for my job, but not like this."

"Well, we just talk. That's about all there is to. I'll ask some questions, but mostly we just talk."

"About what?"

"Well, for starters, tell me about your job. I understand you're a teacher. What's that like?"

"It's, well, it's just teaching. You have teachers, don't you?"

"Certainly, but what made you choose teaching?"

"I like to read – always have – and I like working with the children. I'm an only child, so I never got to have a little brother or sister. Surely, this isn't the kind of thing you're interested in, is it?"

"I want to know all about you, Margaret, your hopes, your fears, your pet peeves, even your favorite color. It's how I do my job. I get to know people."

Margaret told her about her classes, both her first class and her current class of Pox children. She went on about the tier school structures, the tradition of teachers selecting their students and vice versa. Before long, she was going into the detail of her philosophy on her lesson plans and how she felt this was superior to the Chelsea method which had held sway over most schools since the nine hundreds.

In truth, Marcy was not interested in it at all, at least not for her story. This was just to get Margaret comfortable, but her passion for her profession was both genuine and infectious. Marcy let it run on for longer than she should have, but eventually she brought the subject back around to the Teruvian Pox. "As I understand it, you went five days after your initial diagnosis without treatment – seven, really, from the time you probably contracted it. I'm not a medical expert, but that may be a record."

"I wouldn't know, but it's not really true. We did have some Taranex, after all."

"But I was told you were given less than two percent of the normal dosages."

"Yes, but it was at least some treatment. Plus, they were able to keep me going with some other medications."

"Still, I read a report that you endured the Teruvian fire for fifty-six hours. It must have been excruciating. Just the thought of it is terrifying."

Margaret looked down at her hands in her lap. "It was, terrifying that is. Well, both, actually."

"You were afraid you would die?"

She nodded. "Mostly, though, I was afraid so many others would and that they were wasting the medicines on me. Logically, I really didn't think I was going to survive."

"But you never gave up."

"No, I couldn't. My father was out there, and I knew he was coming back. I couldn't give up before he returned. It wouldn't be fair."

"And your friend, Captain Akahele Kalas, what about her? Have you forgiven her for infecting you?"

Margaret shook her head slowly but firmly. "To forgive there must first be sin, and Captain Kalas committed no such sin."

"Not everyone would feel that way."

"May I ask a question? I mean, is that allowed in this kind of thing?"

"Certainly," Marcy replied. She could always edit it out later.

"How did you get the Pox? Who gave it to you?"

Marcy did her best to keep a calm face. Had Akahele told her? "I don't know what you mean."

"Oh, I'm sorry. It's just that with your hair back, I saw the scars."

Marcy reached back and felt her bare neck. Her hair, she realized was mostly pulled up into the little quarantine cap Akahele had given her.

"They're not as bad as mine," Margaret went on. "It's just that I've been seeing a lot of it lately."

In her earpiece, she heard Jose from the next room. "What is she talking about? What scars?"

"How old were you?" Margaret asked.

"I was fifteen," she answered. Kealing would probably get her fired, but to hell with him, to hell with them all. "Dad was a marine, so we were always getting shipped from one base to another, each one with a different local calendar. In all the mix-up, I never got my last booster shot."

"And who infected you?"

She shook her head. "I never found out. Mom and I were on a commercial liner making the run from Rockbolt to Arvin. I didn't even notice it on board, but they caught it at customs."

"And do you blame this other woman?"

"Yeah, I always did." She had spent much of her time in the hospital trying to remember all the faces: the guide, the safety officer, the waitress who stopped to admire her bracelet, a few others. For almost ten years, she had hated them all.

"And have you infected anyone?"

"No," she said forcefully. "They cleared me."

"They cleared Captain Kalas, too."

Marcy looked in through the window to see Jose watching. She thought of dinner with his sister and niece, playing cards with his wife. "I don't know what I'd do if I ever gave it to someone."

"You and Akahele, so quick to assign blame both to others and yourselves. These things happen. It's what you choose to do that matters."

Marcy returned her eyes to Margaret. "And what did Captain Kalas do?"

"She saved me. She saved the colony."

"I think your father had a hand in that, too."

"For the Pox certainly, but for Captain Kalas I meant something larger. She prevented a disaster."

"What disaster?" Marcy thought back over her notes. There had been only the one epidemic.

"What do you think would have happened if she hadn't come back to investigate? What if your survey people never followed up on her report? What if we had made it all the way to Callista Prime? I've been thinking about this quite a bit lately."

"I don't know. I suppose someone else would have infected the colony."

"No," Margaret shook her head. "I'm not talking about the pox. You see, things would be different then. Until recently, I have lived my life with the expectation that I would grow up here, marry here, and raise children here. Each of my children would expect the same, but eventually a generation would come that would grow up expecting to reach our New Providence, of building a new home there. They would have arrived at Callista Prime expecting it to be theirs, and if we had raised them right, they would all be faithful followers of the blessed St. Mason, true children of God.

"I think back to what happened to the old Masonites, the ones our forefathers left behind. If three hundred thousand Masonites came racing in to Callista Prime, would they be seen as a tragedy of lost opportunities or as invaders? And as for our children, would they…" she paused, trying to come to grips with it herself. "Would we just start it all over again?

"But now," she continued eagerly, "now we have a chance for something new, and it has come to us as a gift, not a birthright. We will take such care with it, like barren Sarah and her blessed son Isaac." She looked out to the yard and the sweeping panorama beyond. "For our sons, for our daughters, we have the chance to do something we had never dreamed, that even they would never dream. It is as beautiful and undeserved a thing as the very grace of God. That He chose my friend Akahele Kalas to deliver this gift is a blessing I will not question."

175

Marcy sat silently. This was not the young victim she had come looking for.

Reverend Morris shoveled the mashed potatoes into his mouth. The cuisine on Latera had been exotic, but after ten days of ship-board food, he found he was desperate for Kara's cooking.

"Do you want more?" his wife asked.

He drank more of his ale and considered it. "Tempting, but I don't want to load up after all that time sitting around on little ships."

"But the planet?" she asked. "Tell me again about the oceans."

He took a deep breath, remembering it. "They're vast, Kara. I mean, the whole of our *Chariot* would be like a pebble dropping into the lake, and the storms... I only saw them from orbit, but they spread out over the land like... I don't know. It was beautiful and terrifying at the same time."

"And the people, Tony, what were they like?"

"Once they began to believe us, they were mostly nice. Certainly, they're heathens of every stripe you can imagine – even a large contingent of those idolatrous Catholics – but they were nice. I would even say friendly."

Kara poured him more ale from the bottle. "But were they happy living on a world like that?"

"Honestly, I think most of them were oblivious to their good fortune, but there was this one boy, playing in the surf with me on the beach. I have neither seen nor felt such unrestrained joy in so long. I confess I truly envied him for all his eager abandon."

She reached out her hand to take his. "Perhaps someday our child will have that joy?"

He nodded. "I would like that, Kara, but first we must have one."

She looked down at their joined hands and smiled quietly.

"What?" he asked sharply, almost spraying his ale out of his mouth. "Are you telling me... Kara, are you with child?"

She looked up to meet his eyes. "I found out two days after you'd left. I'll be at twelve weeks on Friday."

"Oh, Kara!" he exclaimed. "I love you!"

Pritchard sat at his dining room table gazing at the holographic display before him. It showed the results of a twelve-variable regression analysis on localized oxygen density at various points on the station. He was evaluating some of the new applications of the computers they had brought back from Latera. This kind of analysis had been too unwieldy for their own systems, and even if they had taken the time to run the program themselves, the results would not have been what he saw before him. The mathematical discipline of chaotic domain remapping had never been discovered on the *Chariot*. It was not his field, but the techs in environmental systems had helped him with the data. Ultimately, an old groundskeeper's theory had been correct: it was the combination of concentrated oak near algae ponds that caused the bulk of the oxygen spikes, but only when the local humidity was above forty percent.

Normally Pritchard would not have pursued this as far as he had, even for the purpose of exploring the new computer's capabilities, but today he had another excuse. Young Cal Johnson had been circling the block for almost an hour, pausing meaningfully in front of the Pritchard home on each circuit but never coming in. Pritchard had a fairly good idea what was on the young man's mind, but he was in no mood to make it easier for him. On the other hand, he was due to leave soon for a meeting with Commander Noland about the engine overhaul, and he did not want to be late. Upon sighting Cal once again, he walked to the front door and opened it.

Cal saw him immediately but took several moments to find his voice. "Tier-father... were you going out?"

"No, but after watching you putter around on the street, I wasn't going to wait all day for you to summon the courage to come in." He walked back to the table and resumed his examination of the display. There was evidently a time-variations as well, so he began to step through the animation.

Cal stood there for a moment as Pritchard ignored him, engrossed in his work. "I would like to have a word with you, Tier-father."

"I know you think you do, Cal," he replied, not looking up, "but you would be better off trusting the instinct that kept you from knocking on my door. I only let you in to stop you from making a spectacle of yourself on the street."

Cal pulled out the chair next to him and sat. "But, sir, I do want this, and you promised me at the hospital that we would have this talk."

Pritchard sighed and paused the display and set aside the input pad. "Cal, my answer today will be no. Until she turns twenty, nothing you say will change that answer."

Cal nodded slowly. "Am I so unacceptable to you, sir?"

"No, Cal, you are a fine young man with good prospects. I think Maggie has chosen well, but I will not bless your union until she is of age. You've waited this long. You can each wait a little longer." He reached for the pad again. "It is not a time for rash actions."

Cal reached out and took hold of Pritchard's forearm firmly, halting its reach. "It is also not a time to let my world be overrun by events outside of our control."

Pritchard looked at Cal's hand on his arm briefly before locking eyes with him. "You forget yourself, boy."

Cal removed his hand, doing his best to keep it from looking like the retreat it was. "My apologies, Tier-father, but the moment is coming when I will not wait."

"When you will not wait? And what of my daughter?"

"We have discussed it. She is a grown woman, Tier-father. She needs your blessing no more than I."

Pritchard shifted in his seat to face the boy. "You would do such a thing?"

"I know it's against tradition, but it is our right under colony law."

"If you could find a parson who would perform the ceremony," he scoffed.

Cal straightened his back and took a deep breath. "I have, Tier-father, and yes, he knows who you are. Don't think you can intimidate him."

Pritchard lurched between disappointment and anger. "You think you're old enough to marry my daughter, but you're obviously not old enough to understand that reputations last a lifetime. For five months of impatience you would forever stain yours as an upstart who would defy the will of a tier-father and a commander."

"With due respect, sir, I do understand."

"Then you are a fool."

Cal stood, doing his best to tower over the seated Pritchard. "In the last three months, I almost lost her. If I am a fool, then so be it, but I will not wait for it to happen again." He stepped back and nodded once before turning to leave. The only sound in the house was the slow creak of the door as it swung shut.

Pritchard picked up the pad again and tried to resume his previous train of thought but pushed it away in frustration. He poured himself a cup of tea in the kitchen and looked out over the back porch to the world beyond. Margaret's school was just visible between the branches of the cedar tree he had planted when she was born.

He was going to lose her. He had always known he would, but today it was different. He could feel it, as inevitable as the turn of the chariot wheel, that it would not be to something so harmless as a young man's passion.

Ackerman and Commander Aaron Soze had already been on their way to the aft engineering sections when the courier's transitory visit was spotted on the bridge. As soon as he heard, he knew what message it was bringing, and that only urged him on to his destination. By the time the call from the *Henley* came, he was already in the compartment for aft-thruster six.

"Pipe it down here," he said. The comm was in a small alcove, shielding it from the din of the crew replacing several fittings. "Captain Campbell, what can I do for you?"

"We just received orders via courier."

"Yes, we saw it come and go."

"There was a mining accident on one of Saragen's outer planets, lots of radiation exposure. We've been called in to help move the patients to better facilities on Rockbolt."

"Are any of your people on board?" The question was purely a courtesy. Since the departure of the bulk of the carrier group, Ackerman had made it a point to be alerted on every entry and departure.

"No, the last shift returned four hours ago. Unless you object, we'll be pulling out shortly."

"Are you taking the *Goliad* with you?"

"No, we did not receive new orders for Captain Conway, so *Goliad* will be staying here for the time being. It was good meeting you, Captain."

"And we are indebted to you and your crew, Captain. I hope to meet again."

"I share your hope, Captain."

The *Henley* was gone within another few minutes, leaving only her shadowy companion *Goliad* behind. By then, Ackerman had finished his cursory inspection and had scanned through Commander Noland's report. Even after four weeks, none of the aft thrusters were operational.

"Commander," he called. Both Noland and Soze turned. "Numbers two and five look like they're getting close – at least closer than the others."

Commander Noland nodded. "I could have them done by the end of the week if you weren't so insistent on the directional thrust."

"That won't do, Commander. I want them back up to full operating specs, including the directional thrust. I believe the original design allowed for a full nine degrees of variance. I want the full range, even if it takes double shifts from your entire department."

Noland scowled. "It's not the labor, Captain. It's the parts. We just don't have any spare field joints. I've got four of my machine shops working on new ones, but if you ask me, we'll be lucky to get six degrees."

"The old joints… are they all bad?" Soze asked.

"None of them are operational if that's what you're getting at."

"No," Soze replied. "I meant are they bad through and through? Can you salvage bits and pieces of them?"

Noland's brow furrowed. "I suppose. Number seven had some pretty good spools on it, but you're talking about disassembling the entire outer assembly."

By then Ackerman was already nodding to Soze. "I see where you're going. That's a good call, Aaron. If we could get thrusters two and five going, it would be worth it."

Noland was taken aback. "But sir, we can't use just two thrusters, especially not those two. They're not balanced against each other. With the rotation of the ship, we'd introduce a wobble. It would tear us apart eventually."

Ackerman nodded his understanding. "But how long before the wobble became noticeable?"

"A day, maybe two, depending on the thrust levels. It's not really long enough to change course in any meaningful way."

Ackerman smiled. "It's long enough. Hell, I'd settle for just one. You get your teams split up on numbers two and five. Rip up the other thrusters if you have to, but get those working. The first team to finish gets the week off. The others have to put the mess back together."

"But Captain," Noland objected, "this makes no sense."

Ackerman merely shook his head and turned to Soze. "Make sure he has what he needs."

He left without waiting for a reply.

Pritchard stopped by Jose Mendoza's guest apartment later that day. The fact that two junior constables were there told him that Jose was home. One was there to safeguard Mendoza's belongings, and other was there really to act as his guide but also as a bodyguard if necessary. A rotation of eight guards had become the standard procedure after one or more angry colonists had thrown rocks through Akahele's apartment window. Hathaway had initially offered some of his Divine Mark officers for the duty, but he later balked for unexplained reasons. Captain Ackerman had covered the gap initially with his own crew security, but ultimately Pritchard convinced enough other tier-fathers to allocate some of their local constables to the effort. Pritchard had considered it something of a personal victory as he learned the inner politics of the House of Fathers.

Mendoza opened the door in response to the constable's call and invited Pritchard inside. His equipment was arrayed around the den with holographic headshots of several colonists floating, frozen in mid-air. Margaret was among them.

Mendoza nodded towards it, saying, "Quite a young woman you raised, sir. She gave a great interview."

"I suspect it is her youth. Having given one myself, I found it exhausting." He picked up a loose imager and examined it. "Tell, Mr. Mendoza, with all this equipment you maintain, do you know much about communications equipment? Not this tach burst stuff, but basic ship to ship, that sort of thing."

"A little. I mean, I took some classes at school, and I worked a year at one of our broadcast points. It's not exactly the same, but it's similar. Why?"

Pritchard set the imager down. "We've been getting an intermittent feedback loop in some of our bridge comm systems ever since we received our new equipment from Admiral Wozniak. I was hoping you could help us track it down."

"I'd be glad to help. I'm trying to finish up a rough cut for Marcy, but I'll be free in an hour or so."

Pritchard silently cursed the man's priorities but could not complain while asking. "I will await your presence on the bridge."

Two hours later, his escort brought Mendoza to the bridge. Lieutenant Thacker had already opened the external communications bay, exposing the bastard mix of the two systems. Mendoza shook his head at the untidiness of it but still sprawled out on the floor with some of his own portable tools.

His first assessment came almost immediately. "Damn, you didn't say this was fleet stuff. I can't reprogram any of this. It's all encrypted."

Thacker piped up. "We don't want you to reprogram it. Just see if you can find the feedback."

He worked for another twenty minutes before Pritchard stopped by for a progress report. "Have you found anything yet?"

Mendoza looked up from one his gadgets. "Uh, no, I haven't found anything yet," he replied, but his expression gave a very different report. Something was clearly wrong.

"You're sure?"

Mendoza did his best to cover his face with a false smile. "I'm still trying to get the hang of it."

After another hour of checking, scanning, and rechecking, Mendoza finally packed up his gear. He walked over to Pritchard with a pad in his outstretched hand. "I'm sorry, Commander," he said, "I just can't make sense of it. This military gear is always ahead of ours."

Pritchard took the pad. It was clear except for one handwritten note. "Commander, the fleet components are transmitting constantly. That is the source of your feedback. I believe anything said on this bridge is being transmitted on an encrypted channel."

He looked up to meet Mendoza's eyes, his face pale. "You're sure?"

Mendoza nodded. "Yeah, you'd need a professional to work on this."

They met Captain Ackerman twenty minutes later in an empty car on a spinward tram. He took the news impassively. "You're positive this wasn't just an unintentional accident?"

"Absolutely," Mendoza replied. "I couldn't crack their programming or anything, but it's clearly transmitting with good power in a non-standard scheme, even for military chit-chat. It's clear they didn't want anyone else to find the signal by accident."

"Can you disable it?" Pritchard asked.

"I could pull it, or even set up to jam it and block its power, but without the program key, I can't do much."

Ackerman held up his hand. "Let's not be too hasty." They both looked at him in surprise. "There may be some advantage to having an eavesdropper." He nodded, smiling to himself. "Especially when the eavesdropper thinks we are unaware."

The wedding of Sharon Pritchard to Albert Hillis was a modest affair, but it was still done in the full Masonite tradition, complete with the honor guard of friends and the release of the single dove. Margaret had received a special dispensation from her doctors to skip her normal quarantine garb and wear the traditional blue bridesmaid dress, as long as she wore gloves and exercised caution. In truth, she did not need to exercise much care, since everyone knew about her condition. She was probably the most famous Teruvian case in the colony.

She did allow herself one dance with Cal, who wore the formal stiff white gloves of the honor guard. Beyond the gloves, Cal himself seemed distant. "What's wrong?" she finally asked at the end of their dance.

He gave his ceremonial bow and led her from the dance floor to a table near the edge. "I had an argument with your father last week."

"He mentioned you stopped by, but he didn't say anything about an argument." She sat down beside him. "It wasn't about the wedding, was it?"

He nodded and looked over at Margaret's cousin Sharon. "That could be you in white, Mags."

Her face lit up in surprise. "He said yes?"

"Not exactly, but he did acknowledge that he could not stop us."

She sighed her disappointment. "There's a difference, Cal. He didn't say yes, did he?"

"No, he did not."

"Well, there's no need to rush," she said. "I'd like my scars to fade a little more anyway."

He twisted in his chair and glanced down at her back. The faint blue scarring had retreated from her shoulders but still covered much of her back between her shoulder blades. "I don't know, Mags, I kind of like the scars. They're exotic."

She was about to reply with something equally playful when Sharon swept by with her new husband. "Oh, Maggie, there you are. I just wanted to thank you so much for bringing that reporter friend of yours. Our wedding is the first one in the colony to be recorded with all those fancy cameras."

Albert nodded his agreement. "Amazing little things. I saw part of your interview on one of her little projectors. It's almost like being in the same room. Have you seen it, Cal?"

"I've seen the interview out on the network, but just on the flat transfer." A rough cut of Marcy Clark's two hour piece had been floating around the colony network informally for most of the week.

"Well, see it if you can," Albert replied. "But you've already seen the best part," he said turning to Margaret. "I really liked what you said about having a new chance, Maggie. You know, I was talking to Greg, you know the Solomon family from your tier, and he was suggesting—"

"Oh, you and politics," Sharon interrupted. "Let's not go down that path." She began to lead her new husband away. "Oh look, there's Aunt Elise."

They watched the dancers for a few moments before Margaret broke their silence. "So, you've seen it then, the interview?"

He nodded.

"What do you think about it, about the colony?"

He sighed. "I think you're getting ahead of yourself, Mags. Sure, it sounds wonderfully exciting, but the reality is going to be very harsh. It'll be some cramped-up station for a while, then some tight little dome on a God-forsaken rock, not just for a year, but decades, lifetimes. Is that really where you want to raise our children?"

She did not answer.

Pino's Hammer was a cold world, but its rich deposits of rhodium made it wealthy. The easy access to the rare metal made it a natural magnet for ship construction, especially the tachyon polarization filters that made the core of their sails. It had also built up the normal support industries as well as those for several shipboard components. However, the intemperate weather still left it as a net importer of food, especially meats.

As such, Torin Graylock had no difficulty in acquiring spare cryo-containers at port. He also had no difficulty in acquiring a variety of modern commercial ship components, everything from computers to scanners and communication gear. He would have liked to have picked up some modest hull-mounted weapon systems, but he was not licensed for their transport, and his freshly minted Takasumi letter of credit was not going to get him far in the black market.

His only real difficulty came on the eve of their departure when the local docking supervisor balked at his loading instructions. "Let me get this straight, Captain Graylock. You want us to put this tech gear into the cryo units?"

Torin nodded. He still got a warm feeling whenever someone referred to him that way. "Yes, is there a problem?"

"Well, just a couple. First, the cold is no good for this stuff – makes 'em brittle."

"Oh, of course. I don't want you to turn them on."

"Ah, I see. Well, the second problem is the size. The walls on these, you see, are thicker – insulation and all – so they're not as big on the inside. It's usually not a problem because they're just packing loose sides of beef, that sort of thing. It doesn't matter if the boxes don't line up because there are no boxes."

"I don't see what you mean."

"All your gear is in half-meter palettes. That's fine for your standard three-meter cargo pod, but these cryo's are only two and three quarters on the inside. It's not all gonna fit, and it's sure as hell gonna rattle around. I mean, we can quick-foam it, but it'll be extra."

In the end, the Jinley left Pino's Hammer with all the gear Torin had bought, but the spare staterooms and both lounges were packed to the ceiling with the extra.

The *Indigo Flame* dropped out of tach with all the precision of a military ship, and she was a military ship of sorts. She had been originally commissioned as the Solarian Union's *Galahad*, a cruiser that saw action in both the second Catai war and the Julosh Insurrection as well as a number of other border skirmishes in the last century. When decommissioned, she was sold to the Celenne Federation, a loose group of independent worlds on the coreward border of the League of Catai. When the Celenne government disintegrated, the *Galahad* fell into unscrupulous hands. Updated and well-crewed as the *Indigo Flame*, she was one of the most potent ships in the Yoshido pirate fleet.

Her companion ships, the *Queen Eleanor* and the *James River*, dropped tach shortly afterwards and not quite so precisely, but they had never been true fighting vessels. They were luxury passenger liners that had fallen on hard times. Sufficed to say that now the times were even harder and much less luxurious, but they were capable of carrying over three thousand passengers each. For human cargo, they were the Yoshido bulk carriers.

Captain Elise Bracken looked over the scopes carefully. The Masonite colony ship was ahead in the distance, while the Confederate vessel hung back slightly off to the side running in stealth mode. "Looks like your intel was right, sir."

Jiro Yu smiled at the prospect. "It always is, Captain Bracken. Activate your Shiantic transponder, please." That had been the arranged signal. Yu was not sure which ships were still defending the *Chariot*, but his information was that none of them would defend against ships from the Shiantic Ribbon. It was common for the Yoshido to sail unofficially under their flag. It gave them an extra level of protection, and the Shiantic fanatics enjoyed the additional pain for the Confederacy.

"We're receiving their challenge now via directed tach-burst."

"Send the reply, and send it on standard comm as well."

Bracken loaded the file and sent it, wondering at the different reaction it would have on the two vessels before them.

"This is the *Crimson Tiger* of the Shiantic Ribbon of Truth, and we are here to cleanse the universe of this Masonite stain and exact revenge for ancient crimes. All Confederate ships are advised to act the cowards they are and leave the area."

Chapter 10

"I once hunted black panthers in the northern forests of Liao's Fist, and I must confess it was as terrifying as it was exhilarating. With all the weaponry, body armor, and vision enhancements we had, it was easy to forget that this supposed prey of mine was itself a deadly predator. The panthers, on the other hand, were more than willing to remind us." – John Kealing, opening remarks to the Stonefall University alumni spring fundraiser, 3398.

Captain Ackerman leaned down on the bridge's central plot table looking at the latest scans as various officers crowded in around him. The three Shiantic ships were shown clearly. The *Goliad* was only marked with a probability cloud based on various communications they had received. He had her captain on the comm, trying both to firm up *Goliad's* position and to convince him to intercede.

"But Admiral Wozniak made it clear to me that you were here for our protection. Are you disobeying those orders?"

"I am not, and your interpretation of what the Admiral promised you is not the same as an order from him to me. If these were simple pirates, yes, but this is clearly a foreign force of greater strength, and I am not authorized to risk my ship in such an effort."

DAN THOMPSON

Commander Pritchard arrived with Akahele and Marcy Clark. Ackerman nodded to them and hit the transmit switch again. "Not even to save our lives."

"You are not citizens of the Confederation."

"But we do have Confederation citizens on board," he replied, motioning to his guest.

"This is Marcy Clark, citizen of the Confederation, resident of Latera. Transstar Media will take a dim view of you abandoning its citizens, Captain."

"I'm sorry, Miss Clark, but I did not put you on that ship. I suggest you get back on that yacht of yours and clear out while you still can. Otherwise, you are on your own."

Commander Dudley Meyers nodded to the Captain. The *Goliad* cloud had shrunk from a vague probability to a region only a hundred kilometers across. It was not good enough for a firing solution, but Ackerman still did not know if he would need one.

"Captain," Ackerman signaled again, "I will be filing a protest with your fleet command at the earliest opportunity."

"You are free to do so, but first you must survive. I suggest negotiation is your best option."

Ackerman clicked off the connection, suspecting that his next words would still be heard by the *Goliad*. "Negotiation? Captain Kalas, what do you make of the situation?"

Akahele looked over the plot and the telescopic views of the force closing in. "For starters, they're almost certainly not from the Shiantic Ribbon. This is too far for them to venture in with anything less than a carrier group. More likely they are common pirates, or perhaps well-financed pirates. I doubt *Crimson Tiger* is even their real name, but the *Goliad* doesn't want to admit it because they're probably outclassed in firepower."

"Well, what will they want?"

"What pirates always want, your cargo."

"But what do we have? Outmoded terraforming gear, recycling equipment?"

191

"There's only one way to find out. Beg enough, and they'll tell you."

He toggled open the second channel. "*God's Chariot* to *Crimson Tiger*, we are an unarmed colony. We do not mean to make war on anyone. Please, show us mercy."

The reply was briefly delayed. Their ships were still a light-second out. "Mercy? Masonites deserve no mercy."

"Please, we'll give you anything you want, mining gear, terraforming equipment, foodstuffs, anything. Just don't fire on us."

The silence on the channel lasted almost a full minute. "There is something you can give us, Captain, and we will spare your lives for now." It was clear now that the other captain was a woman.

"Say the word, and it is yours."

"You have a large population. You will select six thousand women between the ages of twelve and twenty-five. Be sure that some of them have technical training. Have them ready to be picked up within four hours."

"You want hostages?" he asked. The surprise in his voice was mostly an act. He had suspected them of piracy the moment they appeared, and he had read enough history to know that the most valuable cargo was rarely gold.

"No, you simpering idiot, we want slaves, and you are going to provide them."

"I won't."

Another voice came on, a male one, very smooth but with a thick accent. "Look, Captain, it is not so bad. They will be taken to a real colony world. Is that not your goal?"

"Not like this."

"Perhaps not for everyone, but don't you have a few troublemakers, those you would rather be rid of? We'll even take those pox-ridden whores off your hands. It's almost a favor."

Pritchard opened his mouth to speak, but a look from Ackerman silenced him.

Ackerman nodded his silent assurance and keyed the handset again. "I think that can be arranged."

"I suggest haste," came the smooth reply. "The patience of my officers is limited."

"I will spare no effort," Ackerman answered and cut the connection and looked at the plot. The two trailing ships had begun their approach. They were well within the directional range of the one operational thruster, but at six degrees from the center-line, the *Indigo Flame* was close to the edge. For all his apparent treachery, though, the *Goliad's* captain had been smart enough to hold off. *Goliad* was a full twenty-two degrees off the center-line and well outside of their directional capabilities.

Ackerman pointed to the three pirate ships and nodded to Pritchard. "Pass the word, Commander. We're going to give them what they want." He would let the *Goliad's* captain make what he wanted out of that comment. He just wondered whether or not the *Crimson Tiger* was also able to monitor the signal.

Pritchard saluted and left the bridge. They had set up a second intraship communications station two blocks away, well outside the range of any monitoring equipment on the bridge. Commander Soze was waiting in engineering to relay the orders to Noland.

Ackerman looked around at his immediate compatriots, only some of them in on his secret. He noticed that Marcy Clark was wearing her yellow imaging headband. If they survived it would all be recorded for history. Much of the bridge crew, however, had been kept in the dark. The best held secrets were held by few, but if he had had more time, he would have spread it a little further.

Hathaway and Reverend Cooper sat in a quiet corner of the park by Lake Harmony. In the distance, a one-man sailboat made its way back towards the docks.

"I know they seem helpful, High Reverend, but I found these people very strange, almost alien. Beyond their heathen beliefs, their very way of life is disturbing."

"And yet Brother Tony found much of their world charming. He spoke to me in very different terms."

Cooper sighed. "And that is what frightens me the most, that these worldly notions can lead us astray. I urge you, High Reverend, that if we are to accelerate our mission, we do it with as little outside help as possible. If it takes ten generations more, they will be generations well spent. Don't we owe that to the generations that came before?"

Hathaway was about to answer when his phone beeped with his private secretary's priority signal. "What is it?" he asked.

"I am patching Reverend Wallace through for you."

"High Reverend, you've got to get to the bridge," Wallace told him, his voice almost panicked. "Ackerman's gone mad."

"Brother Christopher, what are you talking about?"

"We're under attack, High Reverend. I have a well-placed officer sending me reports, and he tells me three pirate ships are approaching, demanding we hand over six thousand of our young women."

Cooper's eyes went as wide as Hathaway's. "Surely that can't be. The captain would have alerted me."

"It just started, High Reverend."

Hathaway looked up. The bridge complex was a third of the way around and two blocks aft. Everything looked serene. "You're sure about this?"

"I swear it on my wife's ashes."

Hathaway stood. "I'm on my way to the bridge now. Get hold of Reverend Terrence and put out a general alert. The people need to be getting to the shelters." He hung up, nodded a curt goodbye to Cooper, and started running around the aft shore of the lake. He almost ran past the tram station, but his lungs were already giving out. He staggered onto the platform and into a waiting tram. He counted his fortune that it was going in the right direction. The bridge was two stops away.

At the next station, two uniformed crew came on. He saw their side-arms and recognized them as security. The younger one stepped closer. "High Reverend, are you well?"

Hathaway looked at the approaching bridge complex. "Not at all, young man. Terrible work is afoot. I need you to come with me to the bridge, both of you."

They nodded and followed him out at the next station. It had been two years since Hathaway had been to the bridge, and in his confusion, he made two wrong turns, but his escort corrected him and ultimately led him to it. He was nearly there before he heard the general alarm go out from Terrence's communication office.

He passed two more security guards before he burst into the open space of the bridge. "Captain Ackerman!" he roared. "I don't know what you're doing, but you had best explain yourself."

Ackerman's eyes went wide, and he clearly choked back his first response. "High Reverend, I don't know what you've been told, but—"

Hathaway stepped up to the main display plot, his escort flanking him. "I've been told that a fleet of ships is threatening us, and that they have demanded you hand over the innocent as slaves."

Ackerman looked around the table. Hathaway recognized a few of the senior officers as well as Akahele Kalas and that young reporter woman. "Yes, High Reverend, that is in fact the situation."

"And what are you doing? Are you planning to hand over six thousand young souls to these monsters?"

Ackerman scanned his eyes over the rest of the bridge. He looked unnaturally nervous.

"Captain! I'm expecting an answer."

"I am doing what is necessary to save our colony, and I don't have time to explain myself to you right now."

"You will make time, Captain, or I will relieve you of command." He turned to his escort and prepared to issue an order. Only then did Hathaway realize his mistake. These were not officers of the Divine Mark.

Ackerman stepped around the table to one of the two guards. "Jack," he said. "You know me, don't you?"

"Of course, sir."

"Then trust me," he said and pulled the sidearm from the guard's holster.

The other guard's eyes went wide with surprise, but not before another officer, a commander by his insignia, could grab hold of his gun hand. "Don't," he said and slowly took the pistol into his own hands.

Hathaway started backing away, realizing he suddenly had no real authority here. Ackerman tucked the gun into hip pocket. "High Reverend, with all due respect, sit."

Hathaway's face turned red with anger, but he complied, taking a seat at an empty scanning station. Ackerman grabbed a pad and scribbled a quick note on it before tossing it to Hathaway's feet.

When Hathaway picked it up, his face went pale, but he did not speak. It simply read, "This is no mutiny. Be silent and pray for luck."

Pritchard's voice came on the comm. "We're ready, sir."

Ackerman looked again at Hathaway and gave the order that no Masonite captain had given in over a thousand years. "Commence firing."

At the trailing end of *Chariot*, aft-thruster two jumped to life after almost two hundred years of silence. Fortunately, the officers directing the thrust had understood well that the *Indigo Flame* was about to escape from their firing cone, and it was their first target.

On board its bridge, Captain Bracken was lazily monitoring the plot when the thruster came alive. In the ten seconds it took to come to full power and hone in on their position, she was able to ask, "What? Do they think they can outrun us?"

She never got an answer. A two-meter stream of fusion exhaust moving at almost the speed of light swept across her ship. It was the result of taking virtually every atom of interstellar gas across three hundred kilometers and cramming into a tightly focused beam of freshly-born helium nuclei.

While the old warship's hull was strong enough not to come apart instantly, the *Chariot's* officers had been lucky enough in their targeting to hit one of their reactors with that first pass. The stream disturbed the magnetic field enough to cause a small plasma leak, but as many an engineer has stated, there is no such thing as a small plasma leak. It was enough to slag the power line feeding the magnetic field, and in under a second, the entire field had collapsed. In another two seconds, the expanding plasma had reached the other two reactors, and in less than five seconds after that first lucky sweep of the thruster's exhaust, the *Indigo Flame* had been reduced to an expanding cloud of debris.

The *Queen Eleanor* and *James River* were not as lucky, especially their crews. Their hulls melted easily under the intensity of the drive exhaust, and they were split first in two and then into successively smaller pieces as the stream of fusion exhaust swept over them again and again. Eventually it hit the remnants of the engineering sections resulting in massive explosions, but by then the debris had spread out enough not to be consumed by them. Some of the crew had died instantly, but most had been preparing for boarding and were in armored vacuum suits. While a few of them would be later rescued, most died from slow asphyxiation in the depths of interstellar space.

All of this played out on the large screens of the *Chariot's* bridge. Most took it with surprise and exhilaration while Hathaway looked on in horror.

Ackerman opened the channel to Pritchard. "Well done, Commander. Pass my compliments to Commanders Soze and Noland and prepare for the next firing sequence."

Hathaway stood but realized he had no way to intervene. He was powerless.

Ackerman spoke sternly into the handset. "*Goliad,* as you can see we are capable of defending ourselves, and I have reason to doubt your sincerity. State your intentions."

There was no immediate response.

Hathaway slowly approached the table again. He could see a red cone trailing out behind *Chariot* with a cloud labeled *Goliad* off to one side.

Ackerman turned to the armed officer and pointed to the display. "Do we have a lock on their position?"

"Yes, sir," he replied with a shrug. "They're still running that damn stealth system of theirs, but at these speeds their radiation shadow makes them pretty hard to miss."

Ackerman spoke into the handset again. "I repeat, *Goliad,* state your intentions."

Hathaway happened to be looking at the telescopic view when it happened. In a sudden streak of red light, the *Goliad* had left.

Ackerman must have seen it too, for he sagged forward onto the table, his weight supported only by his arms, quivering at the elbow. He then removed the pistol from his pocket and slid it across the table back to the guard. "Thank you, Jack. Meyers, give yours back as well."

He then stepped around the table and stood before Hathaway. "My apologies, High Reverend, but our bridge and communications systems were being monitored. I could not explain that without showing our hand."

Hathaway stared at him in disbelief. "Our hand? No, it was your hand, Captain. You have made murderers of us. Everything we have denied, all for nothing. You've made us just like those we left behind."

"I did what was necessary, High Reverend, for this ship and for the colony. Would you rather I had handed them your daughter?"

The High Reverend leaned in close. "I thought I knew you, Captain, but I was wrong. I will not make that mistake again." He staggered back towards the hatch and left.

Cal ran forward along Carson. The all-clear had just sounded. He still did not know what the emergency had been. He did not care. All that mattered was finding Margaret. Tier Bennet was eight blocks away, but the trams were still on lockdown.

He would have come straight away, but he had already been in the shop basement, and the surge of his coworkers had forced him further down into the shelter. He had tried to get back out, but the airlock doors had already closed. There was no choice but to wait it out. The phones had gone on lockdown as well, reserved for priority traffic only. The emergency had been short, only twenty-eight minutes, but they had been the longest minutes of his life.

Crowds were spilling out onto Carson street from the shelter exits, so Cal angled across a small park towards the school. That was the shelter Margaret would have used. He saw an set of stairs descending into the ground outside, and he headed down, flying two or three steps at a time. He pressed through the line of students coming through the airlock and did his best to follow the signs, looking for homeroom teacher names. Two lefts and then a right, and then he found her at last.

Margaret stood calmly waiting by her young students, telling them some soothing words that mattered not at all to Cal. He ran in, grabbed her by shoulders and pulled her into a tight embrace. "Never again," he said.

She mumbled something into his chest, but he would not let go of her to hear it.

He swore he would never let go again.

Ackerman strolled through the outer office towards his appointment with Hathaway. As always, he was looking for any minor changes, but today there was a much more significant one. Stationed outside the High Reverend's door was an officer of the Divine Mark, but not in dress uniform. Instead, he wore the black combat uniform, complete with the short carbine rifle slung over his shoulder. The officer glared at him silently.

Ackerman paused before him. "May I go in?"

The officer nodded. "I believe the High Reverend is expecting you."

Inside, Hathaway was sitting behind his desk. The stiff-back chair Hathaway normally kept in the corner had been moved out front to face the desk. Ackerman took his seat while Hathaway considered him quietly from the other side of the desk. The silence stretched for a minute. Then two.

"Tell me, High Reverend, should I be worrying about the armed guard at the door?"

Hathaway leaned forward, steepling his hands on his desk. "I thought, my dear Captain, that perhaps you should experience something of the feeling I had when you took a gun into your hands yesterday afternoon."

Ackerman sighed. "Again, High Reverend, I apologize for that. More than anything, I was trying to defuse the situation, and I could not offer a full explanation at that moment."

"So you said, but could you not have offered one before? Could you have not taken a few moments to take me aside one evening and tell me what had been done to your bridge?"

He nodded. "Yes, I could have. In retrospect, I should have, and I can only ask you to believe me that eventually I would have told you, but my primary focus was on operational security."

"And you feel that I cannot keep a secret?"

"Not at all, though I suppose I thought you might choose not to keep it a secret. I worried that you would have taken this to the Confederate officers immediately, the very officers who were eavesdropping on us. You are very trusting man, High Reverend. That has served you well within our colony, but with respect, I fear it has left you naïve."

Hathaway leaned back from his desk again and seemed to consider him for a moment. "And so it seems my education in duplicity has come from you."

Ackerman nodded. There was no denying it. "To my sincere regret."

"And all this talk of a course change, was it merely a ruse to turn us into an armed camp?"

"I was honest with you before, High Reverend, but I confess I did see the dual purpose in getting those engines working again. Something about seeing all those warships arrayed behind us left me feeling vulnerable."

"And you thought me too much the fool to trust me with that decision?"

"Respectfully, I knew your strengths. I thought only to augment them."

"And one of my strengths is my faith in God's plan for us. It is a shame you could not have a similar faith, or at the very least, some faith in me as God's appointed shepherd for our flock."

Ackerman nodded, but he held back his thoughts on blind faith. He had heard the cruelty in that pirate's voice, and he had very few doubts about his ultimate intent. "I will strive for it, High Reverend." It was all he could truly promise.

Hathaway took a deep breath and let it out in a grumble. "Well, enough of the past. As for today, I understand you have collected some survivors from the wreckage."

Ackerman subtly relaxed, but resisted the temptation to slump or cross his legs. "Yes, eighty-four members of their would-be boarding party. At the moment, we're holding them in launch bay A-3."

"Is it secure?"

Ackerman nodded. He had ordered them stripped of the armored suits and left in the outer bay with the knowledge that the doors could opened into space without ceremony. None of his people went in without an environment suit and a safety line. "Secure enough, but it's not a good long term solution."

"And what do you suggest for that?"

"If we do end up on good terms with the Confederacy, I'd like to hand them over, but in the meantime, I would prefer we use our own security facilities to detain them. Perhaps your Divine Mark officers could assist us in that."

Hathaway grimaced. "Forgive me, Captain, but right now I feel a little possessive of my Divine Mark officers. You can work with the tier-fathers to use the various constable buildings. I'm sure you'll find a solution."

Ackerman nodded and silently cursed himself for tripping over that sensitivity. "Is there anything else, High Reverend?"

"No, Captain. You may go."

Ackerman walked past the guard in the outer officer again, suddenly uncomfortable at having him to his back.

The next morning, Captain Patrick Conway stood in the office of Sector Admiral Horatio Nelson at Arvin. He had never actually served under the admiral, but he had heard enough to know two things. First, he did not appreciate the historical jokes about his name, and second, he took disloyalty very personally. Everyone in his academy class had heard the stories of the *Victoria* mutiny, and the man responsible for it sat behind the desk reading and pointedly not acknowledging him. Conway remained standing, not because there was no chair, but because the marines had told him to remain standing. It did not bode well.

"I was just comparing your after-action report, Captain Conway."

"If I may ask, sir, comparing it to what?"

"To your first officer's, Lt. Commander Young."

"My apologies, Admiral. I did not realize he had filed one."

"Yes, it is not standard practice, but I asked for it. He was most obliging, and I found it to be fascinating reading."

Conway stood silently.

"Tell me, Captain, do you feel your report is complete?"

"Yes, sir. It is, of course, leaving out minor details of little importance, but the core of the event is there."

"Really? The 'core' of the event, yes..." he paused to scroll the text on the desk screen. "I take it the identity of the ships was not quite the core of the event."

"Sir, the ships are clearly identified in my report: the *Crimson Tiger*, the *Emperor's Pride*, and the *Adrianna*."

"Yet your first officer felt quite certain that the *Crimson Tiger* was not actually what it claimed to be."

"Perhaps in looking back, Admiral, he had some doubts."

The Admiral smiled weakly. The stories did not go well if the Admiral smiled. "Some doubts, you say? It would seem that he felt strongly about it at the time of the incident. His personal log entry after you tucked your tail makes that quite clear. He says he told you that the *Crimson Tiger* was actually the *Indigo Flame*, a well known pirate vessel."

Conway repressed his curse. "To be fair, Admiral, the computer only gave that match a forty percent probability."

"Oh, only forty percent. I suppose your little calculus did not include the fact that the Shiantic ship *Crimson Tiger* is listed in the database as having been destroyed in the Vassat incident over ten months ago or that the so-called *Adrianna* was a spot-on match for the *Queen Eleanor* which has been long suspected of running the slave trade in the spinward reaches?"

"In fairness, sir, there was not much time."

"Not much time? It was time enough for your first officer, Captain. It would have been time enough for me. I would think it would have been time enough for a trained monkey."

Conway shifted on his feet, trying to find a way out. "To be fair, Admiral—"

"To be fair?" Admiral Nelson interrupted him and rose to his feet. "Let me tell you what's going to happen to you, Captain. You are going to march out of this office and down to the station brig where you will stay until a formal inquiry can be held, at which time I will recommend your full court martial on charges of cowardice, disobeying standing orders on piracy, and possibly even conspiracy to commit treason."

"But, Admiral..." Conway began to object but withered beneath Nelson's glare.

"If you're lucky, Captain, you'll lose your commission and be dishonorably discharged." He raised a hand to signal the marine forward. "But if we were to be fair, well, I'd give you to the Masonites."

They gathered in the plain light of day in the middle of Peace Park, but the meeting still had the feeling of a conspiracy. Around the picnic table sat Richard Ackerman, Carol Ashburn, Neville Catelli, and their informal leader, Gregory Solomon. "There's no going back to the way it was before," he said. "That pirate attack just underlined the point."

Carol nodded vigorously. "They were coming for me. For me, gentlemen. They may not be back tomorrow, but they won't be the last."

"I'm not that worried," Richard replied. "My father seems to have dealt with them handily."

Neville shook his head. "I don't agree. From what Greg said, it was a very close thing. Even then, I don't see your father getting us ready to go. This whole course change thing seems more designed to placate us, to get us thinking of generations instead of starting a new colony right now."

"But he's just the captain. You may think my father has plenty of authority, but he has to do what Hathaway tells him."

"It's not your father," Gregory told him. "And it's not Hathaway either. It's their generation." He paused to let them see it. "I mean no disrespect, but they have spent their careers on carrying *Chariot* forward. I don't think they can see the obvious options before them."

Richard frowned at him. "And you do?"

"I'm not saying I have the master plan worked out, but this is going to fall on our generation. Whether we head off to colonize now or we wait thirty years until we are in charge ourselves, the new world will start with us."

"I like the sound of that," Carol replied. "But we're four people sitting in a park. What are we going to do about it?"

"For starters, we can talk about it."

Richard laughed. "Gregory, I think you're talking plenty already."

Neville shot him a glare. "I think he means more than this"

Gregory looked up at the expanse of the *Chariot* above him. "Yeah, a lot more."

Ackerman stared across the table at the heavy man in the orange prison uniform. When his crew had rescued the would-be boarders from open space, he had paid this one particular attention. By training both old and recent, he was intimately familiar with various forms of rank insignia, from the highly structured to the informal. Most of his prisoners had borne no special markings on their armored suits. A few had one or two red bars on their chests, and one in particular had also included a vertical black sword through three red bars. The man in this cell was not an ignorant grunt but rather Master Sergeant Tano Osrick.

"Miss Clark will be recording this." It was not a request for permission, just a statement of fact. He nodded to her to begin.

Osrick ignored her, focusing his attention on Ackerman instead. He was not the only one able to understand foreign insignia.

"I'm going to skip over the preliminaries of your supposed affiliation with the Shiantic Ribbon. Your men have already spoiled that lie. What I'm more interested in at the moment is the Yoshido organization, who authorized your attack, and who provided you with our precise location."

Osrick shrugged. "I don't feel much like talking today."

Ackerman sighed. "As it stands, Sergeant, you are accused of rape—"

Osrick chuckled. "With all due respect, sir, if I'd raped any of your girls, they'd be thanking me, not accusing me."

Marcy's face reddened in anger, but she held her place. Ackerman had warned her.

"You're welcome to try that defense with the High Reverend," Ackerman answered, "but I don't think he'll take it well. I believe he has always contended that the sin of the heart is more important than the actual act itself."

Osrick shrugged again and gazed around the room calmly.

"And yet," Ackerman continued, "if you cooperate, I think I could get you released to the Confederate authorities."

"That's not much of an offer, Captain," he replied. "I'd likely get life without parole, maybe even death by spacing. No thanks. I'll take my chances with your preacher."

Ackerman sat back with a perplexed look. "You haven't actually met with the tier-son who's going to represent you, have you?"

Osrick shook his head. "Never liked lawyers anyway."

Ackerman cocked his head to one side. "Then maybe no one here has explained it to you, but I assumed you know something of us from your old history."

Osrick shrugged. "Calloway's long gone."

"Yes, but..." he trailed off. He glanced at Marcy and feigned embarrassment. "Of course, it has not been done in my lifetime, but I thought everyone knew the traditional Masonite penalty for rape. Don't you?"

The sudden look of horror in Osrick's eyes told Ackerman he wouldn't need to go into the details. He was learning that there were advantages to Calloway's bloody specter. The interrogation suddenly became much more productive. Osrick had orders, names, timetables, even routing instructions for the would-be slaves.

Afterwards, Ackerman felt confident that there would be no second wave of pirate ships. Osrick was sure that the *Goliad's* departure had been arranged, and it seemed unlikely that something that required both convenient timing and military corruption would be attempted again. Meanwhile, Marcy Clark had an entirely new line of investigation for her story.

"I can't wait to get back to Latera and follow up on this. Father Chessman, really. I'd always heard stories, but nothing like this. There has to be a government connection. I can smell it."

Ackerman nodded. "While I don't wish any problems on your Confederation, I would take some joy in seeing a little bloodletting."

"I think you'll get that, metaphorically of course," she replied. She looked back down the hallway to the row of cells. "Tell me, Captain, what is the Masonite penalty for rape?"

His smug smile took on a feral nature. "You can look it up yourself in the library, but trust me, Miss Clark, your virtue is secure."

Reverend Morris stepped into the tram car and saw Pritchard seated at the far end. "Commander," he called, and Pritchard motioned him over.

"Congratulations on your good news, Reverend. I'd been meaning to come visit, but..." he waved his hand abstractly.

"I know," Morris replied. "It's been non-stop at my end as well." He was on his way to do yet another round of sermon reviews with the parsons in the forward tiers.

"So tell me, when is she due?"

Morris grinned. "January fourteenth." Kara had already extended the calendar by a month so she could mark it red.

Pritchard chuckled. "That's Maggie's birthday."

"I'll take that as a good sign, Commander. She's turning into quite an upstanding young woman."

"Upstanding and outspoken, and if you ask me, I could do with a little less of the outspoken."

Morris nodded. "Yes, I've seen that interview she gave, though I dare say she handled herself better than we did."

"Indeed, I suppose she did." He sighed. "It's just that I'm growing tired of all my fellow officers and tier-fathers asking me which ideas were hers and which were mine."

"I, of course, will give you credit for the best of them."

"You're too kind, Reverend."

He shrugged. "Well, as rough as they are, they are appealing, even to me. Perhaps it's the baby, but I find myself thinking about the future of our children much more these days."

"I'm sure you'll do fine," Pritchard assured him. "If there's anything you need, well, I suppose I can still change a diaper."

"Thank you, Commander, and if there's anything I can do for you or your Margaret, be assured that I will."

The return of the *Jinley* was a welcome sign to all, especially Akahele. She met Torin on the hanger deck. At least the transfer was easier since she had arranged for a proper docking collar to be installed on some of the shuttles.

He stepped off in the dull green uniform of a Takasumi captain. "Captain Kalas," he said. "Are you authorized to grant me access?"

She nodded to him formally. "Yes, Captain Graylock, I welcome you aboard."

Torin stepped down and embraced his former captain. "It's good to see you."

"And you. How's the ship?"

He smiled rather smugly. "My ship is getting along just fine, thank you very much."

She patted him on the back and led him towards the exit. "Did you have any problems getting what I asked for?"

He chuckled nervously. "No, no problems at all."

Unloading took a little longer than expected. One factor was that the Masonites were not accustomed to handling cargo like most ports, and then there was the matter of the loose components being carried over by hand, one shuttle at a time. Nevertheless, the civilian communication and sensor gear was much appreciated. The military gear was quickly pulled and replaced with something that was both simple and documented. Captain Ackerman had insisted on keeping much of the advanced military equipment, but he had been willing to give some of the tampered components to Marcy Clark for her story.

There was another private dinner at the High Reverend's home, though it had much less a celebratory air than the first had been. Gone was the younger generation and family members. It was only Hathaway, Ackerman, and the two captains of the *Jinley*, Akahele and Torin. Also, they had not killed the fatted calf for his return. From the onion flakes marbled into the steak, it was clear this was vat-grown grata meat.

The toasts were short and perfunctory, and they quickly fell to discussing the recent events. Ackerman had thanked him profusely. "While I saw some advantages to tampered gear, I'll be glad to have some equipment on my bridge that I can trust."

"Yes," Hathaway agreed. "I would just as soon forget the unpleasantness surrounding the original equipment. Its replacement was a fine gift."

Torin hesitated, but now was as good a time as any. "Well, High Reverend, it was not exactly a gift."

Hathaway blinked several times and set his wine glass down. "I'm not sure what you mean. We have no money, at least not any of your Confederate currency."

"Well, I'm a trader," he replied. "I was hoping we could make a trade."

"And what did you plan on asking for? As those damned pirates discovered, we have little to offer."

Torin held up his fork with a large bite of grata-steak on it. "I was thinking of about a hundred, maybe a hundred twenty tons of this."

"Grata?" Hathaway laughed. "You want grata-steak? I don't know if anyone has told you, my young Captain Torin, but grata-steak is hardly a delicacy. Certainly, we've dressed it up some, but this is our subsistence food."

Torin popped it into his mouth and savored the flavor. "I mean no disrespect, High Reverend, but I am a professional trader, and I know a market when I see it."

Loading the grata proved to be another challenge since they could not get the cryo pods that far into the ship. Instead, they had to package the meat back at the vats and transport it by tram down to the docking bay. Torin had insisted on a wide variety of the different kinds, ranging from the lean and pure to the fatty and spicy. In the end, they had managed to fit one hundred ten tons of grata into the cryo pods. Another fifty-four kilos of the fattiest and spiciest went directly into the *Jinley's* galley.

Reverend Cooper decried the action, pointing out that the steady loss of matter from their closed ecosystem would rob them of their necessary ingredients, but Torin assured him that he would be willing to make another run sometime in the future, trading them the basic carbon-based matter in exchange for more grata.

After only three days, the *Jinley* was ready to leave again. On the eve of her departure, Akahele dined alone with Torin on her old ship.

"You're doing well, Torin. I'm proud of you. That was a fast turnaround at Pino's."

"Well, it's a familiar ship and a familiar crew. I promoted Semi, somewhat informally, but I'm still really a man short."

She nodded but did not comment. Torin grinned at her silence. He knew she would have promoted Victor instead, but it was his ship now. Finally she asked, "Any difficulties here?"

"Well, only one, and it's a bit of a political one. I've received quite a few requests from some of the younger colonists asking to come with me."

"Particularly the young female colonists?"

"Well, naturally," Torin grinned. "Seriously though, they know what those pirates were after. Beyond the impatience of youth, I think a lot of them are scared."

"Well, let's not push that for now. I don't think the Reverends are quite ready to send their daughters off with the likes of you and Semi just yet."

"I thought as much. I also got a request from that reporter, Marcy Clark, and her technician Jose. She says she's got her story and is ready to go back."

"I know. She's been pestering me, but I didn't want to leave the *Chariot* without a tach-ship in case something came up. You go ahead and take her."

"Of course," he replied but then stiffened into formality. "I mean, after careful consideration, I have decided to accept two Confederate passengers for transport back to Latera."

She smiled at him. "Captain Graylock, you're just loving this, aren't you?"

He raised his glass to her. "Didn't you?"

She raised her glass back. "Even more."

The *Jinley* departed the next morning with Marcy Clark and Jose Mendoza in tow. They were eager to get back. Beyond the interview she had first come for, Marcy suspected she had the start of the story of the year, possibly even a Clio award.

Captain Ackerman waited in the High Reverend's office. As was his habit, he glanced around from his seat, looking for any changes. Most things were static, of course, but today he found one minor change. A worn copy of the *Chronicles of St. Mason* rested on the corner of the desk. Ackerman was considering this as Hathaway swept in from the side hall that led from his private secretary's office. Ackerman rose to greet him, but Hathaway just went right to his desk and set down a small stack of folders.

"You asked to see me, High Reverend?"

Hathaway nodded and sat behind his desk. "Yes, Captain, I needed to catch up on a few things."

Ackerman stood for a moment before realizing that the High Reverend intended to stay behind his desk rather than join him in the more relaxed sitting area. He strode over to the chair before Hathaway's desk and sat. "I am at your service, High Reverend."

"I understand you have completed the installation of the new equipment that Captain Graylock provided. Is it functioning?"

"Yes, we were able to test it with *Rachael's Luck*. Miss Reynolds was kind enough to make a few runs out behind us to let us confirm it. The sensor suite is impressive as well, far better than our old telescopes and radar. We should have an excellent view of just about anyone coming in, perhaps even one of those Confederate stealth ships."

Hathaway leaned back into his chair and folded his hands in his lap. "I always thought our sensors were for looking ahead, to see any hazards to navigation."

"We're using it for that too, of course. I just thought it would be prudent to provide a broader view of possible dangers."

"I see," Hathaway replied. He reached for one of the folders and pulled out a few sheets. "I have a report here from Reverend Cooper. The grata vats are working at twenty percent over capacity, trying to restore the food that was taken. Even then it will be of a lower quality."

"With due respect, High Reverend, my crew and I will gladly eat the worst of it in exchange for our new toys."

"Toys, yes," Hathaway harrumphed. "This other electronic gear Graylock brought us. I understand there was a problem when Tier-father Latham tried to pick up his consignment of these new computers for the administrators in his tier. Apparently, one of your men, a Lieutenant Markinson did not want to give them up. Tell me, Captain, is it a standing policy for your crew to hoard such things?"

Ackerman calmly held back his original response. "No, High Reverend, it is not. I had simply not given sufficiently explicit orders on the distribution of our recently received cargo. I assure you it is a mistake that will not be repeated in the future." He did not mention, however, that he and his crew had in fact hoarded several items, particularly a collection of personal comm units with something called "vari-field encryption".

"And you expect there will be future cargos?"

"Why, yes, High Reverend. This may be the solution to our problem."

"Grata?"

Ackerman shrugged. "Yes, but not just that. I suspect that we have a number of unique technologies. Certainly, we have dealt with quite a few problems that the rest of humanity never encountered. If I may be so bold, High Reverend, we may be able to leverage our resources into quite a bit of wealth."

Hathaway sighed. "I can sympathize with your passion for this, Jim, but it won't be enough, not to found a new world so far from here."

"Forgive me, High Reverend, but I don't think we'll really know that unless we try."

"Try?" he replied. "And what would that do to us? Look at the disruption we've had so far from just a handful of these visits. Would we be sending our best technicians out into this Confederacy to trade for this wealth? Or perhaps you would bring these outsiders here, onto the holy *Chariot* of God, to live amongst us, corrupting our young, leading them astray."

"Captain Kalas has lived here for almost a month now. I don't feel my son is being led astray."

"Your son is not the only child in my flock. Take that Pritchard girl for example. Have you seen that interview of hers? She certainly has some outlandish ideas, and I don't think they came from her father."

"With respect, High Reverend, I found her ideas to be worthwhile, a bit childish perhaps, but not outlandish. This is a gift. It is our chance to fulfill generations of dreams, and to do it now, not when we are mere names in the histories. Don't you want that?"

Hathaway gazed at the book on corner of his desk for a moment. "I do hear you, Jim, and I am not immune to that desire, but it is ultimately my responsibility. You would do well to remember that I alone will decide when it is time to debark from God's *Chariot* onto the Promised Land. Not you, not that girl, and certainly not Captain Kalas. Do I make myself clear?"

Ackerman nodded in a slow bow of his head. "I would not think to oppose you, High Reverend, but I am but a single spoke in the wheel. If it begins to turn, I will not be able to stop it for you."

Chapter 11

"I am the most powerful man in the universe. Like no king or emperor of history, I rule all that can be ruled, for my hand stretches out to a thousand worlds, and none question its authority." – from the diary of First Prime Dieter Leoben, 3194, two years before the Catai Rebellion.

Margaret had not been active in Youth Auxiliary for over a year. As the daughter of a Tier-son – and now a Tier-father – she knew she should have been, but she had always found the chapter meetings to be boring and petty. Even the socials were less about the supposed ideals of faith and duty and more about a chance to find a date. In fact, that was where she had met Cal three years back. Since then, her involvement had dropped mostly to bringing Aunt Jen's rolls to the various bake sales.

So it was with significant confusion that she read Gregory Solomon's note inviting her to a special YA meeting that night. Her first thought was it was just a formality. She was, after all, the only child of their district's Tier-father. It would only make sense for them to invite her to stop by from time to time, but the post-script left her clueless. "Sorry for the short notice, Maggie. Please come. We really need you."

Confused or not, curiosity got the better of her, so after a solitary dinner at home – Father was on an extended shift again – she made her way down to their local tier's community center. She doubted there would be much to it. The last time she had been to a regular meeting, it had only been the five board

216

members sitting in front of an audience of three, one of whom was dating the chairman.

When she opened the door this time, it was standing room only. Over a hundred young men and women filled the hall, chatting in a pre-meeting cacophony. She recognized some of them but not most. Even then, many she did recognize did not live in her tier. Her cousin Sharon and her husband were there from tier Wilson, and she even saw the Captain's son Richard there all the way from tier Drake. On the front dais was the same long table she'd always seen, but it was well lit, and a banner hung beyond it proclaiming, "Colonize Now".

She was still standing in the doorway when Gregory Solomon waved to her from the front. "Maggie!" he called out. She started walking forward and those around her started to quiet, turning towards her with hushed whispers. Gregory spoke out over the quieting room, "I'd like us all to extend a warm welcome to Margaret Pritchard. She's not actually on our local board, but she was kind enough to come anyway." A general applause broke out as Gregory motioned her to the front. He met her at the end of the table as the noise died down.

"Greg, I don't even know what I'm doing here," she whispered.

He shook her hand heartily. "Don't worry, Maggie. I think we're all just brainstorming tonight." He led her to a seat at the end of the table, and he returned to the center podium.

Margaret recognized the woman next to her, Caroline Ashburn from tier Galloway. "What is all this?" she whispered.

Caroline gave her hand a quick squeeze. "I liked what you said to that reporter."

Gregory pounded the gavel twice, and the room settled. "Thank you all for coming. I know some of you had a long tram ride, and I especially appreciate those of you who had to juggle shifts to make it. But the time..." he paused to motion to the banner behind him, "the time is now."

A wave of applause sounded through the hall amid calls of "For our children" and "Amen".

217

Gregory nodded to his audience. "As our good sister Margaret said, we have been given a gift. Yes, truly a gift, but it is also a challenge. Had we not been given this true providence, it would be another six hundred fifty years before any of us would have to study the terraforming techniques our forefathers planned for us. Who here knows much about atmospheric seeding? Or catalytic cascades? Or the different forms of... I believe it's called lichen?"

He was met with grim silence.

"You see my point. It's not enough for us to merely want this gift. We have to work for it, and with a true respect for all of those who came before us, this task will ultimately fall to our generation. It's hard to believe, but the founders of our new world are in this room right now sitting next to you." He paused to take in their reverent awe, and with a deep breath plunged onwards. "So, we're going to need terraformers, engineers, environmental techs..."

"Vat farmers!" someone in the audience called out.

"Yes, vat farmers," he replied.

Margaret leaned over to Caroline and whispered, "Survey... that has to come first."

"What?" came the response, but it was not Caroline. It was Gregory at the podium.

Margaret looked out at the audience. Every face was turned towards her. "Uh, survey. I was saying we're going to need to survey first. You know, map-making, soil samples, scouting for the base camps... pilots, explorers, that kind of thing."

"Pilots," Gregory replied, dumbstruck. "Atmospheric pilots. I hadn't even thought of that." He returned his gaze to the crowd. "As you can see, we're really just getting started, but a few of us have cobbled together an outline of how we can start getting organized. Mark, can we have the first slide?"

The lights dimmed, and the real presentation began. Margaret sat in silence, astounded by the scope of the project but invigorated by the passion surrounding her. By the end of the evening, people were signing up for over dozen exploratory committees, all with the charge to report something back within the month. She slipped away from the table as the meeting was ending, but she could not make a quiet escape. She shook so many hands on her way out if felt like she was back in the High Reverend's receiving line.

When she did finally make it back out the doors, most of the audience was still inside, and those few who had left were moving as though on a mission. The only figure standing in wait was Cal. He leaned against one of the columns surrounding the entryway, his features unreadable in the dimmed evening lights.

"Sweet Chariot, Cal, I didn't even know you were here."

"I sat in the back. You, on the other hand, seemed to be front and center."

She shrugged. "This was really Gregory Solomon's idea."

"His idea? It sounded a lot like your ideas." He nodded his head to the side and turned down the path back to the tram station.

She hastened to follow. "Just because I said something... well, it's not like I made anyone do this. They're doing this on their own."

Cal maintained his steady stride. "On their own, yes, but you seem to be going right along on the same ride."

"Well, yes, I suppose I am. I think they have the right idea. What's wrong with that?"

Cal stopped abruptly and turned to her, grasping her by the shoulders. "It's not your place..." He paused and took a measured breath. "I don't hear any of this coming from the High Reverend. That's a presumptuous lot back there, don't you think?"

She just stared at him a moment. "But just because he hasn't said anything yet..."

"Doesn't give us the right to head off on our own." Cal's grumble was almost a growl. "Greg's got no business making these kinds of plans, and you shouldn't be involved."

She glanced down at his hands on her shoulders. "Cal, I think we do have the right to plan our own lives, and if this is where we want to go—"

"Where we want to go?" he mocked. "Let me tell you this, no wife of mine is going to be involved with that kind of thing!"

She tried to take a step back but his grip was firm. She put a hand on his and pried it off, and then twisted away from the other. "As you're so often reminding me, Cal, we're not married yet."

"But..." he stammered.

"But what?"

He took a step back. "All right, Mags, you can have your fun, but remember this as a warning. There's going to be trouble, and your friends back there are going to be at the heart of it."

She shook her head slowly. "You're making too much out of this, Cal. I can't believe this is going to lead to any real trouble."

He sighed. "Look, I'm sorry I brought it up. It's only that... okay, I'm sorry." He glanced around. "Shall I walk you home?"

"No, Cal. You go ahead and get a tram back to your place. I'll be okay on my own."

"You're sure?" He did his best to put on a smile. "I mean, honestly, I really am sorry."

She nodded. "It's okay, Cal. Just go home."

He backed away slowly before turning back down the path. Margaret watched him until he disappeared through the station gate. No wife of his, indeed.

Marcy Clark was still largely innocent of the world, but even she knew she had just latched onto the biggest scandal since the Copeland assassination attempt. When the *Jinley* arrived at Latera, the news of the "Shiantic" attack had just arrived three days before via Arvin. It was already being described as a likely pirate attack, with hushed commentary that "an internal investigation is underway."

Meanwhile, she had the attack itself on cube, along with the altered military gear and Osrick's debriefing. This was on top of hours of background material, especially her extended interview with Margaret. She had done her final edits on the flight and released it on the public nets as soon as she could find a terminal. Within a day, she was the talk of the media circuit, and many were asking just how it was that the Confederate navy would abandon a young woman as sweet at Margaret Pritchard to a band of slave-traders.

The Masonite Dilemma, as it had been called since Kealing's interview, was starting to reshape itself into the Masonite Injustice. Torin had no complaints about that, because the new sympathy for his clients made for an easy introduction. "I'm Captain Torin Graylock of the *Jinley*, the ship that found the Masonites."

One particular contact he had suddenly found available was Charles Sanders, vice-president of the third largest banking alliance in the Confederacy. He had heard of a Masonite delicacy called "grata" making its way through customs and wanted to sample it firsthand. Torin was only too happy to serve him as formal a dinner as the *Jinley's* galley could muster.

The grata in question was one of Torin's favorites, the garlic and rosemary mix with the mushroom layers. Sanders savored every bite. "You say they make this by the ton?"

"I've seen the vats myself. Each one is over eight cubic meters, and they line them up one after another. Each facility must have dozens, and I looked only at the beef varieties."

Sanders examined a morsel on his fork closely. "Funny, but we've had organ cloning and tissue treatments for... well, for so long I don't even know, but across all our worlds, none of us ever thought to grow meat, let alone with the spices built-in. How's that done again?"

Torin shrugged. "I asked, but the biology was beyond me. It was something about vines forming tissue frames or maybe the other way around, but they know. This isn't some lost art handed down over generations. They're actively managing it and pursuing improved techniques."

"They can cook. I'll grant them that."

"It's more than the cooking, Mr. Sanders. I mean, I certainly wouldn't ask them to do a refit on my tachyon polarizer, but I bet they could extend my life support endurance."

Sanders chewed slowly. "Not to mention that plasma cannon they cobbled together. I'm not really a navy man, but it sure beats the mining drills my brother-in-law uses."

"Exactly. Who knows what other tricks they've managed over the centuries?"

"Tell me, Captain, do your clients have legal representation?"

"Well, Takasumi Lines is handling a number of their contacts, but I admit our legal department here on Latera is a little weak."

Sanders smiled broadly. "Well, a friend from my riding team heads up an excellent intellectual property firm right here in Stonefall. I'm sure she would jump at the chance to help your clients market these technologies."

Torin hesitated, unsure in Akahele's absence. "I'd have to check with, uh…"

"But of course, there would have to be some kind of finder's fee arrangement for Takasumi and its captains, yes?"

Torin perked up at that. "Oh yes, of course. Then I suppose I'll have to send some steaks her way, won't I?"

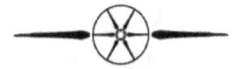

With only an hour left on the main shift, the *Chariot's* bridge was fairly quiet. All of the system tests and reports were complete, and the various officers and their backups were mostly waiting for their evening shift counterparts to arrive to begin the hand-off process. Captain Ackerman was sitting idly next to the main command table, lazily scanning over a power grid diagram.

Commander Noland arrived at his side quietly. "Did you want this in your ready room?"

Ackerman shook his head. "Here is fine. I heard aft-thruster five is back online."

"Yes, sir. At least, it passed all the low-power tests."

"And when do you expect to do the full-power tests?"

"I thought it best to wait until aft-thruster one was finished so that we could run a balanced thrust test."

"I don't want to wait. Coordinate with Pritchard and Soze, but I want it done this week."

"Aye, sir." He no longer asked why there was such a rush.

"By the way, I was impressed by young Lieutenant Carson's idea for that new plasma joint. Once five checks out, I'd like to get his new design fitted on as soon as possible." Ackerman took a deep breath to make sure his next words would carry. "If he's right, our firing arc should stretch all the way to sixty degrees, maybe even further."

"Yes, sir, his design does seem far more flexible, though of course, it is untested."

"Well, I'll want to know that it's solid before we put it on any of the forward thrusters." Ackerman purposefully kept his eyes cast downwards towards the display, doing his best to appear unconcerned of who might overhear him. "I expect an estimate on the refit time by the end of the week, Commander."

"Aye, sir."

The hour ticked down, and Ackerman continued his absent-minded study of various systems. As the shift change approached, he ordered a small dinner from his steward and retired to his ready room. Eventually the evening officers trickled in, and one by one, the main shift slipped away. This deep in crew territory, crew uniforms were quite common, so no one took notice of another officer or two headed in the same direction, especially the five officers who were being discretely followed.

All of them went home, though two of them of them made calls on the tram. They were not overheard, but those two earned extra scrutiny for the rest of the evening. It was of little surprise when an hour later, one of them, Lieutenant J.G. Henry Patterson, went out for a rather odd tram ride, riding the spinward trams more than once around and even backtracking aft before heading forward to tier Reynolds. From there, he walked a third of the way around the *Chariot's* curve before reaching his destination.

In all, it had taken eight officers to follow him, but it was Pritchard who had the luck to see him go in through the servant's entrance to Reverend Wallace's home. Fifteen minutes later, the High Reverend's private tram car arrived on the secondary line serving Wallace's compound. Pritchard could not see that well through the trees surrounding the Reverend's home, but he could recognized Hathaway's stiff white hair moving up the walkway.

Pritchard walked two blocks away before he pulled out his new communicator and punched in his Captain's code. "It's Patterson, sir."

"You're sure?"

"He's meeting with Hathaway right now."

"Thank you, Bill. I'll have updated protocols for you in the morning."

Back in his ready room, Ackerman cursed silently before picking up his pad again. It had already gone into a security-lock mode, but his thumbprint reactivated it. He scanned back down the page to find his place. *My Life as a Spy: Twenty-eight Years of the Covert Confederacy* was as gripping as it was useful.

The *Lady Tenessy* was smaller than her sisters on the main passenger routes, but what she lacked for in size, she made up for in luxury. While she frequently plied a speed run on the Latera-Arvin-Quentis line, it was not uncommon for her to be used in unique charters as she was now. Ostensibly the voyage had been organized by Transstar Media to get some of its own coverage on these Masonites, but then the local parliament offices had gotten involved. In all, four members of parliament had decided to come, as well as staff from six others, and a varied collection of other interested parties.

One such party was Miranda Welch of Barris, Larsen, and Welch, originally a chemist by training but now a lawyer by profession. She sat in the aft observation lounge sipping her tea and watching Latera's main commercial station fall behind them.

"May I join you?" It was John Kealing. He was impeccably dressed, but somehow he looked less real in person.

She nodded and set her tea down. "You're Kealing, right?"

He smiled and sat. "And you must be Miss Welch, the lawyer who's going to teach us to love that vat-grown stuff."

"Among other things. Have you tried it?"

He wrinkled his nose at the thought of it, but did his best to smile it away. "I guess I'll have my chance."

She looked around. Apart from the steward by the hatch, they were alone. "I always make it a point to take in this view, but it's usually much more crowded."

"I think most of our fellows are off on the starboard side. We're about to rendezvous with the *Navarra*. I hear our navy friends are sending over a liaison team for the voyage."

"Good," she replied. "After hearing about those pirates, I'll be glad to have the escort."

Kealing dismissed it with a wave. "I wouldn't worry. My sources tell me they've already dispatched a division of heavy cruisers from Arvin. I even heard that old man Nelson was going out there personally."

Miranda shrugged. "Nelson?"

"Nelson... Admiral Nelson." Kealing stressed it. "I actually did one of his few public interviews a few years back. He's about as steely as they come. He was second officer on the *Victoria* back in '78. The *Victoria*, if you can believe it, and yet he made it all the way to full Admiral."

Miranda stared at him blankly. "The *Victoria*?"

"From the Caspian rebellion? Surely..." he trailed off. "I suppose you were too young."

"And too distant," she replied. "I grew up in the Union."

"Ah, that would explain it. You should read my book sometime. Get a new insight on the Confederacy's history."

She was about to reply when she saw two gentlemen take a table in the far corner. She recognized one as Minister Fowles from the subcommittee on colonization. "I thought Kirkpatrick was supposed to going, but I didn't see him on the passenger list."

Kealing smiled broadly but answered quietly. "No, it looks like he had to cancel. He's far too busy on damage control these days."

"Are the rumors really true?"

Kealing shrugged. "For a newsman, it's almost too good to be true, but I have to give that young Clark some credit. Someone got his hands dirty, and someone's going to take the fall for it." He glanced over at the Minister and his aide. "But if you'll excuse me, Miss Welch, I'm going to go sniff around for a few rumors of my own."

Miranda sipped at her tea again. She cared neither for politics nor old war stories. What she smelled was profit.

Hathaway's weekly executive meeting with the senior reverends was ending. He recited a quick prayer of blessing, finishing with, "And may St. Mason guide us along God's path. Amen."

"Amen," resounded around the table, and the other six reverends rose. Two left immediately, while three others trickled out in conversation. Soon enough, only Wallace and the High Reverend remained.

"You're looking well, Brother. You look like you're sleeping well again."

"By God's grace," he replied. "I was hoping to have a private word with you."

"Of course," Hathaway replied, and shooed his secretary from the conference room. "What can I do for you?"

"This last step by the Captain, High Reverend, it concerns me deeply."

Hathaway nodded. "I share your concern. I have no desire to see our holy *Chariot* turned into something more akin to those ancient war wagons."

"It's not just that. It's the mindset behind it. He has shown himself to be a military man."

"He wouldn't be the first."

"No, High Reverend, but these are perilous times, filled with uncertainty. Men such as him… well, it wouldn't be the first time a military man seized control for himself."

"You're suggesting mutiny?"

"You must admit it's a possibility."

Hathaway shrugged. "I suppose it's always a possibility, but while Captain Ackerman has disagreed with my decisions at times, I have a hard time believing him capable of betraying his oath. Remember, he's been my friend since long before we each held our offices."

Wallace nodded. "I know. That's what you said after he pulled a gun on you during that pirate incident. 'I can't believe it,' you said. 'I thought he was my friend.'"

Hathaway scowled. "That's not what happened. Your sources exaggerated the details. I realize now that I came in unaware, and he did his best to defuse the conflict. In the end, he did yield to my authority." He leaned back from the table, considering it. "But he did surprise me that day. You really think him capable of mutiny?"

"High Reverend, I fear he is already making preparations."

He sighed. "I don't want to believe that could be true, but I confess there is much he has hidden from me, much he could still be hiding. But to charge him with treason? I cannot see it."

"Hopefully not, but hope may not be enough. Respectfully, High Reverend, I think we should be taking our own precautions here."

Hathaway nodded, gravely. "You may be right, Brother. I want you to start working more closely with the Divine Mark. Can you come to my security briefing on Wednesday?"

"Gladly, High Reverend. Gladly."

Admiral Nelson was on the bridge of the CFS *CP-874* when they down tached alongside the *Chariot*. On the small bridge of the courier ship, there was no place for him to sit, so he stood, unwilling to displace Lt. Commander Elliot from his proper place. A courier ship was a trivial command, but it was still a true command post. The admiral was particularly sensitive to that.

Elliot peered over his subordinate's consoles and reported, "All systems nominal. The *Chariot* is the only active transponder. Shall I open a channel?"

The Admiral nodded, and when it was ready, he swallowed his pride and began. "This is Sector Admiral Horatio Nelson of the Confederate navy. I have come to apologize for the cowardly actions of the *Goliad* and her captain. He is currently awaiting a court martial on charges of dereliction of duty and conspiracy to commit piracy. I await your captain's response."

Two minutes passed in uncomfortable silence before the response came. "This is Captain Ackerman of the *Chariot*. I freely accept your apology and welcome you and your officers."

"Thank you, Captain. I have also come to offer you a new escort, if you are willing to accept it. I have seven ships standing by if you will grant permission for them to enter your space."

"Permission granted, Admiral."

"I look forward to meeting you personally." Nelson nodded to Elliot, and the tach burst went out to the rest of the division.

As the pleasantries wrapped up, four heavy cruisers and their support vessels down tached around the *Chariot*. While most stayed well off to the sides, Nelson had ordered the *Hidalgo*, his temporary flagship, to drop in a direct line behind the *Chariot*. The admiral knew that if he was going to win Ackerman's trust, he would have to sleep under the Masonite's line of fire.

Dinners in the High Reverend's private residence were usually a quiet affair, and this night was no different. His wife Louise and daughter Jenny joined him as usual while his son Arthur was now living on his own. The meal itself was a savory chicken-grata pasta casserole with just a hint of peppers. Two servants attended them but stayed discretely out of sight in an alcove by the kitchen.

"Dear, I thought I saw another one of those Confederate officers today. Was I seeing things?"

He shook his head. "A handful of their ships arrived late yesterday."

"Will they stand up to the pirates this time, Father?"

"I believe so." He forced himself to take another forkful. It was excellent, but he did not have much appetite this evening. "This Admiral Nelson of theirs seemed quite apologetic, and from what our Captain says, he's some special admiral or something like that. He should be able to make it stick this time."

"Well, dear, I hope this batch of officers is more polite than the last ones."

Hathaway poked at his food once more and then pushed the plate away.

"Are you well, my dear?" Louise asked. "You barely touched your dinner."

He gave it a brief second thought as he saw it carried away to the kitchen but let it go. "It has merely been a disappointing day."

"What happened, father?"

He shook his head as if to brush away the outside world. "It's these Confederate ships. I grant you we're probably safer with them than without them, but for a while we flew alone once again, and I had enjoyed that feeling."

Louise reached out to take his hand. "I understand, dear, but the world has changed."

He sighed. "So they say, but I find myself having a hard time accepting that. In fact, I find myself wishing we could just carry on as before, secure in the knowledge that in another six hundred years or so our descendents would embark onto New Providence."

"You mean Callista Prime, don't you, Father?"

"No, damn it—" he caught himself. "I apologize, ladies, but God promised our forefathers New Providence, a new world on which to establish His paradise. I have always believed in His good will, and it tears at my heart to think that God has broken that promise." He reached absently for the medallion hidden beneath his shirt. "Forgive me, but some days I just don't know what to believe."

Louise squeezed her husband's hand. "I don't know what to tell you."

He shrugged. "No one does. No one..." He raised his eyes. "No, our Father knows. I will ask him."

Jenny had paused in her own eating. "Do you want to pray again?"

He shook his head. "Not now. I must prepare." He stood and draped his napkin across his uneaten food. "In the morning I will go, and I will pray."

He left the dining room, unsure of himself, but with a purpose.

Ackerman had reserved a corner table in a rooftop diner above the environmental offices to conclude his tour with Admiral Nelson. With the core lights dimming, it made for a picturesque view. They had toured the core power grid, engineering, the recycling complex, and even the grata vats. Notably absent from this tour had been the bridge. After his last experience with Wozniak, Ackerman had felt it best to exclude that, and Nelson had politely not asked after it, even though they had had legitimate reason to stop by. The *Lady Tenessy* had arrived mid-afternoon and made inquiries about transferring visitors. Ackerman had put them off for the day by suggesting they take the night to orient themselves to the difference in clocks.

"That was good thinking," Nelson commented over dinner. "I wouldn't want to deal with them either without a good night of sleep at my back."

"You expect them to be trouble?"

The admiral shook his head. "Journalists and politicians are both necessary in a free society, but I have grown accustomed to the order of military life. I prefer to leave that chaos to others, and fortunately, I have that luxury. I imagine you do not."

"Hardly," he replied. "Fortunately, the High Reverend and I have a good history. Certainly things have been more strained than usual, but I'm sure he'll come around." In truth, Ackerman had tried to arrange a dinner with Nelson and Hathaway, especially with the arrival of the Tenessy and her passengers, but he had been rebuffed. The High Reverend was at prayer was the official explanation, and for all Ackerman knew, it could be true. "In the meantime, I think I can manage most of the inquiries for now."

"I would be happy to send along some of my officers to help bridge the gap. Besides," the admiral said, waving his hand at the view above, "your hospitality is a uniquely exotic experience."

"They would be welcome. You can coordinate that through my Commander Pritchard."

"Thank you, Captain, and I can assure you they will be on their best behavior." Nelson chuckled. "You need not worry about them corrupting your youth."

Ackerman returned the laugh. "That will be most appreciated. Our youth is corrupt enough already."

Nelson nodded. "So you say. I imagine it's a universal condition of the species, though I did see something interesting today as we passed one of your parks. There was some kind youth gathering, complete with signs and banners, something about 'colonize now'. I presume that is a recent corruption?"

Ackerman smiled silently, admiring how deftly Nelson had brought the conversation around to it. At the time, he had done his best to distract the admiral and steer him on to their next destination. "Recent indeed, but I suspect it is merely the unfocused impatience of youth. I have hopes that it will pass, as do all such youthful fancies."

"Ah, spoken with the voice of a father," Nelson replied. "I gather you have a child or two involved in this, yes?"

"Regrettably yes, a son, though at least he seems to be a follower, not an agitator. I have done my best to dissuade him, but as a father I am powerless in this." He had pressed Richard on this days ago, but he had not pressed hard. Their relationship had been suffering these last few years. Hathaway had warned him of this likelihood years ago.

"You're not worried?"

"No. Ultimately, these decisions are adult decisions. My son and his friends don't appreciate all that is at stake, but with time they will grow to understand." He shrugged. "At least, that is my hope."

Nelson raised his glass. "It is certainly a hope worth sharing."

The Hall of the Revered was usually reserved for the high ceremonies and rites of the Reverends, such things as the induction of a new Reverend or the selection of a new High Reverend. It had the shape of a small chapel, but it was rarely used for that. This night, however, was not a typical night.

High Reverend Hathaway knelt before the communion rail, alone. He had knelt there for thirteen hours. He had not eaten. He had not drunk. He had prayed. He had knelt and prayed and wept until he could barely stand.

This was his third day in prayer.

But the answer had not come.

At the arranged hour, the side door opened. It was supposed to be one of the junior parsons come to help him up from the alter, but this night it was Reverend Wallace. He approached quietly and lowered himself to one knee at the High Reverend's side.

"High Reverend," he spoke in a tone as quiet as the room. "May I pray with you a moment?"

Hathaway turned to see who it was and nodded.

Wallace stepped forward and knelt at the rail. "Father, who guides his chosen towards heaven, we revere you and your saint. Make us instruments of your will, so that it may be done on our earthly plane as you see to it in heaven. Help us always to feed our children and those who hunger. Forgive us for our failures, and help us to forgive one another. Lead us not towards the heathen temptations, but deliver us from their evils. In the name of our Father and his most holy saint, Amen."

"Amen," Hathaway responded, his voice little more than a rasp.

"I worry for you, High Reverend. Many of us worry for you."

Hathaway shook his head. "And I worry for you, for all our children."

"May I ask what vexes you so? Surely, when two or more are gathered in his name-"

"In his name... we were made a promise, Chris. Our fathers made us this promise, just as their fathers had made the promise to them, and so on all the way back to the day that our Lord Father made that promise."

"New Providence, yes. I know the promise well. We all do."

Hathaway sagged forward against the rail. "And has God broken that promise? Have we failed Him somehow, displeased Him, so that he would take New Providence from us?"

Wallace reached his arm around Hathaway's shoulders. "Oh, that cannot be. Surely, High Reverend, you of all people must know this."

Hathaway drew a ragged breath. "And so did I think, and yet I have been here asking our Father if he is keeping that promise. For three days I have asked, and for three days He has not answered."

"Come... come with me. It pains me so to see you this way. You who have always had such faith, whose faith has always inspired us."

Hathaway laughed, or at least he tried. "My faith?"

"Yes, High Reverend, your faith. Even before all this Confederacy nonsense, you always spoke of the promise of New Providence as a fact. It was God's will for us on this earthly plane, and it was our duty to walk in faith towards that promise, so that our children's children would someday enjoy the blessings of God on our New Providence. You and I, we are merely faithful stewards of that promise, as were our fathers, and with God's good grace, as will our sons."

Hathaway swallowed hard and dry. "My faith indeed," he whispered.

Wallace gave his shoulder a squeeze. "Yes, my good brother, your faith."

Hathaway began to nod. "How could I..." He trailed off and then folded his hands before his bowed head. "Forgive me, Father, for I was weak, and I doubted You. I must stay true... I will stay true to the promise You have made to us. Please grant me the strength and the vision to see a way through for us, so that our children's children may someday worship you beneath the sky of New Providence. In the name of our Father and his most holy saint, Amen."

"Amen," Wallace responded. "And now, my faithful friend, let us get you to a table and break bread together in celebration of our Lord's blessing."

Hathaway staggered to his feet with Wallace's help. "Thank you, my good brother. You may in truth be the answer to my prayers. Thank you."

Rome was eternally Rome, but Pope Julius IX was dying. His doctors were still optimistic about this latest liver treatment, but he had sealed his own fate when he refused the third regrowth procedure. Without that, it was only a matter of time. After thirty-two years of duty in the Holy See, he had learned to take comfort in his own mortality. He had not regretted that decision at all until Cardinal Mueller's letter reached him.

The letter lay on his desk before him though he resisted the desire to read it once again. There was no answer hidden there, but he had more hope in the council he had summoned. Two cardinals and a councilor sat patiently before him. Cardinal Vazquez of the Congregation for the Doctrine of the Faith seemed the most anxious, so he was granted priority with a nod.

"Holy Father, I must urge you in the strongest terms to reaffirm the Church's long-standing position on these heretics. They are as unrepentant as their forbearers, clinging to the notion that they alone are marked by the Lord's divine blessing, and not through faith but by mere birthright. There is no place in Christendom for such beliefs."

The pope considered it a moment before replying. "And yet from what I read of history, they practice the Holy Eucharist much as we do, acknowledging Christ's sacrifice for their souls."

Vazquez shook his head. "For their souls, yes, but as they would tell you, not for yours or mine. We are mere idol worshipers."

Julius turned to Cardinal Balogh of the Congregation the Evangelization of Peoples. "And what would you say, my brother? Would you extend a hand to those who would cast you down with the Canaanites of old?"

"Well, I do not feel it is my place to judge the piety of their souls, Holy Father. I would remind my brothers that it is not their place either." This drew a grunt from Cardinal Vazquez. "But I will say that it would not be the first time the Church has come to the aid of those who follow a different spiritual path. I need not remind you that only seventy years ago we assisted in the founding of the Samsaran Circle when they broke from the Union."

"But the Hindus have enjoyed good relations with the Church for centuries," Vazquez countered. "These Masonites clearly have not."

The pope eyed his final visitor cautiously. Bishop Laurent's capacity as the Pontifical Councilor for Inter-religious Dialogue gave him an official reason for being in the meeting, but over the years, Julius had come to rely on him for his deeper wisdom in many affairs. "You've been very quiet on this, brother Laurent. My staff tells me you have not even prepared a position statement on it."

"With humility, Holy Father, I felt it best to deliver my thoughts personally."

Julius nodded, but the silence stretched. It was Vazquez who finally prompted him. "Then let's hear it. He isn't getting any younger."

"I know," Laurent replied. "I think that is the point. Holy Father, ultimately this is not about history or precedent or doctrine. We could follow those arguments around the college of cardinals for years without reaching a conclusion, but it is today that you face a choice: condemnation or forgiveness. Some will remind you of all the reasons for which they earned their excommunication. Others will tell you of generations passing, of the need to forgive the transgressions of their ancestors. None of what they say matters. You must decide, and you alone will have to face our Creator and explain that decision."

Julius nodded. "And if you sat where I do, what decision would you want to take to the grave?" the pope asked.

Laurent sighed. "I would want to forgive them, Holy Father, but I doubt I would have the resolve to do so."

Chapter 12

"I never planned on fighting for this. I never planned on mutiny. I certainly never planned on taking up arms against my own people, my fellow officers, and our so-called Reverends. But I wish to God that I had." - Commander Charles McNally, final words before his execution, 852.

The park was decorated in high fashion, almost as if it were Launch Day. With the core lights dimmed for evening, it was lit up like a jewel for all to see. Margaret preferred her own park of course, but she had to confess that tier Bradley really knew how to do a festival right. Lanterns hung from the trees, with ribbons strung between the branches, and a bold banner over the buffet table proclaimed the motto: Colonize Now. Margaret wandered through the crowd and saw that she was not the only one who had come from other tiers. Over a thousand people moved through the park, almost all of them around her own age.

"You're Maggie Pritchard, aren't you?"

She turned and saw a woman in an odd suit. "Yes, I am. Did you come on the Tenessy?" Her hairstyle alone marked her as a foreigner.

She extended her hand to Margaret. "Miranda Welch. I've been meeting with your father, among others. I recognized you from the interview."

Margaret clasped the offered hand firmly by the wrist, though she was still wearing the gloves of her quarantine regimen. "It's nice to meet you, Miss Welch. Is there anything I can do for you?"

Miranda laughed. "Nothing formal, certainly. I was just over there," she waved vaguely towards the spinward curve, "and I saw all the lights. I thought I'd come see what the party was for. Could you show me around?"

Margaret led the way towards the tables and the main stage. She ran into a number of other friends as well as many of the leading organizers of their colonization study. They were all pleased to meet Miranda, especially Gregory Solomon. "This is just wonderful, Miss Welch. If at all possible, I would very much like to meet with you and a few of my compatriots tomorrow. We have some questions about colonial law."

They were lining up for the buffet when Caroline Ashburn passed by with a roll of tickets. She turned sharply and called to them. "Maggie, so good to see you again! This must be that lawyer friend of your father's."

Maggie nodded and completed the introductions. "I see we're having a raffle tonight?"

"Oh yes, it's kind of last-minute, but it's really bringing in the crowds. There's a bunch of officers from the *Hidalgo* over, and we're going to raffle off three of the young ones."

Miranda elbowed Margaret in the ribs conspiratorially. "Raffle them off for what?"

Margaret laughed. "Oh, it's completely innocent, nothing like what I've read of your Confederacy's... well, this is simply a dating thing. You're not married, are you?" Miranda shook her head, and Margaret reached into her pocket for coins. "Caroline, a ticket for Miss Welch, please."

"Why thank you, Maggie," Miranda replied, "but aren't you going to get one yourself?"

Caroline giggled quietly. "Yeah, Maggie, live a little."

Blushing, Margaret counted out eight parsons to Caroline and took the two tickets. "I'm only doing this because it's for a good cause. You know that."

Caroline gave a lustful grin. "Whatever you say, Maggie, but when you see them, you're going to wish you'd bought more tickets."

They passed through the buffet line and took a seat at one of the tables scattered around the central field. They must have passed a dozen foreigners along the way. Beyond the three officers from the *Hidalgo*, four reporters had come, along with several parliamentary aides. Margaret couldn't see them all, but it was easy to tell where they were by the little crowds that milled around those tables, just as they were milling around her own. She did her best to handle the introductions, but after a while it became so overwhelming she excused herself.

From the quiet of one of the park benches, she watched Miranda Welch continue on without her, perfectly confident in the crowd, clasping arms, and taking note of the various names and the research areas of each. She envied her that level of confidence. Eventually Gregory Solomon rose to the podium on the stage and welcomed the crowd. He gave another speech much like the one he'd given at that first meeting, but he was smoother. He also had more facts at his disposal and did a good job at making it sound very possible. She realized that she should not be all that surprised. After all, they had generations of experience in maintaining a livable environment in the harshness of interstellar space.

When he boiled it down, there were only two problems they did not yet have a handle on. The first was the selection of a suitable world. Gregory stressed that Callista Prime was unavailable, but they had already been reviewing the data from various Confederate sources. In fact, they had already narrowed it down to twenty-eight possibilities, most within a hundred light years.

The second problem was money, but Gregory was happy to announce that the evening's festivities were already making a dent in that. "We're going to take tonight's raffle money and clean out a few neighborhood stores of the grata our new Confederate friends are so taken with. Captain Kalas has assured me cargo space on the next Takasumi shipping run, and within another month or two, we will have real Confederate currency. It's not much, but it's a start."

He closed with a few more rousing words, and while Margaret found them worthwhile, she did not listen closely. Instead, she found herself staring at the raffle ticket she held in her hands, number 817. It was completely innocent, she reminded herself, but the fact that she hadn't seen Cal in two days left her uneasy. Still, she sat a little straighter when the raffle began. The officers did indeed look very handsome.

The first was a short but strong security chief, and he was sent off with a giddy Allison Hoskins. The second was a redheaded navigator. Margaret took quite a bit of interest in that. There hadn't been a redhead on the *Chariot* in over two hundred years. Alas, Janet Olsen had the lucky ticket. Clearly, though, they had saved the best for last.

Hidalgo's second-shift communications officer Lieutenant McKay had a strong face, and his athletic body looked simply divine in his deep blue uniform. He reached into Caroline's bag of ticket stubs and pulled one out. She handed him the microphone, and his deep voice boomed out, "I'm looking for the lovely lady with ticket number 122." There was no immediate reaction, so he looked down at the stub again. "I repeat, ticket 1-2-2."

Suddenly Caroline dropped the bag and gave a little shriek. She quickly fumbled through her skirt pockets and held aloft a string of six tickets. "It's me!" she shouted with a little jump. "Sorry, gals, but it's really me!" The young lieutenant bowed to her and led her from the stage.

Margaret tucked her ticket back into her pocket and began the stroll back to the tram station. Perhaps she should have bought more tickets after all.

Reverend Morris filed into the Hall of the Revered along with his fellow reverends. It was only his third time in the Hall, the first being his elevation to the rank of Reverend. The second had been Reverend Jeffries' induction. He knew very well that it was not a place used lightly, and that worried him, because he had not seen nor heard from the High Reverend in several days, and the rumor was that he had been secluded in prayer in this very Hall.

The pews had been moved since his last time there. Instead of facing forward, they faced inwards from along the walls, forming a three-sided rectangle with a single chair at the front. The High Reverend sat in that chair, waiting for them.

The more senior reverends moved to the pews closer to the High Reverend, claiming the right of rank. As the second most recent inductee, Morris found his place along the back pew, near the corner. He leaned back to see his one junior Jeffries giving him a shrug from the other end of the pew. He was just as much in the dark as Morris was.

Or at least, that was what Morris was trying to convince himself. Looking at Hathaway's grave expression, Morris had a sinking feeling this did not bode well for their future, and Morris had been growing attached to the idea of that future.

After a few moments, the shuffling settled into silence. Hathaway's swept his gaze across them all and then began. "My most holy brothers, chosen of the Chosen through the wisdom of God Himself, today we are faced with the most dire threat in our lives. No, not just in our lives, in the entire life of the colony. Our forefathers set us on this path because they saw the sin of the world and would not be part of it. They left it behind to form a new order, a new world, and we have carried on for them for generations, all for the promise of our New Providence. It was to be a world of our own, a world of the Chosen.

"But now we find that the faithless have thwarted us. They have stolen our world. They have stolen the food from our tables. Had they had the chance, they would have stolen our daughters. Yet even now they are here, amongst us on *God's Chariot*, and our home is not merely a ship as they would say. It is holy ground they tread upon. Our forefathers had the strength to break apart from them. Are we to insult that wisdom and welcome them instead?

"I confess that I myself have extended that welcome. I did so, and I am ashamed for it, for succumbing to the temptation of their proposals. The corruption of the soul never comes in a foul-smelling cup. No, it comes in the poisoned glass of wine, the false offer of friendship, and in the betrayal of those once loyal. But still, I should have known.

"And now that we have invited them into our home, what are they doing? They are tempting us, trying to lure us away from our holy path. They are offering us other worlds, new ways of governing, new ways of living, but we know their path leads to eternal damnation. They may be blind to it, but they fulfill their evil roles nonetheless. If we are to be faithful to the wisdom of our forefathers and the promise God made to them, we must not stray from the path God has set for us."

Morris sat in silence as Hathaway began to recite the creed of St. Mason, and it was only the jab of Reverend Lambert's elbow that enabled him to join in for the final, "Amen."

Hathaway glanced around the room before continuing. "Brothers, I ask for your wisdom and support. What would you ask of me?"

The hall was silent but for the creaking of the pews, but Reverend Haggerty spoke first. "High Reverend, I too worry about the influence of these outsiders, but I fear I see no alternatives. They hold Callista Prime, our New Providence. Even if we had a way to reach it, how would we dislodge them?"

Morris let go of the breath he had been holding. Haggerty was a wise man, and while he did not have the High Reverend's gift of charisma, he was well respected among the reverends. If there was a hope at countering this, it was with Haggerty.

The High Reverend nodded. "Ah yes, that was where I first stumbled as well, my brother, but let me ask you a question. When the *Chariot* embarked for New Providence, it was empty, was it not?"

"Yes," Haggerty answered.

"And if we change nothing and continue on our course, our children will arrive in some six hundred years, will they not?"

Haggerty nodded.

"And it was promised to us by God Himself, was it not?"

From across the hall, Reverend Olsen called out, "Amen, High Reverend, it was."

Haggerty sighed but nodded again. "Yes, I concede all of that, but I do not see how that changes the facts at hand."

Morris opened his mouth to support him but could not find the words quickly enough. He covered his mouth as if to cough and slouched back into the pew.

"Indeed, the facts at hand today remain unchanged," Hathaway answered. "But it says nothing about the facts in God's hands some six hundred years hence. He has made us a promise, and I for one do not wish to tell the Lord our Father that I have lost my faith in His promises. Do you? Do any of you?"

A scattered chorus of "No!" came back in response.

Haggerty thought it over. "You expect God to wipe it clean for us?"

Hathaway shrugged and gave a soft chuckle. "Oh, it need not be a divine stroke of vengeance, dear Brother. Six hundred years is a long time. Who knows what might befall them?"

"Amen to that, High Reverend." That was from Reverend Wallace in the front corner. "From what I have seen so far, these Confederates are a vile and deceitful people. It passes beyond understanding that they have survived this long with only two civil wars. They could certainly all perish by the time we arrive at New Providence."

A murmur of assent passed through the hall as many added their own quiet suggestions of the Confederacy's likely demise.

Haggerty sighed. "Forgive me, Brothers, for being such a source of doubt, but I must ask. Are we seeing the full scope of these people? Tell me, Brothers Morris and Cooper, you have been to one of their worlds. Are they truly such a doomed people?"

Reverend Cooper answered first, being the elder and having no trouble finding his voice. "They are indeed doomed, or at the very least I pray to God that they are. Their duplicity and depravity knows no bounds. They led us around like exotic tamed animals, making empty promises but never delivering upon them. The stench of their corruption was palpable." He shuddered briefly. "I consider myself a forgiving man, but I find I have sympathy for our ancient cousins who made war upon the heathens."

Haggerty nodded slowly before turning to look down the row of reverends to Morris in the back. "And you, Brother Morris? What was your opinion of these Confederates?"

He glanced over at Cooper, who waved him on eagerly. "Yes, Brother Morris, tell him about that deceitful Hopkins woman. For all we know, she ordered those God-forsaken pirates after us in the first place."

Morris hesitated. Indeed, he had not been impressed by what their politicians had done for them, but they were only a handful among the many that he had met. There had been the helpful guides driving them through the city, always friendly and eager to talk. The hotel staff had been very courteous and quick to see to their needs. And then there had been the vibrant young boy who had cheerfully led them down to the beach on that last day.

"Come, Brother Morris," Hathaway prodded from his chair at the front. "Tell us."

"Well, my brothers, there were many I found to be helpful. I thought some of them served us well and kind."

"Kind?" Cooper replied. "You mean there were many eager to curry favor in exchange for a few coins. Their idea of charitable friendship is to pretend to be a friend in hopes of eliciting your charity."

Morris remembered it well, struggling with the various rates of gratuity in different situations. How could anyone be expected to do so much math at every social interaction? Yet it had seemed to be a common practice, not much different than praising the cook at his favorite diner in Carson tier.

"Perhaps, but there was the boy at the beach," he countered.

"A beggar child if I ever saw one," Cooper roared back.

Haggerty waved Cooper down. "Let our brother speak, good man."

"Thank you," was all Morris could manage. Every eye turned back to him, and they were not happy eyes, the High Reverend's least of all.

"Apart from this beggar and whatever greedy servants you did business with, what of their rulers?" he asked. "Do you put greater faith in their stability than you do in God's promise?"

Morris looked out at the bitterness that surrounded him. The Confederates were far from perfect, but he would not have wagered his fellow reverends to outlast them. And yet, he knew the reverends would last long enough to crush any dissenting opinion he could offer. He looked to Haggerty, the sole voice of reason, but even he had lowered his head in surrender.

And that was when Morris failed his brothers, his colony, and his unborn child. "No, my brothers, I do not. God's promise must stand."

"Very well then," Hathaway replied. "Are there any others who would speak on behalf of the heathens?"

None spoke.

"So, it is decided," Hathaway announced.

"Then what are we to do?" Wallace asked. "They infest us."

"As most of you know," Hathaway answered, "I have been secluded in prayer for several days, and I think I have an answer. We will do as our beloved St. Mason instructed us. We shall cast out the heathen and live our lives in purity as the

Chosen of God. As for this ill-named Callista Prime, I still believe in the promise of our New Providence. Our forefathers kept the faith for over a thousand years. We can keep it another six hundred. Beyond that I leave in God's hands."

Reverend Terrence nodded in eager agreement. "But what of this Solomon fool and his rabble?"

Wallace raised his hand. "If I may, High Reverend? While I admit the freshness of his appeal, the problem he presents us with is an old one. His faith has stumbled so far that he no longer even recognizes the promise, and in that confused state, he attempts to create a new promise, not of God, but of man. His is not the first heresy in our history, and I think we know how to deal with it"

The word heresy rippled through hall.

"Well said," Hathaway declared. "Well said indeed."

Morris bowed his head as the cries of assent echoed through the hall, but he could not summon a prayer, not when God was letting this happen.

Rachael's Luck was already powered up when Pritchard arrived to see them off. He could make out shadows moving though the forward observation window, but he could not see anyone directly. He walked across the hangar deck to the open landing ramp and peered up.

"Is that you, Bill?" Akahele called down from the hatch. "Come on up. We've still got a few minutes."

He climbed the ramp and met her in the small passenger lounge where she was locking down a few crates in the corner. "I was afraid I might miss you."

"No, we're still waiting on Miss Welch, but she should be here momentarily. She was squeezing in one more meeting with some of your youngsters."

Pritchard nodded. "From what I heard of her schedule, it seems she barely slept."

"That sounds about right. I don't know how Torin found her, but she's sharp. It's not just your grata vats, either. I hear she's even found something unique in the lighting filaments in your central core. I mean... lights, I never would have even thought about it."

"Nor I," he admitted. "But will it be enough?"

Akahele sighed and sat down on the arm of the couch. "Honestly, Bill, I don't see how it could be, not even close. Even if all of this is wildly successful, you'd need ten times that."

"I thought as much."

She forced a smile. "Don't be discouraged. It's a start. If you can show at least some kind of economic viability, we might be able to interest someone in making the investment. From the sounds of it, Marcy's story on Maggie bought you folks a lot of good will."

"And commerce is going to buy you some more," Miranda said from the hatch, her suitcase rolling past her into the lounge. "Sorry I'm late folks. I just had to get a sample of the lubrication you use on your tram guides. Its viscosity isn't all that great by modern standards, but if I'm to believe your maintenance chief, it lasts longer than anything I've heard of." She dropped into one of the lounge chairs. "Everyone else is using magnetic trams, of course, but the industrial applications should be worth a tidy sum."

Pritchard took some comfort in that. "Then I'll let you two be on your way."

He waited a while in the observation room, watching the final preparations as *Rachel's Luck* was lifted upwards into the launch bay above them. He was just turning to leave when Reverend Morris arrived. "Ah, Tier-father, I thought this must be the right one. Am I too late?"

Pritchard nodded. "I'm afraid so, Reverend. You just missed them."

"Pity."

"Well, they're just off to Quentis for a brief visit. They'll be back in three weeks."

Morris frowned. "I would like to think so, but I fear it might not be that simple."

"I'm not sure I understand you, Reverend."

"Well, Tier-father..." Morris paused and then glanced back at the empty hall. "Bill, I don't like this myself, but things are about to get more difficult for people like Captain Kalas, and for your daughter as well."

Pritchard stiffened. "Maggie?"

"This whole colonization thing has the High Reverend unsettled." Morris shifted to look out into the hanger bay. "There are going to be some changes."

"Meaning what?"

Morris sighed. "The High Reverend's sermon this Sunday will be mandatory. You'll see then, but in the meantime, you should have a talk with your daughter. Warn her. I recall that interview she gave, and I fear that a number of things she said may soon be considered heresy."

Pritchard blinked twice in shock. "Heresy?"

Morris nodded. "I don't expect the charges to be applied retroactively, of course, but you understand my concern."

"I see," he replied, regaining his composure. "Thank you, Reverend. Your advice is well taken."

Morris glanced around the chamber. "You also understand that we didn't have this conversation, Tier-father. I was only here to see Kalas leave. Is that clear?"

"Of course, Reverend."

Morris walked to the exit but paused in the hatchway. "I'm sorry, Bill. I wish I could do more for you, but I don't see how."

John Kealing was wearing his trademark smile as he finished up his recording session. "And that's the way I see it. John Kealing, reporting from *God's Chariot*." He held the pose for another five seconds and relaxed.

He has his own recording crew with him, but some of the Masonite technicians were watching along with Reverend Terrence. Terrence was ostensibly in charge of maintaining the colony's communication infrastructure, but Kealing knew a propaganda man when he saw one. After all, he was one himself.

"I wanted to thank you again, Reverend, for allowing me to use your fine facilities here. They add a real professionalism to my work."

Terrence gave a non-committal nod. "I saw some of that Miss Clark's report. Your media is far too distracting for my tastes. All those little facts piling up, your sidelines as you call them. It's amazing anyone can watch for long."

"I completely understand," Kealing replied. He motioned Terrence closer with a conspiratorial look in his eye. "The truth is that we're forced to do that. Our viewers in the Confederacy... they're not as intellectual as your colonists here. We're doing what we can to just keep their attention, so it's all jingles and trinkets."

"Really? You don't like it either?"

"Certainly not," Kealing replied. After thirty years practicing, he could lie with the best of them. "I much prefer a simple presentation. Well, that or a good book. But try not confuse the medium with the message. At some level, we are just trying to get even more information to our viewers."

"Well, I suppose," Terrence replied. "I just wish it were done more..."

"More tastefully?"

Terrence nodded. "Yes, I suppose that's it."

Kealing smiled. "You know, we should do something together. Let me show how we can do this kind of thing right, how it can support the message, not distract from it."

"That's an excellent idea, Mr. Kealing."

Kealing did his best to keep from overplaying it. "I hear your High Reverend has a big sermon tomorrow. Maybe I could help with that."

Terrence reached out and put a friendly hand on Kealing's shoulder. "You know, Mr. Kealing, I'm starting to think my good Brother Cooper may have misjudged you."

Hathaway had left Ackerman standing before his desk as he read down through the edicts. He had known this would be difficult, but to his credit, the Captain had taken it all in silence. He finished the last item with, "Any extensions to a visa's three day limit must come from my office." He looked up from the list. "Do you have any questions?"

Ackerman stood stiffly at parade rest. "May I speak freely, High Reverend?"

Hathaway nodded. "Within the bounds of decorum."

"Then I must protest, High Reverend. I believe these new policies of yours are a mistake of grand proportion."

"I suspected you would, my dear Captain, but you don't actually agree with those Colonize Now heretics, do you?"

"Solomon is a fool and a troublemaker, High Reverend. I would lock him up myself if I thought it would do any good. As for his… heresy, while I cannot agree that we are nearly so ready to disembark as he says, I do believe that we should do this sooner than six hundred years."

"I appreciate your candor, Captain, but I disagree."

"High Reverend, even if…" he paused and relaxed his pose to meet Hathaway's eyes. "John, I can understand if you feel we are moving too fast, and I would gladly support a public moratorium of a year, even ten years, for us to think about this calmly. But all this talk of deportations and visas sends the wrong message. Like it or not, we'll be dealing with these Confederates for years, and yes, very likely six hundred years."

"I hear your words, Jim, but I am not swayed. My decision stands. Will you carry out these orders?"

Ackerman stiffened again. "Please don't ask me to do this."

"Regretfully, I am not asking you to do this, Captain. I am ordering you. Will you comply?"

He came to full attention. "I will carry out your orders in compliance with the Covenant of 774."

"Then make ready, Captain. I will announce these in Sunday's sermon, and they will then carry the force of law."

Ackerman nodded once, turned crisply on his heel and left. Hathaway watched him go. He had had many fruitful discussions with his friend over the years, but this was the first time he been forced to give him an order.

Margaret and her father ate in near silence, more in the company of their thoughts than in the company of each other. It was a chicken grata-variation with a side of rice, their usual Saturday fare. Margaret was debating the merits of two particular colony candidate worlds and idly daydreaming about what it would be like to explore them. Her father, on the other hand, was trying to think of a way to stop her from having those very thoughts.

"We haven't been seeing much of each other these past two weeks," he said at last.

She pointed a chiding finger at him. "Well, you're the one working all the extra shifts, Father, not me."

"As a matter of fact, I was here last night for dinner. You were not."

"I do have a social life, Father."

He took a sip of water, trying to delay the inevitable. "It's not your usual socializing, Maggie, and you know it. All these colonization meetings are premature, even inappropriate."

"And yours, Father? You went to one of their worlds yourself," she accused him with a playful grin. "Was it not to find a new home for us?"

"Yes, but—"

"Then we're just taking the next logical steps. I don't see how you can find fault in it."

"Maggie, it's not me. It's the Reverends. They want to wait, and it would be dangerous to disagree."

Margaret shrugged and started cutting off another slice of the chicken. "Well, that's just their opinion, and I'm not afraid of what any old—"

"Maggie!" he cut her off. It was the first time Bill Pritchard had raised his voice to his daughter in years.

She set down her knife and fork and waited with her hands in her lap.

"This is not a matter for public debate. The High Reverend will be giving a sermon in the morning, and when he speaks on this subject, his word will be law."

"I understand, Father, but—"

"No buts, Maggie. I want you to stay away from that Solomon and his crowd."

She glared at him in silence.

"Look, Maggie, if you're just fighting back... I mean, if you're angry with me for not letting you marry early..." he trailed off, summoning his strength. "It goes against my better judgment, but I'd be willing to let you marry now. I suppose three months won't make much difference."

She looked away sharply, unsure of what to say.

Pritchard looked closely at his daughter, surprised by the lack of reaction. "Would that be enough, Maggie? Would that give you enough to do?"

She sighed. "No, it's not that." She faced him again, but submissively. "You were right before, Father. It would be best to wait, and it is only three months. I still have to make the chapel reservation and all that."

He wanted to question her, but he was not going to overturn his windfall. "Well, that's fine, Maggie. I'll see if I can get Reverend Morris to officiate. You always liked him."

She started cutting the chicken again. "Yes, Father, that would be lovely."

He watched her a moment, trying to read her, but she was inscrutable. When had that happened? "But you'll remember what I said about that Colonize Now crowd, yes?"

"Yes, Father. I'll remember."

Dinner returned to an awkward silence.

Lieutenant Arthur McKay was asleep in quarters when the call came. It was his personal signal, not the general alarm, but he still came alert to answer it. "McKay here."

"Art, you need to listen to this." It was Petros Kasren, his prime shift counterpart. "I'm piping it down to your station there."

McKay moved over to the desk he shared with his roommate and tapped on the flashing icon. The voice that came across was a little distorted but filled with authority, "...presumptuous 'Colonize Now' movement is hereby outlawed. No charges will be filed for past actions, but no further meetings, discussions, or-"

"What the hell is this?" McKay asked.

"It's that Reverend guy. He's really got a fire going."

"...shall be considered a minor heresy punishable by thirty days of public shunning. Subsequent offenses will be considered a major heresy with the full weight of spiritual law." Hathaway blasted on.

McKay shook his head in disbelief. "This is for real, right?"

"Absolutely."

"You're dumping this to storage?"

"Of course. Skipper's listening to the live feed too."

"Damn, I really thought..."

"Yeah, me too, but it doesn't look so good for your girlfriend now."

Hathaway's voice pressed on, "Visitations by the heathens, whether they be Confederate military or civilians, are no longer under crew authority but will require pre-approved visas..."

"No, Petros, it doesn't look good at all."

The steward poured the wine and retreated to the antechamber. Admiral Nelson had had better flag cabins on carriers and dreadnaughts, but the *Hidalgo* was sufficient for entertaining Captain Ackerman. "You've met the other captains now. Are you comfortable with them?"

Ackerman nodded eagerly. "Yes. I was particularly impressed with your Captain Castillo. She's very forthright."

"Good, because you'll be coordinating with her from here on out. I'm heading back to Arvin on the next courier run, probably tomorrow. Your escort will stay, of course."

Pritchard took it calmly. "I see," was his only response.

Nelson sighed. "I imagine you're thinking about the *Goliad* right now."

"Among other things, sir."

"That's understandable, though I hope these captains have inspired a higher level of trust."

"Yes, Admiral, they have."

"And yet..." Nelson prompted, but Ackerman failed to take the bait. "Well, just to state it more clearly, I've ordered them to treat this as a joint fleet operation with you as the command ship. Our rules of engagement won't let me actually put them under your direct command, but I can give you the status of an ally."

"Thank you, Admiral. That's very generous."

Nelson shrugged it off and took a sip of wine. "Another raid seems unlikely, but I didn't want there to be any misunderstandings."

Ackerman also sipped at the wine. It had a particularly mellow flavor for a red. The *Chariot's* limited winery had nothing like it. "I appreciate the steps you have taken, Admiral, and while I do not wish to insult your officer corps with an impertinent question, I am curious. Was the *Goliad* the first time you have ever had to deal with a treacherous officer?"

Nelson set his glass down. "It's certainly the most egregious example in recent memory. I assure you of that."

"And of the not so recent?" Ackerman probed.

This drew a frown from the Admiral. "You are aware, of course, of our most recent civil war."

"The Caspian rebellion."

"You must understand, Captain Ackerman, that many of the officers who joined that misadventure were only doing so in defense of their home worlds. They were misguided, yes, but I would not go so far as to call them treacherous. Many went on to long careers of fine service to the Confederacy."

"But you, Admiral," Ackerman insisted, "you personally have had to deal with such treachery, such... disloyalty."

Nelson sat straight in his chair and studied Ackerman for a moment. "The *Victoria*." Ackerman nodded. "Well, you've certainly done your research, Captain. What are you getting at?"

"I ask, Admiral, because I have a disloyal officer."

Nelson sat in silence for a moment, and when he did speak his words were slow and quiet. "Tell me, Captain Ackerman, are you trying to prevent a mutiny or commit one?"

Ackerman did not speak. His only answer was a slight nod of the head.

Nelson took a deep, slow breath and called out, "Johansen!"

The steward stepped in from the antechamber. "Yes, sir?"

"I won't be needing your services any further this evening. We'll gather my things in the morning."

"Aye, sir," he replied and left. A moment later, they heard the outer hatch open and close.

Nelson looked at Ackerman, studying the little details as if he were evaluating him for the first time. "I don't have to tell you it's not an easy decision."

"No, sir, you do not. I have not yet made it, though, and I hope I will not have to."

"Well, I share your hope because I think you know how these things usually end."

"Yes, sir, but you did succeed."

Nelson shook his head dismissively. "It was more luck than anything. I can't say I'm optimistic for you, Captain. I read a transcript of your Reverend's sermon this morning. Between that and your disloyal officer, I'd say you've already lost the element of surprise."

Ackerman nodded gravely.

"You control the engineering and environmental, yes? What about security?"

"We have our own crew security, but the constables and the Divine Mark outnumber them by far."

"They're under your Reverend's control?"

"The Divine Mark, yes, but his authority over the constables has always been exercised through the tier-fathers. At best, we can neutralize some of them, but not the Mark."

Nelson's face looked even grimmer. "What about communications?"

"Yes. We do have secure wireless communication for the critical people."

"No, that's not what I meant. Do you control the broadcasts like your Reverend's sermons?"

"No, that's under Reverend Terrence. Why would that matter?"

"Well, it's not much, but sometimes a mutiny is just a race to declare victory. The first one to say they've won usually has."

"Is that what you did, Admiral?"

"No," he replied wistfully. "That's what my captain tried."

That same evening, Cal was in his tier-father's home. "Tier-father Silverman, please understand. She hasn't been making sense since the pox."

James Silverman put a comforting hand on Cal's shoulder. "I know, my son. So many were affected, perhaps your Margaret most of all, but we're going to help you. We're going to help you help her."

"Yes, we are," came a new voice. Reverend Wallace stood in the door to the study.

Cal rose immediately. "Reverend Wallace, I... I didn't know you were coming."

Wallace waved him back to his seat while taking one for himself. "I am here to help tend the flock, to guide the lost sheep back into the warm embrace of the faith."

Cal nodded. "Thank you, Reverend, but I wouldn't say she's lost her faith."

"Oh, of course not," Wallace replied, "but she is confused."

"Absolutely. All this talk of starting some new colony right away, and then the High Reverend's edict this morning..." Cal shook his head. "I don't want her to get in trouble. I don't want her to get hurt."

"Nor do we," Silverman interjected. "Like you, we only want her to see things right, to understand God's will."

Cal looked back and forth between them, hoping for salvation. "You'll talk to her then."

"In time, my son," Wallace answered. "I know you love this girl, but there are many who are confused, many sheep that are lost."

Cal nodded. "Gregory, especially."

Wallace glanced to Silverman who replied, "The Solomon boy."

"Ah, yes," Wallace noted. "We're already keeping a close eye on Gregory Solomon, as well as a few others. We have hopes, of course, that the fervor of our High Reverend will have dissuaded most of these youngsters from their folly, but we fear that many will continue on in secret."

"It's a delicate situation," Silverman added. "Unspoken heresy is just that, unspoken, but a whispered heresy can still be heard by many."

"We need to know who still persists in these ideas, my son. Those who let go of it deserve God's forgiveness," Wallace told him. "But those who would continue in defiance of the High Reverend will need our special guidance."

"But, Reverend, I don't know what you want me to do. I'm not one of them, and I pray my Maggie won't be either."

"I understand, my son," Wallace persisted, "but for now, it might be best if she were, and more to the point, if you were also."

Cal shifted away from the Reverend. "You want me to spy on them?"

"In a sense," he answered. "I would ask you to keep an open ear, and if need be, to tell them what they want to hear."

"But... Reverend, you're asking me to lie to them, to Maggie. You're asking me to betray her."

"No, my son, I'm asking you to help us save her."

Cal looked down at the floor, at his hands folded in his lap. He felt the slow spin of the chariot wheel, of chances slipping away. A lifetime later, he looked up to meet the Reverend's eyes. "You'll protect her."

"Yes, my son."

"I have your word on that?"

"Not just mine, my son, but the High Reverend's as well."

He nodded firmly. "Then I'm your man."

Chapter 13

"Performing live theater has a very special quality to it. By opening night, you've rehearsed for weeks, learned your lines and your marks, and you think you're ready. Then you walk out on that stage in front of the audience, and you know there are no second takes, no edits, and no more time to rehearse. That's when it hits you: you're never ready." - Professor Quincy Caruthers, Callistan School of the Arts.

Captain Fiona Palmer of the *Lady Tenessy* fidgeted in her command chair. They were supposed to have been underway six hours ago. She had even brought the tach drive online while waiting for the final shuttle, hoping to leave as soon as it docked, but John Kealing had ruined that plan simply by not being there. At this point, all of their new visas had expired, and when she last spoke to that High Reverend of theirs, he had made it quite clear that they should be moving along.

Only two aides had still been aboard the *Chariot*; rather, the aides plus Kealing. Captain Palmer did not care that much for reporters, Kealing especially, but Transstar Media had chartered the liner, and Kealing was their darling. That last shuttle was supposed to get all three of them, but Kealing had not shown up. Instead, he had only passed along the cryptic message, "Send my regrets to Captain Palmer."

Now she had three senior members of parliament clamoring for her to get underway. The *Hidalgo* had already called twice inquiring about the cause of their delay, and she knew a third call was imminent. The shuttle was refueled and still on standby, but what was she to do, send over a search party?

Right on schedule, the call came in, but it was not the *Hidalgo* this time. "It's Kealing," her communications officer told her. "He wants to talk to you."

She picked up a headset and vowed to stay calm. "Mr. Kealing, you are overdue. I'm sending the shuttle back to get you. Be ready to board it when it docks."

"My apologies for making you wait, dear Captain," Kealing answered, his voice as smooth as his news reports. "I thought I'd made myself clear. I'm staying behind for now."

"Mr. Kealing, we are leaving for Latera, and we are not chartered for a return visit. I repeat: I am sending the shuttle back to get you. Your presence on it is required."

"I appreciate your sense of responsibility, Captain Palmer, but I am my own master. I am staying behind."

"But your visa has expired, Mr. Kealing."

"Special exception," he replied. "Unlike the rest of your passengers, I've actually made friends with the Reverends here, especially the good Reverend Terrence."

Palmer shook her head in derision. Her one meeting with Reverend Cooper had been more than enough. "But what are you doing? If I return without you, your employers are going to demand an explanation."

"There's a real story here, Captain, one that amateur Clark overlooked. It's the eternal clash of the cultures, the very preservation of faith. It's a story worth telling, and as any journalist will tell you, you have to be where the story is."

She looked around at her bridge officers, many of them showing the same disbelief. "Last chance, Kealing. I'm not going to be responsible for you if you don't take it."

"I'll find my way home, Captain. I always do."

She sighed. "Well, best of luck, Mr. Kealing." She put down the headset and turned to her navigator. "To hell with him. We're leaving."

The *Jinley* dropped out of tach a respectable distance from the *Chariot*. Torin had heard the rumors of an escort, and he did not want to spook them. The tach pulse came in from the *Hidalgo* with a friendly query. "Your profile identifies you as *Jinley*. Please respond with registration codes, and stand-by for traffic control."

By the time they had gotten close enough for a reasonable time-lag on light-speed communications, the *Hidalgo* had already relayed the new regulations as laid down by the High Reverend. It was not long before they had Captain Ackerman on the line.

"Can you even give us permission to come over by shuttle?"

Ackerman wavered. "That's unclear, but I'm going to give it anyway. The bays are crew territory and under my jurisdiction. I'll meet you there in three hours."

By the time Torin and Semi had transferred over in one of the maintenance shuttles, Ackerman had secured a visa for Torin only. Semi's had been explicitly refused. "It takes only one man to steal food from our table," Reverend Wallace had argued.

With only the one visa, Ackerman settled for herding them both into a small control room and sealing himself in with them. "I apologize for all this."

"I don't really see it as your fault," Torin replied. "The *Hidalgo* briefed me."

Ackerman shook his head. "Still, there's no excuse for this."

"Is this just temporary?" Torin asked. "Or is this really the new order of things? It's insane to think Callista Prime is going to empty itself by wishful thinking, even in six hundred years."

"I'm still sorting that out myself, but it seems to be the order of things today." Ackerman turned to Semi. "I'm sorry."

Semi merely shrugged, but Torin did not take it so calmly. "I can understand your position, but with all due respect, Captain Ackerman, what are you going to do? Not about Semi, but about your Reverend?"

Ackerman took a sharp breath. "That... is not a question for these walls."

It took two of Torin's three days to arrange for what cargo transfer he could. He could trade only a third of the electronics he had brought, and only the most utilitarian at that. The more entertaining devices had been turned away. He had even gone to a few tier-fathers directly, but it was clear they had been directed not to do business with him. The only cargo he did manage to unload completely was the cheapest he had brought, seventy tons of high-density hydrocarbon blocks. Their traditional use was in some of the various organic terraforming processes, but Reverend Cooper had pushed through their approval as replenishment matter for the grata vats. Even then, he had held the line at giving him only thirty-two tons of a few different grata varieties. He had explained that more could have been made available, but alas, Torin's visa would expire long before it could be readied.

There was no fanfare to mark his departure. No one waited for him at the docking bay. Even the launch bay crew kept its distance from him. He boarded the shuttle on his own and strapped himself into one of the rear seats. Minutes passed with only the sounds of the shuttle being lifted up into the launch bay and the soft puffs of the maneuvering jets firing. They were halfway to the *Jinley* before he finally heard the pilot speak. "Why don't you come up and sit by me?"

Torin recognized the voice immediately. "Captain Ackerman, what are you doing out here?"

"I couldn't let you go without at least a little send-off," he replied.

Torin drifted gingerly forward into the copilot's seat. "I was starting to wonder."

"With everything going on, I didn't want to be seen with you much."

He nodded. "Understandable. My popularity is well off its earlier high mark."

"I hear you didn't come away with many orders for your next trip back."

Torin chuckled. "Hardly. In fact, I got the distinct impression I shouldn't make a trip back."

"Well, I'd like you to," Ackerman replied. He pulled a folded sheet of paper from his breast pocket and handed it over. "I was thinking you could do a little shopping for me at Pinot's Hammer."

Torin scanned the text quickly with disbelief: four hundred Salokor PR-18's, thirty-five crates of matching energy cells, nine crates of directional stun grenades... The list filled the page. "What the hell is this?"

Ackerman repressed a feral grin. "The answer to your earlier question."

Torin let loose a low whistle as he read the list again. "This isn't going to be easy."

"I know. Get what you can, Captain Graylock, and come back quickly. I hope we won't need them, but if we do, my officers and I will be depending on you."

The scale of it came down as a weight on Torin's chest, even as he floated against the straps. "I'll do my best, Captain Ackerman. I promise you that."

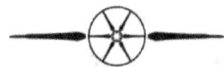

Akahele stared out the window of their train compartment while Miranda organized the files. She could see the starport on the other side of the harbor. She had already called Hannah

Reynolds to prep *Rachael's Luck* for departure. "You're sure you don't want to come back with me?"

Miranda shook her head. "They don't need me there to sign the charter. Any Confederate citizen can act as witness. One of those fleet officers would do nicely, or your pilot for that matter. As for myself, I've already booked passage back to Latera. If they're going to lock any of these planets for a five-year term, I need to start raising the capital."

They had met with incredible good fortune at the Board of Colonization. They had reserved a claim on three reasonably attractive worlds within the Confederate sphere of influence, one of which had just been found by Survey a year before. The real boon, however, was the so-called Bosom of the Angel, named by the surviving crewmembers of the disabled Survey ship that had found it in the last century.

There had been an initial attempt to terraform it in the decades that followed, but that effort was derailed by the Caspian Rebellion. By the time the war was over, the company that had started it was bankrupt. Three other groups had expressed interest over the years, the most recent being an agricultural consortium based ironically on Callista Prime. They had renewed their five-year option four times, and everyone had expected them to renew it yet again. Except that they had not.

There were five branches of the Board within the Confederacy, each the official point of registry for specific colony worlds. Angel fell within the region for Quentis, and it had been posted as available again a mere day before *Rachel's Luck* arrived in the system. The news had just gone out on the Confederate mail courier when Miranda and Akahele put a provisional lock on it for one year in the name of the Masonites.

Its sudden availability had surprised the board members as much as anyone else because Angel was becoming increasingly attractive. For over eighty years the original bacteria had been at work on Angel's surface. By this point, there was enough oxygen in the atmosphere to be breathable with the use of filters, and the once rocky surface was becoming more and more what one could reasonably call soil, especially in the coastal lowlands. The inland areas still suffered very harsh winters, but even with that it was a colonization jewel.

The only problem had been on the reservation form itself. It had to be claimed in the name of a prospective colonist, someone who intended to be part of the initial settlements. Akahele thought about using her own name, but Miranda had pointed out that if Akahele later dropped from the venture, there might be some question to the legitimacy of the provisional reservation. Normally it would not matter as much, but given the value of Angel, there was a much higher probability of litigation.

Miranda brought Akahele back to the present with a nudge. "Here it is."

She took the offered pad and looked over the collection of documents: the application for colonial charter, the draft charter itself, the request for Confederacy protectorate status, and of course, the planetary reservation forms. On Miranda's advice, she had used a different colonist's name for each of the three worlds, but she had chosen them carefully. She tabbed open the one for Angel and read to herself:

> I, Margaret Eloise Pritchard, hereby authorize my agent's actions in placing a provisional reservation of one standard year upon the planetary body SRC-2704-4, known as Bosom of the Angel, under the following terms…

Margaret sat on the tram with her hand in Cal's. Technically, she was still supposed to be wearing her gloves, but tonight she was making an exception for Cal. Besides, there was no one else there to see. "You're sure about this?" she asked.

"How many more times do you need to hear me say I was wrong?" he replied.

She giggled a bit and gave his hand a squeeze. "At least one more time."

He took a deep breath and sat straight. "I was wrong, Mags, and you were right. Still, in my own defense, it didn't look so obvious until the High Reverend went over the edge." He grumbled in indignation. "No official meetings, no private gatherings of more than five, no public gatherings without prior approval. He's practically banned the entire Youth Auxiliary over this. What's next, closing the parks?"

"Well, if he does, he'll just drive us indoors." A few months before, she would have thought the suggestion itself scandalous.

Cal's mouth hung open a moment. "Do you mean that, Mags?"

She flashed him a quick smile. "We'll talk later, but Father is showing signs of flexibility." The tram began to slow. "This is our stop."

They took a path through a small shopping plaza, and at Margaret's insistence they circled through it again to make sure they were not being followed. From there it was two blocks over, a shortcut through a small greenbelt, and up the back stairs of an apartment building. They finally found themselves in the home of Caroline Ashburn.

It was a small three-room apartment she shared with her younger sister. The sister was conspicuously absent for such a late hour, but no one mentioned it. In all, fourteen had come, though to Margaret's surprise, Gregory Solomon was missing. She was about to ask after him when Caroline called everyone into the kitchen. It was a tight fit, but she simply pressed that much closer into Cal's arms.

Caroline sat at the small table with two others. There was also a plastic box of circuits and cables on the table, looking very much like a disemboweled video player with a long wire running up to the ceiling where it hung by a piece of tape. She turned a dial on the casing and asked, "Can you hear me, Arthur?"

The response came from a speaker on the side of the box, "Just fine, Caroline." Tinny though the voice was, Margaret still recognized it as the dashing Lieutenant McKay from the *Hidalgo*.

"Then I'll hand things over to Gregory," she said and laid a grey wristband on the table. Margaret's eyes went wide. She had seen Father wearing the same style of wristband for the last few weeks.

"Thank you all for coming," Gregory said through the encrypted signal. "I apologize for not being there myself, but the Reverends are watching me. They're not too good at it, mind you, but I didn't want to lead them right to the rest of you." A quick flash of grins passed through the room at this.

"So, I hereby call to order the fifth meeting of the executive committee for Colonize Now," Gregory continued, "and no matter what that fool Hathaway has to say, there will be a sixth, and a seventh, and so on. By God, I swear we'll be having them on solid ground someday."

This was met with a heartfelt murmur of assent throughout the room. Even Cal did his part.

"Very well then," Gregory continued, "first on the agenda is a report by the environmental committee..."

Rachael's Luck dropped tach clean and close behind *Chariot*. Unlike most of the recent visitors, she was close enough to receive *Chariot's* traffic control before the escort was able to even send a tach pulse query. The response she got, however, was not what Akahele had expected.

"What do you mean we can't dock? I have urgent business with your captain and the High Reverend."

"I repeat, you are to hold your current..." the voice of traffic control paused and was replaced by Ackerman's.

"Captain Kalas, I am personally clearing you for docking. I should be there shortly."

When they arrived, however, only Bill Pritchard awaited them.

"What the hell is going on here, Bill?"

He shook his head and led her through the now familiar corridors to the trams. A private one waited for them. Only there did he answer her. "The High Reverend has had a change of heart. He has placed all colonization plans on hold."

"For how long?"

"If you were to take him at his word, for six hundred fifty years."

"Sweet Ocean, no... he can't be serious."

"It would seem so."

"Then I doubt he'll want to see me."

"Quite the contrary. I was told to bring you to his office immediately."

"And your captain?"

"He said he would meet you there. Do you have news?"

"Yes, but..." she trailed off, looking out the window at the curved horizon sliding past. "Tell me, how is Maggie doing? Will I get the chance to see her?"

"She is well, but I'm afraid a visit is unlikely. The Reverends have denied your visa."

"My what?"

"It's a long story, but I'll be happy to pass along any message you have for her."

It was supposed to have been a surprise, and for days she had savored the thought of seeing Margaret's face when she told her. Still, she pulled a data card from her jacket and pressed it into Pritchard's hand. "It's a present from me to her. Please tell her I'm sorry I couldn't give it to her in person."

269

The rest of the ride was a rapid exchange of information, from Hathaway's crackdown on the colonization movement to Akahele's success with the colonization board. Given the tone of her arrival, she thought it best to leave out the way she had involved Margaret. Even then, Pritchard's response was cool.

"But, Bill, isn't this what you wanted?"

"Yes, but I begin to wonder if we are indeed moving too fast."

"You don't agree with Hathaway, do you?"

Pritchard glared at her. They were approaching their stop. "All I know is that my world is threatening to spin out of control."

The tram door opened. Ackerman was waiting for them. She gave her news to him as quickly as she could on the short walk to Hathaway's office: three worlds ready to be claimed, one especially so. All they lacked was the money to fund the effort.

The High Reverend was waiting for them in his office, seated behind his desk. He did not invite his guests to sit. Pritchard, it seemed, was not welcome at all. "Tier-father," Hathaway told him, "this is not for your ears. You should go."

Pritchard nodded to his Captain and closed the door behind him.

Hathaway wasted no time. "Captain, you have brought this foreigner aboard *God's Chariot* in direct defiance of my wishes. Explain yourself."

Ackerman stood stiff, almost braced to attention. "High Reverend, given the news I knew she would be bringing, I felt it critical for you to hear it."

Hathaway made a noise somewhere between a huff and a growl. "Then let's hear it and be done with it."

Akahele felt sure she would have little time, so she plunged to the heart of the matter. "I have found a new colony world for you, High Reverend. It is a prime world, already partially terraformed. Within a generation, it could be a paradise."

"A paradise?" Hathaway mocked her. "What do you know of paradise?"

"By your meaning, very little, High Reverend. By your standards, yes, I am a heathen, but I have known many worlds, and if I were to call any a divine gift, it would be this one. I felt so strongly on the matter that I already reserved it on your behalf."

"Why should I need your reservation any more than I need your world? We already have a world. We have our New Providence waiting, and it was reserved for us not by mere mortal authority but by God Himself."

"But Callista Prime—"

"Will be wiped clean by the wrath of God if necessary!" Hathaway roared as he stood.

Akahele blinked through the shock of his fury and took a deep breath before daring to reply. "High Reverend, forgive me, but..."

He waved her to a halt. "No. No, Captain Kalas. My patience for you was born of your honest wish to help us, but your help is no longer desired. I thank you for your passionate effort, but I bid you to go now. You are not of the Chosen. You are no longer welcome here."

"But I..."

"A brother of mine will escort you back to your ship. Do not tarry."

Akahele looked one last time to Ackerman, but he only nodded. With her shoulders slumping, she left the office. Wandering past the armed guard and the glaring secretary, she wondered if there were any friendly faces left here at all.

Back in Hathaway's office, Ackerman stood silently before the High Reverend, waiting for Hathaway's fury to quiet.

Looking at the *Chronicles of St. Mason* sitting on the Hathaway's desk, he had reason to worry about his own rage as well.

Hathaway sat again and adjusted a few files on his desk. "You will see to it that her ship departs."

Ackerman took a deep breath to calm himself, but he could not let this pass. Instead, he stiffened to attention. "With respect, High Reverend, I will not."

Hathaway paused, his mouth hanging in surprise. "You won't?"

"No. High Reverend, you can chase her back to her ship, but the docking bays are crew territory. By the Covenant of 774, that is my domain. Within it, I will exercise my own judgment in the interests of the colony."

Hathaway's breath quickened. "You walk a thin line, Captain. The Covenant also puts you under my formal command. I can issue you such a command."

"Yes, you can. And when I refuse it you can have me arrested and replaced."

"What am I missing then? Why shouldn't I do just that?"

"Because at my trial I will have to testify before our people that you betrayed them by refusing Kalas' offer."

Hathaway rose slowly. "Me? Betray? You forget, Captain, that I speak with the authority of the Almighty Father."

Ackerman took a step closer to Hathaway's desk. "And who do you think they will believe, High Reverend?"

Hathaway stared at him in disbelief. "Has it come to this, my old friend? You would call me an enemy before our people?"

"It would bring me no pleasure, High Reverend. I..." His voice faltered. "John, it doesn't have to be this way."

"You leave me little choice."

"But you do have a choice. You can choose to wait. I implore you, take a few days to think. As you always urge others to do, you can pray upon the matter."

"And what, let you walk free in the meantime? Let you wander amongst the people, sowing dissent with the serpent's promise of a new and better world? I think not."

"If you will take the time to think, I will not speak of this new world. I give you my word of honor."

"Honor?" Hathaway laughed. "I should respect honor from a faithless man?"

Ackerman closed his eyes and clenched his jaw a moment before he admitted his deepest heresy. "Honor is my faith, High Reverend, and in that respect I am as faithful a man as you. Do as you wish, but I will stand by my oath."

He turned and left without uttering another word.

The brother waiting for Akahele was Reverend Anthony Morris. He stood by the open door of a private tram car. "Captain Kalas, I was asked to escort you back to your ship."

They rode in silence for a few minutes as Akahele was still processing the shock of the High Reverend's dismissal. She could not believe it was truly ending this way. They were halfway back to the docking bays before she looked up to find Morris studying her from across the car.

"Captain Kalas, I realize this is a difficult time." He paused, casting his eyes around in despair. "In fact, I realize this could be the last time we speak."

"That's not for me to say," she replied.

"Nonetheless, I cannot let this opportunity pass."

"What do you mean?"

"Once, a few months ago, I insulted you. It had not been my intent, but I did it nonetheless. You spoke to me honestly of a reverence for your home world, for its oceans, for its very essence, and I belittled you and your beliefs. I was wrong to do so, and I apologize."

She nodded, more surprised by this than anything Hathaway had said. "Apology accepted, Reverend."

"Thank you, Captain. If I may ask one indulgence…"

"Yes?"

"I ran into Tier-father Pritchard as he was leaving. He spoke of a new world you had found. Can you tell me about it?"

"But why, Reverend? Your Hathaway has made it quite clear to me none of you will be going there."

"Because I…" he paused, forcing the tremor out of his voice. "It would seem, dear Captain Kalas, that you are not alone in longing for the embrace of the sea."

She took another hard look at him. Perhaps there were still friendly faces to be found here.

Pritchard and Ackerman sat together, leaning close around the main plot table on the bridge, speaking in hushed tones. The one spy they knew about was gone, but they did not want to tempt fate. "Why provoke him so?"

Ackerman shook his head. "I don't know. Maybe I just lost my head, but damn it, Bill, we need her. Besides, I think he was ready to move anyway."

"And now?"

"It's been six hours, and he hasn't arrested me yet. I think I bought us some time."

"Enough?"

Ackerman sighed. "Is it ever?"

The scene was similar to their last meeting, though this time it was Cal's kitchen table that held Caroline's makeshift radio.

Greg Solomon had managed to elude his watchers this evening, so he was able to chair it in person. "As promised," he said, "this is our sixth meeting, and with a nod to Maggie's news, we may be holding these on solid ground sooner than anyone thought. Maggie, it's your show."

She plunged through the facts as quickly as she could. No, Bosom of the Angel had not been on their original list, but it was far better than any of the others. The last survey report was three years old, but it looked like they would not even need environmental suits. Headgear and supplemental oxygen tanks would be sufficient. The soil samples at the time showed that with the right fertilizers, they could actually start seeding with real plants. It was more than just a possibility for some future generation. It was real, today, and it was already earmarked for them.

"And it's only eighty light years away," she concluded. "In a ship like *Rachael's Luck*, we could be there in a month. Captain Kalas got us the charter, the application for protectorate status, everything. All we really need now is the money."

"We'll hear from the finance committee in a moment, but first, any other questions for Maggie?"

Her cousin Sharon raised a hand. "What about the High Reverend?"

Gregory pounded his fist on the table. "To hell with Hathaway!"

"That's not what I mean," Sharon insisted. "It's these Confederacy folks. Will they even honor the reservation without the High Reverend's authorization?"

"She's got a point," Lieutenant McKay's voice crackled through the speaker. "If it was reserved in Hathaway's name, it's his call who gets to go."

Margaret held her head high and smiled. She had saved the best part of Akahele's gift for last. "Yes, that is exactly the point, for you see, the Bosom of the Angel is not reserved in the High Reverend's name. It is reserved in my name, and I say we go."

In the next room, Cal tried to drown out the celebratory cries with fervent prayer.

Torin stood out on the loading platform watching the Pino port crew load his cargo. There was nothing really for him to do at this point. He had only been able to get a little over three hundred of the rifles and barely enough energy cells even for those. The stun grenades would have taken another three days for the license checks. The rest of the list was similarly spotty. He was going back with very little, but he was going back with something. He remembered the urgency of Captain Ackerman's voice and tried to impress it onto the cargo handlers with his eyes.

Semi joined him and watched for a moment before speaking. "I just got our clearances. We'll be out of here in four hours."

Torin nodded. There would be another six hours navigating the traffic patterns out to a minimum safe distance from the gravity well before engaging the tach drive, and then six long days back to the *Chariot*.

"Do you think our customer will still be there, Captain?"

Torin kept watching the loaders crawl up the ramp. "Just make sure we're ready to leave the minute our window is open."

"Aye, sir," Semi replied and left.

Six and a half days was a long time.

The *HHM Ephesians* dropped tach a full three light-hours behind the *Chariot* and her escort. The data on *Chariot's* precise vector was four months out of date and understandably inaccurate. That did not matter much, at least not to the

Ephesians' captain. He was here to deliver a message from his Holiness, Julius IX. He could do that just as well from this distance, both by tach pulse and by the slower light-speed channels.

However, it did have an unexpected impact on the times at which different people received the word. The first to receive it was the *Hidalgo* on rear picket duty, specifically in the person of Lieutenant Arthur McKay. He forwarded it to his Captain immediately and handed the console to his backup while he went for his dinner. Sufficed to say, his mind was focused less on dinner and far more on passing the message on to his conspiratorial girlfriend aboard the *Chariot*.

A fractional second after the *Hidalgo*, it was picked up by *Rachael's Luck* resting in docking bay three of the *Chariot*, but none of *Rachael's* three occupants were on the bridge to observe it. An hour would pass before Hannah Reynolds found it in the logs, and it would be another thirty minutes before a trusted crewmember could put a copy of it in Ackerman's hands.

It was just over three hours before it reached the High Reverend, and then only because John Kealing had loaned his portable scanner to Reverend Terrence. By then, of course, events were already in motion. As Hathaway was shouting his first curse at "the idolatrous swine", the seventh meeting of the banned Colonize Now executive committee was being called to order.

They all held the papal message in their hands. "This is it, my friends," Gregory Solomon addressed them. "I am open to suggestions for action."

The responses came in rolling over each other. "I say we just leave." "Wait for Hathaway – he might still act." "It's time for our own mutiny." "The Captain is bound to do something."

Gregory chewed at his lip. "As tempting as it is to get up and leave, this will never work as a world of a few dozen. We need to take the colony with us, not just hundreds, but thousands... tens of thousands. I say we force the issue."

"How?"

He held up the message for emphasis. "We post this on the public nets along with everything we've got on Maggie's little Angel."

As the vote was being taken, Ackerman was addressing his seven commanders in a hastily arranged meeting in the core, two miles above at bulkhead intersection 14J.

"I say we move now," Commander Meyers urged.

"I don't see how we can," Soze countered, "not without the cargo *Jinley* is bringing. It's-"

"Important," Ackerman filled in. "The cargo is important."

"I don't care what cargo the *Jinley* is bringing us," Carleton replied. "She's three days away at least. I don't see how we can wait that long. It's not safe."

"We can wait," Pritchard said. "The High Reverend may be misguided, but he's not completely blind to reason. He could still make the right choice."

"Is that a Commander speaking," Meyers asked, "or a tier-father?"

"Tier-father or not, he's right," Noland countered. "We should give Hathaway the chance."

"That's enough," Ackerman cut them off. "We wait. Until the *Jinley* returns, we have no reason to make the first move. In the meantime, gentlemen, no one do anything stupid. Understood?"

Six minutes later, as Hathaway was first speculating on Ackerman's likely actions, Gregory Solomon's fiery manifesto went out onto the public net. That was how most of the colony first read Julius IX's message of peace:

> To my brothers and sisters in faith,
>
> A millennium has passed since anyone on Earth has spoken the name Masonite as anything but a historical epitaph. I fear you must stack all manner of vile insults to equal the bitterness with which most speak it even today. It is a mournful truth of humanity that we can hold such hatred for those long since dead. I am sadly

not surprised that for some the passions are already rising, and it is to my bitter shame that I feel it myself.

But it serves me as a reminder of Christ's lessons of love and forgiveness, for while you are distant and may distrust me as much as your ancestors once did, you are still my neighbors. I can do nothing to restore Callista Prime to you, but I can offer to help you find a new home. To that end, I authorize the release of Church funds of up to 70 trillion Solarian credits, and I have instructed Cardinal Mueller to spare no effort on your behalf.

I know we may never be able to reconcile the gap between our two faiths. I leave that to my successors. For today, I ask only that you accept my offering of Christ's love for you.

His Holiness, Julius IX

Chapter 14

"You say that God has failed me. Your mockery is itself blasphemy, for God can never fail. It is I who has failed God, but at least I go to my end knowing that I did what I could to carry out His divine will. Remember that when you toil in hell." – Nathan Calloway, final transmission from Gabriel's Wrath, August 14, 2302

No one slept much that night. Hathaway's own sleep was shattered by recurring rage-filled dreams, and every time he woke, he pressed his subordinates for updates. No, Gregory Solomon was not yet in custody. No, there were no obvious signs of crew mutiny. The only observable signs of the looming storm were an abnormally high absentee rate for many of the night shifts and unusually high residential voice traffic for the overnight hours.

Ackerman and his officers spent night quietly organizing. To the two officers of the Divine Mark given the task of watching Ackerman's home overnight, all was dark and silent. They did not see him crouched over a small table in his bedroom closet, nor did they hear him speaking into his encrypted radio. "That's forty-seven by my count. And you're sure you can get a weapon to each of them?"

"Most of them, sir," came Meyers' response. "But the ammunition is going to be the harder problem, particularly for the officers. We don't have many of the chem-stun or rubber rounds, not unless you want to involve more of crew security."

"It's too soon for that. What about target rounds? They're not supposed to be as lethal."

"Good thinking, sir. I'll see what I can round up, but either way, this is going to be bloody."

"That's what I'm afraid of." He looked down at his own revolver, his official Captain's gun, handed down to him privately through the generations. In a not so subtle defiance of the Covenant, it was traditionally loaded with quite lethal copper-jacketed slugs. "Just find what you can and get it to Soze. He has the primary target."

"I'll do what I can, sir."

He put in another call to Commander Soze. "What can you see?"

Soze's voice was hushed. "I've circled the main communications office twice now. Security is definitely stronger here than before, at least fifteen of the Mark. There's also a lot of coming and going, but with the nets going wild tonight with that Solomon firebrand, they may just be trying to get a handle on that."

"Is Reverend Terrence there?"

"The light is on in his office, but the only face I've seen so far is that Kealing character."

"Understood. Stay hidden for now. I'm trying to get the troops lined up. Hopefully things will look better in the morning."

"I hear you, but Captain, I think we're well past stupid now."

In the quiet of his closet, Ackerman chuckled. "No, Commander, it's that Solomon boy has gone past stupid. We, on the other hand, are merely preparing to be stupid."

"Yes, sir. I'll be in touch if things change here."

His next call was to Akahele who had good news. "These yachts are used for ferrying the executives around, and the last one Hannah had was a something of a hunter, but not too serious about it. He'd brought plenty of firepower for his safari guests but left one of the crates behind. We have five rifles with scopes and plenty of ammunition for them."

"I'll have someone there soon to get them, but I want you to get moving now. Ensign Caruthers should be there by now, and she'll guide you through some of the engineering spaces to get past the Divine Mark."

Gregory Solomon and his band spent most of the night moving from home to home setting up call trees to get the word out. They would march on Hathaway's home at 08:00.

About the only person who truly slept well that night was Margaret Pritchard, who spent the night curled up in the arms of a nervous Cal. She knew it was taboo to sleep under his roof before the wedding, but she was beyond caring about taboos.

The warning reached Hathaway before he could hear the growing crowd, but when he climbed to the third floor balcony and looked out, he could see them filling the streets. It was not merely the few hundred misguided youths he had been expected. It was clearly in the thousands, and from what he could see along the distant curves of his world, even more were coming.

"Get me Reverend Wallace on the line," he told his aid. "Franklin, too." This was going to take more than just a few extra officers of the Mark. They would need the as many of the priesthood and constables as they could get. Around the curve to his left, he could see another tram pulling into one of the Long-4 stations. He silently cursed himself. He should have shut down the trams last night. He would need to lock down the civilian nets as well.

The aid returned with a phone. It was Wallace. "We're already stretched pretty thin, High Reverend, but I'm sending you everything I can."

"What about Solomon?" Hathaway demanded. "You said you had an inside source!"

"We almost caught him two hours ago, but he slipped away."

"He's probably outside my house right now, Brother. This has gone beyond law enforcement. I'm looking at open rebellion."

"I was afraid of that. High Reverend, my Mark officers are asking for permission to use lethal force. I think they should have it."

Hathaway looked out at the advancing crowd. Many were carrying broom handles and other makeshift weapons. A few were throwing what appeared to canned goods. It seemed ludicrous until one of his perimeter guards went down from a solid hit to the head. "Not on the crowd."

"But for Solomon and his zealots?"

In the courtyard below, several officers were stacking the stone benches from the garden in front of the gate. "Only his so-called committee. You know the names better than I, Brother, but you have my authority."

"Bless you, High Reverend. It will be done."

Ackerman was in his ready room off the bridge when Soze made the call. "Most of the Mark is leaving. The High Reverend must be rallying them to him."

Ackerman cursed, though not as silently as the High Reverend. Three days. He had only needed three more days. It would have been easy then. He could have disabled the Divine Mark with non-lethal weapons. He could have taken the constables out of the equation with an appeal to the House of Fathers, and he could have confronted Hathaway with a well-armed core of officers at his back. Even if Hathaway had refused at that point, taking over the civilian comm center would have been simple and bloodless. But with Solomon's mob, the day was shaping up to be anything but bloodless.

He cursed again. Mutiny it would be, and it would be today.

He raised the wristband to his face again. "Has Broussard reached you yet?"

"Yes, but only seven of us are armed."

"Commander, I know that what I'm asking for is difficult."

"Don't worry, Captain. We can manage it."

"Then do it. I am authorizing Plan B."

"Aye, sir," Soze replied. "I understand."

He called Meyers next. "Dudley, I need something quick, but it's now or never."

"Name it, Captain."

"We're going to go today, and right now Hathaway's trapped. If I can, I want to blind him too, cut him off from his resources. His data lines should run along the Lat-7 tram line to the main C trunk. Can you get there?"

"Checking." Meyers' voice was replaced by a distant roar. "It looks pretty bad from here, but I should be able to get in. How precise do I need to be?"

"I don't care if you take out the whole ring. Just figure something out and be ready on my command."

"Aye, sir. And you?"

"I'm getting Captain Kalas. With luck, we can still end this quickly."

He cut the connection and walked out onto the bridge. There was one last detail to attend to. "Lieutenant Patterson, I would like to speak to you for a moment."

The young officer calmly stood and walked up the steps to Ackerman's ready room. Ackerman followed him in and closed the door. "Have a seat, Lieutenant."

Patterson sat in one of the chairs facing Ackerman's desk while the captain paced behind him. "What can I do for you, sir?"

"Time is short, Mr. Patterson, so I'm going to dispense with the pleasantries. You're Hathaway's man. There's no point in denying it."

"But... I, I mean..." Patterson stammered. "Aren't we all in service to the High Reverend?"

"Not everyone's duty includes late night visits to Reverend Wallace, Mister."

Patterson's shoulders slumped in a moment of resignation before returning to a stiff defiance. "From what I see on the streets this morning, I only wish I had done more to stop you."

Ackerman leaned in close, his face inches from his officer's ear. "That's not my doing," he snarled. "The High Reverend has betrayed our colony and its mission, and thanks to that Solomon idiot now the people know it."

Patterson kept staring forward, and eventually Ackerman backed off to resume his pacing.

"Mr. Patterson, I was reviewing the tapes from the pirate attack, particularly the visual images recorded by Miss Clark. She had a particularly good view of your station, and yet as many times as I watch it, I cannot see you signaling Hathaway about what was happening."

"That's because I didn't," he replied.

"Then who did?"

The lieutenant did not answer.

"Mr. Patterson... Henry, I want you to think about the people out there, the people who at this moment are marching against your High Reverend, and then remember everything I have done to protect them. If you have any love at all for this colony, tell me who the other informer is."

"You make a pretty speech for a heretic, Captain. The ranks of the faithful are vast."

Patterson had no warning of the attack. By the time he even registered Ackerman's hand on the back on his neck, his face was slammed down and pressed into the desk. The cool muzzle of a pistol rested against his temple. "I'm going to ask you one more time, Henry. Only once, understand? Who else is working for Hathaway?"

Patterson's lips peeled back in a wicked grin. "You'll never see it coming. Burn in hell, Captain."

Ackerman shook his head twice and slammed the butt of the pistol into the side of Patterson's head. The lieutenant grunted once and went limp. Ackerman holstered his gun and strode onto the bridge. Jack Logan was standing at his security post by the rear hatch.

"Petty Officer Logan," he said, loud enough to be overheard. "Place Lieutenant Patterson under arrest."

He blinked twice but replied properly. "Aye, sir. May I ask the charge?"

"Insubordination," he answered, "and depending on the rest of the day, I just might tack on mutiny." With that, he left the bridge.

Margaret could no longer see the front of the crowd. She had briefly gotten close enough to see the line of priests and officers of the Mark blocking the way, but that was all. She had had a heavy jar of pears ready to throw, but she could not get the space to properly cock her arm. Now, the bodies pressed in around her and jostled her back and forth. The shouts of those around her mixed together in a blur of sound, punctuated by cries of "Hathaway is Calloway!" and "To the Angel!"

"Mags," came the call.

She turned and saw Cal. "I couldn't get to the front," she croaked, her own voice hoarse.

He squirmed between the bodies and took hold of her arm. "We have to get out of here, Mags. It's not safe."

"No, we have to keep going."

Cal leaned close. "Susan and Daniel already went down."

"How bad?"

"Abby took Susan to the hospital," he answered. From next block over, another flaming bottle flew towards Hathaway's garden wall. This one scored a solid hit and briefly engulfed one of the Mark in flames. "Daniel wasn't moving, Mags."

"He knew what he was doing, Cal. Hathaway has to give in!"

The crowd surged forward again. Cal almost lost his grip on Margaret's arm, but he managed to stay close. "It's not working, Mags. Gregory called a meeting. We have to go."

She frowned but started working back against the tide of bodies. Within a block, there was enough room to start running, dodging back and forth between those just arriving.

She was three blocks away when the first shot was fired.

Ackerman paused next to the maintenance port in the park to look up and over to Hathaway's home, the smoke spiraling up around the core. He had read of the wildfires on old Earth, but this did not seem to be getting out of control. The roar of distant voices masked the sound of the shots, but he could tell something was happening by the way parts of the crowd fled.

He made a rapid round of calls for status checks. Carleton had a firm control of environmental, and Noland reported that the docking bays were secure. Meyers was almost in position. Soze, however, was meeting continued resistance.

"Broussard is dead," he said. "Four others are wounded, so we're down to just the nine of us, but at least now we're all armed."

"Are you in?"

"We're on the ground floor, but they have they have the elevators locked down, and the damn Mark set up barricades in the stairs."

"How well defended?"

"Well enough. That's where we lost Broussard. We're going to try going up the elevator shafts."

In the distance, he could just make out the occasional spark of a muzzle flash around the High Reverend's home. "Be as quick as you can. Things are going badly at Hathaway's."

"Aye, sir".

Ackerman turned his eyes away from the carnage and climbed down the ladder into the maintenance tunnels. He was only two sections away from Akahele by now.

Hathaway had retreated to his office phone. "Brother Terrence, you're sure it's crew?"

"Yes, High Reverend," he replied, the fear audible in his voice. "I saw them on the lobby camera. It's Aaron Soze."

The High Reverend had received sporadic reports throughout the morning, but he had ignored them all until now. The break-in at the Mark's target range had seemed to be the work of vandals. The loss of communication of his men in the central core had been written off as a side effect of the lockdown of the communication networks. Now, however, it was clear.

"Mutiny," he said it at last. "This whole scene with the mob is just a distraction. Damn him!"

"What should I do?"

"Hold out as long as you can. I'll send you what I can. Ackerman must be trying..." he paused, remembering something Reverend Wallace had told him. "Brother Terrence, listen carefully. Some of young Solomon's committee were using radios, something outside the normal wireless network. Ackerman must be as well. Can you use our wireless system to disrupt them?"

There was a delay while Hathaway could hear a muffled conversation in the background. "Yes, my technician says we can blanket the colony with a jamming signal, but we'll lose our own wireless system, too."

"It doesn't matter. We can still use the hard lines. Do it."

"I will, High Reverend, but please hurry with the Mark. I don't know how much longer we can hold them off."

Commander Meyers stood guard just inside the door to the little shack. The mob had dispersed, regrouped, and was coming back again in pieces. The occasional priest wandered nearby, but so far he hadn't seen any of the Mark come close. "Have you found it yet?" he asked the older Lieutenant Everette.

"I believe so," he replied from amidst the racks of wiring. "If we take out this unit here, we get his entire block."

Meyers tapped out the code for Ackerman on his wrist comm. "Myers, here. We're ready, sir." There was no response. "Sir?"

He tried Noland next, then Soze, but he still got no response. He checked his normal pocket comm unit. It was dead. All the wireless systems were down, even the priority crew channels.

"That tears it, Everette. Pull the box now."

Cal Johnson stood by the window in the back bedroom of Caroline's sister. He was supposed to be keeping an eye on the mob still on the attack, but he was really watching the entrance to the apartment building. When he saw a dozen of the Divine Mark charge up the far steps, he knew it was time. As calmly as he could, he walked back towards the kitchen.

There were only eight of them now, counting Cal. "I can't get through to the *Hidalgo*," Caroline said. "All I get is static."

Gregory shook his head nervously. "We've got to get some troops somehow. The damn crew doesn't seem to be doing anything."

"Mutiny's not an easy thing," Richard Ackerman replied. "I told you we should have waited."

"Well, was your father going to do anything?" Gregory shot back.

"And if he were, Gregory, do you think he would have told me?"

"Mags," Cal called to her.

Margaret pulled away from the table. "What is it?"

"I just saw something. I need to show it to you."

She took a few steps towards him. "What is it?"

He leaned close and whispered in her ear. "I think it might be your father. Come see."

She followed him back into the bedroom, and he yanked her towards the closet just as chaos erupted in the front rooms. "What?" was all she got out before Cal forcibly dragged her down to the closet floor.

Margaret struggled against him, but he kept her buried under his weight and silenced her with a hand over her mouth. All they could hear for a few moments were loud crashes and incoherent screams. By the time it settled, Margaret had as well. Words were being spoken by a voice she did not recognize, but it was all muffled through the walls.

And then a gunshot.

"My father will—" Richard's shout was cut short by another shot.

The screams began again, punctuated by shot after shot.

It was brief. The last was Caroline's voice, sobbing. "Please," was all that made it through the walls before one final shot silenced her forever.

A moment passed as Margaret's eyes stared up at his in terror, tears streaming. "I, I…" she stammered, but before she could finish, she saw an officer of the Divine Mark step across the light, his short carbine rifle sweeping across the closet door.

"They're back here, Reverend."

Cal rolled off and looked up to see Reverend Wallace by the guard. He also wore the black uniform of the Mark with the green sash of his office draped across his chest. It was speckled with blood. The pistol was still in his hand.

Another officer arrived. "The area is secure, Reverend. There were only six of them."

"Six?" Margaret asked, still dazed on the floor beside him.

Wallace looked down at them and nodded. "You did the right thing, Mr. Johnson."

She turned her face back to him, her eyes damning him. "Cal... you didn't. Tell me you didn't."

"Mags, I..." he stammered. "It was the only way I could protect you."

"No, Cal. No." Her voice was barely a whisper.

"Don't be hard on him, girl," Wallace commanded. "He saved your life today."

A uniformed arm reached down and pulled her up and away. Cal tried to follow but Wallace blocked his way. She was already out of sight before he heard her screams. "No, Cal! No! You lying bastard! No!" The last of it faded as she was pulled further and further.

"Where are you taking her?"

"She'll be all right, son. We're taking her to the High Reverend himself. He will teach her the error of her ways."

"But you said—"

"I said she would be safe, and she will be. Now I have other duties to attend to. You stay here until I send for you."

Wallace left, two of the Mark trailing behind him. Cal could hear talking in the outer room for a few minutes, and then that fell to silence as well.

On shaky legs he staggered out into the living room and saw the carnage he had triggered. He could identify Gregory only by the clothes he had been wearing. Richard, Bradley, and Philippe had gone quickly it seemed. Neville had taken several shots to the chest, a kitchen knife still in his hand. He found

Caroline slumped against the kitchen wall at the far end of a blood trail. One bloody hand rested against the wound on her leg while the other gripped her makeshift radio. Her death mask was the most disturbing so far, completely serene but for the solitary hole in her forehead.

Cal dropped to his knees and vomited.

The House of Fathers was a placid scene compared to the mob still visible above it, but it was still chaotic. Only fifty-two of the eighty-four tier-fathers were present, and that fluctuated from moment to moment as many came and went. The net links were down, but a steady stream of runners was bringing news both for the assembly and for individual members.

Tier-father Berman held the chair as the most senior member present. It was a role normally filled by Tier-father Holmes, but no one had heard from him in over an hour. He read the latest dispatch. "Dr. Sidel reports sixty-eight dead and over five hundred wounded. He is asking for a secondary location to send the non-critical cases. Who here has a suitable facility?"

Tier-father Johannes stood and answered, "I do, Father. If a runner is available…"

Berman nodded and turned to the aid next to him. "See to it." He then looked down at a list before him. "I believe Father Pritchard is next. Pritchard, are you still here?"

Bill Pritchard rose from his seat and strode down the steps to the lower podium. He grasped the lectern in his hands, calming himself with the feel of the textured wood. He had been sent with his captain's agenda, but now he did not even know where to start.

"Bill," Berman prodded from the dais, "are you all right?"

He nodded slowly and raised his gaze to the faces of his fellow fathers. "Legend has it that this lectern is carved from Earth wood. Earth… not long ago it was ancient history, but last night a letter from there plunged us into this crisis. History, it seems, cannot be outrun even by *God's Chariot*.

"Do we stay or do we leave? I think back to the last time this question was raised to such a crisis. It was a question that divided our people. The details of that debate are lost to history, but we do know it tore us apart. Son from father, brother from sister, and yes, even husband and wife.

"Today we fathers face a choice, and I find myself unsatisfied with my options. High Reverend Hathaway has called upon us to offer up all of our local constables, our tier-sons, and yes, even our very own sons to rally to him and against both the crew and the people of our Holy Chariot. I cannot in good conscience do that."

A cry of "mutiny" rose from the scattered benches, but it was short-lived.

"Yes, mutiny. Beneath my tier-father's cloak I wear the uniform of a commander, a Captain's man. I would be lying if were to say my loyalties were not torn. I... I was sent here..." he trailed off, lost between oaths. He held his audience with a gaze, but the whispers were already starting. "I was sent here," he repeated. "I was sent here by my captain to rally you to his cause, to mutiny, but I cannot do that either."

"Choose your master," came another cry.

"Yes, choose I must, as must you all, but I will not urge you to add to this bloodshed. I will not tell you to rise up against our Reverends, nor will I tell you turn on my fellow officers. If my words can reach you, I urge you simply to go home. Call back your constables. Bring in your tier-sons. Send your people home and tend to your wounded. If either of my masters is to meet his doom today, let it be of his own making. We are Fathers, the wisest of our people. Let us be the cooler heads today."

He stepped back and nodded once to Berman before he left. He was already in the outer hall before the applause began.

"Father Pritchard," came the call, but not from behind him. It was a runner coming in from the foyer. "I have news for you."

"Let's hear it."

"I'm sorry, Tier-father, but your daughter Margaret was arrested."

"When?"

"Just now, sir. Reverend Wallace and the Mark took her."

"Where is she?"

"I believe they were headed to the High Reverend."

Pritchard headed for the exit.

"But, Father, what should I do? Tier-son McKenzie wanted to know if we should go after her?"

Pritchard paused in the doorway. "No, tell him to get all of our people home. I'll take care of Maggie myself."

Ackerman limped up the stairs towards light. The encounter with the Divine Mark had not been part of his plan. He had wounded two of them, but in the process, he had twisted his ankle as he had ducked into one of the crawlspaces.

Above him, Akahele stood guard with one of the hunting rifles. She was aiming it into the air, using the scope to survey the curving ground above them. "I still can't see anything definite from your Commander Soze."

"We'd know if it was good news. That's the only place they could be jamming us. If he takes it, we'll get our comm back."

She handed him a note. "Ensign Barris brought this for you."

He read it. They had lost control of the environmental systems. That meant Commander Carleton was probably dead. "We should get over and help Soze. That has to be our priority now."

"Captain!"

Ackerman wheeled back around and aimed his pistol back down into the dark.

"Sir, wait! It's me, Noland."

Ackerman holstered his pistol and beckoned him up. "I'd hate to have lost you, Commander, but I'd also have hated to waste a bullet on you."

Commander Noland climbed into the light. "You're low?"

"Down to five," Ackerman replied.

"And you?" he asked Akahele.

"I've still got nine rounds."

Noland pulled out his own pistol. "Sir, I've still got a full clip, 9mm chem-stun. What's yours?"

Ackerman shook his head. "7mm."

Noland gave a hint of a smile. "I'll trade you," he said, holding his own gun out butt first.

"I'll take that offer," he replied, drawing his own. "Thanks, Stephen."

The exchange was made, but as soon as Ackerman held the heavier weapon in his hand, he knew something was wrong. It was something about the balance. The barrel was too heavy, or the stock was too light. Or the magazine was empty. By the time he had put it together, Noland had already shifted out of reach behind Akahele and was pointing Ackerman's gun at her head.

"Nice and slow, Captain Kalas. Just let the rifle slide to the ground."

Ackerman aimed and pulled the trigger anyway, hoping against hope that he had guessed wrong. He had, but not about the ammunition. He had trusted the wrong man. Lieutenant Patterson was right. He had never seen it coming.

Akahele did as she was told and backed away to let Noland pick up the rifle and carefully sling it over his own shoulder.

"Why?"

Noland nodded. "It's the natural question at this point, Captain, but it's one I've been asking for quite some time. Why would the High Reverend put his trust in someone with no beliefs? Why should I build you a weapon to turn us from a colony into a war machine? And why should I follow you into mutiny just so you can prove to us all that you're right and he's wrong? Well, I have my answers now."

"You're a fool, Noland."

He laughed. "You're the one who handed over your gun, Captain."

Ackerman lunged for him, but with his ankle, he was far too slow. Noland took three quick steps back and had the pistol leveled at his head. "No, Captain. It's not going to happen that way. You're going to the High Reverend. You're going to face his justice, not mine."

Reverend Morris waited in one of the hallways off the emergency entrance to the hospital, holding a bag of ice against his head. The bleeding had stopped with a pressure bandage, but the swelling was still profound. The nurse told him there might still be small particles of glass in the wound, but it might be some time before they could clean it properly. He had shooed her off, feeling guilty enough taking one of the chairs while others waited on the floor.

He had never seen who had thrown the jar. In fact, he had not even been the target of the attack. He had just turned a corner when the jar exploded against the brick wall, sending glass shards flying against his head and face. Still, he had counted himself fortunate to be coated only in applesauce and not something flammable.

His good fortune was impressed upon him again and again as he sat in that hallway, watching the wounded roll past him. He had stopped counting long before. There were too many. Instead, he focused on those who had been left there, those like him who could wait. They lined the sides of the hall, some on gurneys, some merely laid out on the floor. Two other head wounds sat to his right. A chubby man sat on the floor to his left, his leg in a field-splint made of fence pickets and a pair of suspenders.

And across the corridor, much to Morris's surprise, lay Justin Wheeler. Morris stood and shuffled over. His balance was coming back to him. "Justin, my boy, I don't think I've seen you since your confirmation." Had it already been a year?

The boy opened his eyes. "Reverend," he replied weakly.

"What happened to you, Justin?" Justin was a boy who had once shown the same kind of exuberant energy as had that boy on the Latera beach. A boy like the one he hoped Kara was carrying.

"Not sure," he answered. His breathing was labored, each intake sounding a raspy note. "I think... something fell on me."

Morris looked him over. There were no obvious bandages, no signs of bleeding. "You probably just broke a rib or two, son. You'll heal up just fine."

"Thanks," he said. "It doesn't... hurt as much... as before."

"Well good. It means they're taking good care of you." Morris looked up and down the hall, hoping to find a nurse he could talk to about the boy's breathing. He saw none.

"I haven't seen you at any of my churches, Justin. Are you still helping with the services?"

He nodded. "We moved... to Drake."

"Oh yes, I know the area well. I have a cousin..." he trailed off. The boy's eyes had fluttered briefly and rolled upwards. "Justin, is there something wrong?"

He did not answer. Morris quickly leaned his ear to the boys face. He heard no breath, nor did he see his chest moving.

Morris scanned the hallway again. "Nurse," he called feebly. He took one last look at the boy and strode down the hall. "Doctors!" he called. "That boy isn't breathing!"

They pushed past him and immediately put a mask to his face and began to pump it. "Curtain seven," one of them called out. Morris tried to follow, but another gurney came pushing down the hall behind him. It was another gunshot wound.

He was left, standing in the hallway, the wounded staring up at him.

"No," he said. "This will not do. This simply will not do."

The mob was recoiling from what would be its last surge. Pritchard struggled through them, not so much buffeted by the bodies as he was grabbed at by all those who warned him not to go forward. "They're shooting everyone, Father," one of them warned. Many of those he passed were wounded in one fashion or another, and many of them were being carried by the other survivors. The last he passed were the hardest, the wounded who had been left behind, each calling out to him for help. He was about to abandon his mission to do that when the stern voice of an officer of the Mark called out to him.

"You there, Tier-father, the High Reverend wants to speak with you." He followed obediently, passing through the haphazard fortifications erected in the streets.

He saw Tier-father Garret resting against the garden wall, and he grabbed him by the shoulders. "Paul, listen to me. There are wounded out in the streets. You need to get them to the hospital."

Garret blinked at him, dazed. "But... the High Reverend..."

"Forget Hathaway. Those people are depending on you as their father. Grab as many men as you can and help them."

He did not wait for a response. He just followed his escort onwards.

Captain Castillo gazed around the table at her officers. "Our information is very limited. It could be anything from a mutiny to civil war, but they're not navy, nor are they Confederate citizens. The regs don't give us much leeway here."

Major Osgood nodded. "It would be a tricky assault anyway. We'd need them to open the airlocks. If we breach them ourselves," he shrugged. "Well, we could easily do more harm than good."

Commander Markinson nodded. "And with this damn jamming, we're not even getting their traffic control signals. Who knows if they'd open for us or not?"

Castillo turned to Lieutenant Kasren, her prime communications officer. "Is there any way we can cut through this?"

"No, ma'am. Not from here anyway. Even our suit comms could have difficulty if we went over."

She looked down at the end of the table, to young Lieutenant McKay. "I'm sorry, Arthur. I know you like this girl, but I don't have the authority to order an assault."

"But, Captain," he pleaded, "they have applied for protectorate status."

"That's not quite true, Captain," Markinson said. "They have an do application for protectorate status, but it's for that Angel world, not the *Chariot*."

The table fell silent for a moment, and Castillo was about to adjourn when Osgood raised a stalling hand. "Lieutenant, you say they have the application. Have they actually filled it out?"

McKay nodded. "It's in the name of Margaret Pritchard."

"But it hasn't been filed," Markinson countered.

Osgood held out his hand for it, and the pad was passed down to him. He scanned down the pages briefly. A hint of a smile cracked his grizzled face as he passed it over to his Captain.

She read the highlighted portion in silence for just a moment before standing. "Under section 9-c, as a commissioned senior captain in the Confederate navy, I hereby provisionally accept this application for protectorate status for ninety days. This applies to both the physical world and all support ships holding the colony citizens." She set the pad back on the table and turned back to Osgood. "So, Major, get your troops ready. We're going to take both pinnaces over. It's about time I meet this colony's only official citizen."

Margaret sat quietly in the corner with her hands stuffed into her skirt pockets. It was her first time in the High Reverend's office. It was bigger than she had imagined. Hathaway sat nearby on the corner of his desk, lecturing down to her with the *Chronicles of St. Mason* clutched in his hand.

"Yes, the Bosom of the Angel is quite a name, and I can understand how tempting that would be, my child, especially after everything you have been through these last few months. But the name was not given it by God, nor one of His Chosen. I hear these heathen have even called one of their worlds Eden as if it held the very Tree of Life." Hathaway shook his head. "Such misguided and casual blasphemy. Surely, child, you see this now."

She dared to look up at him. "But if God has placed it before us, does it matter who named it?"

His grip on the book tightened. "You seem so sure that it was God. Did not Satan tempt the Christ of old with sumptuous rewards?"

She nodded. "Yes, and he was right to refuse them, but I believe this gift to be from God, Himself."

"And why?" he demanded, brandishing the book in the air as if to strike with it. "By what divine insight do you claim this? Why do you hold out this false promise to our people?"

She looked down to the floor and whispered. "My mother told me."

"Your mother," he shouted down at her, "is dead! And if you persist in your blasphemy, you will join her."

She thought of her mother in the garden, waiting for her on New Providence. "That is my hope."

John Kealing heard the muffled sounds of the mutineers pounding at the barricade blocking off the outer room. Reverend Terrence and the sole remaining technician were struggling to position one more bookcase in front of the door to the master control room where they were making their last stand. A shot fired in the outer room. They all ducked, and the pounding paused for a moment, but it picked up again soon, louder than before.

Terrence crawled over to him and pushed a revolver into his hands. "It's only got four rounds left. When the time comes, make them count."

He nodded. Was this how his story was going to end, as one of the final tragic defenders of the faith? He did not particularly like the way that would play, especially considering the faith in question. He hefted the gun in his hand. Hero of the revolution would get much better ratings.

Pritchard reached the High Reverend's outer office only to hear Hathaway's shouts muffled through the wall. The private secretary opened the door for him, and Pritchard saw his daughter cowering beneath the Hathaway's towering figure.

"Maggie!"

"Father!" she cried out.

Hathaway glared at her. "I'm not done with you yet, girl. Keep your seat. There is more for you to learn here."

She nodded intently and sunk further into her seat, her hands digging into her pockets.

"High Reverend," Pritchard objected, "my daughter is not a part of this."

Hathaway accepted a handful of dispatches from his secretary. "Your daughter is indeed part of this, Tier-father, and her fate hangs on my patience and understanding." He began turning through the pages. "Do not test them."

Pritchard took a few more steps towards Margaret, but she glared at him with an intensity he had never seen. She nodded towards the High Reverend and subtly shook her head.

The aide stood waiting. "The others are here. Should I send them in?"

"Yes," Hathaway answered. "We'll have a lovely little reunion."

His secretary stepped to the door and waved a signal. Hathaway paused on one of the dispatches. "Quite a speech, Tier-father, one we shall have to discuss, though I suppose I should at least grant that you refused your captain's plot."

"High Reverend, I only meant—"

"In there," came a gruff voice. An officer of the Divine Mark shoved Captain Ackerman through the door and dragged Akahele behind him by the arm. Ackerman was still limping, and both were bound at the wrists.

"Sit," Hathaway commanded. "You, too, Tier-father."

The officer bowed briefly before the High Reverend and presented Ackerman's revolver. Hathaway slowly set the worn copy of the *Chronicles of St. Mason* on his desk and took the gun into his hands. "The Captain's gun... I'd always heard rumors, but I never believed them."

"Should I stay?" the officer asked.

"No," Hathaway replied. "I want you back on the perimeter, and tell Reverend Wallace I want the House of Fathers closed." He took a firm grip on the pistol and sat again on the edge of his desk, facing out at his opponents. "And the rest of you, sit." The guard and private secretary exited the room, leaving only the five of them. Akahele settled into the far armchair as the mutinous officers sat on the long sofa.

Hathaway looked back and forth between them for a moment, accepting the silence of their defeat. "I was just thinking," he said, "of the first time we were here in this office. I suppose young Margaret didn't join us, but I think it's time for the younger generation to learn some of the difficult realities we face."

Ackerman lumbered back to his feet. Hathaway took a step forward and leveled the gun at him. "I told you to sit, you traitorous devil!"

"High Reverend, I alone am responsible for this mutiny. Whatever punishment you intend should fall on my head alone."

Hathaway lowered the gun slightly but maintained his stance. "Still playing at the honorable man, I see. It suits you, James, and at some level I think you truly believe it. That would make things so much simpler between us. We could have settled it, you and I, no longer as friends, but at least between us. But you did not act alone – far from it. With the exception of that faithful Noland and possibly the Tier-father here, they all made quite a go at it."

Ackerman turned his head and glared at Pritchard. "What does he mean?"

Pritchard swallowed hard and looked up at his captain. "I'm sorry, Captain. You see…"

"No," Ackerman cut him short. "You were right, Bill. Save yourself and your daughter. I was a fool."

"No, James," Akahele said from her chair. "Hathaway is the fool here."

"Don't make this worse, Akahele," Ackerman warned.

"No," she said, raising up her bound hands, "fuck this! It's not like he's going to give us a trial. You saw the carnage out there. He's going to gloat over us and then put that gun to our heads. And for what?" She turned her attack on Hathaway. "For what? You can't go back to the way it was before, you ignorant ass. They're always going to know that world is waiting for them. Maybe you've won for today. Maybe you'll even last a year, but someday, even if it takes a generation, they're going to pack up and go."

She stiffened herself in her seat as she glared at Hathaway fuming. "I once pitied you, Reverend. Now you don't even deserve that."

The High Reverend looked down at the gun in his hand and then back to Akahele. "You're right, Captain Kalas. I cannot turn back the clock, but I can do what I should have done the first time I saw you." He took another step forward and aimed the gun.

"No!" Ackerman cried out and leapt.

The gun fired, but by then Ackerman was already crashing into Akahele. The bullet passed through his chest and into her shoulder. The two tumbled backwards over the chair, taking the end table down with them.

Hathaway stepped quickly and kneeled at their sides. Ackerman still lay across Akahele, the blood spilling out of him, spreading across his uniform. Akahele lay still with a bloody gash in her head as well as the shoulder wound.

Ackerman looked up at Hathaway, barely seeing him. "I only wanted us..." he gasped, "to stand beneath..." The rest was lost in a gurgling rasp.

Hathaway rose to find Pritchard facing him. "It is time for you to choose, Bill. Is your loyalty to your captain or to me? Pretty words aside, you cannot have it both ways."

Pritchard met Hathaway's eyes. "You once told me, High Reverend, that my loyalty must always be to the colony and its mission, not to any one man. I cannot follow you."

Hathaway raised the gun at Pritchard. "I regret that it had to come to this."

They were the last words he ever spoke. Before he could pull the trigger, his torso evaporated in a spray of flesh and bone that splashed against the far wall of the office. His head dropped the floor, the surprise never even registering on his face.

In disbelief, Pritchard turned to see Margaret standing with arms outstretched towards where Hathaway had stood. She blinked a few times and lowered her aim to the floor. In her hands, she held Akahele's old Jansky-7. Carefully, she turned the dial back from the highest red setting back down through the greens and slid the short barrel back into the safety position.

"Maggie?" Pritchard questioned.

She looked blankly at her father and sank to her knees, the little device rolling out of her hands and across the floor.

He stared at it and back to her.

"Captain?" came a muffled voice. "Captain, are you there?"

Pritchard turned. The sound had come from Ackerman's wristband. He stepped over the bodies and pulled it from his captain's wrist. "Is that you, Soze?"

"Pritchard? We got through and cut the jamming. Where's the Captain?"

He checked Ackerman for a pulse. It was a formality. "He's dead."

A crash sounded from the outer office followed by raised voices and two shots.

Pritchard's eyes scanned around for a weapon, and he grabbed up the Jansky just as the door swung open.

It was Reverend Morris, flanked by two guards. They were crew security, not officers of the Mark. "Tier-father," he began but froze, taking in the scene.

Pritchard looked at what was left of Hathaway and at Margaret trembling on the floor. "I had no choice, Reverend," he said. "It was self-defense."

Both Morris and Soze had the same question. "What do we do now?"

He answered them with resolve. "We end this. Now."

Chapter 15

"Friends have asked me to travel to see the Bosom of the Angel, but I have always refused. I have many regrets, but that is not among them." – Cal Johnson, 3462.

Bill Pritchard stood outside the open hatch to docking bay four, watching the young colonists walk past. They were headed out with little more than a few keepsakes and a change of clothes, but really, he wondered, what more would they have ever taken anyway? He could see the shuttle beyond them. The *Lady Tenessy* had indeed made a return trip after all, the first of many. Part of him still wished he could go.

"Father," Margaret called out from the line. "I thought I'd missed you!"

He held out his arms for an embrace. "Far from it, my little Mag-pie."

She slid into his arms. "That's the last time you get to call me that, Father."

He held her tight for a long time, longer than he really should have but still not long enough. "The last time?"

She took a half-step back and waved a finger at him. "The last time until you come see us on Angel."

He nodded. "That's fair enough."

"So, can I mark it on my calendar?"

"Soon," was the only answer he could give. "Are you sure you're ready for this?"

She closed her eyes and nodded. "I need this, Father. Too much has happened here. I need a fresh start. Besides," she said, meeting his eyes again, "it's my name on the papers. I have to go."

"I know, but a father can worry, can't he?"

"No more than a daughter can. How will you manage all alone?"

"I'll be all right. Your aunt Jen is still here, and I have my memories."

"Mother," she said.

"Yes, I was just thinking about her last night."

"As was I, Father."

"And I was thinking about your dream."

Margaret gave a quick look askance, fearing a rebuke that would no longer come. "I think about it, too, Father. Often."

"Maggie, if you…" he paused, the fear of blasphemy so ingrained in him. "If you see her again, tell her I…"

Margaret nodded. "I know, Father, and I will. I promise."

He looked up and saw that the line was dwindling. "Well, you'd better hurry. You don't want to be last on board, do you?"

She gave him one last quick hug and skipped off.

"Remember," he called after her, "always keep an extra set of air filters with you. You can't have too many."

She spun around and smiled at him, answering him in a teasing sing-song, "Yes, Father, I'll remember."

He watched her progress down the line through the hatch into the bay.

"She's a sweet girl," Akahele said from beside him.

Pritchard gave her a brief glance. Her hair had regrown enough to cover the stitches on her scalp, but her left arm was still in a sling. "How long have you been there?"

"A little while. I didn't want to interrupt."

"Well, it's not easy for a father to let go."

"I understand. Dad was the same. I suppose there's no point in trying to change your mind. I could take you on *Rachael's Luck*."

"No," he replied. "Someone has to stay behind and pick up the pieces. We have to find a way forward."

"I understand, but you will come someday, won't you?"

"I believe so. They're still trying to decide what to call my new office, but one thing I'm insisting on is that it's not a lifetime appointment. We've had enough of that, so yes, someday."

She nodded. "My vote is on 'Revered Father', but no one listens to me anyway."

He laughed. "Sorry, but the rumor is running towards 'Father Captain'. At least that's the rumor I'm spreading."

She jabbed him with the elbow of her good arm. "Speaking of rumors, I hear that you're actually going to change course and take the *Chariot* to the Bosom of the Angel directly."

He flashed a brief smile. "We're still working on the numbers, but yes, it's quite possible that in another eight hundred years the colony will be whole again."

She gave a low, drawn-out whistle. "Eight hundred years. You people sure have patience."

He shrugged. "It's long enough to plan a celebration." He glanced back up the line. "Speaking of celebrations."

Reverend Morris spotted them and stepped forward. "Bill, Captain Kalas, it's good to see you. I was wondering why you were absent from the farewell gauntlet."

"We're merely the last of it," Pritchard replied.

Akahele tilted her head in confusion. "I didn't think you were going this early, Reverend."

Morris smiled broadly and swaggered a bit. "It was a last minute decision, really, but Kara wants me to go. I'm going to have a son, Bill, and she wants me to go make a place for him. You'll keep watch over them until I return?"

"Of course," he answered. "Just as you'll watch over Maggie."

Morris clasped him briefly on the shoulders. "With pride, my friend, with pride."

They watched him go through the hatch as Akahele chuckled. "He sure is full of surprises."

"Yes, fortunately for us."

They watched in silence as the last of them filed through the hatch. "Bill, you never told me what really happened in Hathaway's office after I blacked out."

"No," he replied, "I never did."

A moment passed before she surrendered. "Okay, I see how it goes."

"You will keep an eye on Maggie, won't you?"

"Yes, Father Captain, I will."

Margaret took an open seat near the large bay window in *Tenessy's* forward observation lounge. She could just make out the dull glow of the *Chariot* in the distance. She knew most of the people in passing, and there was a general nod of greeting.

The last seat beside her was taken by a young man with meek features but strong shoulders. "Hi, I'm Darren Whitford."

She took his hand by the wrist. "Maggie Pritchard."

"I don't know if you remember, but we met at the fair."

The memory flashed in her mind. "Yes, I do remember. You're Carl's cousin, aren't you?"

He smiled playfully. "Guilty as charged."

"Then welcome aboard, Darren."

"Thank you." He glanced around the lounge as most of the eyes were still directed to the window. The stars were starting to shift to the left. "So, what do you think it will be like? You know, standing on real ground, looking up at a real sky?"

She took one last look at her home as it shifted out view. The stars suddenly stretched, and they were on their way. "I don't know, Darren, but we're going to find out."

ACKNOWLEDGEMENTS

There are a multitude of people to thank for encouraging me to write. These include teachers, family, friends, and other authors. If I were to list them all, this book would need another forty-eight pages. Suffice it to say, I would not have gotten to page one without them, let alone page three hundred, so thank you all.

For this particular book, however, I can narrow it down. I want to thank the folks at National Novel Writing Month (nanowrimo.org), because thanks to them, this went from a vague notion to a first draft back in 2005.

I want to thank my wife Julia who encouraged me to finish it as well as put up with my roller coaster of angst and mania along the way.

I want to thank my beta readers: Julia, Rose, and Andrew. I want to single out Andrew who read it twice, and I will say that his advice is largely responsible for one of the major plot lines in the book. I could say which, but I'd rather you just assume it was your favorite.

I also want to thank Rose again, who has politely poked at me to actually get this out the door. So... (*gulp*) now it is.

And one last piece of thanks should go to Muffy Morrigan, who did the final pass of copyedits. The book is much cleaner thanks to her. Any remaining typos or misspellings are my fault. I'm sure some things are wrong, but apparently I wanted them that way.

If you enjoyed the book, please tell a friend or leave a review someplace. If you hated the book but still slugged on through to reach the acknowledgments, then I suppose you've earned the right to complain about it too. But either way, thanks for reading it. I got into this to tell people stories, and thanks to you, I've just done that.

ABOUT THE AUTHOR

Dan Thompson started writing fiction at age ten. Luckily for the world, all copies of that early Star Wars rip-off have been lost to time and Sith retaliation. Moving on from that six-page handwritten epic, he wrote short stories through the 1980's and 1990's, and sold a few to magazines that rarely lived past his story's publication.

After three or four abandoned novels, he finally started finishing some and decided they should do more than collect dust and red scribbles. Because of the shakeup e-books have brought to publishing, he decided to pursue self-publishing for the time being. Thus Quantum Forge Press was born.

He lives near Austin with his wife and three children, drives old police cars, wears kilts when the weather permits, visits with friends as much as possible, and is generally considered to be the weirdo next door. Fortunately, the neighbors don't know how weird he really is.

For more from Dan Thompson,
check the website

DanThompsonWrites.com

and sign up for the mailing list.